Ben Elton's career encompasses some of the most memorable and incisive comedy of the past twenty-five years. His TV writing and performing credits include such multi-award-winning shows as *The Young Ones*, *Blackadder*, *Saturday Live*, *The Man from Auntie* and *The Thin Blue Line*. His three hit West End stage plays are *Gasping*, *Silly Cow* and *Popcorn*, which won the Olivier Award for best comedy. He wrote and directed the feature film *Maybe Baby*, starring Hugh Laurie and Joely Richardson, which was based on his novel *Inconceivable*. He has also written three stage musicals including the global phenomenon *We Will Rock You*, which he created with Queen and which he also directs worldwide.

He has written ten internationally bestselling novels including *Dead Famous*, *The First Casualty* and *High Society*, which won the WH Smith People's Choice Award. He recently returned to stand-up comedy after a gap of almost ten years and his new show, *Get a Grip*, played to packed houses in the UK, Australia and New Zealand.

High Society

'As I raced to the end, I found myself applauding Elton. This is a tough subject tackled with courage and commitment'
Will Hutton, *The Observer Review*

'A fix of high comedy from a writer who provokes almost as much as he entertains'   *Daily Mail*

'Tremendous narrative momentum . . . genuinely moving'
The Times

'A return to Elton's top fiery form'   *Glamour* magazine

'Very racy, a compulsive read'   *The Mirror*

'Full of passion and plenty of one-liners'
Scotland On Sunday

'A joy to read . . . a startling head of narrative steam'
Evening Standard

'A throat-grabbing thriller which also manages to savagely satirise this high society we all live in . . . Excellent'
Ireland On Sunday

Dead Famous

'One of Ben Elton's many triumphs with *Dead Famous* is that he is superbly persuasive about the stage of the story: the characterisation is a joy, the jokes are great, the structuring is very clever and the thriller parts are ingenious and full of suspense. And not only that – the satire (of Big Brother, of the television industry, of the arrogant ignorance and rabid inarticulacy of yoof culture) is scathing, intelligent and cherishable.

As House Arrest's twerpy contestants would put it, wicked. Double wicked. Big up to Ben Elton and respect, big time. Top, top book'
Mail on Sunday

'Brilliant . . . Ben has captured the verbal paucity of this world perfectly . . . devastatingly accurate in its portrayal . . . read Elton's book'
Janet Street-Porter, *Independent on Sunday*

'Elton has produced a book with pace and wit, real tension, a dark background theme, and a big on-screen climax'
Independent

'Very acute about television and the Warhol-inspired fame for fame's sake that it offers . . . certainly delivers a readable whodunnit'   *The Spectator*

'One of the best whodunnits I have ever read . . . This is a cracking read – a funny, gripping, hugely entertaining thriller, but also a persuasive, dyspeptic account of the way we live now, with our insane, inane cult of the celebrity'
Sunday Telegraph

Inconceivable
'Extremely funny, clever, well-written, sharp and unexpectedly moving . . . This brilliant, chaotic satire merits rereading several times'   *Mail on Sunday*

'Extremely funny without ever being tasteless or cruel . . . this is Elton at his best – mature, humane, and still a laugh a minute. At least'   *Daily Telegraph*

'A very funny book about a sensitive subject. The characters are well-developed, the action is page-turning and it's beginning to seem as if Ben Elton the writer might be even funnier than Ben Elton the comic'   *Daily Mail*

'This is Elton doing what he does best, taking comedy to a place most people wouldn't dream of visiting and asking some serious questions while he's about it. It's a brave and personal novel'   *The Mirror*

Also by Ben Elton

STARK

GRIDLOCK

THIS OTHER EDEN

POPCORN

BLAST FROM THE PAST

INCONCEIVABLE

DEAD FAMOUS

HIGH SOCIETY

PAST MORTEM

THE FIRST CASUALTY

and published by
Black Swan

CHART THROB

Ben Elton

BLACK SWAN

TRANSWORLD PUBLISHERS
61-63 Uxbridge Road, London W5 5SA
a division of The Random House Group Ltd
www.booksattransworld.co.uk

CHART THROB
A BLACK SWAN BOOK: 9780552773768

First published in Great Britain
in 2006 by Bantam Press
a division of Transworld Publishers
Black Swan edition published 2007

Addresses for Random House Group Ltd companies outside the UK
can be found at: www.randomhouse.co.uk
The Random House Group Ltd Reg. No. 954009

The Random House Group Ltd makes every effort to ensure that the
papers used in its books are made from trees that have been legally
sourced from well-managed and credibly certified forests. Our paper
procurement policy can be found at:
www.randomhouse.co.uk/paper.htm

Typeset in 11/12pt Melior by
Falcon Oast Graphic Art Ltd

Printed and bound in Great Britain by
Cox & Wyman Ltd, Reading, Berkshire

2 4 6 8 10 9 7 5 3 1

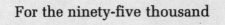

For the ninety-five thousand

And Still to Come

Some years from now

The nation had watched Shaiana cry so many times. Heard her voice crack as she struggled to complete her sentence.

'I just want this so much. I really, really want it *so much*. It's all I ever wanted. Since I was a little girl . . . It's my . . . It's my . . .'

She couldn't do it. Words failed her. Her lip quivered, her nostrils flared and a watery film spread across her eyes. The lids closed in an agonized grimace and squeezed out a glistening tear.

Just a tear, a single tear, but such a tear. One of the most scrutinized tears that was ever shed. Few tears in all history would be seen by so many and so often. Over and over again it had teetered momentarily upon the thickly mascaraed lashes of Shaiana's lower lid before tipping forward and rolling heavily across the downy expanse of that now nationally familiar cheek, tracing its course through the heavy blusher with which the make-up artist had struggled in vain to cover the tiny blemishes on Shaiana's quivering face.

The people in their millions had absorbed this scene immediately before the last break and also before the break which preceded that. They had seen it at the very beginning of the programme and in the trailers that had played throughout the earlier part of the evening. Those with access to the digital channels

11

had been able to watch the tear for nearly a week already and grainy stills of it had appeared in the press. It was also possible to download it to one's mobile phone by accessing the 'preview highlights' section of the *Chart Throb* website.

But despite all this massive exposure, up until now that tear had always been a future tear, a tear which, in the endlessly repeated phrase of Keely the presenter, was 'still to come'.

'And still to come, it's all too much for Shaiana.'

'Still to come, Shaiana struggles to keep it together.'

'Is Shaiana's dream turning into a nightmare? All that and more, *still to come*.'

And so the tear had teetered. A maybe tear, present and entirely familiar but nonetheless a tear in waiting. But now finally it had arrived. No longer a tear that was 'still to come' but all of a sudden a clear and present tear, a tear that was on its way. And for the first time (but most certainly not the last) the viewing millions saw it disappear beneath the square white plastic nail of Shaiana's outstretched finger as she rested her chin upon Keely's gorgeous skinny shoulder, and failed to find the word for which she was struggling.

'I just want this so much,' she repeated. 'I really, really do. I want it so much. It's all I ever wanted. Since I was a little girl . . . It's my . . . It's my . . .'

At the very last linguistic hurdle, emotion defeated Shaiana and words failed her.

'Dream?' Keely coaxed. 'Is it your dream? Is that what you're trying to tell us? That it's your dream?'

'That's right, Keely,' Shaiana sniffed. 'That is *so* right. It's my dream.'

Keely's bronzed, cadaverously muscular arms enfolded Shaiana's shoulders. Momentarily entwined, they made quite a contrast: the golden girl and the girl with the dream. It all looked slightly uncomfortable as

12

Shaiana's arm (the one which she had raised to wipe away the famous tear) became trapped in Keely's skeletal embrace. Briefly Shaiana's hand rested in the hollow of Keely's armpit and Keely's teeth rattled against Shaiana's big hoop earrings. Neither woman seemed to notice the awkwardness or if they did, they did not care. Emotions were running too high. It was all too much.

'You go, girl,' Keely whispered. 'Just you go, girl.'

'Yeah,' Shaiana sniffed, raising her eyes towards what would have been the stars had it not been daytime and had she not been indoors. 'God gave me this chance and I'm going to rock their asses!'

Calvin Simms

Some months earlier, one of the asses whom Shaiana intended to rock had been quivering with violent fury as its owner, Calvin Simms, came to the shocking realization that he, the ultimate manipulator, the man who with a single glance knew a person better than they knew themselves, had been had. Calvin always believed that he could read anybody. Anybody, it now turned out, except the woman he had married.

'A divorce?' he stuttered.

'Yays, Calvin,' his beautiful American bride of just two weeks drawled in her sexy, sultry Southern accent. 'Ah want a dee-vorce.'

They were standing in the hallway of the vast detached mansion in Belgravia that Calvin had assumed would be his and Dakota's marital home. Numerous items of matching luggage surrounded them. The two drivers who had helped them into the house had only just closed the front door behind them. He had *carried* her over that threshold not two minutes before. His passport was still in his pocket, he still had sunscreen on his neck, he was still wearing *shorts and sandals*, which made him feel particularly ridiculous in the light of the shocking revelation that the honeymoon was most definitely over.

'We've only been married a fortnight!' he protested.

'Way-ll, believe me, darlin', it felt lahk a ye-ah,' Dakota purred.

'Why bother with the fucking honeymoon then? Why not dump me outside the church?'

'Gotta consummate, pussycat. Cain't have you claimin' Ah withheld ma fay-vers an' gettin' a judge to declare our *nerp*tuals null an' void.'

Like a big win on a fairground coin cascade, the pennies in Calvin's head were tumbling down. *That* was why she had made such a racket in the sack! Screaming and shouting and beseeching the Lord Almighty to give her strength. She'd never made love that noisily when they were courting. In fact previously she had been rather clinical in her approach to sex, which, being a very busy man, Calvin had always appreciated. Suddenly, however, she'd seemed to feel the need to let the whole world in on her exertions. There had been complaints from other guests, and Calvin had been forced to book the surrounding rooms and compensate a middle-aged couple who claimed to have had no sleep at all. He had wanted to honeymoon in one of his many holiday mansions but Dakota had insisted on their staying in a very public hotel. Now he knew why.

'Ah do believe eva'body in tha whole o' Venice knows how *insatiably* you used ma poh weak body, Calvin. Ah wuz lil' more than a sweet young virgin chile an' you done jes about furked me intah a *coma*.'

Calvin stared at his wife. There were many ways one might have chosen to describe her, but 'sweet young virgin child' was not one of them. Thirty-four years old, well over six feet tall, glamorous, sophisticated and now, it turned out, cunning as a snake. They bred them tough, those girls of the Confederate aristocracy. It had after all been only six generations since their great-great-great-great-grannies had been left with nothing but their looks and their well-bred gentility to survive in a cruel new world.

'Ahm dee-vorcin' you, honey,' Dakota purred. 'An' Ahm filin' in tha city of Angels, which means o'course Ah git half.'

Calvin's mind was reeling. Could she do it? A *two-week marriage*, for heaven's sake. Half? Surely not.

'On what grounds?' he asked.

'Mental cruelty.'

'Mental cruelty!' Calvin exploded.

'Uh-huh.'

'When was I ever cruel to you?' he protested.

'You ain't bin, honey, 'ceptin' *boring* me half tuh death 'bout how clever you are an' all,' Dakota sneered. 'We both know thay-at. But fortunately for me nobody else knows it, an' since you have so carefully curl-tivated an image as tha nastiest, cruellest, most *brutal* man on television, Ah don't imagine that a dee-vorce court will need merch persuasion tah believe that you treat yo' sweet virginal bride tha same as you treat yo' dumb contestants.'

Realizing he was still holding his cabin baggage in his hand, Calvin put it down on the polished marble floor.

'Shall we go in and sit down?' he suggested.

'Nuh. Ahm leavin', ma car's outside.'

'What? Immediately?'

'Sooner if possible.'

'Have you been planning this from the start?' Calvin asked.

'O' course.'

'The very start? Three years ago?'

'Uh-huh.'

'You mean you *never* loved me at all?'

'Duh!'

Calvin's mind was filled suddenly with memories of their courtship. That spilt glass of champagne at the Versace show which had first led him to talk to her . . .

'Ah am so sorry, suh! Did Ah wet yo' pants? Ain't I a fumble-fingers?'

Had she engineered it? She had seemed so disarmingly frank and honest at the time, so cool and assured, wiping him down with a napkin and giggling in that confident, proud way that girls of the Southern aristocracy seemed to perfect in the cradle. It couldn't have been a set-up. And yet it seemed it had been.

'What about the Bay of Biscay? You really didn't love me then?'

'Double duh!'

The sunset had been so fabulous and they had found themselves alone and she had said she loved him. That was when he had proposed.

'Please, Calvin,' Dakota said, sounding almost bored. 'Don't look so *downhearted*. After all, honey, *you never lerved me.*'

Actually this was true, although he hadn't realized she had been aware of it. He had never really loved anyone but he had *liked* her enormously.

'Of course I loved you! Why else would I marry you?'

'Same reason Ah married you, Cotton Candy. Ta git sermthin' you didn' haive. You wan'ed a *wahf*. You'd *dern* your bachelor thing. Yew wan'ed a beautiful *wahf*. Fer kids, fer premières, ta make your parents happy. Ta git rid of all those gay rumours once an' fer all.'

Calvin could only gape. She was articulating his inner thoughts better than he had done himself. It was true: at forty-two, obsessed with work and dripping with wealth, he had decided that a witty, intelligent, glamorous companion of childbearing age was what he required to complete his carefully constructed life. At the wedding, when they had the famous reading from *The Prophet* about twin pillars, Calvin had thought it very apt, for what he wanted most from his life companion was support, support that would enable him to continue unhindered with his world-conquering career. Now it turned out that instead of a pillar to prop up his life, he had got himself a wrecking ball to smash it to bits.

Remembering the wedding day brought another thought to his mind.

'You do realize *Hello!* magazine is going to want its money back, don't you?'

Dakota assumed an expression of infinite superiority.

'Ah have always despised yo' *common* and *grubby* side, Calvin. Thankfully Ah no longer have ta bear it. Ah'll see you in Californ-yuh!'

The beautiful, stately 'blonde bombshell', as the papers had not been able to resist calling her, turned on her four-inch heels and laid her hand on the door handle.

'You'll never get half,' Calvin shouted. 'Not even in California!'

Dakota turned back to look at him once more.

'Ah will git half, Calvin. Ah haive bin made a *fool* of. Ah wuz se-*dooced* ba yo' charms into sur-rrenduhrin' mahself. Se-dooced ba a may-un, a dirty *English* may-un who then *brutalized* me and shamed me unnatterally.'

'You wouldn't claim that?'

'Ah would, Calvin honey! Ah'll say you demanded unnatteral acts an' when Ah refused that you *beat me*!'

'You can't! It'll be your word against mine!'

'Exactly! Tha word of a sweet tearful Southern

17

Baptist girl aginst tha word of the most famous bastard in the world! Smug, sneerin' ol' Mr Mean from tha biggest show on TV. No jury in America is gonna have any trerrble believin' that you tried to stick yo' nasty *English* rapier where no Christian wahf should let it be sterck.'

'This is outrageous! It's theft, pure and simple. You are trying to steal from me.'

'Oh, come on, Calvin, yo' a thief yo'self. Why, evabody knows that *Chart Throb* is jest *X Factor* with differen' judges. *Nastier* judges. *Much nastier* judges. You stole it! An' now Ah'm stealin' from you.'

If Dakota had been attempting to make Calvin even angrier she was certainly succeeding, for this was his sore spot, the one fly in the sweet ointment of his vast fame and wealth. There could of course be no doubt that Calvin's show, *Chart Throb*, the latest in a whole series of wildly successful television talent shows, had been lifted pretty much wholesale from the shows that preceded it. Calvin never denied it, nor that he had cast himself in the Simon Cowell mould as the rude, acerbic English judge. Nor did he deny that he had gone out of his way to recreate the elements that made up a successful judging panel. He had hunted down a mumsy reality TV star with a publicly dysfunctional family. He had found himself a pleasant-faced pop professional who had been looking for television exposure. He had studiously recreated all the elements that had made *X Factor* such a triumph, and had been so successful in doing so that *Chart Throb* had eventually eclipsed the original model. This was the point that Calvin never tired of explaining to people. It wasn't that he had done anything new, only that he had done it better.

'There *is* nothing new anyway,' Calvin protested. 'I didn't rip off anything that hadn't been ripped off before. *X Factor* was just *Pop Idol* and *Pop Idol* was just *Pop Stars*, which started in New Zealand as it happens, and it all comes from *New Faces* and *Opportunity Knocks* . . .'

'Whatevah, Calvin!'

'No! Not whatever! Rob me if you like but I'm not having you insult me like this. The reason my show's the most successful is because I'm the best at doing it! Why do you never hear about *X Factor* any more? Because of me. I'm the King now, because I do things my way!'

'OK. So you're better than the last guy at bein' a rude, sarcastic lil' shit on camera. Big deal, Calvin, whoopidingdong.'

'There's a world more to it than that and you know it,' Calvin snapped. 'It's what I do *behind* the scenes that makes me the best. I have the *touch*. I *understand* the process. When it comes to manipulating the public I am fucking *Goebbels*, mate. I *make the fiction real.* Nobody gets it like I get it.'

'Goebbels, eh?'

'Yes, Goebbels.'

'Yo' mother must be very proud.'

Yet again Dakota turned on her heel to leave, but Calvin grabbed her arm.

'All right, darling!' he said. 'How about this? You want half of everything I've earned?'

'Tha's raht, Calvin. Ah do, an' Ahm gonna git it too.'

'How about I give you a chance to get *all* of it?'

Dakota leaned against the front door.

'Ahm listenin' . . .'

'You say *Chart Throb* is just a rip-off. That I'm just another rude English guy who got lucky. I say I bring a unique talent to my show. I say it's what I do *behind* the cameras that matters . . .'

'Ah know, Calvin. You *never* tire of tellin' me.'

'Well, we're currently doing the preliminary vetting sweep for the new series of *Chart Throb*. I challenge you to name a ringer. Put up anyone you like and I will ensure that they win the competition. If I succeed, you walk away with nothing. If I lose, you get it all.'

Dakota looked thoughtful, clearly taken by surprise. This was a bold challenge indeed, much bolder than anything she might have been expecting.

'Ah cain choose anybody?'

'Well, they have to be British or Irish . . . and not a paedophile. Even I couldn't swing a Gary Glitter!'

'Thait's yo' only stipulation?'

'Yep. Put up anybody you like, except a paedophile, and I will turn them into this year's Chart Throb.'

'Well, Ah must say, this does appeal ta ma gamin' instincts.'

'Thought it might.'

Dakota's family, among other things, bred horses and twice a horse named in her honour had won the Kentucky Derby.

'O' course Ah couldn't allow you ta weight the other candidates.'

'What? You mean pick eleven other people with even less chance of winning than the one you nominate? I could do that, I suppose, but it would make a pretty shitty show. Let's say this last year *Chart Throb* averaged eight and a half million viewers. If we drop below eight this time, even once, I lose the bet by default.'

'You'd risk everythin' on this, Calvin?'

'I'm risking nothing. I know I can win. I'll give you a day to nominate your ringer.'

'Well. OK then. Ah accept yo' bet. An' Ah don't need a day to choose either. Ah've already decided.'

Beryl Blenheim

'What do you mean, the pig won't shit?'

'The pig won't shit, Beryl, what can I tell you?'

'We should have used one of my own pigs.'

'We thought we had a better chance of a decent shit this way. The people at the animal acting agency said they fed this one up big.'

Beryl Blenheim had been hanging about for hours, standing uncomfortably in a pair of gold stilettos and a Stella McCartney evening gown. Beside her on an antique coffee table lay a pair of Marigold rubber gloves and some Spray & Wipe disinfectant. The bucket of hot water had gone cold and been replenished any number of times. The afternoon was disappearing. Already Beryl had been forced to cancel a consultation with her plastic surgeon, who was a very busy man and had many bottoms besides hers to lift and therefore would have difficulty fitting her bottom in again at any other time that week. Yet still the pig would not shit.

'Give her something to make her shit.'

'We did. It didn't.'

'I have a life, Arnold!'

'And I have a crew and if this pig takes much longer to take a dump we'll be running into some serious overtime here.'

The crew in question were attempting to shoot a scene for the final episode of the current season of *The Blenheims*, a 'reality' television show featuring the 'real life' trials and tribulations of a dysfunctional show business family. One of the most popular themes of the show had proved to be the ubiquitous incontinence of the family's numerous pet pigs and when storyboarding the closing episode everybody had agreed that pig shit must provide the principal source of humour.

It had all sounded so good at the pitching meeting.

'So Beryl is all dressed up to go with Serenity to the Recoverers' Ball, right?' Arnold explained. 'But the new pig keeps taking a crap so poor Beryl has to keep getting down on her hands and knees in her jewellery and evening gown to clean it up and when she finally gets into the car to go to the ball she still has her Marigolds on! And Serenity says, "Oh my God, Beryl, people will think we've come to clean the toilets," although it will sound so much funnier when she says it.'

'Do you think Serenity can remember that many words?' Beryl had enquired.

Arnold assured her that it was actually funnier when she didn't.

And so the shoot had been planned accordingly, though not for the day of the Recoverers' Ball. Obviously, if Beryl Blenheim did clean her own house, which she didn't, she wouldn't do it on the day when all of LA's première casualties gathered together to celebrate their collective triumph over the self-inflicted wounds with which decades of gargantuan personal indulgence had marked them. Beryl Blenheim, ex-druggie, ex-alchie, ex-food addict, ex-sex addict, ex-rock star and, most famously of all, ex-man, was after all the poster transsexual for the whole grand affair.

The plan was to shoot the pig shitting and Beryl cleaning it up a week earlier, when Beryl had an afternoon window, and then pick up the pay-off shot of Beryl going out still wearing her gloves on the actual night of the ball, which would have the added bonus of giving Beryl's wife Serenity a week to learn her line. Accordingly, on the day in question the crew had assembled at the Blenheim mansion to shoot the footage.

When the show had first begun, three seasons

earlier, the camera crew had spent a substantial amount of time with the family, but as things progressed it became easier and easier to plan and storyboard the shows, until a tight professional working pattern had been established that was economical with both time and money.

'I've scheduled an hour for Flossie,' Arnold had said as he and the crew arrived. 'We have three cameras, so she only needs to shit once and we can use three different angles to establish the three separate craps. We only need to tie you to the first one, Beryl, we'll take the other two shits on close-up. Then we can use chocolate pudding to clean up.'

Unfortunately the pig had refused to cooperate. The crew plus Beryl had been following the little pot-bellied creature as she wandered about for two and a half hours and still she would not defecate.

'Look, I don't have time for this,' Beryl finally snapped. 'You'll have to use some stock footage, then shoot me cleaning up the pudding separately.'

Arnold was dubious.

'The whole point of you being here in your party gown, Beryl, is to *tie you to the turd*. If we have to shoot you and the turd separately we really don't have a story at all. The audience is just too media-savvy these days. Remember when we got burned cutting in shots of Serenity snoring through an all-night family row and forgot to adjust the clocks? "All night" was clearly only five minutes and those shots are still all over the internet, making me look like a dick.'

'Well, I can't stand here all day waiting for the pig to shit!'

'Stock footage is high-risk strategy, Beryl. I mean every shitting shot we have is *out there*. They are TV *classics*. We have them featured on a special bonus DVD. I just don't think we could get away with using them again.'

'I knew when we started this we should have gone with shitting dogs like the fucking Osbournes did.'

'Please, Beryl, *as if*. The whole pig thing has *so* given you the edge. They're much more rock 'n' roll and their DNA is really close to humans', which helps you with the mum thing.'

'I don't *need* help with the mum thing. I'm a fantastic mother. I've won awards.'

Beryl Blenheim was extremely sensitive on this issue. No matter how hard she worked to establish herself as an iconic matriarchal figure and truly modern mum, she would for ever be handicapped by the fact that she had, for most of her life, been a man. Her offspring were not hers by blood, but Serenity's, by a previous marriage. When Beryl had met her (his) wife, Serenity had been married to the owner of a chain of fried chicken franchises in Missouri, which Blaster Blenheim (as was) would patronize when swinging through the Heartlands on his Seventies Rock Revival tours. Blaster's heart had been won by Serenity's space-hopper-sized false breasts and ability (when drunk) to fart 'The Battle Hymn Of The Republic'. Serenity, for her part, had been wooed by Blaster's English accent and the fact he could get an entire red-hot chilli chicken into his mouth. They had run away together and Serenity had obtained a quickie divorce, having threatened her husband that if he forced her to sue for it she would claim infidelity and name a long-horn bison as co-respondent.

Blaster and Serenity were married at the Love Me Tender Chapel in Las Vegas and in the years before his sex change Blaster had been a loving, if drunken, step-father to Serenity's twin girls, whom they had renamed Priscilla and Lisa Marie. Serenity had naturally been surprised when Blaster, in an effort to revive interest in his flagging career, had announced he adored fanny so much that he wanted one of his

24

own, but being an amiable sort and completely fucked up on drugs and fried food she had gone along with the new arrangement. Priscilla and Lisa Marie had suddenly found themselves with two mothers, a situation which they were forced to deal with very publicly after Beryl (née Blaster), enamoured of her new role as housewife and matriarch and jealous of the success of other self-publicizing rock mothers, had taken the decision to place the entire family on reality TV. There weren't many children who were forced, as Priscilla and Lisa Marie had been, to go to school knowing that the previous evening all their classmates had watched their stepmother demonstrating with the aid of a sausage and two new potatoes how she had had her dick removed.

'Forget the pig,' Beryl snarled. 'Put some pudding down and I'll discover it. Then stick the pig outside in a hedge and shoot her like she's trying to hide.'

'Once maybe but three times, Beryl? Three times you clean up the pudding but we never see the pig shit? That is *so* lame. This is our final programme of the season. If we're to buy the fact that you're late for the big dinner because three times you had to clean up pig crap then *we have to see the pig shit with you in shot.*'

'Well, it isn't happening, is it, Arnold?' Beryl shouted, pulling on her Marigolds. 'And I have a doctor's appointment. So just lay down some chocolate fucking pudding and I'll wipe it up.'

'I just think that this is the most horrendous artistic compromise,' Arnold protested.

'Do it!' Beryl replied, picking up her bucket and her Spray & Wipe.

Just then, the pig shat.

'Shit,' said Arnold.

'Did you get it?' Beryl asked.

'What do you mean, did I get it? I'm standing here in

front of the camera. This is a *reality* TV show, Beryl, you can't have the director in shot.'

'Don't talk to me like that. I sold forty million albums when I was a man!'

Just as things were beginning to turn nasty the cameraman pointed out that Flossie was still hovering about admiring her steaming shit and that if Arnold gently edged himself out of the shot and Beryl then walked into it they could still tie the star *and* the pig to the turd.

'That's right,' Arnold agreed, hurrying behind camera. 'If we can get you, the pig and the turd in the same shot, we have our story even if we didn't see her shit. So take two steps back . . . Is Beryl out of frame?'

The cameraman announced that she was.

'OK, Beryl,' Arnold continued. 'Step back in shouting, "I'm coming, Serenity . . ." then see the pig, see the big mountain of shit, curse the pig and clean up the turd.'

It worked like a dream. The agency pig even co-operated by suddenly positioning her back end over her turd as if having just dumped it and then, as Beryl entered shot, turning round and sniffing it in what looked like a deeply satisfied manner.

'Coming, Serenity!' Beryl shouted convincingly as if reacting to some angry off-camera summons. 'Don't be so fucking impatient! You want me to look fabulous, don't you?'

Then she stopped dead and looked down at the pig in horror.

'Flossie, you flea-bitten little ratbag. I'll have you sliced up for bacon burgers.'

And then with genuine abhorrence, for this was after all a real pile of shit, Beryl knelt down and cleaned it up. When she had done so she even had the presence of mind to coo at the pig in her famous sexy mumsy voice.

'I forgive ooo, ickle Flossie-wossie.'

When the shot was complete there was much joy and celebration.

'We can dub on a beeping car horn later and shoot Serenity calling for you next week,' said a jubilant Arnold.

Then a small voice piped up.

'Sorry, but I don't think we can use it.'

The voice was that of the continuity girl.

'What do you mean, we can't use the shot?' Arnold cried impatiently, for it was the lot of continuity girls always to exasperate their directors by pointing out that supposedly perfect takes were unusable because somebody had changed hats or walked out of the wrong door.

'Beryl had her rubber gloves on as she *entered* shot,' the girl replied miserably. 'I tried to say but you'd already turned over.'

'What's the problem?' Arnold demanded. 'She's supposed to be cleaning up shit, isn't she? You want her to do it with her bare hands?'

'Well, no, but our story is that Beryl is on her way to the car when she *discovers* the doo-doo. She's even shouting at Serenity that she's coming. Why would she be wearing rubber gloves to the Recoverers' Ball *before* she sees that the pig has been to the bathroom on her floor?'

There was an angry pause as everyone worked the story through in their heads and was forced to conclude that the girl was right.

'Fuck,' said Beryl.

'Maybe she'll do it again,' Arnold said, but Flossie had already retreated. In the end they were forced to make what for Arnold was the heartbreaking compromise of shooting all three of Beryl's cleaning shots using chocolate pudding – with no pig in shot at all. After that, Beryl rushed off to try to retrieve her cosmetic surgery appointment and one of her Mexican maids cleaned up the chocolate pudding and pig shit properly.

The Other Bloke

'Any messages, Maureen?'

Rodney Root was trying to sound casual and relaxed as he strolled into his Berwick Street office. As if it was all the same to him either way; messages, no messages, whatever, he was far too big a fish to worry about whether anybody wanted to communicate with him. Sadly, the truth was the opposite. Rodney was not busy, he was not in demand. He knew it and Maureen knew it, but the fact was never acknowledged. It was the elephant at the dinner table of their professional relationship. Rodney had spent nearly two hours over breakfast at Soho House, delaying his arrival at the office until almost 10.30am, in the hope that by mid-morning something interesting might have come in. He had eaten a full English fry-up, sausage, bacon, black pudding, soda bread and two eggs, putting on countless kilos he could ill afford, and for what? Nothing. Nothing had happened.

'Your dress suit is ready at the dry cleaner's,' his faithful secretary told him, attempting to make this innocuous piece of information sound urgent and interesting.

'Right. Good. Very good. That's good,' Rodney replied, as if his suit's condition was all part of a larger game plan and everything was falling into place nicely.

'And Iona rang. She wants you to call her.'

Rodney's face darkened. If there was anything worse than no messages, it was a message from Iona. Nothing excites a man less than the object of a passion spent, particularly one to whom many promises were made and a shedload of guilt is attached. Rodney had come seriously to regret his affair with Iona Cameron, which had blossomed so publicly after Iona's band, Shetland Mist, had been ignominiously ejected from last year's series of *Chart Throb*. Rodney had been, briefly, deeply infatuated with the pale young Scottish girl and, like many infatuated men before him, had made something of an arse of himself. Lost in the rosy haze of love he had publicly announced that, despite Beryl's bullying contempt and Calvin's studied lack of interest, Shetland Mist would surely be stars and that he, Rodney Root, pop Svengali and the ultimate rock 'n' roll insider (as Keely habitually referred to him), would make it so. Rodney's gushing pronouncements on live TV of faith in Shetland Mist's talent had been accompanied by an equally clear and slightly toe-curling enthusiasm for Iona's personal charms.

'Iona's a gorgeous, gorgeous girl,' he had said with tears in his eyes. 'And she deserves to be a big, big star. She *will* be a big, big star. She should have a contract, she *will* get a contract. The whole band will have a contract and Iona will be a big, big star.'

'And you're going to make that happen, are you, Rodders?' Calvin had teased wickedly in the time-honoured manner of judges' banter.

'I shall make it so,' Rodney had replied pompously. 'These kids deserve better than you and Beryl have given them and I intend to see that they get it.'

Iona had been absolutely thrilled with Rodney's gushing attention to her and also of course his passionate and highly public commitment to her band. After all Rodney had once been a big recording star, one half of The Root and The Branch, an early-eighties techno pop outfit which had scored a respectable number of hits and had even charted once in the

States. Admittedly Rodney had been the less celebrated member of the team. In those days techno duos had often been made up of one nerdy instrumentalist who stood almost motionless behind an assortment of keyboards occasionally depressing a key, and a flamboyantly homosexual vocalist who strutted about in various PVC outfits grabbing all the limelight. Rodney, as the songwriter, had ended up behind the keyboards while The Branch, who was, in fact, a heterosexual lorry driver from Aberystwyth (whom Rodney had recruited via an advert in *Time Out*), pulled on the pink plastic hotpants.

Rodney's virtual anonymity within his own band had been a source of massive irritation to him for nearly twenty-five years but nonetheless he had once been a star of sorts, and he had gone on to write a number of identikit hits for various boy bands before sinking into complete obscurity in the mid-nineties. His career had been given a second lease of life when Calvin asked him to become a judge on *Chart Throb*. Calvin had hoped to find a genuine pop manager who had actually developed real recording careers, but unfortunately all the real players in the industry had got wise to the dissatisfactions of playing second fiddle to a charismatic bully and Calvin had had to settle for Rodney.

Rodney and Iona had embarked on a very public affair which in the early weeks went as far as an *OK!* magazine cover shoot with heavy hints of an engagement to follow. Rodney's ardour, however, had soon evaporated. What was Iona, after all? A struggling part-time singer who worked in a shop. During the brief explosion of publicity that had surrounded Shetland Mist's appearance as *Chart Throb* finalists she had seemed glamorous and fresh, a real star and a fitting consort for an important man such as Rodney. But the life of an instant celebrity is short indeed, and within weeks Rodney found himself attached to a woman who added nothing to his equation but herself, which he was quickly tiring of. Apart from anything else, she was not half so cute without the *Chart Throb* costume and make-up department's constant attentions. During the white heat of the *Chart Throb* finals Rodney had scarcely seen the object of his passion apart from when she was performing with her band or being filmed for the inserts. It was this television creation that he had fallen in love with. Poor Iona looked very different when dressing herself in the bedroom of Rodney's penthouse flat while he lay in bed staring at her critically over the dome of his middle-aged spread. Suddenly Rodney noticed the tricky legs, the slightly asymmetrical boobs and the droopy bottom. Suddenly the Scottish accent that he had briefly found so musical and charming was saying things he didn't want to hear.

'My ma and da are coming to London, can we take them to dinner? The band has a gig at the Islay Folk Festival, everybody's really hoping you can make it.'

The Islay fucking *Folk Festival*! Islay was *six hundred miles away*.

Love had quickly died and irritation set in, irritation that this rather ordinary girl, with an ordinary life and an ordinary family, had gatecrashed his important and busy existence. Rodney quickly concluded that he did not want her in his life and he most certainly did not want her in his bed. She was suddenly turning him off as violently as she had briefly turned him on. So he dumped her.

'I just think we were both a little mad there for a while,' he told her. 'This was never truly meant to be.'

Iona had taken it with dignity, although she was devastated, having imagined that she loved him.

'Will I still see you?' she asked. 'Will you still be helping us out with the band?'

'Of course,' Rodney assured her. 'Of course, of course, of course. I *believe* in you guys . . . although sadly I can't make Islay.'

All that had been last year and was now for Rodney a deeply embarrassing memory. He had done nothing for Shetland Mist and probably couldn't have done much even if he had tried. Contrary to the *Chart Throb* myth, Rodney was not the 'hitmaker of pop' and with the best will in the world success is not something that can simply be invented. Iona still occasionally tried to contact him – after all, he was still technically their manager, a job he had announced for himself during the *OK!* magazine interview – but Rodney never took her calls.

'Nothing else?' he enquired airily.

'Well,' Maureen replied, 'I had an email from the agency dealing with the marketing for Tesco. They are interested in using you in an advertising campaign.'

Rodney lit up like he'd swallowed a light bulb.

'Tesco? The supermarket?'

'Yes but . . .'

'The *biggest supermarket chain* in Britain? Thirty per cent of UK retail? Currently masterminding an audacious attack on Wal-Mart's supremacy in the USA?'

'Well, yes but . . .'

'For God's sake, woman, why didn't you say so before? I would *love* to work with them. I'm *exactly* what they need, I'm loved, trusted, down to earth, instantly recognizable. Tesco and I would be a terrific combination . . .'

'Rodney, it isn't just you that they want.'

Instantly the light inside Rodney dimmed. He should have known, of course. Had it been genuinely good news Maureen would have called him the moment she had got it; instead she had buried the message behind his dress suit and a call from Iona.

And why? Because Maureen was well aware that an offer where they did not want just him was worse than no offer at all.

'They want the three of us?' he said, unable to conceal his disappointment.

'Well, that's certainly their base-line position . . .'

'Do they want me to approach Beryl and Calvin?'

'They have written to them separately but . . .'

'They've received no response and so they've decided to try going through me?'

'Sort of . . . Reading between the lines I think that's the position.'

Why? Rodney simply could not understand it. He was one of the three judges. He got as much air time as the others, he was in all the promotional clips and press releases. Yet Beryl was advertising everything from toilet cleaner to haute couture, Calvin was too busy but could probably get himself elected Pope if he wanted to, while he, Rodney Root, hitmaker of pop, Svengali of Denmark Street, was offered nothing.

'Do not flatter them with a reply,' Rodney said, summoning up all his dignity. 'I shall be in my office.'

HRH

The heir to the throne sat over his solitary breakfast and contemplated the morning's newspapers. They made for depressing reading. He was currently enduring one of those periods of media frenzy in which he was used to being engulfed. He had once thought that he might one day get used to the casual brutality with which the most extraordinarily cruel accusations were regularly hurled at him but he had finally come to understand that he never would.

Today had been intended to be rather a special and important day for him, for the youth charity to which he had devoted a large part of his life was to be honoured by the United Nations. However, this exciting piece of news was nowhere to be found because the ongoing scandal of his 'crown jewels' was still dominating the popular agenda. He was being accused by a disgruntled ex-employee (who had been dismissed for stealing teaspoons) of requiring members of his staff to attend to him during the performance of his bodily functions. The more aggressive tabloids were enjoying themselves hugely, painting lurid pictures of liveried footmen standing to attention while nervous chambermaids scurried about with silken napkins that bore his personal monogram.

'They'll have me selling tickets next,' the Prince lamented to his long-suffering aspidistra, 'like Louis XIV.'

The Prince was of course famous for speaking to his plants. Many people considered this evidence of an eccentricity bordering on madness but in fact it was merely that he could be reasonably sure that an aspidistra would not allow itself to be corrupted by chequebook journalism.

'Ignore it, darling,' he muttered, playing for a moment the role of the plant.

'I can't. I bloody can't,' he protested back at himself.

Possibly he *might* have been able to laugh off lavatorial madness but the more sinister accusations he had to endure were getting out of hand. Rumours had suddenly emerged that he was plotting to kill his mother out of impatience for the throne.

'If only people knew the *real* me,' His Royal Highness lamented, marmalading another slice of oatmeal bread cut from a loaf he had baked himself, with flour ground from oats that he grew in the window boxes of his Scottish estate.

'If only they knew the *real me*.'
Just then the telephone rang.

Priscilla Blenheim

After her consultation with the best arse man in West Hollywood, Beryl Blenheim hurried down to the Virgin Megastore on Rodeo Drive, where her stepdaughter was already midway through an album signing.

It should have been such an exciting afternoon for Priscilla Blenheim. After all, how many seventeen-year-olds get to cut their own album? How many teenage kids get to stand on their own little podium in a top record store while hundreds of other kids call out their name and thrust CDs towards them for their signature? That was the position Priscilla was in. Of course it would have been a lot more fun if some of the CDs that Priscilla was being called upon to sign had actually been hers rather than her stepmother's, in the days when she had been a man. And if most of the kids standing in line had actually bought a CD for her to sign, any CD instead of the crumpled collection of library tickets, student cards, Burger King cartons and till receipts that had been hastily produced. The majority of the kids were not fans at all but merely curious shoppers who had been drawn towards Priscilla's signing table simply because someone famous was in the store.

Then the shop manager had made it worse by announcing to the line that Priscilla would only be signing copies of her album. Instantly there had been boos and catcalls. The crowd was furious. This was not the Priscilla they knew from the TV. Priscilla was meant to be one of the kids, her whole pose on

TV was that of a straight-talking teen, as yet un-corrupted by all the bullshit.

'Hey, Priscilla!' a voice called out, dripping with contempt. 'Why don't you *sell* autographs like some fucking baseball player?'

'Doesn't your *mommy* give you enough fucking bread, Priscilla?' cried another.

Suddenly kids were screwing up the pieces of paper they had been holding into little balls, flicking them at her and turning away.

'Why did you *say* that, you dick?' said Priscilla, turning on the hapless manager.

In fact he had said it because Priscilla had spent the previous half-hour bitching about how she was only signing bus tickets, but he did not point this out. Instead he called out to the diminishing crowd, 'Priscilla is happy to sign whatever.'

Unfortunately this apparent capitulation impressed nobody. 'Then fucking sign this!' a young man called out, pulling down his trousers, and Priscilla found her-self facing a pimply adolescent backside spread aggressively and graphically wide. 'Kiss my chocolate starfish!' the youth shouted through his parted legs before being bundled out of the store by the security guards. Beryl, who had arrived just in time to witness the debacle, brought the embarrassment to a close and the celebrated mother and daughter took refuge in the stock room until what was left of the crowd dispersed.

'They booed me, Dad!'

Priscilla knew how much Beryl hated being referred to as 'Dad'.

'Don't call me Dad! I'm a mum. I've won awards!'

'That jerk showed me his butt,' Priscilla replied, almost in tears. 'And they hardly bought any albums.'

'We sold some, darling. I have a stock report.'

'Eight, Mom! We sold eight and I was here an hour

and that includes two checkout chicks. Which, by the way, is also *so* pathetic: they have like thirty kids working in this store and I am here, *in the store*, signing and even most of the fucking staff don't want to buy my record.'

Beryl turned on the shop manager, who was trying to hide behind the coffee and mini muffins.

'Why the fuck didn't any staff get an album signed?' she shouted into his face. 'You call yourself a record store! You have a major celebrity recording artist here today and none of your fucking staff are even interested. What the fuck is going on here? Borders were *begging* me to deliver Priscilla! We are doing Virgin a fucking favour here!'

The manager could only stand and whimper. 'I guess I'd like one signed,' he said finally. 'I'm a big fan.'

'What? Such a big fan that you don't want a record until my mom toasts you?' said Priscilla. 'Fuck off.'

Later, heading home in the limousine, Priscilla's disappointment gave way to tears.

'I'm a joke, Mom. A fucking joke.'

'Well, rock 'n' roll's a tough game, darling.'

'I'm not in rock 'n' roll. To be in rock 'n' roll you have to *sell* an album, not just *make* one. You're supposed to be a fucking "rock tutor" on that show of yours in England, you're the Queen of Rock, the fucking teacher, the *fucking mentor*. How about mentoring your own daughter for a change?'

'Oh, get over yourself, Priscilla.'

Priscilla lapsed into silence for a moment. It was tough to be a seventeen-year-old star and already washed up.

'Mom?' she said finally.

'What?'

'Do you think kids don't buy my album because I'm like a reality TV star or because I'm actually a crock of shit?'

'Hey, you wouldn't have got to *make* an album if you weren't a reality TV star.'

'That's not what I'm asking. Do you think I'm shit?'

'What a stupid question, Priscilla. You're my daughter, of course I don't think you're shit.'

'I'm your stepdaughter; I didn't get your talent, I only got your name. My real dad fried chicken.'

'Fucking good fried chicken!'

'Come on, what do you think of me, as a singer? I mean, you're my manager, you must have an opinion. Can I sing?'

'Listen, babes, I do deals these days. That's my job. I got you a deal. What you do with it is your responsibility.'

A Star Is Born

Calvin had declined to inform the Prince of Wales's office on what business it was that he wished to see His Royal Highness. In another age this would have presented an impossible breach of protocol and no invitation would have been forthcoming. These days, however, things were different. The royal heir was on the ropes, the unhappy subject of almost daily polls calling upon him to do the decent thing and bugger off altogether, leaving the way open for his more telegenic son. HRH needed friends like his organically farmed non-cross-bred English roses (grown from eighteenth-century seeds supplied by the Kew seed bank) needed rain. Particularly a friend like Calvin Simms, arguably the most famous man in the country, a man whose intuitive grasp of the popular zeitgeist had made *Chart Throb* into the broadcasting colossus that had crushed *Pop Idol*, *X Factor*, *Strictly Come Dancing*, *Celebrity*

Morris Dancing and all those other shows into dust.

Calvin, who was more than aware of his own position in society and entirely realistic about the Prince's, had been confident that His Royal Highness would want to see him and he had been right.

'Hello, hello, hello,' the future king said, leaping from his seat in the window of the drawing room of his London town house. The Prince had long since ceased to reside at St James's Palace, hoping that if he lived in a house instead of a palace the press might stop banging on about how much money he cost. They hadn't, of course; they continued to catalogue his expenses as if they reflected the lifestyle of an emperor of Ancient Rome.

Only that morning he had found his modest fishmonger's bill trumpeted in the press. *Forty quid for a fish supper, sir!* the headline had screamed. *Guess who knows his PLAICE.*

'Hello, hello,' the Prince continued. 'How very kind of you to come. Have you come far? Was the traffic awful? I imagine it was. It always is, isn't it? I did a talk about it and how we need *people-scale* planning for our cities. Didn't do any good, of course. Nobody listened. Just old buggerlugs *banging on* again. Heigh-ho. Who'd be a prince? Have you been offered tea?'

There was then a lengthy hiatus while the Prince attempted to summon somebody to bring tea. Eventually he succeeded and a young work-experience girl brought in a tray.

'Ex-offender,' the Prince explained. 'One of the youngsters from my charity, aren't you, Kira? I just find you need to give young people a sense of purpose. Don't you agree? I'm sure you meet a lot of young people in your line of work. Biscuit? I bake them myself from stone-ground sunflower seeds and raw sugar. People think I'm mad, you know, but what's mad about a home-baked biscuit? Kira, do pass them over, would you? Don't worry, she's not one of the ladies of the toilet! Ha ha ha!' The Prince roared with laughter. 'Good to laugh, don't you think?' He wiped his eyes with a handkerchief he pulled from his sleeve. 'Sometimes I think if I didn't laugh I'd go stark raving bananas. Do you know they try to record my phone calls so they can publish the transcripts? Can you imagine anything more beastly or low? When I was at school that was called eavesdropping.'

Calvin realized he had not spoken once since entering the room. Clearly the Prince was used to filling in the gaps in the conversation.

'Sir,' he said.

'Yes, Mr Cowell?'

'Umm, Simms actually, sir. Calvin Simms. Cowell's another bloke. He used to do a show like mine. That's gone now. We're bigger.'

'Really? Extraordinary. Well done.'

'I wonder if I might explain why I've asked to see you, Your Royal Highness.'

The Prince leaned forward attentively. 'Please, call me sir. Everybody does.'

'Well, sir, I hope you won't think me forward if I say that it strikes me you have a PR problem.'

'Yes. Yes, I rather think I do. I was saying so to my wife only this morning as we de-snailed the herb garden. Sometimes it seems as if every bugger in Britain's got it in for *yours truly*.'

'Yes, it does, doesn't it? Let's face it, you are routinely ridiculed as a pampered dilettante who has a personal bum wiper, consumes 90 per cent of the nation's tax revenues, eats a raw fox for breakfast, smears the fresh blood on his children and then goes off to deliver a lecture about how all post-nineteenth-century buildings are complete rubbish.'

'Yes, that's me. God knows where I'm supposed to find the time.'

40

'I think you're due for a change, sir.'

'Well certainly. But what, if you'll forgive me for asking, Mr Simms, has that to do with you?'

'I can make you popular again. Bigger than your grannie was. I can make you a star.'

The Prince's gentle manner hardened ever so slightly. He knew all about set-ups. He was still trying to live down the incident when he had received the Dalai Lama at Sandringham, only to discover that it was a Radio One DJ wrapped in a sheet.

'Is this a joke, Mr Simms? Perhaps I am to be the subject of some hidden camera prank?'

'Not at all, sir. The simple fact is that I want to see you win the next series of *Chart Throb*.'

'Goodness gracious. Whyever would you want that?'

'Because I'm a monarchist, sir,' Calvin replied.

'No! Really?'

'Yes, sir. I have a deep and abiding loyalty and affection for the great historical institutions of this country and I despair to see how low they have fallen in public esteem.'

'Gosh, don't we all!'

'What is more, I am in a unique position to do something about it. I produce a show that speaks directly to the public. There's no press or spin involved. I create stars. Real stars. Stars in the truest sense of the word, popular favourites, people with whom the public genuinely identify. I want to turn you into just such a star.'

'You want me to audition as a singer?'

'Exactly.'

'But I am to be head of state, Mr Simms. That is a high and serious office.'

'What's serious any more? George Galloway, the nation's foremost anti-war activist, went on *Big Brother*! The leader of the Conservative Party was asked on a chat show if as a lad he'd wanked over Mrs

Thatcher! Politics isn't serious any more, it's showbiz. Nothing but sound bites and razzmatazz. You're a man of conviction and it frustrates you that nobody listens to you . . .'

'They don't, it's *maddening*.'

'Well, sorry to have to tell you, sir, but people don't want convictions, they want *personalities*. That's why the Prime Minister's on *Parky*.'

'Did you see it? I thought he was rather good.'

Calvin did not wish to discuss *Parkinson*. He was an astute judge of human nature and he was about to arrive at the point where he was certain the Prince would be unable to resist.

'Your problem, sir, is that nobody knows the *real you*.'

The Prince's face lit up with an expression of surprise and joy.

'Goodness gracious,' he exclaimed, 'I was only saying *exactly* that yesterday to my favourite aspidistra. How remarkably *clever* of you to spot that, Mr Simms.'

Calvin smiled. He knew it was not clever at all. He had never met a single celebrity who did not lament the fact that people did not know the *real them*. From weather girls to rock superstars, the condition set in the moment a person was first reported or described in the media. Instantly they felt misrepresented, and the more the media represented them the more misrepresented they felt, until their whole lives were consumed with the passionate desire that people might somehow come to know the *real them*.

'I am offering you a fresh chance, a chance to reach a regular audience of *eight and a half million people*, sir. Think of that, eight and a half million people every week. Predominantly *young people*, sir, don't forget that. Our demographic is a prince or a politician's dream.'

Calvin knew that if there was one phrase above all

42

others which was likely to appeal to the very soul of a modern prince that phrase was 'young people', that massive group of supposedly disenfranchised, disillusioned, dispossessed citizens who were already two generations away from any residual respect for the great institutions of state.

'But I'd have to sing for it,' the Prince replied.

'What's wrong with singing? People like singing. *Can* you sing, by the way?'

The Prince hesitated. His was a generation not raised to boast.

'*Can* you sing, sir?' Calvin pressed, sensing weakness.

'Well, I confess I have been told that I have a pleasant light baritone. Nothing to shout about, you understand.'

'There you are then. Come and sing on *Chart Throb*. You'll have plenty of opportunities for sound bites, every bit as long as they'd give you on the news. While all the other contestants will be saying they're singing for their mums or for their kids, you can say you're singing for your charities or sustainable cities or to promote awareness about soil.'

Calvin had nearly pushed it too far.

'You're being facetious, Mr Simms,' HRH protested.

'No, I'm not. You are one of the few people in public life who still has the *conscience* to set themselves apart. To rise above the hysterical orthodoxy of the celebrity-obsessed media agenda and talk about things that *matter*. Architecture, soil, mutton, good vegetables, a lost generation becoming increasingly cut off from society and turning to crack cocaine and knife crime. You are that rare thing, a public figure of real *conviction*!'

'I say, do you really think so? That *is* kind.'

'Of course, it's obvious to anybody who cares to think about it. But nobody ever does think about it. And why?'

'Because I'm just *boring* old *buggerlugs*?'

'No!'

'No?'

'No! It's because your voice has been *crushed* by media hype and the celebrity culture.'

'Well, do you know, I rather think it *has*.'

'And what I'm saying to you is that if show business has conquered conviction, isn't it high time that conviction conquered show business?'

'Goodness!'

'The monarchy is in crisis, sir!' Calvin had stood up now, his teacup rattling in his hand. 'Destroyed by the very people it represents! It is time to reach out to those people, sir! Reach out to them and save their treasured national institutions from the ridicule they have allowed them to descend into!'

'By appearing on a nationwide talent show?'

'Yes! By appearing on the single most influential, ubiquitous and powerful cultural institution in the country. You, sir, with the help of your passionate commitment to organic farming, high-fibre diets and full youth employment, and your pleasant light baritone, can save the monarchy as surely as Queen Bess did at Tilbury. This, sir, is your duty!'

'My duty?'

'Yes! Your duty!'

'To appear on *Chart Throb*?'

'Yes, sir! Your country needs you.'

His Royal Highness did not reply. For a time he sipped his tea in silence, seemingly trying to come to terms with the enormity of what was being suggested.

'Sir,' Calvin said with heavy significance, 'we are living in a *post-modern world*.' This was a phrase which Calvin used regularly and with great effect, despite having no idea what it meant.

Still the Prince remained silent.

'*Plus*,' Calvin urged, laying his trump card down on the table, 'people will love you again.'

His Royal Highness looked up.

'Do you . . . Do you really think so?'

It seemed to Calvin that there was a wealth of weariness in his sad eyes.

'Of course,' Calvin said quietly. 'Everyone loves the winner of *Chart Throb*.'

'Winner?'

Calvin had almost revealed too much of his hand.

'Well, perhaps not *winner*, sir, that of course will be up to the public to decide, but as the country's foremost judge of talent and personality I am convinced that you could go a very long way. At least far enough for people to have the opportunity to see the *real you*.'

Once more the Prince fell silent for the time it took to nibble a biscuit. When he spoke again Calvin knew he had his man.

'I've never seen *Chart Throb*,' he said, 'but I remember my boys watching *X Factor*.'

'And?'

'I believe they received upwards of seventy-five thousand entrants.'

'We got ninety-five last series.'

'Well, forgive my stupidity, Mr Simms. How do you propose to convince people that having auditioned all those ninety-five thousand the best potential pop star you could come up with was *yours truly*?'

Calvin was actually surprised. He had imagined that, having been a part of the cultural establishment all his life, the Prince of Wales might be a little more astute than the average punter. He might have just a modicum of media savvy. Some simple common sense even. But it turned out that he was wrong. The heir to the throne clearly still believed in the tooth fairy.

'Ninety-five thousand people?' Calvin said.

'Yes.'

'And you think we audition them all?'

'I was under the impression that that was the *whole point*. Don't you?'

'No.'

'You don't audition them?'

'No, we don't.'

'Oh . . . I'm not sure I follow.'

'Sir. Please. Just do the maths.'

The Maths

Ninety-five thousand people.

Three judges.

Twelve finalists.

Just one Chart Throb*!!*

That was the breathless message with which (accompanied by the urgent, pounding, *Chart Throb* theme music) the lovely Keely would preface each episode of the show. Reminding the public yet again of the gigantic number of applicants and the three stern, unbending arbiters of poptastic excellence whose arses each and every wannabe star must attempt to rock in order to reach the finals.

Ninety-five thousand people.

Three judges.

Twelve finalists.

Just one Chart Throb*!!*

Keely would shout it over footage of impossibly long escalators crowded with gurning hopefuls. She would yell it in front of leisure-centre reception areas packed with a cheering, chanting throng of stars in waiting. She screamed it as the dizzying, whirling crane shots spun over the heads of vast crowds in car parks. She shouted it again as the endless queues snaked their way forward so that the thousands of hopefuls might be numbered, badged and registered at the long trestle tables.

And after the crowds came the moody and dramatic shots of the three judges, dressed in black, arms folded, staring into the cameras with those grim, unsmiling faces. Faces which said 'We will see you, we will judge you fairly, you *will* get your chance. But do *not* fuck with us because we will *not* be taking any shit and only the best and the toughest will survive our ruthless selection process.'

Ninety-five thousand people.

Three judges.

That was it, the whole show in a nutshell. The connection made loud and clear to the meanest intelligence.

Ninety-five thousand hopefuls. The mad and the sad. The sublime and the ridiculous. The tragic and the gifted. The beautiful and the damned. The good. The bad. And the very, very ugly. And then the ruthless Politburo of Pop. Calvin, Beryl and the other bloke, who would after an exhaustive audition process choose twelve finalists to be offered up to the nation.

It was all very simple. And it was all complete fiction.

'Sir,' Calvin explained, 'when most of those ninety-five thousand hopefuls get rejected they won't even be in the same *country* as Beryl, Rodney and me, let alone the same room.'

'Really? That's *extraordinary*! Have I been terribly *naïve*?'

'Don't you read the celebrity magazines?'

'I sometimes find them in the *loo* when my lads' girlfriends have stayed.'

'I thought you considered yourself a man of the people, sir? Anyway, if you did read them you'd know that I spend half the year in LA! I am a *huge* star over there. *Chart Throb USA* is the biggest show in the world.'

'Goodness, *well done.*'

'So how could I possibly find the time to wander around provincial Britain personally considering the star quality of *ninety-five thousand* nobodies?'

'Well, perhaps not you, but . . .'

'Maybe the other two, you think? Beryl lives in America full time! It's public knowledge that she looks after the entertainment ventures of the vast Blenheim family business. Rodney's around, of course, but even he has a *life* of some sort. How could you, how could *anyone* possibly imagine that the three of us could arrange to meet up and conduct ninety-five thousand auditions?'

'Well, I suppose I hadn't imagined that you actually *auditioned* them *all.*'

'Maybe you think we open the envelopes? Maybe you think we read ninety-five thousand of these?'

Calvin handed the Prince a copy of the *Chart Throb* entrance form. In that carefully worded document the applicant was required to promise to abide by the rules of the competition no matter how often they might be changed and never, on pain of criminal prosecution, to discuss any aspect of their experience with the press.

'Every single person who fills in one of these,' Calvin continued, 'does so because they want to prove to me, Beryl and Rodney that they have *what it takes* – that X, that It, that Pow! which will propel them from the humdrum inadequacy of their current existence towards that mythical nirvana called the "celebrity lifestyle". They all think they have a *chance*. That once they get themselves in front of those three famous judges they have a *genuine chance*, no matter how small, of all their dreams coming true.'

'Well, I'm sure they do.'

'But they're not going to get in front of us, are they,

sir? At least about ninety-four thousand of them won't. The chances of any of them actually getting to perform for me, Beryl and Rodney are tiny.'

'Goodness gracious,' the Prince said, genuinely surprised, 'so it's all a *lie*?'

'Of course it isn't a lie, sir! It's show business. It's entertainment. We don't deceive anybody. The information is there for people if they want to see it, they only have to *do the maths*. Ninety-five thousand contestants, three judges. How could we *possibly* consider even a fraction of that number? Say we did ten an hour, that's nine thousand five hundred hours. Assuming we worked a ten-hour day, that would be nine hundred and fifty days! That's nearly *three years* we would have to be sitting there behind a trestle table saying, "I think you need to find yourself another dream," to an endless stream of idiots, and that's if we worked flat out without a break.'

'I suppose it does all seem a bit *improbable* when you come to think about it,' the Prince conceded.

'Of course it is. People can work it out if they want to. They only have to *do the maths*. But they don't want to do the maths and why should they? Any more than they would want to watch a film that reminded them that it was only actors reciting a script. We are an entertainment show. My researchers scloot tho most interesting and entertaining personalities to bring before the judges. I am in no doubt, sir, that you would be selected, with or without my help. Just as I have no doubt that you will make it to the finals. Then it will be between you and the public. *Your* public. Your people. This is about the soul of the nation, sir. It's 1940 and the barbarians are at the gate. Britain is holding out for a hero. Will you accept the challenge, sir? Will you be that hero?'

49

Shaiana

For the hundredth time she began the sentence anew.

How could she do it? Put down in ten words her hopes, her dreams. Her *hunger* to be a singer.

I want it so much, she wrote.

Even as she set down the words, she knew that they were hollow and uninspiring. Why would anybody care that she wanted it? Everybody wanted it. What was not to want? But did they want it like *she* wanted it? Did they want it *so much*? That was why they *had* to choose her, because of how *much* she wanted it. They simply had to recognize her ferocious desire to show the world that she was not a nothing, a joke, a nobody. *That* was what made her different. *That* was why she could be a star. Because her performance would be fuelled by the passion of a thousand slights and sneers.

I want it so much – five words.

That left her with five more to write. Perhaps she could redeem her application with those. Come up with some brilliant, sparkling, seductive little sentence that would hide her pain and show her to be the brilliant, sparkling, seductive young woman she so wished herself to be.

Instead, once more she wrote *I want it so much*.

Now she had ten words. Or rather she had five words, twice.

Shaiana reached for her pills and swallowed three. The bottle was nearly empty but she knew that she could get more. There had always been drugs in her life, drugs and booze. Even as a little girl she had never known a time when those bittersweet panaceas had not been part of the furniture in her family home.

The pills helped but Shaiana craved a much stronger drug. She was certain that if she could just prove herself as a singer, if she could be a star and in so doing distance herself from the demeaning life that had created and defined her, then she would no longer need to find comfort and escape in those pills.

Once more she tried to focus her tired eyes on the application form, as if hoping to find inspiration from the cold hard commands that she already knew by heart.

I want it so much. I want it so much.

With a start Shaiana realized she had written the words on the form itself. Up until that point she had been writing her sentences out in rough on a big block of ruled A4 that had once been intended to contain her schoolwork. Now, suddenly, she had committed herself.

Not really, of course. She could download another form easily enough, she could download a hundred. But she didn't. Perhaps this was a sign. Perhaps the truth was what she was *meant* to write. Shaiana took up the form, filled in her details, signed it, attached her photograph and slipped it into an envelope.

Emma and the Clingers, Blingers and Mingers

Two weeks later the envelope was being opened at the offices of *Chart Throb* in London. The person opening it was called Emma, a researcher on the show. Emma was good at her job and destined for advancement. On the last series three of her initial picks had actually been chosen as finalists, which was, of course, every researcher's dream. Born with a naturally sympathetic personality, Emma had always been alert to people's anxieties and dreams, understanding when they were unhappy and required support. This gave her a real edge in sensing the neediness that was such an essential element in the emotional make-up of the successful *Chart Throb* applicant.

Shaiana's form struck Emma immediately. Of course they all wanted it, in fact the very phrase *I want it so much* had become something of a *Chart Throb* mantra, but to write it *twice*? That was interesting; Emma had never seen that before. It was so inelegant, so raw, it smacked of real desperation and Emma knew that Calvin *loved* real desperation. She looked down at the section where Shaiana had been asked to describe herself. It was a small box with three blank lines in it, just twenty-five centimetres in which to write. These boxes were usually very full; most applicants managed to fit in as many as twenty words and the record was forty-four.

Shaiana had written only three: *I am me.*

Emma looked at the photograph which, as instructed, had been stapled to the top right-hand corner of the application form. A tense, forceful-looking face, not beautiful but pretty enough, in a plain Jane sort of way. The eyes were big and Emma thought that the girl was holding them unnaturally open. *Look at me!* those eyes seemed to be saying. *Can't you see I want this so much?*

'I think we should see this one,' Emma said, handing the form across the table to Trent. Trent, the most senior researcher on the show, made all the final decisions at first-round stage and answered directly to Calvin.

Clingers, Blingers and Mingers were the three types of entrant that *Chart Throb* researchers looked for.

'The Clingers are the desperate ones,' Trent had explained on Emma's first day at work.

'Aren't they all desperate?' Emma had enquired.

'Of course not. They're all hopeful but they're not all desperate. Clingers are *desperate*. They have just enough talent to be utterly self-deluded . . . actually, sometimes they manage to be self-deluded without having any talent at all, which is *really* good telly. Calvin *loves* that. Clingers cry and plead and beg. *God* gave them their dream, you see. It's *that* important. Personally I hope that if there is a God he's got better things to do than arrange the recording career of some barmaid from Solihull.'

'So Clingers are women?' Emma had asked.

'Normally, but they can be male. Middle-aged guys who just want to give their kids a better life than they've had. Club singers who've done their time and paid their dues and want one last shot at the dream. You'll start to spot them easily enough.'

'What about Blingers?'

'Blingers are the extroverts. The show-offs. The type of weirdly self-confident lunatics whose unshakeable faith in their own powers to fascinate actually *makes* them sort of fascinating, in a kamikaze kind of a way. They say things like *Hey, what's wrong with being a little crazy?* They strike poses. They flirt with Beryl. They think they're sexy. Women Blingers tend to be plumpers but they're comfy being curvy and in-variably turn up half naked.'

'And Mingers?'

'Ah, now *that's* entertainment. The life's blood of *Chart Throb*, the most essential element. Without the Mingers *Chart Throb* would be nothing.'

'And who are they?'

'The true casualties, the saddos, the uglies, the comically short-sighted, the cleft-palated, the mis-shapen, the obese, the educationally challenged, the emotionally stunted and the spotty nerds. The most vulnerable and inadequate members of society.'

'It all sounds rather exploitative,' Emma had said.

'*Hello!*' Trent sneered in reply. 'Duh! Do you think we run a charity? Of course it's exploitative. It's a business. McDonald's for the senses. What truly successful business doesn't exploit its customers by pandering to their desires? We've turned the whole country into one vast medieval village so that we can all stand in the market square and laugh at the idiots.'

'The Mingers.'

'Exactly. Quasimodo time. They sing their little song and do their little dance, desperate for the laughter of the mob because at least it means somebody has noticed them.'

'And what about singers, aren't we looking for them too?'

'Good question.'

'Well, it is a singing competition.'

'Yes, a lot of people make the mistake of thinking that. Actually singers are by far the least interesting group. Singers enter in their tens of thousands but we select very few for real consideration. Being a singer, no matter how good, is simply not enough. To be considered as a singer you have to fit into one of the other categories too. We'll take Clingers, Blingers and Mingers who aren't singers and give them a good run too, might even put one in the finals, but we would never even *consider* a singer who was not also a Clinger, a Blinger or a Minger.'

That conversation had taken place the year before. Now Emma was as practised at spotting the categories as any researcher on the *Chart Throb* team.

'This girl's a Clinger,' said Trent, referring to Shaiana's entry form. 'Shame she's not fatter. We're still a bit short of SOPs.'

Emma winced. SOP was office shorthand for Sad Old Plumper. She had never quite got used to the casual cruelty with which her colleagues discussed the applicants.

'You know Calvin likes the heavier ones,' Trent went on. 'They're more real.'

'This girl's got Clinger eyes,' Emma insisted. 'They put pounds on her.'

Trent shrugged and for a moment Shaiana's application hovered between the recycling pile and three much smaller 'first audition' piles. Finally Trent made his decision and the form was placed on the pile marked 'Clingers'.

Emma opened another envelope.

Two ugly girls who thought they were 'different'. Not different enough, not ugly enough. Recycling.

Next envelope. Pretty black boy who claimed to sing like Michael Jackson. Not as pretty as the half-dozen other black boys who claimed they could sing like Michael Jackson and who were already on the Blinger pile. Recycling.

Another envelope. Suki. Peroxide hair. Surgically enhanced boobs. Fake tan. Pussy pelmet for a skirt. 'Hates being judged for her looks alone.' Emma stared hard at the glossy photograph. Beneath the make-up, the tan and the false eyelashes, Emma thought that Suki looked tired, bitter and was almost certainly a prostitute. A Minger and a Clinger pretending to be a Blinger. Could work, not bad telly. Emma passed it to Trent.

'Too many Bobbies already,' he replied.

Bobbies was office slang for Blonde, Big Boobs.

'It's our year for the truly sad slappers,' he lamented. 'They all think Calvin will want to shag them.'

'Well, we certainly pushed that idea last series.'

'And aren't we paying the price! Every fucking crack whore in Barnsley's dreaming of a fat fee from the *News of the World*. Recycle her.'

Emma stared into Suki's eyes. Here was a woman on the verge of disintegration. Her whole adult life had clearly been built on a tawdry glamour and two-dimensional sexuality that within five years or so she would no longer even be able to fake. No doubt Suki had been pretty at school, pretty enough for her to conceive the dream, the dream that would ruin her

life: that she could be like the girls in the magazines.
Hates being judged by her looks alone.

Yes, thought Emma, particularly these days since you look like a sad washed-out old dish rag.

Emma was about to put the application on to the recycling pile but then, noticing that Trent was absorbed in his own research, she decided on a whim to give Suki a shot. If she featured on the show as a three-second Ming Bling it might double her stripping fee for a month or two and, God knows, it looked like she could use the money. Emma slipped Suki on to the Blingers pile and picked up another envelope.

Inside it was an application from yet another enormous West Indian mother of six with an 'infectious laugh' whose friends had told her to apply. Recycling.

Three more, all Theatre Arts students. Recycling. Recycling. Recycling. Seventeen more. All recycling. All those hopes, all those dreams, all those desperate pleas from desperate people asking to be saved from the lives they were leading and which they hated so much. All recycled.

Emma poured herself another cup of coffee and wondered about going outside for a cigarette. You had to stay focused, couldn't afford to drift off, any envelope could be the one. Calvin's rule was that every envelope must be opened as if it was the very first of the day.

For a moment Emma found her thoughts fixing on Calvin. He was such a *clever* man. Of course he knew it too but there was nothing wrong with that, within reason. Confidence was sexy.

Emma sipped her coffee, stretched wearily and took another envelope from the pile. Even before she had finished reading the form she knew that Graham and Millicent would receive an invitation to audition. Emma did not even bother referring the application to Trent before putting it on the Minger pile. Time was precious, the team had certain rules and Graham of the singing duo Graham and Millicent definitely had what it took.

Graham and Millicent

'I'll leave you two to it then,' said Graham's mum as she closed the bedroom door behind her. It was the bedroom of a music-mad lad: piles of CDs were stacked along the walls, while on the desk an iPod stood in its dock, connected to two enormous speakers on either side of the bed. There was a vinyl deck too and a decent-sized collection of old-fashioned LPs all lovingly catalogued. There were electric guitars, bongo drums, tuning forks, an iMac and the usual Pro Tools paraphernalia. The only difference between this bedroom and that of the majority of other music-mad young men who dreamed of pop superstardom was that there was absolutely no mess. This room was perfectly ordered, with everything in its proper place, where it could be located instantly. And there was nothing on the walls. No posters, no pictures, no framed drumskins signed by members of heavy metal bands, in fact nothing at all.

Millicent sat down beside Graham on the bed. Graham had his acoustic guitar on his lap but Millicent reached out to take it from him.

'Come on,' she said firmly. 'We have to sing unaccompanied, you know that.'

'But it's so stupid,' Graham replied. 'We're so much better with the guitar.'

'It's the same rules for everyone, Graham. You know how much you hate special treatment.'

'I only hate it when it's an excuse for denying me

normal treatment,' he replied. 'I don't mind cheating.'

'I wrote and asked them. They said we can use instruments later, if we get through the opening rounds.'

'Of course we'll get through. I mean how good are we?' Graham posed this question in the modern, rhetorical sense, meaning that he was quite certain in his own mind that they were very good indeed.

Millicent took hold of the guitar and as she did so her hand touched his and for a moment each of them exerted a tiny pressure.

'We shouldn't really be skiving off college, you know,' she said.

'You don't get an audition for *Chart Throb* every day of the week, Milly, and anyway we won't need qualifications when we're stars,' Graham replied.

'Don't get your hopes too high, Graham.'

'We're good, Milly. Everybody says so.'

'Yes, and everybody who goes on that show says that everybody says they're good. Come on, I thought we were going to rehearse.'

They began to sing, warming up as always with 'Just Like A Woman' by Bob Dylan. Milly loved the way Graham put the little croak into his voice even though she knew he only did it to cover up the inadequacies in his pitching. It was Milly who had the stronger voice. Graham's real passion was his instruments.

After 'Just Like A Woman' they did Woody Guthrie's 'This Land Is My Land', and after that Graham suggested a cup of tea.

'We've only sung two songs, Graham. You're not concentrating.'

It was true, Graham did not seem to feel much like singing. He had something on his mind.

'Milly?'

'Yes?'

There was a pause. Whatever it was that Graham wanted to say was not coming easily.

'What do I look like?' he said finally.

Millicent was quite taken aback. She had known Graham for many years and yet he had never asked her that question before.

'What do you look like?' she repeated, feeling foolish.

'Yes. I mean I know I have brown hair and Mum says I'm handsome . . . whatever that means, because mums always think their sons are handsome.'

'Well . . . you are handsome.'

'No, come on. What do I look like?'

Millicent was bright red. She wondered if Graham could sense it; she felt suddenly so hot that she imagined he must be able to feel the throbbing heat rising off her.

'I don't know,' she said. 'Why are you asking now? We're supposed to be rehearsing.'

'Well, if we do well at our audition, millions of people will end up seeing me, won't they? And yet I've never seen myself. That's kind of weird, isn't it? I want to know what they'll see.'

'Graham, it's only an audition.'

'I know what you look like, Milly.'

'Oh, do you? And what do I look like then?'

'You look beautiful.'

And Graham reached up, found her face and drew it towards his. The kiss lasted a very long time, as first kisses often do.

And for Graham it really was his first kiss. Not just between him and Millicent but between him and anyone, and as he lashed about with his tongue inside her mouth he never wanted it to end. Millicent also entered wholeheartedly into the spirit of things. She was not entirely without experience but she was hardly practised and the two of them made up in pressure and energy for what they lacked in style and finesse.

Eventually they parted, Millicent having declined

for the time being to allow Graham to put his hand up her jumper.

'Your mum's downstairs,' she whispered.

'Who cares?'

'I do, Graham. Besides, this is all, well . . . I just want to get my breath, that's all.'

'What do I look like, Milly?' he asked.

His sunglasses had been knocked off during the lengthy face-wrestling in which they had indulged and now Graham was sitting there with those strange, dark unseeing hollows that she so rarely saw and which when she did she felt she would never get used to. Except now, suddenly she felt that she was used to them. Perhaps interpreting her silence for embarrassment or even revulsion, Graham began to feel about for his shades.

'Don't put them back on, Graham. Nobody except rock stars is allowed to wear sunglasses indoors. And you're not a rock star yet. Oh, by the way . . . you look beautiful too.'

The Four-Z

After Graham and Millicent, Emma had opened another thirty or so envelopes before deciding upon The Four-Z.

Michael, the leader of The Four-Z, had written down his full name as instructed. Michael Robert Harley. Age nineteen.

Next Michael was asked for an address. Michael had considered applying for a PO box number because the postman did not always venture all the way along the corridor on the vast low-rise development in Birmingham where he lived with his mother and sisters. The name of Michael's estate had at one point been Aneurin Bevan, then briefly Nelson Mandela. Now it was Collingbrook, so called because of the stream that had once bubbled and gurgled across the land upon which the estate was built and which now formed part of the sewage system beneath it. Michael called it hell.

When he was growing up, there had been only two ways whereby a boy (particularly a black boy) might reasonably expect to get out of Collingbrook: crime (mainly dealing drugs) or sport. Now there was a third, *Chart Throb*. To Michael, forming a boy band certainly seemed a more attractive proposition than buying a gun or training as a boxer and so The Four-Z was born, and it was going to get him and his family out of hell.

There had of course been endless debate about the naming of the group and the name was still not considered entirely satisfactory. The problem was that people kept referring to the boys as The Four Zed when it seemed obvious to Michael that what they wanted to be called was The Force.

'Why don't you spell it The Force then?' Michael's mother asked.

'Because then people would miss the pun,' Michael replied. 'There's four of us see, The Four-se.'

'Yes but if you spell it with a Z that makes it fourz like in paws, not force like in Morse. A Z isn't an S.'

'Yeah, I *know*, Mum, but a Z looks cool. Look . . .' Michael took a piece of paper and wrote down Four-Z and beside it Four-S. 'I mean come on, which looks cooler?'

'People aren't going to be reading it, they're going to be hearing it,' his mum pointed out.

'Not on this form, Mum. They'll be reading this form and I need to give it the best shot I have.'

So Michael wrote down The Four-Z, and when Emma sent the boys an invitation to attend the

Birmingham audition she believed she was booking a group called The Four Zed.

Next on the form came the instruction to describe yourself or your group in ten words. Michael and his fellow group members had imagined that listing ten adjectives instead of forming a sentence was an original approach.

They wrote *Bitchin', Blingin', Badass, Beautiful, Bodacious, Ball bustin' Boy Band.* Emma had read many such exhortations but she did not think the worse of The Four-Z for it. When thousands of people are asked the same question and given only ten words with which to answer it even Shakespeare would be hard put to come up with something unique.

The final question was *Why should we pick you?* In answer to this, Michael wrote, *This is our dream. It is all we ever wanted. We will work hard. We will learn and we will grow. We will make you proud and we will rock your arse!*

Just like tens of thousands of others who, like Michael, had learned *Chart Throb*-speak from the previous series.

Having agonized for so long over the band's name, its description and the question *Why should we pick you?* Michael would have been surprised to discover that the thing which interested Emma most about what he had written on the entry form was his address. It is probable that if Michael had done as he had considered doing and used a PO box for his correspondence The Four-Z would never have been sent an invitation to audition at all. Nineteen other entirely similar-sounding black boy bands from the Midlands had already emerged from their envelopes, one even called The Fource, but none came from such a notoriously hopeless place as the Collingbrook Estate. Collingbrook was a byword for everything that had gone wrong in post-war town planning, a drug-saturated war zone into which the police were fearful to venture. Emma knew that the contrast between the lives these boys must currently be leading and the 'celebrity lifestyle' of which they dreamed was what Calvin would definitely call good telly.

Emma placed The Four-Z on the Blinger pile.

Like buses, successful application letters seemed to come in groups and the very next envelope that Emma opened after The Four-Z was from Peroxide. Another nod-through, which Emma placed directly on to the Blingers pile without even reading it or referring its contents to Trent. Emma had been expecting to hear from Peroxide; it had, after all, been her who had encouraged them to re-apply.

Same Time Last Year

Peroxide's story had begun the year before. They had been a promising prospect plucked from the stands during one of the stadium audition days. Stadium days very rarely bore fruit, it being pretty much impossible to form a useful opinion about anything when twelve thousand people were all trying to grab your attention. The stadium days were little more than stunts, set up partly to get the biggest of the crowd shots for the opening credits and partly to lend a whisper of credibility to the central *Chart Throb* fiction, that thousands of people were genuinely considered for inclusion. These were entirely open calls, where anyone who felt like it could turn up and wait in the stands while teams of researchers hurried along the lines picking out anybody who caught their eye, seeing as many of them as possible in conveyor-belt manner at twenty- to thirty-second intervals. Of necessity snap decisions were made and the harassed and sweating teams could do little more than go by appearance. Peroxide, two near-naked blonde teenagers, had been selected and had thereafter done a surprisingly good audition before the three judges. It turned out that their embarrassingly inept attempts at sexuality were not their only promising feature. They could actually sing and suddenly everybody had got rather excited about them.

Emma could still remember the production meeting that had taken place the previous year when Calvin had announced his plan for them.

'We'll chuck them out after the next round,' he explained, to everyone's surprise. 'You have to play the long game.'

'I thought you might put them in the final,' Beryl remarked. 'Thought they were just your type. They can sing at least as well as half the other finalists, they're cute and they're absolutely fucking desperate. What could be better? I mean, did you see the way they cried when we put them through?'

'Exactly, these are Alpha Clingers, particularly the younger one,' Calvin agreed. 'They cry even better than they sing. If they cry like that when they win, *imagine* what's going to happen when they lose.'

'Why not give them a bit of a run then, so they can lose big time?' Beryl had persisted. 'They're lovely-looking girls and quite frankly we're way over quota on Fatties and Dogs.'

'The long game, darling, the long game. You have to ask yourself, what's the story?'

'And what is it?'

'Well, we could certainly give these birds a run, as you say, and I've no doubt they'd be good TV.'

'Plus all the cunty ex-boyfriends crawling out of the woodwork to talk about the girls' insatiable man-hungry needs and eight-times-a-night marathon sex sessions,' Beryl chipped in.

'That's right,' Calvin replied. 'It's all there for the taking and I'm sure you all think we should grab it with both hands. But how about *this*? We build them up on the first round, big stuff, give them the whole "You two are the best thing to come through that door all day" and "Thank God for some real talent" bit. *Then*, shockingly, we dump them almost immediately, straight after round two. Nobody's expecting it, least of all them. You're horrified, Beryl, the girls weep, you hug them, shout at me, throw water over Rodney, but I am immovable and of course Rodney votes with me because he does what he's fucking told. Just kidding, Rodney.'

'Ha ha.' Rodney grinned, as if he loved nothing more than this gentle joshing from his great mate and equal.

'Outside with Keely in the holding area,' Calvin continued, developing his theme enthusiastically, 'it all gets even more hysterical. Peroxide's hearts are broken. Keely can't *believe* they've been dumped, she wants to walk straight in there and give me a piece of her mind. Beryl is now threatening to quit ... Lots of shots of Rodney looking grim, *knowing* Beryl's right and that he's made the wrong fucking decision *again*.'

'Ha ha,' Rodney laughed woodenly.

'Even I'm suddenly looking doubtful,' said Calvin, barging on. 'Did I make the right choice? The girls certainly know the answer to that! They go to the Bite Back Box and shout into the camera that they *will* be stars, breasts heaving, mascara running, belly-button jewellery jiggling with emotion. "Just you wait, Calvin Simms!" they shout. "We'll be *huge* and then you'll be sorry." We milk it for a week, debate it over and over again on ITV2, try and tease the papers into running a "Support Peroxide" campaign. Feature the whole thing heavily on the Christmas DVD ... *Then*,' and

Calvin grinned triumphantly at his own cleverness, 'we bring them back *next* year. Now *that's* a story that has what it takes.'

Peroxide

Ten months after this conversation, Georgie's parents were sitting in their small sitting room listening to the sound of the toilet flushing upstairs. They had not heard their daughter Georgia vomiting but that was only because she always played loud music when she went to the toilet to puke.

It had started again the moment she got the phone call.

'Yeah, hi, Mr Costello, it's Emma from *Chart Throb*, remember me? How's *gorgeous* Georgie, we so *love* Georgie. We are such big fans. Is she there?'

Georgie was the younger of the two members of Peroxide, a pop duo which she and her friend 'Chelle had formed while attending Saturday morning drama classes and which the previous year had triumphantly sailed through the first round of *Chart Throb* only to be sensationally dumped in the second. Georgie had been just seventeen at the time, too young, in her father's opinion, to be appearing half-naked on television.

'If it's a singing competition why can't you wear some clothes?' he asked.

'The show's all about having what it takes, Dad,' Georgia would reply, standing on the living-room carpet in little more than her underwear. 'Calvin's always saying it . . . do you have what it takes? Well, this is what it takes.'

The skimpy costumes had been 'Chelle's idea. At

nineteen, she was very much the senior partner in the act.

Georgia's parents were firmly of the opinion that their daughter's eating disorders had begun with those costumes. 'Chelle was a natural exhibitionist who would happily have worn her hotpants and bra top to the pub, but Georgia had what her school counsellor called 'body issues'. She was a slim girl who, when she stood before the mirror, saw a fat girl staring back. Despite being generally acknowledged as very pretty, Georgia could never quite convince herself that her body was good enough to be displayed alongside the confident 'Chelle's and so she began to punish it for its inadequacy.

After Peroxide's sudden and brutal ejection from *Chart Throb* Georgia had become convinced that they had failed because she hadn't been thin enough. The more people expressed surprise that she and 'Chelle had failed to advance to the Pop School stage of the competition, the more she believed that it was her fault.

In the weeks following the ejection Georgia's parents had watched in despair as their beautiful daughter had gone to war with her own body. At first they had hoped that as the notoriety faded she would regain some sense of balance in her life, but the extinguishing of the media spotlight served only to increase Georgia's self-loathing. The comments in the street went from support to pity to contempt and finally to indifference, and it was this last that seemed to hurt Georgia most. For a moment she had imagined that she meant something and then she had discovered that she didn't. It was all the fault of her traitorous body.

It had taken six months of family pain, together with the money for private help that her parents could ill afford, to bring Georgia back from the brink, and now it was all beginning again.

'Hi, Georgie!' Emma chirruped. 'How's it all going with Peroxide? We *love* Peroxide.'

Nothing had been promised. Emma had been extremely careful not to commit herself or her employers in any way but nonetheless she was gently encouraging. Subtle hints were dropped that everybody on the team thought an injustice had been done the previous year and that the girls owed it to themselves not to be beaten by it. They were two strong ladies and it was up to them to come back fighting.

'Chelle and Georgia had been thrilled. 'Chelle had gone straight to the local Ann Summers shop to start work on their new costumes and Georgia, whose breasts had only recently returned to their normal shape and whose periods had still not become regular again, had gone straight to the toilet to begin the process of getting back into shape.

And so her parents sat and watched as the same old signs crashed back into their lives. The gorging, the flushing, the ever-present smell of toothpaste on her breath. It was Georgia's way of maintaining control: if she could influence nothing else in her life she could at least hold sway over her own body, forcing it to shrink, consume itself, punish it for having failed the last time and showing it what would happen if it failed again.

A Royal Request

Three hundred envelopes, four coffees and two cigarettes on from Peroxide and Emma's head was seriously beginning to spin with too many hopes and dreams when suddenly she picked up an envelope that brought her up short. It was such a surprise, a shock even, and for Emma a deeply depressing one. The envelope was marked Balmoral and had been franked by the Buckingham Palace Post Office. It was embossed with a triple-feathered crest.

The Prince of Wales was applying to be a Chart Throb.

She could hardly believe her eyes when she saw the name on the application form and read the personal description beneath it. *Organic farmer. Charity worker. Heir to throne.*

Emma felt like she wanted to cry. This was simply *too much*. It wasn't that she was a fervent monarchist but she had a real affection for an institution that had lasted so many hundreds of years and was in any number of ways unique in the world. When Emma had been a little girl, the Queen had visited her school and everyone had had the most splendid day. All the little girls had carried flowers and felt themselves to be princesses in the presence of a real queen. Of course that had been nearly twenty years before and nowadays the monarchy was no longer the stuff of fairy tales. Nonetheless in a world of enormous breast implants, radical facelifts and reality television, Emma had continued to respect what the royal family stood for. And now . . . now the *Prince of Wales* was applying to be a Chart Throb.

'Fuck!' she could not help exclaiming. 'My *God*!'

'What's up?' Trent enquired as everybody around the big paper-strewn table turned to look.

'Nothing,' Emma replied.

In an instant she had made her decision. She would not put him through. She would save him from himself. Hiding the monogrammed envelope, she casually tossed the royal application on to the recycling pile.

'It's nothing at all,' she repeated.

But it was too late.

'What was that?' Trent enquired.

'Nothing, I said.'

'So why shout "fuck" and "my God"? Come on, Emma, what's on that form? Your mum?'

'Oh, it's just a stupid hoax, somebody pretending to be the Prince of Wales of all people. I'm binning it.'

'Show me the envelope.'

Attempting a shrug of indifference, Emma handed over the envelope with its embossed fleur-de-lis and royal franking. Trent studied it carefully.

'I think this is fucking genuine,' he said at last.

'Oh come *on* . . .' Emma began.

'Because if it is a hoax it could only come from somebody with access to the Buckingham Palace post room and what would they have to gain? Either way we need to find out. Get me the number of the Prince of Wales's office.'

Fifteen minutes later the story was confirmed. His Royal Highness had indeed decided to volunteer for the experience of *Chart Throb* and hoped to be selected for audition. It was stressed that he wished to be treated in exactly the same manner as all the other applicants and that if he wasn't he would withdraw.

'The clever bastard,' Trent exclaimed.

'What do you mean?' Emma replied. 'It's simply ridiculous. How could he possibly be a pop star?'

'It's a last throw of the dice, isn't it? The guy's finished anyway, every single poll says *everybody* wants him to stand aside for the next generation. So what does he do? He applies to *join* the next generation. It's so audacious it isn't funny! The clever, clever *bastard*.'

The more Emma thought about it the less she wanted any part of it. She was a girl who went to museums and visited castles. She was a member of the National Trust and the History Society. Tradition and the past *meant* something, surely? Except if the heir to the throne was to appear on *Chart Throb*, clearly they didn't.

'Let's reject him,' she said, trying to sound cool and casual.

'What?' Trent demanded, astonished.

'He'll just turn himself into even more of a laughing stock.'

'And?'

'Well . . . I mean, it might make us look stupid too.'

'Uhm, I don't *think* so, Emma. You have clearly lost the plot. This will be *brilliant*. Fucking hell. He actually thinks he can *use* us. They all do, don't they? All those desperates who go on *Celebrity Big Brother* and *I'm a Celebrity* and *Shag Me, I'm Famous*, they all think they can use the process to get what they want. Haven't they learned yet? Don't they remember George Galloway? We will *eat* them. We will chew them up, swallow them down and *shit them out*! This guy actually thinks we'll make him popular. He probably thinks it will make him seem down with the kids! Is he going to get a shock when Calvin's finished editing *his* stupid royal arse!'

Beryl Is (Briefly) There for Priscilla

Beryl perched gingerly on the very edge of the back seat of her black stretch Humvee truck, wearing no seat belt in order to be able to sit as far forward as she could. She was of course breaking a state law and putting herself at risk of being stopped and fined by the LAPD, but Beryl was rock 'n' roll and played by her own rules. Besides which, the Humvee was equipped with reflective windows and so she was totally safe from detection.

Beryl was perching on the front of her seat because

71

she had finally been able to fit her arse into her celebrity surgeon's busy schedule, where it had been subjected to a particularly brutal treatment of lifting, underpinning and cellulite-sucking. The surgeon had thrown in a complimentary rectal bleaching, which had stung like hell. She had also had more work done on her false vagina, which had been an ongoing project ever since her sex-change operation. Further work had been done on the imitation clitoris the surgeons had built for her out of the nerve endings which had been left hanging about after her dick was removed. Beryl's ambition (as she had confessed to Oprah) was one day to be in a position to pleasure herself with a big black dildo.

'Honestly, Oprah, I haven't had one off the wrist since I gave old John Thomas a last slap in pre-op before they cut it off.'

Such indulgences were, however, in the future for Beryl and currently she was reluctant even to trust her full weight upon her bruised and battered under-carriage. Not that that weight amounted to much, since in another part of her obsessive body-management programme Beryl consumed a weekly fat pill which absorbed almost everything she ate before emerging from her like a seal stuck in a sewage pipe.

Having recently had the fat sucked out of your buttocks and what had once been your dick nerves knotted into a small bun to make a clitoris is not likely to put a person in the best of moods, but Beryl would have been tetchy even without having to sit on a sucked-out arse. For a start she was stuck in traffic and, like most people of her phenomenal wealth and power, Beryl could never quite work out why it was that traffic jams applied as much to her as to the rest of the human race. *Why* did she have to sit in traffic? Every other aspect of her existence was improved by her wealth but the trip out to LAX remained a frustratingly egalitarian experience. That couldn't be right. Surely something could be done? But drum her fingers, swear at the windows and wriggle her sore arse about on the rich leather upholstery though she might, Beryl could think of nothing. Even *she* could not afford to build a private road from her house out to the airport and so the freeway remained her only option.

And that was another point. Why was she on the freeway anyway? Because she was on her way back to the UK, which she absolutely hated. The UK was where she had come from and (as she never tired of telling people) she had come from a dark, dark place. Backward, parochial and frustratingly devoid of good and attentive staff.

'So why are you going?' her wife Serenity had mumbled through her obscenely inflated inner-tube-like lips as she bade Beryl farewell from the marble steps of their mansion that morning.

It was a good question. Why go and work in shitty old Britain when you have a huge career and a huge house in sun-drenched California?

Deep in her heart, just above the groaning fat pill and behind the breast implants, Beryl knew the reason. Vanity, vengeful vanity. It was payback time. She wanted all the sad, dowdy, permanent residents of the dark little island from which she had come to see just how big a deal she was these days. All the people who, in her own mind, had shat on her and on whom she had most certainly shat would have to eat it. That was why she was going back to Britain: hate it though she most certainly did, there was nowhere on earth where her success mattered more to her.

Unfortunately for Beryl she was going to miss her flight and if she had been in a bad mood on her way *out* to the airport, that mood was sunshine itself compared to how she felt on her way back into town, having been urgently summoned to return to Beverly Hills. The call had come just as Beryl was finally beginning to relax and to think about a gin and tonic in the VIP area.

The call was from Claude, her personal assistant.

'It's bad news, I'm afraid, Mrs Blenheim. Priscilla's been caught on camera buying coke.'

'Fuck,' Beryl gasped. 'How's it spinning?'

'Not great. Fox is trying to be nice . . .'

'Of course they are. We're all under contract to them. I suppose everybody else is going for the jugular.'

'Kind of. Maybe just a tad,' Claude replied, trying to project a grimace of sympathy over a cell phone. 'She says she needed it for the pain of her new breasts.'

'Priscilla had new breasts?'

'Yeah.'

'How do they look?'

'OK . . . Kind of big.'

'*Tacky* big?'

'Sort of.'

Beryl pulled down the favourites menu on the car's computer and clicked on Priscilla's website. Sure enough, there was her stepdaughter, now augmented by two enormous new breasts.

'Fuck. She got herself a couple of Pammies.'

'And some.'

'Takes after her mum. Serenity gets new tits like most girls get new bras . . . Actually, you know, they look OK. Tacky but kind of punk. Like Courtney Love or something. I always say if you're going to get new tits, get "Fuck You" tits. I know I did. She'll have them removed when she gets bored.'

'What do you want me to do about the drugs thing?'

Beryl had momentarily forgotten about this added complication to her life.

'That idiot. If she needed drugs why didn't she ask her fucking mother! Juan!' Beryl shouted, rapping on the glass partition that separated her from her driver. 'Turn around!'

If there was one thing Beryl prided herself on as a mother, it was her ability to handle a domestic crisis. Perhaps not mundane domestic crises, such as leaky taps, bee stings and tummy upsets. For that she would get her office to call a plumber or hand the kids over to a member of staff. But in terms of a *real* family crisis, like if one of her stepchildren was caught buying drugs after having inappropriate cosmetic surgery, for instance, and was subsequently engulfed in a media feeding frenzy which threatened to swamp the entire family franchise, Beryl was a mum in a million.

'Where is she?'

'At the precinct.'

'She's been *busted*?'

'Maybe just a tad.'

'Which precinct?'

'Beverly Hills.'

Beryl breathed a small sigh of relief. Buying drugs in Beverly Hills was a very different thing to buying them in South Central.

'Frank thinks it'll be a caution pending social reports,' Claude went on. Frank was the Blenheim family lawyer. 'I called him first. He's down there with her.'

'You're a star, Claude. Call him again, tell him Priscilla is not to leave until I get there to pick her up. Her mother needs to be there.'

'Of course, Mrs Blenheim.'

Once more Beryl shouted at her driver. There was actually no need to shout as the Humvee had an intercom, but Beryl was naturally disposed towards ostentatious displays of authority.

'Juan, you dozy tortoise! How long to Beverly Hills if you risk your licence?'

'It's clear heading back in, Mrs Blenheim, so forty-five minutes top.'

75

Beryl checked her watch. It was 11.03.

'OK, then take it a little easy because I want to be pulling up outside the police precinct in *exactly* one hour.'

'12.03. You got it.'

Beryl returned to her conversation with her PA.

'Claude, call the networks. Tell them I have cancelled my UK trip and will be picking up Priscilla personally. I will arrive at the precinct at 12.03.'

'I see where you're coming from, Mrs Blenheim.'

Claude understood that Beryl was anxious to ensure that the promptness with which she was spreading her mother hen's wings and 'being there' for her 'troubled' daughter would play live as breaking news midway through the top stories on the noon bulletin. 'Next, call the Betty Ford Clinic, book Priscilla in as of this afternoon then release a statement in my name saying that Priscilla is actively seeking help to deal with her problem, which has been brought on as a result of media pressure and poor self-image. After that, call the *Larry King* office and get me and Serenity on to tonight's show. They're bound to bump someone for us, particularly now that Priscilla's been busted.'

'Will do. You got it.'

It all went like clockwork and exactly an hour later Beryl Blenheim was meeting her errant daughter on the steps of the Beverly Hills police station among a level of media frenzy that, twenty years before, would have been reserved for a visit from the president.

'We got into this as a family and we will get through it as a family,' Beryl said grimly from behind her dark glasses. 'Priscilla fully realizes she needs help at this time to deal with her issues and to learn and to grow. She is reaching out and she will not reach out in vain. In closing I should like to thank the wonderful LAPD and everyone else for the support that we have received during this difficult time.'

A phalanx of security guards whom Claude had dispatched to the scene held the press back while mother and daughter clambered into the long black Humvee. Priscilla was not happy.

'You might have let me say *something*, Dad,' she griped.

'Mum!'

'It was my fucking bust after all.'

'Oh, shut up. You've done *quite* enough already today, young lady, and *what* is with the new tits?'

'At least I didn't get a new dick.'

'I am a transsexual. You are just a screwed-up teen.'

'I needed something to give me back my confidence after my album.'

'If you're going to get a job done every time an album flops you'll end up with the tits of a sperm whale.'

Beryl scrolled through the radio news stations. They all carried the story.

'Priscilla Blenheim, stepdaughter of legendary British satanic rocker and transsexual Beryl née Blaster Blenheim, and star of Fox Network's hit Osbournes-style reality show *The Blenheims . . .*'

'Osbournes-*style*!' Beryl shrieked. 'We shit *all over* those lightweights. They don't know what dysfunctional is!'

'C'mon, Mom. We stole the idea from them.'

'What? Like jerking off on the TV is something new? You think turning your life into a show is *original*? Did Jessica Simpson steal from *The Osbournes*? Did Tommy Lee? Did Britney? Everybody puts their life on TV, baby. We are so not the Osbournes.'

'Yeah, maybe you're right, Mom. For one thing, the Osbournes survived, they loved each other, they stayed together. I'm gonna divorce you the first chance I get.'

The radio reports continued to pump out the bad news.

'Priscilla Blenheim caught on camera openly purchasing . . .'

'You fucking idiot, Priscilla,' Beryl snapped.

'C'mon, Mom. One wrap of coke. What's the big deal? You used to get your groupies to blow more than that up your ass with a straw.'

'Now listen here! Firstly, it was different in the eighties. Secondly, when I was a man nobody expected me to act like a lady. But thirdly and most importantly, you are a member of a family. You have responsibilities.'

'I just can't believe you're trying to kick my ass here, Dad!'

'Mum!'

'You and Mom get up at meetings every week and talk about how much shit you've done and you ain't telling me you never bought off a street dealer.'

'It is one thing buying coke in the street, it is quite another getting yourself caught *on camera* doing it.'

'Everything I do is caught on camera. Maybe you forgot that.'

'Don't be a smart arse with me. You're not too old to slap.'

'Oh yeah, like I wouldn't sue your fucking ass.'

'Don't mention my arse, it's had quite enough to deal with recently and now you drag it into a mess like this. I am *working*! I am supposed to be on a plane to England.'

'Nobody asked you to come and get me.'

'You think I could let you handle this on your own?'

'Mom's here.'

'Oh yeah. That would be great, wouldn't it? Her wandering round saying a skip full of coke a day for thirty years never hurt her! I don't think so. We have a new season upcoming!'

'Everybody takes drugs.'

'*Exactly*, Priscilla! It is not as if cocaine is hard to

78

find in this town, yet *you* decide to buy it off some sleazoid in a parking lot.'

'I wanted to find out what it felt like to be a normal kid.'

'Oh, very funny. Well, let me tell you now, Priscilla. You are going straight into rehab to spend an *entire* fortnight getting in touch with yourself, growing, learning, taking time to heal and facing up to your issues.'

'Two weeks! *But Dad!*'

'*MUM!* Please do me the courtesy of respecting my gender change.'

'All right, *Mom*. But I am not going back into rehab. I just got out.'

'You are going back in . . . *And* when you come out you are going to volunteer for a downtown youth programme working with deprived kids!'

'*Mom!*'

'Priscilla, you have been *busted*. The cops have to decide whether to prosecute. You could be sent to Juvenile! Did I not just remind you *we have a new season upcoming*?'

'You'll get me off. Frank will get me off.'

'*Not* without your cooperation, young lady. You'll do your time and like it and thank your lucky stars you're at Betty Ford getting carrot juice and a shiatsu massage instead of in prison having your muff munched by some giant lezzer whore who's doing life for cutting the dicks off her tricks.'

'You are *so* gross.'

Having deposited a very angry and reluctant Priscilla at the Betty Ford Clinic, Beryl returned to LA to continue to deal with what was a surprisingly negative media reaction. She had not expected this, for the Blenheims had made a career out of cheerful dysfunction. Both Serenity and Beryl openly confessed to decades of alcohol and drug abuse and the

79

children made no secret of their pointless, slobbish, dilettante existence.

It was the reason people liked them.

'I guess it's kids and the drug thing,' Larry King opined to Beryl when she and Serenity appeared on his cable chat show that night. 'You know, Priscilla's still very young and . . .'

'Look, Larry,' said a tearful Beryl, 'I've had enough, I've really had enough. We do not deserve this and we do not have to take it. What normal family doesn't have to deal with crap like this? But their daughters don't get treated like criminals. And don't forget, Larry, we *are* a normal family, just four people who love each other very much trying to get through all the crap families have to get through and we will be strong and positive, we *will* help Priscilla and we will learn and grow and heal together. In the meantime, I am appealing to the media to just back off and give us some space. Priscilla's just a kid, for God's sake. I'm just a mum. Serenity's just a mum. We're not perfect . . . who is? But we have a right to privacy just like anyone else. Don't forget, Priscilla is also dealing with new breasts right now. It's always an emotional time for a teenage girl to develop breasts and, well, our daughter is going through that for *the second time*.'

Larry looked as if he was about to cry. He turned to the camera. 'So how about it, guys?' he said, eyeing the lens sternly. 'You all have kids. You know what it's like, kids do dumb stuff and it's Mom and Dad who have to pick up the pieces. So how about cutting Beryl and Serenity some slack here. Let's back off and leave these people to learn and to grow and to heal, huh?'

After this appeal for privacy, the channel cut to a break featuring a trailer for the repeat run of *The Blenheims*, airing weeknights at ten.

Friend and Acquaintance

On the evening Beryl finally arrived in the UK, Rodney arrived in London also, having returned from a month's golfing in Portugal. The following day all three judges were booked to do a pre-record day for the new season of *Chart Throb* and so, for the first time since the end of the previous series, they were all not only in the same country but in the same city. While Beryl went from studio to studio in her ongoing damage limitation exercise, Rodney dined with Calvin. The dinner had been booked at Rodney's extremely heavy-handed insistence.

'Just to map out some parameters for the new series,' he had said over the phone.

'What parameters?' Calvin enquired when he could no longer avoid taking Rodney's call and was trying to think how to get out of actually having to meet him.

'The ones for the new series.'

'But they're the same as the last series.'

'That may be the case but either way I should like to map them out.'

In the end even Calvin's legendarily thick skin was not thick enough to withstand Rodney's anguished entreaties. He was forced to sacrifice a precious evening he had hoped to spend with his wine merchant selecting purchases for a massive new cellar he had built on his Sussex estate, in order to meet up with his fellow judge.

'Good to see you, mate,' Rodney said as Calvin bustled in very late.

'My driver couldn't find the place,' Calvin replied testily. 'How, incidentally, did you?'

'Oh, I always come here. My little secret. Avoids all that media shit. What I say is if you can't find it then nor can the press, eh?'

Rodney had indeed deliberately booked a small and

anonymous Soho restaurant for very good personal reasons. He'd had plenty of experience of being caught in media scrums with Calvin in which he had been virtually ignored and even elbowed out of the way as the press pursued his world-famous colleague. He was not going to put himself in that position by booking them a table at Nobu or the Ivy.

'Whatever,' Calvin replied. 'Let's order, shall we, lot of prep still to do for tomorrow.'

'Of course, of course. Me too, very busy, tons of stuff going on.'

Calvin took up his menu and began to study it. Rodney, who had arrived about as early as Calvin had arrived late, had had ample time to read the menu some twenty or thirty times and so had made his choice. He was now forced to wait while Calvin read the entire menu carefully and then proceeded to try to negotiate with the waitress. In Calvin's mind anything was better than talking to Rodney.

'I want to order off-menu,' he said.

'Uhm. Off-menu?'

'Ask Chef to do me some oysters.'

'We have oysters Kilpatrick.'

'Yes, I can see that. I want them *au naturel* with a little lemon and a drop or two of Tabasco. OK?'

Of course it was not OK, this after all was England. Living in LA, Calvin had developed the local power habit of ordering off-menu and, like many other returning expats, found it difficult to get used to the agonizing slowness with which the British were adopting American habits and manners.

'We have oysters Kilpatrick,' the waitress repeated. 'They're very nice. Chef serves them with grilled bacon, chopped chives and Worcester sauce.'

'I know what oysters Kilpatrick is, darling.'

'Well . . . Would you like them?'

'I would like oysters *sans* Kilpatrick.'

'Umm . . .'

'Here's what Chef does, my love, OK? Chef takes the oysters, Chef *doesn't* add the bacon, Chef *doesn't* add the chopped chives, Chef *doesn't* add the Worcester sauce and Chef sends them to me. Meanwhile you, my darling, pop over to the bar and grab me a couple of wedges of lemon and the Tabasco sauce. How's that?'

The poor girl was not paid to operate on her own initiative; all she could think of was the nightmare of trying to reprogram the computerized billing system which had all the dishes and prices pre-set.

'I think we'll have to charge you for the Kilpatrick bit, sir. I mean, we won't be able to deduct the price of the bacon from the overall price.'

'That will be fine,' Calvin said. He seemed to feel that the fact that he could afford to buy the restaurant entitled him to act as if he had *actually* bought it.

The minutes ticked by and Rodney squirmed with impatience as, slowly but surely, Calvin plodded through the ordering of his main meal and then, having summoned the wine waiter, insisted on discussing with him the virtues of almost every wine on the list including the stickies. Eventually, however, even Calvin's considerable powers of procrastination were exhausted and he was forced to enquire as to what might be on Rodney's mind.

Rodney took a deep breath and prepared to deliver the arguments he had so often rehearsed.

Then Calvin's phone rang.

'Sorry, Rodney, better take this,' Calvin said, without bothering to conceal the fact that he had not yet checked the digital display to find out who it was. Rodney was left to conclude that Calvin would talk to anybody else in the world rather than him. In fact the frown that passed across Calvin's face as he did now glance at his Nokia seemed to suggest that Calvin now regretted committing himself to take the call.

'Damn,' he said, 'Christian.'

'Ahh,' Rodney replied, nodding in a knowing manner. He knew very well why Calvin might wish to avoid conversing with Christian, it had been all over the Bizarre page in that morning's *Sun*. Christian's contract was not to be renewed.

'Hi, Chris,' Calvin said with a grimace but attempting a light, airy tone, hoping to imply that this was just another call. Calvin might have built a reputation as a pitiless Rottweiler, TV's answer to Richard III, the man who made Simon Cowell look like a pussycat, but he was in fact nothing of the sort. He was tough certainly and horribly corrupted by his immense power, but he still had feelings and like any other person he disliked confrontations and scenes. He disliked having to tell a perfectly decent young man that his dream was absolutely and irrevocably over.

Rodney felt the sadness too, for he had also liked Christian. On the other hand he was deeply annoyed. He had had Calvin's attention, Calvin had actually invited him to speak his mind, and now he, Rodney, a major figure in the industry, a *player*, would have to hover on the sidelines, nursing his Campari while Calvin wasted his time talking to somebody whose second (and final) album had stalled at forty-eight.

'Yes, Christian, it's true. We won't be renewing,' Calvin was saying. 'Of course I was going to call you myself, I've no idea how the *Sun* got hold of it . . . Christian, please, keep it together. It's an album deal, nobody died.'

But of course somebody had died. Christian Appleyard, pop star, had departed this earth and what was left was a pathetic creature indeed. Christian Appleyard, sad act, loser, joke. The distance between fame and notoriety, between adulation and derision, cannot be measured in feet and inches; the tipping point is merely a moment, a moment when suddenly the consciousness of the public changes. Crowds are fickle in a way that individuals can never be. An individual has a conscience, while a crowd can afford to follow its rawest, basest instincts and its instincts were clearly that Christian's fifteen minutes were well and truly up.

'Screw 'em,' Calvin was saying. 'So some builders laughed at you. So what? Did they ever get a number-one album? You did, mate. Nobody can take that away from you.'

It was true, nobody ever could take that away, not even Christian himself, although he would come to wish he could.

'Look, Christian mate,' Calvin continued. 'You've had a lot of fun, we've all had fun but, you know, parties come to an end . . . Brad's still selling albums, Christian, you're not, that's why he still has a deal, that's the reality of the business.'

Bradley Vine, runner-up to Christian's winner on the first ever *Chart Throb* two years before. Apparently he still had it, Christian did not.

'The mums like him, mate, what can I tell you?' Calvin explained. 'You had the kids, he had the mums. Mums have more loyalty than kids and that's life.'

Calvin looked at his watch. He should not be having this conversation. He should never have given that lad his number, but it had all been so exciting that first time around. They had all felt like a team, judges and contestants together. Even Calvin had got carried away a little. For a moment even he had half believed that what was being created was real.

'Look, I have to go, Christian. We'll talk again, OK . . . I don't know when, but we'll talk.' Calvin pressed red and put his phone down.

'Wants to know why you've dumped him?' Rodney enquired.

'I didn't dump him, the public did,' Calvin replied.

'So . . .' said Rodney, anxious to return to his interrupted agenda.

Calvin's phone rang again. Both men glanced down at the display and saw the word 'Christian'. Calvin let it ring.

'So, you were saying?' Calvin enquired. 'There was something you wanted to discuss?'

But Calvin was still not really listening because when the statutory four rings were over he took up his phone, pressed 'names' and scrolled down to the C's. Christian was nestling between Christina Aguilera and Christian (Coldplay), two steps up from Chris Evans. Elevated company indeed, the sort of company among whom, one year before, Christian Appleyard might almost have expected to be in reality, but now those days were gone. Calvin pressed delete, the gap between Christina Aguilera and Christian (Coldplay) closed and Christian Appleyard was gone.

No More Mr Nice Guy, Please

Finally Rodney was able to make his point.

'I feel I need to show the public more of the real me,' he said.

'The real you?' Calvin enquired.

'Yes. I think the public's ready for it.'

'Ready for it?'

'Yes.'

'The real you?'

'That's right. I get a lot of comments. You know, feedback.'

'Asking to see the real you?'

'Well, more of it. You know, people say that they

want to see me really, really . . . show them, to really show them . . .'

'The real you.'

'Yes.'

Calvin squeezed his lemon wedge over his oysters. 'Oh . . . Sorry, mate. Never could aim a lemon.'

'That's all right,' said Rodney, wiping juice from his eye.

Calvin chewed an oyster and quaffed deeply at his wine, letting Rodney stew for a while.

'So, Rodney,' he said finally. 'Exactly which bit of the real you do you think the public's missing out on?'

'The tough bit. The two-fisted, straight-talking hard man with the rapier-sharp putdowns bit.'

'Wow. Big bit.'

'I feel I've become bland.'

'You've *become* bland?'

Whatever Calvin might have meant by his heavy intonation, Rodney chose to ignore it.

'Yes, always being so nice. I think it's getting boring,' he said, developing his argument.

'Isn't it nice to be nice?'

'Well, you certainly don't seem to think so, Calvin, with your worldwide Mr Nasty franchise.'

'You know, good cop, bad cop and all that, with Beryl in the middle. It's the classic judging line-up. Worked for *Pop Idol*, worked for *American Idol*, worked for *X Factor* and it works for us.'

'I've been looking at old tapes. They used to ring the changes a bit. Louis Walsh used to get to be mean occasionally on *X Factor*. They did a whole episode based around it.'

'That was before the formula got absolutely nailed. We nailed it. We don't deviate. That's why we're number one now.'

'Well, anyway. I don't think it's you and me with

87

Beryl in the middle. I think it's you and Beryl with me on the periphery.'

'I see.' Calvin chewed thoughtfully for a moment. 'And you think the answer is for you to be mean?'

'Well, sometimes yes. I mean last series I was pretty much *always* nice. I just want to vary it a bit, you know, surprise people. Shake things up.'

'You think you could pull it off?'

'Of course I can, I'm creative, a songwriter, I did lyrics. I'm good with words.'

'I remember – *Sex baby. Sex baby. Saturday night. Yeah. Ooh baby. Ah baby. Saturday night.*'

'Exactly. Number four in Belgium. I'm *good*, Calvin, really and I want to do more of the putdowns. I've been writing some. I'm quite pleased with them . . . "If you were any flatter, darling, we could use you as a coffee table." '

There was a pause. Calvin looked at Rodney, his face a blank.

'I'm sorry?' he said finally.

'What?'

'I don't understand what you're saying, what do you mean use me as a coffee table?'

'Not you.'

'You just said you could use me as a coffee table.'

'Not you.'

'Who?'

'One of the contestants.'

'Which contestant?'

'Any contestant, a hypothetical one. That was one of my putdowns.'

'What was?'

' "If you were any flatter we could use you as a coffee table." Flatter. Singing flat. It's a joke.'

Calvin paused for a moment, clearly working the idea through in his head.

'Oh, I *see*,' he said finally. 'Well, good luck, mate.'

'Umm, thanks.'

The two men ate in silence, with Rodney trying to work out whether he had made any progress. Calvin decided to change the subject. He had not intended to bring up his plans for Rodney's ex-girlfriend over dinner but as he could think of nothing else to say he did it anyway.

'I'm bringing Iona back, by the way.'

Rodney choked on his wine.

'Please don't tell me you're surprised.'

To Calvin it was the most obvious move in the world. So much drama, so much tension. The encounter would be excruciating.

'You do understand I have to do it, don't you, Rodders? I mean you two having been an item and then you dumping her and all that. Brilliant telly, her coming back to audition once more in front of the very man with whom she once shared a bed. Just fantastic. Then of course there's the fact that she needs to come back and audition at all, having got absolutely nowhere in the last year. Can't let you off the hook on that one, Rodders. Not after everything you promised.'

Rodney's face showed he understood exactly where Calvin was going with this. After all, both Calvin and Beryl had rubbished Iona and her band, while Rodney had publicly stated that he intended to make them into stars. Iona's return to the *Chart Throb* audition process was going to brutally demonstrate that Rodney had not made her into a star.

'Calvin,' Rodney stammered. 'I'd really rather you didn't . . .'

'Oh, come on, Rodney. All right, Beryl and I might tease you a bit but so what? One of the consistent themes of *Chart Throb* is broken promises and out-rageous predictions. Every week one or other of us gravely informs some wide-eyed innocent that they could sell a lot of records and the public never seems to mind that almost none of them ever do. Tell you what, mate. Here's a thought: you want to be mean, how about this, we bring her back but you tell her to dump her crappy band. Plenty of drama there and it will certainly make you look tough.'

Calvin looked at Rodney as he thought it through.

'Yes. I suppose you're right actually,' he said finally.

'That's my job.'

'Like, I'm the hard-bitten professional. OK, so we had our thing, but that's dead and gone . . .'

'Get over it, babes. I have.'

'Exactly. Move on.'

'Walk away.'

'Can't build a future if you're living in the past.'

'No way.'

Rodney was growing enthusiastic.

'So if she comes back solo we give her another chance?'

'Exactly, and you can show just how tough you've become by giving your ex-girlfriend, to whom last year you were almost engaged, a really, really hard time.'

Once more doubt clouded Rodney's features.

'A really, *really* hard time?' he asked nervously.

'Great telly, Rodders. Great telly.'

Flight of Fancy

The next morning found Calvin, Rodney and Beryl squashed together in the rear section of a private jet circling high over RAF Brize Norton. They were squashed together because the front section of the plane was occupied by a camera crew, which consisted of a camera operator, a sound recordist, a continuity girl, costume and make-up mistresses and the director. Trent and Emma, senior researchers, were also present because it would be their job to stitch the material taken that day into the overall edit. They were shooting the 'travelling' sequences, those earnest, dramatic shots of the three judges diligently sweeping the country day after day, week after week, in search of potential Chart Throbs, those raw young talents whom they would mentor and mould into superstars.

They had been airborne for about ninety minutes and although the plane in which they were travelling had never been more than twenty miles from Brize Norton they had already visited Glasgow and Newcastle and they were just leaving Manchester.

'All right,' Trent called out from the confusion of cables, clipboards, laptops and costumes in which he was crouching. 'We're flying out of Manchester and heading for Birmingham. Can we change position, please? Beryl and Rodney swap seats.'

'Why do we have to change position?' Beryl complained, for the aircraft was small and moving about in it was not easy and involved unpleasantly intimate contact as the three judges attempted to squeeze past one another.

'Because it's a different day, Beryl.'

'I know that, Trent. I am acquainted with the magic of television, you know.'

'Yes, of course, Beryl, I . . .'

'Do you have an Emmy? I don't think you do, do you? I've got an Emmy, in fact I've got fucking two, darling, so don't talk to me about how to make television.'

Emma smiled ruefully at the sound recordist with whom she was crammed into the plane's tiny toilet. He smiled back. They all hated Beryl. They didn't hate her for being an arrogant, bullying bitch, although she was. They were used to that, putting up with that was what they were paid for. They hated her for the way

91

she *pretended to be so fucking real*. When it suited her she was everybody's friend, just one of the girls, no airs, no graces, just big-hearted old Beryl, but God help you if you crossed her, or if she took against you for no reason at all, or if you forgot for one moment that she was the Empress of Popular fucking Culture and the people's darling. What was most frustrating for those who worked with her was that she truly believed the popular conception of her was the result of her own special talents and fabulous personality. She thought the public believed her to be sexy, mumsy, caring, playful, emotional, honest, sensitive, hard but fair and totally down to earth because she *was* all those things, whereas Emma, who had spent many, many weary days in the edit suite cherrypicking the handful of shots that made her look so good, knew that Good Old Beryl was the creation of her editors and production teams. Be they in America working on *The Blenheims* or stuffed into the tiny toilet of a private jet hovering over RAF Brize Norton for *Chart Throb*, it was the crews who created Beryl Blenheim. Perhaps that was why she treated them with such contempt.

'I just don't see why, because it's a different day, we all have to sit in different seats,' Beryl moaned as Hair and Make-up got to work on the subtle changes they had planned so carefully in order to create the fiction of a progression of days. 'I get on planes all the fucking time, I don't get on thinking, oh, I must sit somewhere different from yesterday.'

'Yes,' Rodney added. 'I think we'd have kind of got our set places by now. You know, we'd have sort of claimed our own little space.'

'Yes, but we need to *show* the viewers it's a different day,' Trent argued, looking anxiously at his watch.

'That's what the costume changes are for, darling,' Beryl replied. 'I've changed my jacket, it's a different day. I don't need to change my seat. I'm not fucking moving.'

Trent sent an appealing glance towards Calvin, who was staring out of the window and so missed it completely.

'Calvin,' Trent said. 'Beryl doesn't want to change seats for Birmingham.'

Reluctantly Calvin engaged his attention.

'Problem, Beryl darling?' he enquired.

'Every time we cover a different day, this prick makes us swap seats. Why would you always sit in different seats?'

'Not *always* in different seats, Beryl,' Trent protested. 'We only *have* six seats after all and you "visit" five cities so the combinations are—'

'I am *talking* to Calvin.'

'Well, darling,' Calvin smiled, 'it's like this. Quite a lot of rather careful storyboarding has gone into this morning's shoot and we are attempting to create rather more than the impression that the three of us spend months together travelling the country looking for talent. For instance, during the Manchester auditions you and Rodney will have had a fight about Rodney being mean to a talentless sweetie . . .'

'I'm going to be mean?' Rodney enquired, brightening up immediately.

'Yes, Rodney, you're going to be mean. You can use that "sharp as a coffee table" putdown if you like.'

'Flat.'

'Whatever.'

'Yes, anyway. Terrific.'

'What's your point, Calvin?' Beryl snapped.

'Well, darling, when we leave Manchester you are all angry and sad. Your mother instincts have been roundly provoked by this sweet disillusioned little girlie being brutalized by smug old Rodney.'

'Smug?' Rodney enquired.

'Witty,' Calvin corrected himself. 'And you, Beryl, are sitting apart, in that single seat at the back, lost in thought. You don't like this job any more, you are even wondering about resigning. That's why Trent wants you in that seat where Rodney had been sitting on our way *into* Manchester.'

'Why was I sitting on my own on my way to Manchester?' asked Rodney, his suspicions aroused.

'Because Beryl throws a glass of water over you in Newcastle.'

'Oh *no*, Calvin! We agreed . . .' Rodney protested.

'*You* agreed, Rodney.'

'Yes! I *said* I don't want Beryl throwing water over me this year.'

'It's a theme, Rodney, the public expect it.'

'I hate doing it anyway,' Beryl moaned. 'It was that Osbourne woman's thing on *X Factor*.'

'And if a thing's worth doing, darling,' Calvin said gently, 'it's worth stealing. Old showbiz rule.'

'I think I should punch him in the mouth. You know, a little bit of the old Blaster in me coming out.'

'Maybe next series, darling. I don't want to tease them with your masculine side until your beard line's completely gone.'

'Fuck off. I'll bet Madonna shaves her 'tache more often than I do these days.'

When the storyboarding had been explained to her, Beryl agreed to change seats and, with her hair and make-up revamped, she was filmed staring angrily out of the window.

'Try to look like you're thinking of resigning,' Calvin instructed.

'No problem there, mate,' said Beryl, imagining that she was sounding tough and witty, unaware that everybody in the plane had long since worked out that she would die rather than resign from this brilliant job that had done so much for her.

Once the shot was in the can, Hair and Make-up again adjusted Beryl's look while the camera swung across to Calvin and Rodney, who were sitting next to each other at a double table.

'What's the next story, somebody?' Calvin shouted.

'You and Rodney looking at each other like naughty schoolboys because you've annoyed Beryl,' Emma shouted back, squeezing past the sound recordist and poking her head round the toilet door.

'Thank you, darling,' Calvin said and he smiled directly at her.

Emma blushed. Then, looking away in some confusion, she dropped her pen. As she bent forward to pick it up, her glasses, which had been perched on top of her head, fell on to the floor while her bottom pressed back into the toilet against the sound recordist.

'Watch out, Emma,' the recordist protested. 'Your arse nearly deleted the last take.'

Emma stood up quickly and bumped her head on the door frame of the toilet cubicle, yelping and dropping her clipboard.

'Steady on, darling,' Calvin smiled. 'Focus.'

Emma blushed more furiously than ever.

'I'm fine. Fine. Sorry, Calvin,' she said, then: 'SHIT!' She had trodden on her glasses.

'What?'

'Nothing.'

'Could we *please* get the fuck on with it,' Beryl called out grumpily.

'Yes, absolutely, Beryl,' Emma replied, clearly trying to remember where they had got to.

'It's Rodney and me looking naughty,' Calvin said, giving Emma another smile.

'Thanks, yes, I knew that,' Emma replied gratefully, returning the smile.

'And after that are we done with leaving Manchester?' Trent enquired.

Emma pulled herself together and looked down at her notes.

'No, Trent,' she called. 'We need Rodney on the phone.'

'Rodney on the phone?' Rodney enquired.

'Yes, Rodney,' Calvin explained. 'Terrific stuff, old *X Factor* idea, hasn't been used since and anyway we'll do it loads better. Lots of on-air time for you.'

'Great, how's it work?'

'Well, while in Birmingham we'll have seen some hopeless old Blinger bird who can't sing and has a face like an appendix but loads of personality . . . You know, big laugh, "My friends think I'm just like Tina Turner", that kind of thing.'

'Ye-es,' said Rodney, suspicion once more growing inside him. 'Who is this woman?'

'We don't know yet, obviously, but we'll find one.'

'Got about twenty contenders marked down from the envelopes, Calvin,' Trent assured him. 'We're spoilt for choice. Emma will find you a good one in pre-select, won't you, darling?'

'Of course,' said Emma, poking her head out once more from the recesses of the toilet but clearly not much liking Trent's patronizing tone.

'Good girl,' said Calvin, winking at her. Perhaps Emma did not like Calvin's patronizing tone either but for some reason she blushed.

'So what's the idea with me and my phone?' Rodney asked again.

'Well, Beryl and I will have taken one look at this sad old dinner lady and said no, but you decide she has potential. Of course I'm amazed and say, "Rodney, you can't be serious!" and Beryl just laughs at you.'

'Because this woman is a hopeless old Blinger bird who can't sing, has a face like an appendix and an irritating laugh?'

'Exactly.'

'Why do I think she has potential?'

'To make the joke work.'

'What joke?'

'That's what I'm telling you. We can't believe that you think she's any good but the more we laugh at you the more you insist that you think she has a bit of *X*, a bit of *Pow*, and in the end I turn to the Blinger and give her your phone number.'

'My phone number?'

'Yes, I tell her that since you believe in her so much she should ring you and you'll try and build her a pop career.'

'My phone number?'

'Not your actual phone number, Rodney. We'll give you a phone and every now and then during that week's show it'll ring and it'll be her asking when you're going to make her into a star.'

'So the joke's on me then?'

'Well yes, I suppose it is in a way but come on, Rodney, it's a lot of screen time and let's not get precious about things. It's a laugh.'

Rodney wanted to say no. He *so* wanted to tell Calvin to stuff it. But he knew what Calvin would do. Calvin would do what he always did when the people he chose to work with tried to say no, or asked for too much money. He'd dump them. Where were the judges who had worked with Calvin on the shows that had preceded *Chart Throb*, *Pop Goes the Minor Celebrity* and *Rock 'n' Roll Cooks*? Gone, that was where, back to radio or print. What had happened to the presenters who had preceded Keely? Dumped, that was what, hosting reality TV round-up shows on digital channels.

'All right,' said Rodney, attempting to look like he was enjoying the gag. 'Let's do it.'

'Top man!' Calvin replied. 'Trent, take us through

the storyboarding. No, Emma, you're reading the Blinger, you tell us.'

And so once more Emma found herself straining to see round the toilet door and finding her eyes momentarily met by Calvin's. He smiled a special little smile and nodded to her to proceed.

'This is scheduled for episode three,' said Emma. 'You've all left Manchester and Beryl is angry because she thinks you've been mean to the little sixteen-year-old.'

'Yes, yes, we've been through that, Emma,' said Trent rather testily, perhaps a little put out that Calvin was appearing to favour his junior colleague. 'Aviation fuel isn't cheap, you know.'

'Right,' Emma replied hurriedly, glancing down at her storyboard notes. 'After that Rodney and Calvin exchange amused but guilty glances . . .'

'Shot that as well. Emma, can we *please* cut to the chase,' Trent snapped.

Once more Emma seemed confused and risked a glance at Calvin, a glance that could only be interpreted as an appeal for his support. Then her face hardened, as if she was angry with herself for being so weak. If she had been hoping for sympathy she would have been disappointed, for Calvin merely raised a questioning eyebrow.

'Well, then Rodney's phone rings,' she said hurriedly. 'He answers it and when Calvin and Beryl hear him greet the Blinger they crack up laughing . . .'

'Ah!' Rodney butted in eagerly. 'How can we do that? We don't know her name yet.'

Once more Emma checked her notes.

'Calvin will have called her Tina Lite at the audition and that's how she'll introduce herself.'

'You're going to coach her?'

'Well, yes . . . obviously,' Emma replied, nervous at

having to spoonfeed one of the famous judges. 'We always do.'

'Can we *please* get on with this?' Beryl shouted. 'I have a flight scheduled back to LA tonight. My step-daughter is in *rehab* and dealing with enormous new breasts, if anybody cares.'

And so the fiction was arranged. Emma handed Rodney the mobile phone that was to double as his and dialled the number. It rang and Rodney was about to pick it up, but then he hesitated.

'Hang on. I shouldn't have my phone on, should I? I mean I'm on a plane, that's irresponsible . . . Come to think of it, *you* shouldn't have your phone on now. We might crash.'

'Please, Rodney,' Calvin said. 'I thought you wanted to be tougher on this series? Isn't keeping your phone on during a flight being tough? Playing by your own rules?'

'You think it would make me look tough?'

'Of course, the naughty boy, the rule breaker.'

'Well, all right then . . . But I don't want to actually do it . . . I mean, I don't mind *pretending* my phone rings but I don't want it to actually ring. It's dangerous.'

'You want Emma to turn off her phone and speak the ring?'

'Yes, of course. These rules are made for a purpose. Don't you listen to the safety announcements? Mobile phones may interfere with the aircraft's navigation system.'

'No, no. You're absolutely right,' Calvin replied. 'Emma, please speak the ring.'

Just then Beryl's mobile phone rang.

'I have to take this, it's my US agent.'

'Beryl, it's *dangerous*.'

'Fuck off, Rodney.'

For the next few minutes everyone was forced to sit through Beryl's half of a discussion regarding the timing of the new season of *The Blenheims*, which

Beryl was anxious to postpone because she was planning further surgery on the clitoris that she was having built out of the remains of her penis.

'And tell them to put some fucking thinner in the Botox,' she ordered. 'My face hasn't fucking *moved* since the last injections.'

When the conversation was finally over the team went back to work.

'Ring ring. Ring ring,' said Emma.

Rodney feigned surprise.

'Should have turned this off, I suppose,' he said, playing his role. 'But what the hell, I make my own rules. Live fast and leave a beautiful corpse, eh?'

'*Ring ring. Ring ring,*' Emma repeated insistently, knowing full well there would be no time to use Rodney's part-building in the final edit.

Rodney pretended to answer his phone.

'Hello?'

'Hello, is that Rodney Root?' Emma enquired from inside the toilet cubicle, keeping her voice as flat and toneless as possible so as to make it clear that she was not attempting in any way to adopt a character.

'Yes, this is Rodney.'

'It's Tina Lite here, darling. Ha ha. Ha ha. Calvin told me to call. Ha ha.'

'Oh, hello there, Tina Lite,' Rodney replied and Calvin and Beryl both pretended to splutter with laughter. Trent had wanted them both to choke on their drinks but Beryl feared for her lip gloss so only Calvin actually spat water.

'What can I do for you?' Rodney enquired, improvising gamely.

'Well, darling, ha ha. Ha ha,' Emma replied woodenly. 'Maybe you should think about what *I* can do for *you*, ha ha. Ha ha. Because if you make me a star like you said you would, you gonna find out! That's for sure! Ha ha. Ha ha!'

'Well now, listen, Tina, it's lovely to speak to you. I have to rush now, thanks for calling. Bye.' Rodney pretended to hang up his phone.

'There,' said Calvin, staying in the scene. 'You *said* keeping your phone on during a flight was dangerous!'

'Great punchline, Calvin!' Trent gushed. 'Everybody covered?'

When all departments had agreed the material was in the bag they moved on. Beryl disappeared behind a coat once more to change her costume, and there was a new shirt each for the men. They moved seats, they stared moodily at each other, they stared moodily out of the window and they all sat together to show what great mates they really were.

Finally Trent and Emma had no more shots left on their storyboard lists.

'That's a wrap, guvnor,' Trent announced.

'Thank fuck for that,' said Beryl. 'Can this thing take me straight to Heathrow?'

'Just one more shot,' Calvin insisted. 'A new one.'

'What's that, chief?' Trent enquired.

'Leaving Glasgow. Rodney sitting alone.'

'Fine, chief,' Trent replied. 'Any storyline? Any attitude?'

'It doesn't matter. Let's just take the shot.'

Rodney duly sat in the seat that Emma's storyboard said was his for leaving Glasgow and the camera was pointed at him.

'Right,' said Calvin. 'So, Rodney, we want you a little bit tense, a little bit shocked, OK?'

Rodney knew exactly what he was supposed to be shocked about.

'Calvin,' he said, trying to sound unconcerned, 'you know what, mate? I've been thinking about this one and I'm not sure it's such a great idea.'

'Look, we may not even use it, mate. I just want to be covered.'

'What's all this about?' Beryl asked rudely. 'I thought we were finished?'

'It's just a wicked little thought of Calvin's,' said Rodney, still trying to make light of it but clearly slightly worried. 'He wants to bring Iona back.'

'No!' Beryl gasped. 'Not Iona of the awful Shetland Mist, *who you fucked*?'

'Yes, although I thought they were . . .'

'And *having* fucked her you then fucked off!'

'Well, our relationship ended by mutual . . .'

'The ones you publicly prophesied would be big stars and that you would *make it so*?'

'Yes, well, I . . .'

Beryl roared with laughter. 'Oh, this is *brilliant*, Calvin. One of your best yet.'

'I must say I thought it had potential,' Calvin agreed, smiling.

'Potential! It's better than that. Come on, Rodney, you dug yourself into this one. Leaving aside the fact that you shagged the ass off that poor little Scottish Minger then dumped her, you *said* you'd make her crap band into stars and you didn't. You're *always* saying some zero or other could be a star and they *never* are. It's about time you explained yourself.'

Rodney sat, biting his lip, his eyes half furious, half confused.

Calvin winked at the cameraman, who understood exactly what was expected of him and swung his lens round to cover Rodney.

'Got it?' Calvin enquired quietly.

'Got it,' the cameraman replied.

'OK, Trent,' said Calvin. 'That's a wrap, let's get Beryl to Heathrow.'

Rodney was surprised. 'Aren't we going to take the shot then?' he asked, relieved.

'No, don't worry about it.'

Who's That Girl?

Trent accompanied Calvin back to London in Calvin's huge Rolls-Royce. Driving through the car park they passed the coach upon which Emma was about to embark with the rest of the crew. She was standing by its front door, struggling with a large bag containing the various files from which she had been working, her broken glasses perched on her nose. There was a goodish breeze blowing and it filled out her hair most attractively.

'That girl,' Calvin said, staring at her through the blacked-out window. 'The blonde one who was stuck in the toilet on the plane. I remember her from the last series. She did well, didn't she?'

'Yo, boss,' Trent replied. 'She's a good kid. Got some prospects into the finals. We made her a senior.'

As the car passed, Calvin eyed her in silence. He did not know why he had asked about Emma; he employed any number of pretty girls and he never asked about any of them. Emma was not even his type. Far too short. His soon-to-be-ex wife was six foot four.

'Her name's Emma,' Trent continued after a pause. 'Emma Lee-Murray. Still happy with her? Did she fuck up today? Anything you want me to say?'

'No. Nothing. Forget it.'

He remembered her clearly now. She had come to his attention towards the end of the previous season, working on the studio finals. Very little had passed between them but he did remember that he had noticed her. She was very . . . very . . .

Sitting back in his car Calvin wondered what she *had* been. Why had he noticed her then? Why was he thinking about her now? What was she very . . . ?

Was the word 'nice'?

Calvin rather thought that it was. The girl was nice. He had noticed her being nice to the crew. He had

103

noticed her being nice to the contestants. Not professionally nice. Not 'I need you to do what I tell you so I'm going to be nice' nice, but genuinely nice. God knows, he had even noticed her being nice to the studio audience and that was a hard thing to do in the complex mayhem of a finals night when five hundred lunatics had been whipped up into a gladiatorial frenzy.

She had even been nice to him in a funny sort of way.

Not that there had been many opportunities for pleasantries between the busiest and most successful man in show business and one of his army of employees, but nonetheless he remembered that he had felt her warmth. She was honest, which he liked, and her smile was real.

Yes, he had certainly noticed her. And now he had noticed her again.

Funny, that. He had not given her a thought in the intervening nine months. How could he? He had made an entire series of *Chart Throb USA* while also developing any number of new additions to his worldwide entertainment empire. And he had got married. Yet here he was, noticing her again.

Of course she *was* pretty in a small, cute-ish sort of way. But definitely not his type.

Not his type at all. She was too . . . nice.

Birmingham

'It's show two and the search has taken our intrepid judges to Birmingham, where enormous crowds of hopefuls have gathered.'

Whatever Keely might have claimed in her

breathless introduction to episode two, on the day on which the enormous crowds had gathered in Birmingham our three intrepid judges were nowhere near that city. It would *look* like they had been in Birmingham on the same day as the crowds of hopefuls because the footage taken of that crowd, when broadcast, would be preceded by the footage taken in the private jet of Calvin, Beryl and Rodney looking moody high over RAF Brize Norton.

The deceit was not absolute. As Emma often said to her friends when taxed on the subject, it wasn't *really* a lie at all, the three intrepid judges *would* eventually go to Birmingham, on another day, a day much further on in the selection process when the 'crowds' had been reduced to a more manageable few dozen. But they would go. Of course, when they did, they travelled separately up from London by car.

Shaiana had arrived an hour before her appointed time and then queued for another two hours while she and those around her were invited to grin and wave for the ever-present cameras. Shaiana had dutifully done as she was told but she hadn't enjoyed herself as much as she was pretending to. She was a serious singer after all, not like these other gurning fools.

When she finally edged her way to the registration table, Shaiana was directed to go and sit among a group of about sixty people who had been separated from the main crowd.

An oldish man sitting in the seat next to hers turned and smiled.

'Hello,' said the Prince, offering Shaiana his hand. 'How *are* you?'

When Calvin had been 'surprised' to hear the extraordinary news that the heir to the throne had applied to be on *Chart Throb* he had given strict instructions to Trent and his team that the early auditions for His Royal Highness were to be handled as much as possible like any other element of a *Chart Throb* day. Calvin knew that he had a huge mountain to climb if he was to turn the nation's favourite whipping boy into its number-one pop star and he reasoned that the best way to start was to make it plain that the Prince must be seen to receive no special treatment. The Prince himself had also been very clear on this point.

'If I play, I play fair,' he said. 'Dartmouth rules. When I went into the navy I got no special treatment and that's how I wish to play this too.'

'But isn't him turning up going to cause a terrible stir?' Trent had said to Calvin.

'I honestly don't think so. Everyone at our auditions is concentrating on just one thing, themselves. They're not interested in anybody else. Why would they give some sad elderly man in a tweed jacket a second glance? After all, he certainly won't be the only eccentric-looking old bloke hanging around, will he? If people do spot him, what will they think? They'll think that bloke looks a bit like the Prince of Wales. They're not going to think it *is* his nibs, are they? Not unless we start making a fuss of him, which we won't. How many David Beckham lookalikes turned up last year?'

'Eight. And eleven Poshes.'

'And some of them were pretty good, weren't they? But nobody thought it was them, did they?'

'No.'

'And there you're talking about *serious* celebrities. Not some fucking prince. Just let him turn up and treat him like the rest and we'll see how we go, eh?'

The Prince of Wales had duly been sent an acceptance form and instructions to attend Hall E3 of the National Exhibition Centre in Birmingham. He was instructed to be prepared to sing, unaccompanied, one verse and a chorus of a song of his choice. He had therefore rescheduled visits to two primary schools, a regimental dinner and a mosque, and his plans had been entered into the court circular as 'cultural'.

He arrived on the appointed morning in the first of two black Daimlers. This had caused many heads to turn, but only because people had imagined for a moment that Calvin Simms himself was arriving. When only a stooped, sombre-looking figure in a big old-fashioned overcoat got out, all interest was lost. The only obvious thing of note about the man who then made his way nervously into the crowded audition hall was that he was accompanied by two serious-looking persons in cheap suits that bulged at the armpit.

'Look, an old boy band,' someone had quipped as they made their way as directed to where Shaiana was already sitting.

'Hi,' Shaiana replied to the Prince's greeting, but she scarcely looked up. She did not really want to talk to anybody. Today was about her and her alone.

She had to stay focused because she *just wanted it so much*.

'What song have you prepared?' the Prince enquired. 'I'm doing "Jerusalem", which I do hope won't offend anybody. People often make the mistake of thinking that it's a *Socialist* song but I disagree. I'm quite sure that when Blake penned his towering lyric he had *humanism* in mind. It's a song about love of one's fellow man and of one's country, and I do think that's important, don't you?'

Shaiana, like many of the contestants assembled in Birmingham that day, had selected 'The Greatest Love Of All', which is about love for oneself.

The Prince's number, 8,900, was written in felt-tip pen on a big white label that had been stuck to his chest. Shaiana's number was 16,367. Despite the fact that there were scarcely five hundred auditionees present in the hall, all the numbers displayed on the entrants' chests ran to at least four figures, commonly five.

'I am not a number!' the Prince joked loudly, glancing about in a comradely fashion. 'I am a *human being*.'

Neither Shaiana nor any of the others nearby paid any attention. They were all lost in their own thoughts, running through in their heads the verses and choruses which might just change their lives for ever.

The Prince's further efforts at integration with his future subjects petered out when an already familiar amplified voice boomed from across the hall. 'OK, people! It's Gary again,' the voice shouted. 'Say "Hi, Gary!"'

'Hi, Gary!' the crowd responded but with little enthusiasm.

'Oh goodness, not this *fool* again!' the Prince muttered. 'He really is the most prize buffoon.'

'Say, "Hi, Barry!"' boomed a second voice.

'Hi, Barry,' they echoed.

'Come ON,' Gary shouted. 'That was TERRIBLE! Say, "Hi, Gary and Barry!"'

The crowd dutifully replied with slightly more animation this time.

'Hi, Gary and Barry!'

In fact it was not just the Prince who was heartily sick of Gary and Barry; by now everybody was. It was their job to cajole the crowd into supplying the production crew with the hysterically excited mob shots that made up the opening montage of the programme.

'*Ninety-five thousand people. Three judges. Twelve finalists. Just one* Chart Throb!!'

Somebody had to make those crowds shout and clap and wave and it was Gary and Barry, two amiable ex-drama students who wanted to be comedians, who had got the job.

'OK, people, listen up! If you want to be a Chart Throb you gotta ACT like a Chart Throb! You gotta live it, breathe it, OWN it and owning it starts right now. Calvin is watching you! He is the Dark Lord of Rock and he is everywhere! So you have to put everything you've got into this! Let me hear you say, "YO-OH!"''

'Yo-oh!' everybody said, except the Prince.

'I won't do it,' he muttered. 'This isn't bloody communist Russia.'

'Let me hear you say "OH YEAH!"''

'OH YEAH!'

All afternoon Gary and Barry had been working the crowd, gathering them into groups to shout the name of the show, moving them about the hall en masse, getting them to wave, jump, twist and jive in front of huge banners bearing the *Chart Throb* logo. Anything, in fact, to imply that an almost impossibly large number of people were having the time of their lives and loving every minute of their *Chart Throb* experience, as opposed to five hundred people hanging around in an empty exhibition hall.

On the occasion when they had interrupted the Prince's efforts to befriend Shaiana, Gary and Barry were attempting to tutor the crowd in the difficult job of physically spelling out the word C-H-A-R-T. The 'C' and the 'T' were pretty simple and the 'R' was doable, but turning the body into an 'A' was hard and an 'H' pretty much impossible.

'Do the "H" with your fingers!' Gary commanded. 'Like the "W" sign for "whatever".'

'And then we all throb, right?' Barry added.

'Yeah, that's it!' Gary shouted. 'We all spell out C-H-A-R-T then we all thro-o-o-o-b-b-b! Right!'

At the planning meeting the previous evening there had been some discussion as to how the crowd should be instructed to perform a throb. In the end the team had agreed on a sort of general agitation of the arms and body which everybody knew was not a throb at all but a shake, the problem with a genuine throb being that it was rather a ponderous and uniform thing and simply not good telly.

'C-H-A-R-T thro-o-o-o-o-b-b-b!' went the crowd, all shaking and shivering at the appropriate moment.

'Thanks, you're brilliant,' called Barry.

'Absolutely brilliant,' Gary agreed. 'Now let's do it again!'

They did it four times, after which the crowd stopped throbbing and returned to their places in the queue.

Then the two camera teams covering the crowd scenes made their way over to the smaller, separate group, among whom Shaiana and the Prince were sitting. Emma came too. She carried a clipboard and looked rather harassed. Trent, in the vision control truck out in the car park, had just shouted at her that they were already an hour behind.

'Can I have the Quasar please?' Emma called out.

A muscular, confident-looking man jumped up from behind Shaiana.

'Well hello, ba-a-a-a-aby!' he said, grabbing his crotch and thrusting it forward. 'You can 'av the Quasar any time you likes, princess, you nah wha' Ahm sayin'?'

The Quasar spoke in a hybrid Euro-American accent that sat somewhere between Morocco and South Central LA.

'We'd like a little chat on camera.'

'Then the Quasar is ready to rock!'

'Great,' said Emma, smiling weakly, 'that's what we like to hear.'

Quasar bounded forward. He was dressed in skin-tight black jeans, Cuban-heeled snakeskin boots and a red silk shirt, which was unbuttoned almost down to his navel. Emma, followed by the camera teams, led

Quasar towards the queue and placed him in among the crowd.

'Why're you picking *him* out?' a couple of girls screeched. 'We haven't even been auditioned yet.'

'You'll get your chance, ladies,' Emma called with exaggerated cheeriness. But she knew that they almost certainly would not. Most of the real Cling, Bling and Ming prospects had already been identified either from their application forms or by the teams of production staff patrolling the queues. Everyone else would, of course, be given thirty seconds or so in front of a junior researcher to avoid a riot but the chances of somebody showing sufficient weirdness, ugliness, desperation, tartiness, arrogance, emotional or intellectual dysfunction (or even, very occasionally, talent) at this stage to jump back into contention were not great. The National Exhibition Centre was not a cheap hall to rent and Emma and the other members of the hard-pressed production team had only a day in which to process the whole crowd, while at the same time attempting to pick up as many drop-in shots and pieces to camera as possible.

However tough a day Emma might be having, Quasar was loving his and he certainly did not allow the sullen resentment of the other contestants who had been bunched around him to dampen his spirits.

'Wha'appen, babes?' he shouted at Emma, flexing his buffed muscles.

'How are you feeling here today?' Emma shouted back from behind the camera.

'I'm feeling *wicked*!' said Quasar. 'Because I am a *geezer*!'

'Are you the best, Quasar?' shouted Emma. 'Tell us you're the best there is.'

'I'm the best there is!' Quasar replied dutifully.

'Tell us again,' shouted Emma, 'but louder.'

'I'm the best there is!' yelled Quasar.

111

'Can you do a little move with it? Uhm, grab at your trousers or something?'

'You betcha, babes!' shouted Quasar, once more declaring he was the best there was, but this time grabbing at his crotch, spinning round and then dropping to do the splits.

'Fantastic, Quasar!' shouted Emma. 'Tell Calvin that you're going to rock his ass!'

Quasar needed little encouragement. He stepped towards the camera, pulled his shirt completely open, pointed down the lens and said:

'Calvin Simms, the Quasar is gonna rock your ass!'

'That was great, Quasar,' Emma assured him before ushering him back to his seat. 'Good luck.'

Emma's fingers were massaging the packet of Marlboro Lights that was wedged into the top of her cute hipster jeans. It would be a long time yet before she would get a fag break and the work was exhausting. Summoning up all her energies, she re-applied her fixed grin and referred once more to her clipboard.

'Shaiana?' she called out.

Nervously Shaiana identified herself.

Emma looked at her, remembering her application form. Emma didn't always remember the applicants that she put forward for audition, but she remembered Shaiana. *I am me*, Shaiana had written.

And this was her.

During her university days Emma had been a volunteer trauma counsellor for the Student Union. Her distressing duty had been to lend a sympathetic ear to the victims of assaults, burglaries, harassment and occasionally rapes. Emma had looked into the eyes of many victims in her time and she knew the signs. But in her counselling days Emma had met victims *after* the trauma. Shaiana looked like a victim already, even though so far nothing had

112

happened. She was a victim *waiting* to be assaulted.

Emma felt like a mugger but what could she do? Shaiana was television gold. She just wanted it *so* much. So much that she wrote it twice.

Gulping hard and feeling once more for the comfort of the cigarettes clamped to the spray-tanned flesh at her hip, Emma led Shaiana away.

Really, Truthfully, How Much DO You Want It?

'Back in the holding area,' the gorgeous Keely would say the following day when she arrived to film her links, 'every hopeful has a song to sing, and lawks! We just can't stop them singing it!'

Shaiana, who had been placed amid another group of hopefuls, sang 'I Am Woman' just as Emma had asked her to do. When it was over, the people around her applauded as they had also been instructed to do.

When the carefully staged impromptu performance was over, Emma took her place once more behind the camera to shout her questions.

'How much does this mean to you, Shaiana?' she asked.

'It means everything to me, Emma,' Shaiana replied.

'Not "Emma", Shaiana. Don't say "Emma".'

'Why not?'

'Because I'm not here.'

A shadow of confusion fell across Shaiana's face. 'I don't understand.'

'I'm not here. Keely's here.'

'Is Keely here?'

A sudden excitement gripped everybody standing

nearby. Was Keely here? The real blonde beautiful Keely off the telly? So far the crowd had been bitterly disappointed not to have seen anybody from the show, not even Rodney, and now it seemed that the gorgeous presenter was in the building.

'Keely's here!!' The rumour had crossed the floor of Hall E3 in a moment.

'No!' shouted Emma. 'Keely's not here.'

'You said she was,' an aggrieved voice shouted back.

'Yes,' Shaiana agreed, 'you said it to me.'

'Look, I'm just saying that I won't be asking the questions on the actual show. Keely will be asking you the questions.'

'So she is here?'

'NO! No, she's not . . . It's just that we'll record her later and . . .' Once more Trent shouted into her earpiece that time was slipping away. 'Look, Shaiana, just say what I tell you to say, OK? Repeat after me, can you do that?'

'Of course.'

'Good, let's go . . . "I want this so much." '

'I want this so much.'

'Louder, "I want this SO much!" '

'I want this SO much!'

'Brilliant. Now in your own words. Come on, tell me, *really tell me*. Bearing in mind just how much store the judges set by passion and commitment, come on, really, truthfully, how much DO you want this?'

And so Shaiana told the world how much she wanted it. How it was all she had ever wanted. How it was what God had made her for and that it meant just everything. Absolutely everything. It was her dream. Shaiana needed little prompting. With a gentle push from Emma, tears welled up in her eyes.

'Everyone thinks I'm a nobody,' Shaiana said. 'I'm going to prove to them all that I'm a somebody.'

'Yes. Yes, I'm sure you are, Shaiana,' Emma said, her

hand holding tight to the cigarettes at her hip as if fearful that if she once let go of them she might let go altogether and shout: No you're not, Shaiana, you're *really, really not*, with your desperate face and your not bad voice. You're *not* a somebody, you're just any old somebody, we all are. So run, babes! Run, before we break your heart.

More Maths

Quasar took the seat beside the Prince that Shaiana had vacated.

'Quasar, geeza,' Quasar said cheerfully.

'The Prince of Wales,' His Royal Highness replied.

'The fresh Prince of Wales. Wicked! You Welsh then?'

'Well, not really, no . . . you don't really need to be *from* Wales to be prince of it. Isn't that an *extraordinary* thing? It's like my mother is Queen of Australia. I always laugh when I think of that, because she's not a *bit* like any Australians I've ever met. Lovely people, of course. So *down to earth*. Don't you think?'

The Quasar smiled a broad smile.

'Oh, I gets it, yeah, babes,' he said. 'You is doing the whole lookee-likee thing. Wicked! West side! Ouch! Is you with an agency, geeza?'

'Well, no, I don't suppose I am really. I sort of bumble along on my own.'

'Geeza, you is *insane*! There is big bucks in the lookee-likee biz, parties, singing telegrams. I 'as a babe who is a Jennifer Lopez, don' look a bit lak 'er 'cept for 'er big bum but she makes a shitloada money anyways!'

Clearly the Prince had not the faintest idea what his

115

companion was talking about but decades of experience of one-sided communications through which he had smiled and nodded had taught him to change tack rather than probe too far.

'One simply has to be *so* careful,' he often observed to his wife. 'You only have to ask someone how nylon is actually *made* or what Hip Hop actually *is* and you can be there for *days*.'

The Prince looked about him for a moment before observing: 'That was quite a show you put on there for the camera, young man.'

'Well, you gotta big it up, geeza, innit?' Quasar responded with a wide grin. 'I reckon we is *in*, I mean I reckon we is *through*, which is well 'ard. You know wot I'm saying?'

'Uhm, not entirely, no.'

'They's filming us, right? Like, you know, on our first day, man.'

'Yes?' the Prince enquired. 'But surely that's the purpose of the exercise, to cover the selection process – or perhaps I'm getting the wrong end of the stick.'

'Geeza, *check it out*. There is 'undreds of us here, right? An' we is all here for our auditions, right? But they is only filming a few of us in the queue, innit?'

A few metres away they could see Shaiana. She had been placed in front of a small group of applicants and this time she was singing 'Will You Love Me Tomorrow' while the people around her were being encouraged to clap along supportively.

'Well, I suppose it's inevitable that they can only film a few of us, Mr Quasar,' the Prince observed politely. 'They could not possibly cover everybody, there must be five hundred people here. One presumes they simply get what they can.'

'You is crazy, geeza! What you talkin' 'bout?' Quasar grinned. 'In't you seen the show, man?'

'Uhm, well, actually no . . . I thought I had but that was the *X Factor.*'

'Where 'as you bin, geeza! That is so last year, babe! *Chart Throb* is where it's at an' you ain' sin it?'

'I *know*, it's awful of me, isn't it? I *am* a dunce. Apparently it's being repeated on UK Gold too. I asked my equerry to tape an episode but he can't work our Sky Plus any better than I can and the memsahib's no help because she says she'd ban all television to-morrow if it was up to her.'

'Well, if you 'ad sin it, geeza, you would be hip to the fac' that all the people who gets put through to Pop School 'as already bin *seen in the queue*, man! We seen 'em from the start. Like last year, the geeza what *won the fucking final*, man, he was there on the *first show*! He was there in the crowd saying 'e was gonna rock Calvin's ass, right? Even though he was *still only in the queue for 'is first audition*!'

'Uhm . . . I'm not sure I follow the point you're making, Mr Quasar. If there *is* a point? I mean it doesn't matter at all if there isn't . . .'

'That *is* the point, geeza! They ain't filming *every-body* in the queue, is they? They ain't even picking out one in fifty. How *could* they, guy? We'd be here till we was dead! But when Calvin an' Beryl and that other prick choose the people what is goin' through to the next round they's always *already been seen in the queue*, right? They's got shots of them right from the fucking car park, guy! On day one! Think about it, geeza. How would they know to film them if they 'adn't already chosen 'em? We 'as bin *picked*! We is *looking good*.'

The Prince of Wales had been privately educated at great expense and had then gone to Cambridge, while Quasar had left school at sixteen without qualifi-cations in order to become an exotic dancer. But it was Quasar who had done the maths.

117

Graham and Milly in the Car Park

'The journey to stardom is never easy. But for some it's much harder than others. Graham and Milly are two young singers with a dream. Nothing special about that, you might say, except for one thing. Graham has been *blind since birth*.'

That was what Keely would be saying, some months later and a hundred miles down the M6, in a sound recording booth in Soho as she voiced the narrative links for episode three.

Meanwhile the accompanying footage had to be shot and that was down to Emma and her little camera crew. Having ticked off Shaiana on her clipboard she had collected Graham and Millicent from the same area as the Prince, Shaiana and the Quasar and asked them to go back into the car park.

'Why?' Graham asked.

'We'd like to see you arriving.'

'But we have arrived. We've been here for three hours.'

'I know but we didn't see it . . . I mean *witness* it,' Emma said, suddenly struck by the strange embarrassment of the sighted who find themselves using the word 'see' to a blind person.

Graham and Millicent returned dutifully with Emma and her camera team to the car park of the exhibition centre. The moment she was outside Emma clawed at her cigarette packet, almost tearing the top off in her haste. The whole crew were doing the same; theirs was a high-stress occupation.

'Right,' said Emma, trying to speak and inhale at the same time. 'We'd love to see Millicent leading Graham through the parked cars to join the end of the queue.'

'What queue?' Milly enquired.

Emma had been so intent on getting her Marlboro lit that she hadn't noticed that the car park was now almost empty of people.

'Where's the queue?' she asked a colleague, Chelsie.

'Inside,' Chelsie replied. 'We've got them all in.'

'Well, get them all out again!' Emma demanded. She was not by nature a bossy or demanding person but Chelsie (who was new) had a rather supercilious manner. It annoyed Emma that she seemed unaffected by the urgency of their task. 'They can't turn up to an empty car park, can they? They have to join the queue! Haven't you watched the programme?'

'Yes, Emma, I have,' Chelsie replied. 'Which is why I tried to get them filmed when they *actually* arrived and we still had a queue out here for them to join, but you were off somewhere having a fag.'

Chelsie turned on her heel so there was no opportunity for Emma to reply even if she had wished to. Shortly thereafter the junior researcher returned leading thirty or so grumpy-looking contestants. Emma took one look at them and sent for Gary and Barry.

'You'll have to get them going again,' she told the two would-be comedians. 'This lot look like they've come for a lynching.'

Leaving Gary and Barry to remind the crowd that Calvin was watching them, that a true Chart Throb was never off duty and that they should see this as just another chance to shine on camera, Emma took Graham and Millicent to the far side of the car park.

'All right, Millicent,' Emma explained. 'So you've just arrived in—'

'But this isn't our car,' Millicent interrupted. 'We parked in the disabled bay right by the front door.'

'Walked straight in,' Graham added.

'Yes, yes,' Emma said, trying to be patient. 'But don't get too hung up on specifics. We're here to

119

demonstrate a broader truth which is that you're blind, OK? In fact we might take a shot of the disabled bay with a car in it . . .'

'My car?' Millicent enquired.

'It doesn't matter which car,' Emma almost snapped. 'It's just to show that the disabled bay is always full when a genuine case requires it.'

'But it wasn't, it was empty and we used it!'

'I KNOW!' said Emma and this time she did not bother to conceal her irritation. 'Look, we'll forget the car bit, OK? It was just a thought. Wait for our signal and then go with Graham towards the queue. Can you do that?'

'Yes, of course.'

The team then retreated to set up their camera. Emma called 'Action!' then 'Cut!' almost immediately after.

'Millicent,' she said, 'do you think you could possibly *lead* Graham?'

'What, by the hand?'

'Yes.'

'I've got my stick,' Graham shouted. 'And I can hear Milly. I don't need leading.'

'Yes but . . . well, it looks . . . it looks better.'

In the end Graham's desire to please the TV people overcame any wounded pride and he allowed himself to be led by Milly through the car park to join the end of the 'queue', which Gary and Barry had carefully placed by the front door and by some miracle managed to persuade to look cheerful.

When the shot was completed Emma leaned on a car and lit another cigarette.

'Long way to go yet,' said Chelsie.

'Yes. I know.'

'Better get a move on, hadn't we?'

Emma did not move. For a moment she closed her eyes, inhaling deeply.

120

'Did you see that girl Shaiana?' she asked eventually.

'Yes, of course,' Chelsie replied. 'Absolute nutter.'

'Did you think she was a bit *too* intense? A bit scary?'

'I didn't think there was such a thing on *Chart Throb*?'

'Yes,' said Emma, laughing slightly too loudly. 'I suppose if she kills herself we can always lose it in the edit.'

'Bollocks, Calvin would put it in the trailers.'

Mission Statement

Next came the part of the afternoon Emma had been dreading most of all. It was time for her to play her role in the final humiliation of a person whom she saw as a decent and hard-working old man who just happened to be heir to the throne.

'Wales!' she called out, following Calvin's instructions to treat their celebrated entrant no differently to the others.

'Good afternoon, young lady,' said a gentle voice almost at her elbow. 'Wales here, reporting for duty. All present and correct.'

Emma could hardly believe it. He had been not four metres away and she had not even noticed him. Among the wall-to-wall pulsating egos screaming for attention he had simply become invisible, and his detectives even more so.

Emma curtsied. She had not meant to, and she had not expected to. She had not, after all, curtsied to any of the other contestants and she was supposed to treat them all the same but she could not help herself. This was *the Prince of fucking Wales*! To her at least this man meant something. Despite the endless embarrassments, the constant erosion of his dignity and authority, the comically anachronistic nature of everything about him from his trousers to his very office, he *meant something*. Not *him* so much as his position. He was history. His family embodied the nation. A collective focus that stretched back a thousand years.

Emma cared about that. Despite living in a world where anything that was not beautiful or fashionable was deemed worthless, Emma considered this man important. She *wanted* to be respectful to him. That was surely the point of having him. As far as she was concerned if you're going to have a Prince of Wales, play the game and curtsey. Otherwise spend the public money on something else.

This man was the *heir to the throne*.

He was also, it seemed, an embarrassingly naïve wannabe media celeb and she was the Mephistopheles who was soon to hang his sorry, terminally compromised arse out to dry.

'Uhm, hi, hello, uhm, sir . . . I'm Emma.'

'*Hello*, Emma. How *nice* to see you. How *are* you? Are you well?'

'Yes. Yes, sir. I'm fine. It's . . . it's an honour to meet you, uhm . . . Mr Wales. To have you here.'

'Oh no really, I'm just happy if I can *do my bit.*'

'Well . . . we'd like to get a few words to camera, please.'

'Certainly. Certainly. Absolutely. Where would you like me?' he replied, with a deprecating laugh. 'After all, nobody ever accused muggins here of being *bashful with his opinions*, eh? Some people think I should just *pipe down.*'

'Uhm, this way, sir,' Emma said.

Together with the camera crew, Emma, the Prince and the detectives made their way over to a section of the crowd that Gary and Barry had assembled in order that His Royal Highness might be 'discovered' in it.

'I heard you speak once, sir,' Emma said. She had not meant to bring it up but she somehow couldn't help it.

'I expect I was *awful*. Was I? Did I make a *hash* of it?'

'It was at a Holocaust Day ceremony. You spoke about the need for greater understanding and integration in multicultural societies.'

'Bloody obvious really but worth *saying*, I always think.'

'You were very inspiring.'

'Was I? *Thank you*. One does *try*,' the Prince replied, clearly delighted.

'You've always struck me as a man of principle, sir.'

'Well, as I say, one *does try*.'

'So . . . may I ask you something?'

'Yes, yes of course.'

'What are you doing here?'

'Oh, that's *very* simple. I want people to get the chance to see *the real me*!'

It broke Emma's heart. She wanted to cry. How *could* he be so stupid? A man who had met and spoken to *everybody*, making such a foolish mistake as that? Of course they all did, everybody, great and small, rich and poor. From *Big Brother 12* to *Politicians in the Jungle*, everybody thought that if only they could get in front of a camera they could show people the *real them*. Had they learned nothing from watching the very shows they aspired to be on? Could they not see that between them and the public whom they wished to influence stood the *edit*? And the edit would make of them what it pleased. It would not necessarily be brutal, it might as easily create a hero as a villain, but what it would never *ever* do was show anybody as they *genuinely were*.

By this time they had arrived at the appointed place and the Prince of Wales, unable to suppress the instincts developed over decades in public life, turned his attention to the group of people who had been assembled.

'Good afternoon . . . hello . . . hello there,' he said, leaning towards people with an expression of rapt fascination. 'How are you? Do you think it will rain? I must say I had no idea this hall was so *vast*, had you?'

'Sir . . . I mean, uhm . . . Your Royal . . . uhm, Mr Wales?'

Everybody laughed at Emma's confusion, including the Prince. The crowd were, of course, amused at Emma's efforts to think of a way to address a person who was so obviously a lookalike, and an extremely good one at that.

'Perhaps you could speak to us?' Emma continued.

'Yes, yes *of course*,' the Prince replied, apologizing to the people around him. 'Excuse me, I'm afraid I have to speak to this lady and her camera. I've enjoyed meeting you so much. You've all been *marvellous*.'

From the breast pocket of his waistcoat HRH produced some handwritten notes. He spoke first of the 'much-maligned' celebrity culture and of the need for community leaders and politicians to embrace its values rather than condemning them.

'Canute could not turn back the tide and nor can we,' he stated firmly. 'If we cannot go where young people go, if we cannot engage with them in a language that they understand and on subjects that interest them, we risk being left behind. I believe that children are the future.'

For one horrified moment Emma thought that the Prince of Wales was about to launch into 'The Greatest Love Of All' but in fact His Royal Highness had been unaware that he was quoting from that *Chart Throb* favourite.

'Young people have been intellectually and politically disenfranchised,' the Prince continued.

124

'Conventional news and current affairs programmes do not reach them, because they do not watch them. That is not their fault: the responsibility lies with the broadcasters, the politicians and those like me who have the privilege of high office. We have a duty to find a way of reconnecting with a lost generation.

'I do not believe that young people are stupid,' the Prince continued. 'Nor do I think them shallow, self-obsessed and interested only in fame and fashion. They are the life's blood of this country and they need to be taken seriously. I look forward very much to meeting with and talking to as many of the contestants here today as possible. I'm certain that I can learn something from them, just as I hope perhaps they can learn something from me. I imagine that many of them will not have considered the organic option when preparing their shopping lists, nor perhaps will many of them have given much thought to the urgent need to preserve our historic buildings and to consider the *human scale* in town planning. They may possibly not even be aware of the healing power of herbal infusions or the fact that in many of our inner cities young black boys are as likely to find themselves in prison as in employment. These are things I can share with them just as they can share their knowledge and their experience with me. In conclusion, of course I am mindful of the fact that this show is about having fun and there is nothing wrong with that. I may be heir to the throne but I'm also a pretty mean crooner and I look forward greatly to what I believe is called shaking my booty and strutting my funky stuff.'

'OK, that's great,' Emma called out. 'Thanks, that was brilliant.'

She realized he actually meant it. He truly believed what he was saying and that some significant part of his three- or four-minute speech would find its way on to the programme. How could anyone be so stupid?

Emma knew exactly what part of his carefully prepared statement was likely to make it through the edit. The last sentence:

'I may be heir to the throne but I'm also a pretty mean crooner and I look forward greatly to what I believe is called shaking my booty and strutting my funky stuff.'

Telly did not get much better than that. If Emma knew Calvin she was pretty sure that the public would be seeing the Prince of Wales utter that ridiculous line many, many times in the weeks to come. In fact she imagined it would probably form the core of the teaser trailers that would herald the upcoming season.

The Bites

Emma returned the Prince to his place feeling sad and shabby and her mood was in no way improved when Chelsie appeared with the news that the 'Bite' team were ready to rock.

'What do you want first?' Chelsie asked. 'Clingers, Blingers or Mingers?'

Emma swallowed hard and felt once more for the comfort of her cigarette packet. Gathering the 'Bites', as they were called, was hard and emotionally draining work.

'I *hate* doing this,' Emma said.

'Best bit,' Chelsie replied. 'You need to see it as a hunt. Besides, this is what they *want*. They've come here to get on the telly. The ones you should feel sorry for are the ones we *don't* choose.'

'They came here to sing,' Emma replied. 'Bites don't get to sing.'

'They came here to get on the telly and the ones we choose will get on the telly.'

It was true that Bite selection was the last chance rejected candidates had of national exposure. They were the amusing rejects, the one-shot wonders with which the shows would be stitched together. Anyone who had shown any *real* talent at Cling, Bling or Ming (or even Sing) had been picked up at their audition and sent to join the pre-selected group marked down for more concerted exploitation in front of the three judges.

'Have I got time for a fag?' Emma enquired.

'I can do this on my own if you want,' Chelsie replied.

Emma was not having that. She might have been finding her job increasingly draining but it was still her job, she was the senior researcher and Chelsie was the new girl.

'No, let's get on with it.'

Bite selection was tough work. It was no easy task to locate the shortest, fattest, ugliest people in the crowd and then persuade them they really wanted to announce to the world that Calvin Simms had missed his chance of discovering the next Robbie Williams. That, however, was what classic Bite selection was all about. The collection team would trawl the growing number of rejects, searching for those personalities who not only looked the most pathetic but who were also most likely to deliver an entertaining sentence or two which would make them look deluded and stupid. Those selected were then taken to the Bite Back Box and cajoled into making fools of themselves.

The important thing was to gain the trust of the victim. The Bite collector needed to form an instant sympathetic bond with their prey, assuring them that they felt their pain and empathized with their outrage. It was probably the part of the job that Emma hated most but Chelsie enjoyed it, viewing it as an amusing game, a challenge, and she had already proved herself particularly adept at it. Chelsie positively revelled in persuading middle-aged female midgets that it would be a good idea to claim to be a cross between Jordan and Nicole Kidman. She would lurk among the rejects and quickly assess their visual potential, then she would pounce.

'How do you feel about it, babes?' Chelsie would ask, flinging an arm round her victim. 'Do you feel devastated? Angry? Used? Bet you do, babes, don't you? And I'm not surprised, I was listening at the door and I thought you were brilliant. I can't believe they've blown you out, you're *so* much better than the others. Why don't you come with me into the Bite Back Box and you can tell that Calvin Simms exactly what you think of his crappy show?'

The ones who complained and protested that their talent had been overlooked went into the Blingers group, those who cried and spoke of God and how hard they had worked went with the Clingers and the old, the stupid, the ugly and the physically and mentally challenged went into the Mingers.

Emma and Chelsie began to make their way towards the Bite Back Box.

'Let's get the Clingers out of the way,' Emma sighed. 'I always feel so *mean.*'

And so she and Chelsie sat together in the booth as one Clinger after another was brought before them.

'It's all come to nothing, hasn't it?' Emma breathed sympathetically.

'The dream's over,' Chelsie whispered. 'You're going home with nothing.'

'How do you feel?' cooed Emma. 'You must be gutted, you must just want to break down and cry.'

'Why don't you tell us that God gave you a gift and Calvin has hurled it back into God's face?'

And with any luck the person who had spent

months dreaming of stardom would cry and wail and another stitch in the tapestry of distraught sad acts would be created.

Next came the Blingers.

'Do you think you've got it?'

'Yes, I've got it, I've got what it takes.'

'Could you be a star, babes?'

'Yes. Yes, I could, I could be a star!'

And the Mingers.

'Do you think you're sexy?'

'Yes.'

'Don't just say yes, say it all, tell the world, say, "I think I'm sexy."'

'I think I'm sexy.'

'Repeat after me, "I am one badass, kickass, rock-steady mother lover and I am going to rock the world with or without you, Calvin Simms!"'

Sometimes Emma and Chelsie would cheat, cajoling from their victims words which, when edited, could be placed in an order that would entirely misrepresent the speaker. These were called Frankenbites.

'I am not claiming I'm the next Elvis' could easily be cut down later to 'I'm the next Elvis'.

After all, every candidate had signed a form saying that they would abide by the rules of the competition no matter how often the producers changed them, 'including and at any time, verbally', as the form made clear. The producers could do exactly what they liked and it made Emma feel deeply uncomfortable, almost ashamed.

'You're in the wrong job, babes,' Chelsie opined with exaggerated sincerity. 'What you've got to realize is that whatever we do to these people and however we misrepresent them, they are *still* getting on the telly and that is always better than not getting on the telly. No matter what.'

Emma was not so sure.

Peroxide and Blossom

Emma looked at her watch. The day was getting away from her and she still had three 'stories' left to shoot. What was more, they all required crowds and the crowds were thinning. People were drifting away and who could blame them? Their great day, the day of which they had dreamed for weeks and weeks, was clearly coming to an end and what a disappointment it had been. Hours of standing around and being ordered about had been rewarded for the most part by a minute or so in front of a bored-looking stranger. Some posh girl had heard them sing their song, thanked them, possibly taken down a few details and basically fucked them off. There had been no Calvin, no Beryl, not even any Rodney. No chance to proclaim their self-belief, no opportunity for banter with the judges, nothing. Yes, there was still hope, they had after all been asked to wait around, but the brighter minds among them were beginning to notice that those who had been seen were rarely seen again. They just sat about, stood about, milled about and occasionally Gary and Barry would ask them to shout, clap or cheer. The day was definitely losing its fizz. A couple of students dressed as Danny and Sandy from *Grease* (in 'The One That I Want' mode) had begun to write an article for their college paper about the way they were being used. It was at this point in the day that Trent always made his little speech, gently but firmly reminding everybody of the Terms and Conditions part of the entry form which they had of course signed.

'Listen up, people!' Trent said. 'Hey, you all love *Chart Throb* or else you wouldn't be here. You know that we are a great entertainment show and each year we make dreams come true. Now of course, like with any telly show, not everything you see on screen reflects *exactly* what happens off screen – that's show-biz. And what we don't need is any killjoys and spoilsports pissing on the parade, OK? Every magician has his tricks and yes, we have a few up our sleeve, but that doesn't make our show any less true or real. We DO make stars. We DO find talent and if this year it wasn't you, hey, watch the show, enjoy the dream and better luck next year. And always remember, that con-tract you signed is a *legal document*. Anyone who breaks it breaks the law and believe me, the full weight of the law will be brought to bear upon them. Calvin Simms will *take your house*! He will *bankrupt you*! He will *close you down*! Read the contract again before you leave. Don't forget, you may not talk to *anybody*, about *anything* that happens here today. OK? That's it. There's coffee and biscuits coming, enjoy the rest of your day.'

Emma always thought that Trent laid it on a bit thick about Calvin closing people down. She believed it was more of an act with Calvin.

Chelsie came bouncing up to her. 'We're ready for Peroxide. Where are they?'

'Peroxide please,' Emma called out. 'I need Georgie and Michelle.'

'Meanwhile in the holding area,' Keely would explain when the episode was edited, 'two old friends of the show have turned up unexpectedly. Who could forget Georgie and 'Chelle, better known as Peroxide!'

The truth was that meanwhile, in the toilet, one of the old friends of the show was throwing up. The other one was standing outside the door, waving at Emma.

'She's all nerves,' the older member of Peroxide said as Emma and the crew scuttled over. 'Come on, Georgie. Emma wants to do a piece to camera.'

As an old *Chart Throb* hand, Michelle knew exactly what was expected of her. She also knew how busy the

131

production team were and was anxious not to miss her slot.

'I'll only be a minute,' Georgie called from her cubicle, her voice sounding harsh and rasping.

Emma transmitted the news to Trent in vision control.

'Move on to Blossom,' Trent barked back. 'We'll try to hoover up the slappers later.'

Emma winced at the casual contempt with which her colleagues referred to the contestants, although looking at Michelle she could not deny that 'slapper' did rather sum things up. The girl was wearing nothing but erotic lingerie, stiletto heels plus lacy knickers and bra. The only mild concession she had made towards costume was a short and entirely transparent sarong knotted on her hips. She had a coat but she was carrying it, being of the opinion that if it was worth flaunting at all then it was worth flaunting all the time.

'We'll get back to you,' Emma said to Michelle, then she shouted: 'I need Blossom Rochester.'

Turning on her heel, Michelle Peroxide disappeared into the toilet, screaming blue murder and instructing her younger partner to get her fucking fingers out of her throat and mind not to get any puke on the sarong because the silver sheen would certainly not stand the stomach acid.

'Meanwhile, in Birmingham,' Keely would later explain, 'life may be about to take an unexpected turn for Blossom, a singing cleaning lady, who had no idea the auditions were taking place at the exhibition centre but has decided to have a punt.' It was true that Blossom was a cleaning lady, but not at the exhibition centre. She worked up the road at the Birmingham Symphony Hall, but when her application came in it struck Trent as too good an opportunity to miss.

'We're not actually *lying*,' he had told Emma. 'She is

132

a cleaning lady and she didn't know where the auditions were being held. The fact that she's turned up in a nylon housecoat with a mop and bucket is her business, and if the audience choose to infer that she has been cleaning the exhibition centre then that's theirs.'

So Emma dutifully set up the shot with Blossom, a big jolly lady, standing over her mop and bucket and shrieking with laughter at the end of every sentence she uttered.

'Yes, I'm just a cleaner,' she cackled. 'But under this coat maybe there's a star! So when I saw they was auditioning for that *Chart Throb* I thought why not. Now I'm going to put away my mop and go in there and rock their socks!'

Blossom had in fact auditioned earlier in the day, when she had turned out to have a pretty useful voice, and that and her 'story' now ensured her passage through to sing for the real judges.

Having got Blossom out of the way Emma returned to the ladies' toilet, where Georgie was just emerging. She looked different from last year, Emma thought, more drawn, her cheekbones more prominent. On the other hand she was a year older, girls did change at that age.

'Hi, girls!' Emma said. 'We don't have long so let's get straight over to the queue.'

Emma led the two girls across the hall to where, with some difficulty, Gary and Barry had managed to assemble a small group of 'contestants', all of whom had been given extra biscuits and promised 'fun bags' that would contain *Chart Throb* merchandising.

Having placed the girls in the middle of the group, Emma made ready to shoot.

'Hang on,' cried Michelle. 'Get your coat off, Georgie.'

Georgie took off her coat and Emma could not help

133

gasping. She was so *thin*. All her ribs showed beneath the bra, which was obviously padded. Her collar bone stood out from her shoulders and the hips upon which hung her silver-sheened sarong came to two little bony points.

'Well, *hello!*' she heard Trent exclaim over the radio. 'God, she looks *fantastic!*' Glancing down at the television monitor in her hand, Emma had to admit that Georgie did look good on screen. The camera always added a few pounds and by the standards expected of young female entertainers today Georgie filled the bill. In real life, standing only ten feet away from her, an almost naked eighteen-year-old with not an ounce of fat on her, she looked distinctly worrying. Once more Emma felt that she was looking at a victim but, unlike Shaiana, this was a victim upon whom the assault had already begun. Georgie had been attacking herself.

First Time

On the drive home to Leamington Spa, Millicent and Graham struggled to get over their mutual feelings of anticlimax.

'I suppose it was pretty stupid to imagine that we'd get up in front of Calvin and Beryl, first shot,' Graham said.

'It wasn't stupid. That's what they make you think is going to happen,' Millicent replied grumpily.

'Yes, but if you think about it, it's obvious it can't,' said Graham. 'I mean you only have to do the maths.'

Conversation lapsed for a while. Graham turned on the radio, tried a number of stations and then turned it off again.

'Milly,' he said, 'let's get a room.'

'Oh my goodness, Graham!' Millicent could feel herself reddening as she said it. Whatever it was that she would have liked to say to such a suggestion, 'Oh my goodness, Graham' was not it. But it was such a surprise. The truth was that neither of them had referred to the kiss they had shared since the day it had happened. They had both wanted to but failed to do so when they next met, so the opportunity had been missed. As the days went by, it had become more and more difficult to think of a way of raising the subject, until both of them had begun to wonder if it had ever happened at all.

'Because when we kissed . . .' Graham continued. 'We did kiss, didn't we? I didn't make it up?'

'No, Graham,' Millicent said. 'We definitely kissed.'

'Well, when we kissed, I liked it . . . and I thought you liked it too. Did you like it?'

'Yes. I liked it.'

Conversation lapsed once more. Graham could think of nothing to add and Millicent could find nothing to say in reply. After a while Graham felt the car slowing and pulling off the road.

'It's a service station,' Millicent said. 'I expect they'll have some machines in the toilets. They usually do. Have you got some pound coins?'

Graham searched in his pockets and, having found his change, felt for Millicent's outstretched hand. Briefly he touched her and she was gone.

When she came back, they drove on in silence until once more he felt the car slowing.

'Travelodge,' he heard her say. 'Not very romantic.'

'You make your own romance,' he replied and they both laughed.

They went inside, booked a room, bought two Bacardi and Cokes from the vending machine and made their way upstairs.

Afterwards, lying peacefully together, they spoke once more of their audition.

'If only they'd let me play my guitar,' Graham said. 'You know I can't sing.'

'They won't, not until the later rounds. We just have to get that far. You can sing a bit.'

'You carry me, we both know that. I'm a musician, a songwriter.'

'Yes, and if we can just do well enough to get through the early stages then maybe people will listen to your songs.'

'You're the singer. You should have entered on your own.'

'Graham, I only want to do it if it's with you.'

'Supposing they try to break us up? They do that sometimes, when they think one of a group is better than the other.'

'Graham, I would never leave you . . .'

'Why not? I mean if it was one of us or none of us. You're a great singer, you love to sing.'

'Because . . . because I love you.'

There, she had said it. It was out at last.

'I love you too,' Graham replied, and he reached for her again.

I Will Survive

Beryl and Serenity were working on story ideas for the upcoming series of *The Blenheims*.

'How about we get a sit-on lawn mower?' Beryl suggested.

'Don't we have a sit-on lawn mower, sweetness?' Serenity mumbled through her massively inflated lips, like two glossily painted draught excluders. 'Isn't that what Juan mows the lawns with?'

Once more Beryl attempted to explain to her wife the realities of 'reality' television.

'I *know* we've got a sit-on lawn mower that Juan mows the lawns with, babes,' she said gently, helping her to open the can of Diet Coke with which Serenity, with her talon-like false fingernails, had been struggling for the previous few minutes. 'But in our show we don't have Juan, do we? We don't have any servants because we're just a good old ordinary family, aren't we? So who do you think mows the lawn, babes?'

'Uhm . . .'

'*You* mow the lawn, babes.'

'I've never mown a lawn in my fucking life, cherry ripe. I don't even wax my own legs!'

'Exactly. Which is why it will be so funny when we decide that the lawn needs mowing and we get you a sit-on mower and you run over a dog and drive it into the swimming pool!'

Serenity pushed a straw between her semi-lifeless lips and sipped her Coke thoughtfully.

'OK, honey. Whatever you want me to do.'

At that moment a burst of Gloria Gaynor's 'I Will Survive' interrupted their conversation.

It was Beryl's phone.

Beryl loved 'I Will Survive', believing that if ever three words were required to sum her up those three would do it. She had thought about asking in her will for them to be written on her gravestone, until Priscilla had pointed out that this might present something of a contradiction in terms.

Nonetheless 'I Will Survive' was Beryl's motto and her theme tune because Beryl Blenheim saw herself as a fighter, a survivor, a battler, a martyr to the shit that happens. She never tired of assuring people that she had had it tough, she had taken the knocks, *hard* knocks. The crap that she had had to deal with would have defeated a lesser woman. It would have defeated anyone. But Beryl Blenheim was not a lesser woman, nor was she just anyone.

I am a strong woman and I have survived was the opening line of her celebrated autobiography. *I even survived being a man.*

The fact that she was enormously rich and had never wanted for anything in her entire life only seemed to add to the mystique of her fabulous gutsiness. The fact that the majority of what shit she *had* had to deal with had been self-inflicted, brought about by her own greed, jealous ambition, hedonism and relentless self-promotion, never seemed to occur to her, nor did it to the numerous interviewers who nodded knowingly as Beryl, with tight-lipped sincerity, catalogued her tough life as a businesswoman and working mum. It was simply and uncritically accepted that Beryl's education at the University of Hard Knocks had actually been *further* complicated by all the weirdness and heavy shit that inevitably accompany wealth, power and fame. That it was these things which had in fact created the tough lady with the big heart that the world loved so dearly.

Beryl retrieved 'I Will Survive' from the depths of a handbag that would have cost her two thousand pounds had she not got it for nothing from the goody bag at Elton John's post-Oscar party.

'It's Priscilla,' Beryl said, glancing at her mobile's display.

Beryl stuck the Bluetooth in her ear.

'Mom, you fucking bitch,' her daughter shouted down the phone without even giving Beryl a chance to greet her. 'We debuted at forty-eight, you swore we'd be top forty on pre-orders alone!'

'What are you doing with a fucking phone? They don't allow you a phone!'

'I fucking checked out. Mom, the album is a turkey. I wanna die!'

'You *checked out*?'

'I *just said* my album is a—'

'Priscilla, you have a drug bust hanging over your head! I told the media you were working through your problem! Dealing with your issues!'

'Mom, that was *six fucking days ago*! Do you think anybody remembers any more? It's history. You wanna know what's front page today? Another sleazoid thrash metal singer selling downloads of Paris Hilton sucking his dick. The world moved on.'

'Well, you'd better be right because we have a new season coming up and you're in it and we are *not* allowed to film in state correctional institutions.'

'Mom, listen to me. Didn't you hear?' Priscilla's voice was suddenly less strident, less confident. 'My album stiffed. I'm a fucking failure.'

The contrast in accents between the two women was startling: a Swindon battler and a Los Angeles princess. Nobody would ever have picked them for members of the same family had not Beryl arranged for their private lives to be broadcast in weekly instalments on the Fox Channel.

'You're not a failure, darling,' Beryl cooed.

'I am, I am. I can't sing. I have no talent.'

'Of course you have talent, darling. You're a big star. My God, you should count your blessings. How many magazines have you been on the front of, young lady?'

'Do you think I can sing, Mom?'

'Of course I do, darling. I'm one of your mothers.'

'No, but really?'

'Yes, yes, yes, dear. You can sing. You can sing. You can sing. Now I'm sorry that the album flopped but it isn't the end of the world . . .'

'I'm, like, so embarrassed.'

'No, darling, don't be embarrassed. We'll spin it, buy

139

fifty copies in Albania, get you to number one and say you're big in Europe. Now did you get me in with your London surgeon?'

'Yes, yes, yes. He does everybody, he's the best.'

'Good, because I want to get in straight after the *Chart Throb* final and before we start *The Blenheims*.'

'Did Fox agree to postpone our start date?'

'They will. I'm working on them.'

'Mom?' Once more Priscilla's voice softened and the brittle accent could not disguise the yearning. 'Do you *really* think I can sing?'

Not in Love

After Birmingham, Emma, Chelsie, Trent and the team visited Glasgow, Newcastle, Manchester, Dublin, Belfast, Bristol and London, reducing the few thousand people who had been selected from the thousands who had sent in applications or attended the mass audition days to those whom they would offer up to Calvin for selection to feature in the show.

The night before the final selection was scheduled to begin, Emma went out for a curry with friends. She had been intending to stay in and study her character notes but she badly needed a break. The general selection process had been *so* gruelling, much worse than the previous year, and sometimes beer and chicken tikka masala was the only answer.

'I think it's because I understand the workings of the show so much better,' she explained. 'I *know* what these people are getting into.'

'I thought that was going to make it easier,' her friend Mel replied. 'That's what you said: forewarned, forearmed. I'm sure I remember somebody who looked *exactly* like you sitting in that *exact* same chair four months ago swearing that she was going to remain aloof and not get emotionally connected this time.'

'I know, I *know*,' Emma replied unhappily. 'But it's hard. There's this girl Shaiana, she's so *intense . . .*'

'God, where do they get these names?' Mel's boyfriend, Tom, butted in. 'I mean how do their mothers *know*? It's as if when they're born everybody says, twenty years from now she's going to be making a fool of herself on *Chart Throb*. Better give her a fucking stupid name.'

'And there's a girl who's coming back from last year who's anorexic, or at least I think she is.'

'Look, Em,' Tom said, 'you said it was a freak show. They told you that when you started. Clingers, Blingers and Mingers . . .'

'And *some* singers,' Emma protested. 'It's not *all* freaks.'

'Have it both ways. You always do.'

Emma found it very easy to be critical of her situation while becoming defensive when others agreed with her.

'Some people really do get something out of the whole thing,' she said. 'Last year's winner sold a lot of records and three or four of the other finalists are still singing professionally.'

'Where?'

'Oh, I don't know, hotels, cruise ships. That's good, I think. We've got this blind boy who is obviously *obsessed* with music. I think *Chart Throb*'s one of the few places where his disadvantage can actually help him.'

'Emma, *listen* to yourself!' Tom protested.

'Let's change the subject,' Mel suggested, having heard this conversation before.

'No!' Tom insisted. 'Emma is basically saying that because her fucking show is going to exploit this bloke's blindness somehow they're doing him a favour!'

'Well, aren't we?' Emma snapped. 'Certainly Calvin will be interested in the human sympathy angle but so what? He'll still get to sing, he'll still be heard. I'm sure every time his blindness puts him at the back of the queue Graham must be *thrilled* that at least nobody's *exploiting* him. Yes, we take the piss out of saddos and we get to play on people's emotions but we're the only show on TV where a saddo gets even half a chance. What have *you* ever done, Tom, to give a break to somebody with a massive disadvantage in life?'

'Oh, sorry, Emma, I had no idea Calvin Simms was running a charity. There was me thinking he was a cynical, manipulative, money-grabbing shit. You should have *said*.'

Emma bristled further. 'God! Why is everybody I know so down on Calvin?'

'Come on, Em,' said Mel. 'You've often said he's a bully.'

'He *plays* the bully. I don't know that he actually is one.'

In answer to this Tom merely shrugged and ordered more poppadoms.

'The point is he's an *entertainer*. An act, putting on a show. And he *loves it*. That's the point, he loves pop and he loves TV and he loves . . . He loves *entertaining*. And he does it bloody well, which is why he's so huge and also why everybody's so *jealous* and *mean* about him.'

'Well,' said Mel after a pause. 'We're very defensive of Mr Simms these days, aren't we?'

'No. It's just . . .'

'Just what?'

Emma didn't reply, concentrating instead upon her food. Her silence was enough.

'Oh my *God*!' her friend exclaimed. 'I *thought* so. You've got a crush on Calvin bloody Simms!'

'I have *not*. Don't be ridiculous.'

'Emma,' said Tom, 'you *can't* fall in love with Calvin Simms!'

'I haven't!'

'It's the Dad thing *yet again*.'

'Tom. Fuck off.' Emma lit a cigarette, ignoring the fact they were all eating. 'Every fucking time I show an interest in a man you bring up my dad.'

'Because you always show an interest in arrogant middle-aged bastards.'

'Shall we not go there?' Mel appealed. But of course they had already gone.

'Don't you understand, Tom? My dad *walked out*. He dumped me and my mum. I *hate* him for that. The *last* thing on earth I'm going to try and do is replace him!'

Tom raised his eyebrows, while Emma sucked furiously on her cigarette.

'It's so ludicrously oversimplistic,' she said finally. 'Freud for fucking five-year-olds.'

Not in Love Either

'No one *noticed* him,' Dakota drawled through exquisitely glossed, half-closed lips that hovered lazily at the salty rim of her margarita. 'Ah confess, Ah am most surprahsed!'

She and Calvin were in Sardinia, having a breaking-up summit aboard their boat, a seventy-foot, ten-berth fun palace with a hot tub and bar on the foredeck, and Dakota Simms had made no secret of the fact that she was looking forward to taking possession of it the moment Calvin failed in his mission to turn her chosen ringer into the winner of *Chart Throb*.

'So far anybody who bothered to look at him at all thought he was a lookalike. It's amazing, he's just such an unassuming man and when you put him in a crowd of crazy pop hopefuls he sort of fades into the background.'

Dakota's sparkling, ice-cold eyes narrowed with suspicion.

'Hey, if y'all sell him as a lookalike tha bet is ahff. Ah said you had ta git tha Prince o' Wales ta win, not some guy *preetendin'* ta be tha Prince o' Wales, even iffn he really *is* tha Prince o' Wales. Ah hope Ahm makin' sense, precious, because tha agreement we drew up is verrah verrah specific.'

'I know what we agreed, Dakota. Don't worry, the minute we go to air the whole world is going to know just how low fame and rank has fallen in its ambitions to meet the standards of celebrity.'

'An' then you are gonna be *furked*, Calvin, because evahbody *hates* thait *poh*, dull may-un. Did you see tha papers this mohnin'? Ah declare Ah was *sharked*.'

That morning's papers had indeed presented more unpleasant reading for the beleaguered heir. In the latest royal 'revelations', an unnamed source 'close' to the Prince had suggested that the Queen Mother's death at the age of a hundred and one had not been from natural causes, as previously thought, but that the Prince had cunningly poisoned her with a Duchy Originals organic pistachio and nutmeg biscuit which he had intended for the Queen. The papers were quoting 'palace insiders' as saying that the Prince's general air of gloom and melancholy of late was due to his being increasingly racked with the guilt of having murdered his much-loved grannie when he had in fact intended to top his mum. Stories had also surfaced claiming that he'd spent countless thousands of pounds of public money having heating devices installed in his sporrans so that he might wear his kilts in the traditional manner without risking chilblains on his crown jewels.

'I'm well aware of the depths to which His Royal Highness's stock has sunk,' Calvin replied. 'But I accepted your challenge and I intend to follow it through.'

'We-ell, you'd better 'cos it's all or nerthin' fer you an' me, baby, an' Ah plan ta git it all.'

Calvin stared at his beautiful soon-to-be-ex wife and wondered how he could ever have been such a fool as to marry her. Everything about her that had seemed so *right* when he had proposed now seemed so utterly wrong. Her sophistication was exposed as nothing more than cynicism, her joy in luxury mere greed, her wit and intelligence just low, sly cunning and even her glamorous beauty was now an ugly maggot baiting the steely hook of her soul.

Why couldn't he have chosen somebody *real*? A sweet girl, a pretty girl. An honest girl. A girl like . . . like . . .

How strange, he thought . . . Why had he thought about *her*?

'Whart you thinkin' 'bout, honey?' Dakota enquired.

'Nothing,' Calvin said quickly, surprised and angry with himself at what he *had* been thinking about. Calvin did not like his mind to wander; above all things he liked to stay *focused* and in control.

'Well then, Ah'll thaink you not t' sit there lookin' lahk you swallowed a June bug, Calvin. Jerst because we are no longer *close* does naht preclude us bein' *civil*.'

Suddenly Calvin was angry. Furious, in fact. Perhaps it was thinking of the other girl that made him so frustrated with Dakota.

'Oh, do fuck off with all your hypocritical airs and

graces!' he snapped. 'You're not a lady, Dakota, you're a lying, cheating tart.'

'We-ell, Calvin,' Dakota drawled across her glass, 'mebby Ah aim, bert iffn Ah *aim* a tart, thain Ahm a tart who's fixin' ta furk you rigid.'

Later that day Calvin took a private jet home to London, leaving Dakota to enjoy the spacious luxury of the boat that she was certain would soon be hers and hers alone. Sitting on his plane in solitary splendour, Calvin attempted to turn his mind to the game plan he must prepare in order to achieve his goal of making the Prince of Wales popular and fashionable. A huge task, a seemingly impossible task. A task which he must accomplish while simultaneously creating another smash-hit series of *Chart Throb*. A task upon which, therefore, he must *focus*.

And yet he could not focus, for his mind was *wandering* and a wandering mind was something Calvin could not afford.

He was thinking of Emma. The girl from the office. The girl whose skirt and hair had been lifted by the wind in the car park at Brize Norton. The *nice* one whom he had smiled at when she dropped her glasses on the plane.

Calvin frowned angrily and lit a cigarette. He had no business to be thinking of Emma. He had no business to be thinking of anything other than the enormous task in hand. He did not *want* to think of Emma, he didn't know the girl, he did not *wish* to know the girl. The only girl he needed to be considering in the near future was the Southern princess whom, like a lunatic, he had married and who was currently attempting to *furk him rigid*.

Calvin continued to frown for the time it took him to smoke three cigarettes, lighting one from the other. He drummed his fingers and paced about the cramped confines of his jet. The smartly uniformed hostess enquired if she could get him anything but he ignored her. Finally he sat back down and took up his telephone.

'Trent?' he said. 'I want you to do something for me.'

Arranging for a Lift

Having dealt with her stepdaughter's artistic self-doubts, Beryl called Carrie, her long-suffering American agent, to discuss the timing for the next season of *The Blenheims*.

'I don't care if it is two in the fucking morning,' Beryl snarled. 'Has Fox agreed to the delay? I'm starting to look like Cruella De Vil again and I need to get my eyes softened. There's not time before we start work on *Chart Throb* so I need to squeeze it in afterwards.'

'Beryl, you're crazy. You look great, you don't need any more work done . . .'

'Yeah, you were saying that when I still had a scrotum. Listen, we're scheduled to start with *The Blenheims* straight after we're done with *Chart Throb* but I need a one-week window for my eyes. Priscilla has found me a new guy who she says is absolutely the best, he improves *teenagers*, he could have turned Mother Teresa into Jessica Simpson.'

'Can't you just get a little collagen refill? That takes a day.'

'Can't have any more collagen, Carrie. You know that. I already have trouble pulling any expressions, it's like my face is set in plaster. I have to do a facial workout before I can smile. I need a little lift and Priscilla's guy has me booked for the fortnight after the finals. I just need a one-week delay on *The Blenheims*.'

'Fox have their schedule locked, Beryl, this is very

147

hard for them. Can't we make the first episode about your face work?'

'Fuck OFF, Carrie! I have that work done so I *won't* look shit on TV. You think I'm going to invite the cameras in while I'm Frankenstein's monster? You *never* show people the process, that way they can half believe it's natural. I need that postponement.'

'OK, OK, I'll talk to them again, see what I can do.'

'Do it now.'

Refocusing

Emma rose early and picked out her wardrobe with care. She had originally intended to wear a short skirt and possibly even a cropped midriff-baring T-shirt but decided eventually on some slightly less flirtatious figure-hugging jeans and a pretty blouse. She then put her glossy, freshly washed hair into a cute ponytail, smoked a cigarette, brushed her teeth and set off for the tube station.

By tradition, inner London's commuters call the Northern Line the misery line, but on this particular morning, as Emma took her seat and tried to focus on her research notes (one of the very few advantages of living so far out was that she did at least get to board the train before it turned into a sardine can), she could not stop an involuntary smile from flitting across her lips.

Soon she would be in the same room as Calvin. She had not seen him since sharing a cramped private plane with him over RAF Brize Norton. He had not noticed her much then and she was realistic enough to believe that he would not notice her much today either. Nonetheless she was happy that morning and she was happy because of him. It was truly shocking to Emma how quickly this obsession (for how could she call it love when it was so entirely one-sided?) had come upon her. One moment she had thought him an attractively roguish bastard whom any sensible girl would do best to avoid and the next she was sitting dreamily on the tube, falling prey to romantic musings in which he whisked her off to isolated moorland cottages where he would see to her needs like Heathcliff ought to have seen to Cathy's. It was so strange, she had gone through the whole of the previous series without any such thoughts, although if she were honest she had to admit to herself that towards the end her feelings had begun to grow. On this series, however, it had hit her with the force of a sledgehammer and, ridiculous though it was, she knew she was in love.

Emma emerged from the tube at Tottenham Court Road, made her way along Oxford Street and, after picking up the obligatory pint of coffee-flavoured froth at Starbucks, joined the throng of other attractive young people crowding into the beautiful offices of CALonic TV, the company Calvin had turned into a global entertainment colossus. Contemplating the golden legs and naked midriffs of the majority of her colleagues, Emma could not avoid a feeling of jealous resentment. Did these girls have to be so *obvious*? Most of Calvin's employees were attractive young women, but unlike Emma they were generally tall. Calvin famously liked tall women.

Emma was about to enter the crowded meeting room when a voice behind stopped her.

'Emma, could I have a word?'

It was Trent. He led her into his private office and half closed the door behind him.

'There's no easy way to say this so I shan't attempt to find one,' he said. 'Calvin is no longer happy with your work. You're to leave the company forthwith.'

Emma did not reply. She couldn't, she was too shocked.

'Of course you will receive your full entitlements and the company will supply you with a reference.'

'Not happy with my work?'

'That's right. I'm sorry. It does seem unfair but, as you know, Calvin acts on his instincts. Human Resources will be contacting you to discuss your departure package but of course we are all on short-term contracts.'

It was finally sinking in and Emma was blinking back the tears.

'Calvin is firing me?'

'Yes. Now. You're to leave immediately.'

For a moment she stood still, seemingly unable to move. The blinking was faster now.

'Please don't cry,' said Trent. 'There's any number of options out there.'

He looked at his watch. He seemed nervous, impatient to be rid of her.

Emma turned to go.

'Oh, could you leave your research notes please, Emma?' Trent said.

'What?' she asked distantly.

'Your notes. I want them.'

'My notes?'

'Yeah, in fact they're not really *your* notes as it happens. They belong to CALonic. I mean, you were paid to make them, legally they're ours . . . I don't need the folders. They belong to you, of course.'

Without speaking, as if walking in a dream, Emma took out the sheaves of notes upon which she had been working over the previous months and handed them to Trent.

'Thanks,' he said. 'Keep in touch, right?' And he rushed out of the office.

Emma followed him and made her way towards the

stairs. Standing at the top of them, she paused. Some instinct made her turn and look in the direction of Calvin's office. The door had been closed a moment before but now it was open a few inches. She saw his face, watching her, and then it was gone and the door closed once again.

Her face reddened. She strode towards the door and knocked on it. Receiving no answer, she knocked more loudly. She put her hand on the handle and half turned it. Then she stopped. Glancing round, she saw that a number of her ex-colleagues were looking at her.

Then she left the building. She went to Soho Square and sat down on a park bench, where finally the tears which she had fought for so long flowed freely.

Final Selection

Bang on the appointed hour Calvin burst into the room holding a coffee, a croissant and a cigarette all in the same hand.

'Morning, all,' he said, lighting his cigarette, which was of course illegal in a crowded workspace but nobody would have dreamed of complaining. Everybody knew that Calvin played by different rules. It was what made him so special. It was because he played by different rules that they were all in work, and not just any old work but working on the most successful and talked-about show on television.

'Morning, Calvin,' the team replied and there was applause and one or two whoops.

'Yes, yes, yes,' Calvin said impatiently. 'We're not in America, for God's sake.' He looked around at the smiling throng. 'Right. Let's get on with it, shall we? Trent?'

'Yo,' Trent replied, jumping up and bounding towards the end of the room where the audiovisual equipment had been set up.

'Yay!' squeaked one or two of the younger girls as he passed. 'Go, Trent. Bring it on! Yay!'

The room burst into more applause. Everyone was excited. Months of painstaking research and development were about to blossom into another smash-hit series of *Chart Throb*, the biggest show on TV, and the room was alive with a back-to-school buzz.

'Steady on, girls,' said Trent, smirking. 'Easy now. Keep it real. Lotta work to get through, *long* way to go.'

At twenty-eight Trent was the senior member of the team. He had been there at the beginning, three years before, when everybody had been saying that this kind of TV was just stupid and demeaning crap and that it was all wrung out anyway. It was impossible to imagine now but there had actually been a time when people had even questioned the commissioning of *Chart Throb*, asking whether television really needed another talent show. They didn't question it any more, not now that it had saved terrestrial TV. Not now that even the Prime Minister admitted to having voted in the final of the previous series.

Not now that the *Prince of fucking Wales* was going to appear.

Impeccably suited and booted, Trent stood before the enormous plasma screen like the favoured son. His high-button collar, knitted tie and Dolce & Gabbana spectacles gave him the air of a hip intellectual, which in a way was what he was, as he had done an MA in FMZ (Film, Media and Zeitgeist) at Hull. He made a sweeping gesture towards the table on which lay four stacks of photos and biographies accompanied by a pile of DVDs. 'Calvin. May I present to you our Singers, Clingers, Blingers and Mingers?'

'*Prospective* Singers, Clingers, Blingers and Mingers,'

Calvin corrected. 'Don't get ahead of yourself, the only one who's through for sure is his royal nibs but we'll discuss him separately.'

A shiver of anticipation rippled across the crowded room. Of course everybody on the team was aware of the exciting news about the Prince but they had all been ordered not to discuss it. If at all possible, Calvin wished for the penny to drop live on air. His plans for a royal victory partly depended on creating the impression that the supposedly pampered and dilettante Prince was doing things the hard way.

'Yo, boss,' Trent replied, taking a DVD from the top of the Mingers pile and slipping it into his computer. There followed a brief pause while the machine opened its programme.

'Might have helped to have had this prepared,' Calvin said, drumming the table.

'Yo,' said Trent.

'And stop saying "Yo" all the time. You're not black and you don't come from LA!'

'Y . . . yes, boss,' said Trent, laughing and trying not to look like he had just been punched in the face.

People in the room shifted nervously. Off screen, Calvin was normally an easy-going sort of person and not prone to ostentatious displays of bullying.

After a few seconds an image appeared on the plasma screen, an image of a plump but personable young woman frozen in the act of drawing breath.

'Glasgow girl,' Trent said. 'Can sing. Sweet laugh. Cling, with Bling rising.' He pressed play and the woman leaped into life.

'Hi, Calvin,' she said. 'Hi, Beryl, hi, Rodney. My name's Molly Townsend and I'm going to rock your ass!'

Then, screwing up her face, she launched into the opening bars of 'The Greatest Love Of All', explaining with a fearsome passion that in her opinion children were the future.

'Fine, we'll see her,' Calvin snapped after the girl had sung a dozen words. 'Pretty anonymous but could be a useful filler. Next.'

The girl up next also sang 'The Greatest Love Of All', if anything with an even more fervent commitment to the sugary lyric, attempting to put at least three notes (sometimes three octaves) into each word she uttered in the manner made famous by Mariah Carey.

'Fine. Bring her in,' Calvin barked angrily.

Many hopefuls followed in quick succession. Some were selected, others were equally quickly rejected, every decision taken within a verse and a chorus. There was no other way to do it. Calvin was well aware that he was almost certainly missing the odd potential winner, but even after the massive winnowing process that had preceded his arrival he still had an impossibly large number of prospects to consider.

'Darth Death Raider,' said Trent as a black-cloaked figure appeared. 'Comical Minger, claims to be an alien born in a separate dimension to ours.'

Trent pressed play and on screen Darth Death Raider began to sing 'Dead Babies' by Alice Cooper.

'How many Goth Mingers have you got for consideration?' Calvin asked over the noise.

'Not as many as we'd have liked,' Trent replied. 'I think this one could be quite useful. Very, very full of himself, genuinely thinks he's scary and he's got a pierced penis.'

'Fine, we'll take Darth. Next.'

Next up were Graham and Millicent.

'Why's he wearing the shades?' Calvin enquired, viewing the nervous-looking boy and girl on the screen. 'Wanker?'

'Blind,' Trent replied proudly.

'Good.'

Whenever Calvin saw kids auditioning in sunglasses he dared to hope they might be blind but ninety-nine times out of a hundred they were just wankers trying to look like Bono. Wankers were OK of course, wankers could be very good telly, wankers were the backbone of the Christmas *Greatest Auditions Ever* DVD. But in the long run wankers were rarely anything more than one-gag wonders. Blind, on the other hand, if properly developed, could be TV gold. Blind was a *story*.

'*She's* not blind too though, is she?' Calvin asked, suddenly looking worried. 'A sightless *couple* would be *way* too much for Saturday evening prime time. I mean that's just weird. Too many issues. Too many questions. *Way* too many worms in that box.'

Trent glanced down, trying to find the appropriate notes. Graham and Millicent had been Emma's prospects.

'Uhm . . .'

'No. She's not blind,' Chelsie chipped in from the back of the room.

'Thank you.'

'Good,' said Calvin. 'A blind boy and a sighted girl is human drama. A blind *couple* is a freak show.'

'Yes, well, the girl is definitely sighted,' Trent added unnecessarily, trying to draw the focus back from Chelsie, at whom he had noticed Calvin smiling.

'Can they sing?'

It wasn't the first question that the assembled employees expected Calvin to ask. On *Chart Throb* an ability to sing was not the central issue.

'I spend my life trying to avoid singers,' Calvin never tired of reminding them. 'They accost me in the street, push tapes on me when I'm trying to eat my dinner! Break into song when I'm shagging them, for God's sake! I am *stalked* by singers. *Loads* of people can fucking sing. If we wanted the best singers we could go and see fucking *Chicago* or *My Fair* fucking *Lady* or *The* fucking *Lion King*. London is full of sexy kids who can sing, they're all queuing to get into the chorus of *Mamma Mia* and we don't want 'em!'

What really mattered to Calvin was backstory and personality. But the one time singing really mattered to him was when real talent was *combined* with a great backstory; that was gold, that was *his* dream, to combine a heartbreaking family history with real talent. Such a thing would validate the entire series and silence for ever those carping critics who claimed that his great achievement was just a tawdry, manipulative pile of old schlock.

If these kids could *sing*, the entire Righteous Brothers back catalogue beckoned.

'So can they?' Calvin asked once more.

Once again Trent did not know the answer. Once more Chelsie did.

'Yeah, they have really sweet voices and they're lovely kids.'

'Trent?'

'Don't get excited, boss. They can both hold a tune but the harmonies are thin, mate, very thin.'

For a moment Calvin seemed distracted, his mind elsewhere, and wherever that was was not a happy place. His mood remained dark.

'Trent,' said Calvin, 'this is *Chart Throb*, not the Royal College of Music. If they can hold a tune and sing a harmony, no matter how fucking thin, this kid and his girlfriend can sing.'

'She's not really his girlfriend, I'm afraid.'

'They're just friends,' Chelsie added.

'Has she ever been his girlfriend?' Calvin asked.

Trent leaped in once more. 'Possibly,' he said. 'They spend a lot of time together, rehearsing their act.'

'Trent,' Calvin snapped, 'read my lips. Has – he – ever – shagged – her?'

'Uhm, well, I don't know,' Trent stuttered, coming to regret forcing his way back into the centre of Calvin's focus. 'We don't normally go into their sex lives, do we, boss?'

Whatever it was that had dented Calvin's normal good humour was still on his mind, for he responded ferociously.

'There is no normal, Trent!' he said, raising his voice despite the pin-drop silence all around. 'I had thought that perhaps, after three years working with me, you might have worked that out. If there was a NORMAL I could get the IT department to write a selection program and we could run the applications through that. Then I would not have to spend vast amounts of money employing hordes of dimwits like you to turn up at final selection meetings with no fucking clue about the prospects they have chosen. Every case is different, sex matters *sometimes*! Does it matter with game old grannies singing "Daisy, Daisy"? No, I don't think so. Does it matter with a single mum struggling to bring up three gorgeous little kids who are SO proud of her? Probably not, although maybe. Male Mingers trying to rap? No. Dwarf breakdancers singing "Eye Of The Tiger"? Not on my show. Cute boy bands that we drop at round three? No. But does sex matter with blind young men and their devoted, pretty female accomplices? Yes! Yes! Fucking YES! How are we supposed to plan a story for these two if we don't know if they're sleeping together?'

'But . . . but . . .' Trent began.

'Now listen up, ALL of you.' Calvin surveyed the room as every senior researcher, junior researcher, production assistant and secretary attempted to exude alertness so that the great man might be assured that they at least were giving him their most rapt attention.

'What is this show *not*?'

The answer would have surprised the show's legions of fans but everyone in the room knew it.

'A talent show,' they all said in virtual unison.

'That's *right*. We are *not* a talent show. What are we?'

'We're an *entertainment* show,' his people replied.

'My job, your job, *our* job is to *entertain*. If dumping the best singer is more entertaining than keeping him then that is what we do because the public are *not interested in the singing*. The singing is a necessary evil. The public are interested in the *singers*. The *people* singing the songs. Pop is dead. People think I'm so clever because the winners of our show will be signed to my record company. Oh wow! Look at me! I'm *such* a Svengali. Big deal. I get to make Joe Nobody's one and only fucking record. Fuck that! I make more out of *five minutes of telephone voting* than I will out of the entire recording career of most of this year's finalists. Yes. Think about it. He, she or they are worth more to me *before* they win than they ever will be after. Do you know what sort of sales it takes to get a number one these days?'

They did know, for Calvin had told them, often.

'Some weeks you can get there with twenty-five thousand sales! It used to take *half a million* in an ordinary week. Twenty-five thousand CDs or fucking *downloads*, God help us, doesn't pay for their own marketing! Singles are worthless, they're meaningless, they're history. The *only* reason we need our winner to get a number one is to validate the process, to give the show some semblance of meaning. We are a *people* show and if I could find a format where we could do *without* the singing, if I could find a way to attract eight million viewers and two million phone calls a week *without* having to sit through a bunch of deluded pricks murdering "The Greatest Love Of All" and "Unchained Melody", believe me, I would. And, my God, haven't people tried? There's been cooking, dancing, *fucking skating*, for Christ's sake, which sort of worked, but none of them have proved themselves as neat and simple a way of introducing the public to our menagerie of clowns, dysfunctionals, egomaniacs and emotional casualties as singing a song!

'We are a *people* show!' Calvin repeated. 'And 99 per cent of our job is to find the right people. The Singers. The Clingers. The Blingers and the Mingers! Now most people aren't very interesting, are they? No. You lot have just spent six months sifting through nearly a hundred thousand of them and I'll bet you're bored shitless. I'll bet that you're even bored shitless by the few hundred you've whittled the final selection group down to. I'll bet you're wondering whether out of this tawdry bunch of inadequate fuck-ups we even have the makings of a show. Am I right?'

Once more the group were reluctant to answer but it was clear from the embarrassed manner in which some of the younger ones stared at the carpet that Calvin was right. The research team had indeed been driven nearly mad with boredom searching through the endless similar applications and they had most definitely at times despaired of discovering a sufficiently interesting group of contestants to maintain the high standards that the public had come to expect from *Chart Throb*.

'Of course I'm right,' said Calvin. 'And that's because, in spite of the myth which this show was invented to propagate, the world is *not* teeming with undiscovered Aretha Franklins and Elvis Presleys, nor is the average person who *believes* themselves to be mad, amusing, charismatic or sexy *actually* mad, amusing, charismatic or sexy. We're all the fucking same! Everybody has a dream, everybody wants it all and everybody's mum is either dead or will at some point die. Our job is to find something, *anything*, on

159

which to build, on which to hang our stories, to *create* our characters. If some dick once spent a summer driving a tractor on a dairy farm he's an ex-cowboy, if some bird was a movie extra she's an ex-body double. Every cancer scare is a "life and death struggle" to us and two parking fines is a criminal past from which the sinner is struggling to release himself through song. And *you*, Trent, you come to the final selection meeting, the point at which decisions have to be made and our audition group assembled, and tell me that you have a blind lad and his pretty partner but you don't know whether they're having sex!'

'I don't think he's given her one,' Trent said. 'Leastways that's how I read it. No exchange of fluids so far.'

'Why not?' Calvin asked. 'You said you didn't know.'

Trent's eyes flicked down once more to Emma's carefully prepared, neatly handwritten notes.

'They belong to the same choir.'

'You think people in choirs don't have sex? What do you think they join choirs for in the first place? Because they can't get laid, that's why.'

'Well, maybe they'll get round to it,' Trent replied, trying to sound confident and knowledgeable. 'I reckon this singing thing's a surrogate, gotta be. Two nineteen-year-olds meet in a choir, he's blind, she's . . .' he was reading verbatim now, 'member of the school council, Duke of Edinburgh Award recipient, first-year theology student.'

'A *theology* student? Fucking hell,' Calvin mused. 'This is *nice*. Normally only the black ones go on about God. The show could use a bit of non-ethnic faith.'

'He's her project,' Trent continued. 'She thinks she's Helen Keller. Imagine what school was like for this chick. She's a swot, she's in a choir, she's a fucking Christian, for God's sake! The other chicks must have *hated* her. Then she meets the blind kid . . .'

'Graham, his name is,' Chelsie chipped in. She had, after all, been working with Emma and was anxious to remind Calvin that now Emma was gone this research initiative was not Trent's, it was hers. 'Graham and Millicent.'

'Millicent!' Calvin barked. 'This is perfect!'

'Yes, and actually she's nineteen and he's eighteen.'

'She's older, better and better. I like it.'

'That's my point, boss,' Trent barged back in. 'He's younger than her! She's colonized him.' Trent spoke as if he'd been aware of the age disparity all along, indeed he spoke as if he'd planned it. In order to ward off any further attempts by Chelsie to elbow her way on to the agenda he pressed Play and Graham and Millicent leaped into life on the screen.

'Hi, everybody,' said Millicent with a little wave. 'I'm Millicent.'

'And I'm Graham.'

'Hi, everybody,' they said together, waving at the camera. 'We're Graham and Millicent.'

'Loving the décolletage,' Calvin observed, pressing the pause button. 'Nothing sexier than girl nerds in glasses trying to work their tits.'

'Yes,' said Chelsie with a defiant stare at Trent. 'She definitely thinks she has nice boobs, I could tell when I interviewed her that she likes to give the boys a little squiz.'

Millicent, although primly dressed in jeans, blouse and pale green cardigan, was obviously proud of her bosom and had deliberately chosen to leave the tell-tale third button open.

Calvin pressed Play and the voice of the sacked Emma could be heard speaking from behind the camera.

'Hello, you two,' Emma said. 'What are you going to do for us today?'

Calvin scowled but said nothing.

'We'd like to sing "When Will The Good Apples Fall" by the Seekers,' said Millicent with the slightly overassertive confidence of someone who had only recently been head prefect.

'Yes, that's right,' Graham agreed, with considerably less aplomb.

'Oh, *yes indeed*,' muttered Calvin. 'The Seekers, I *like it*!'

Emma had been right, they weren't bad at all. They could hold down a two-part harmony and still deliver the tune, but Millicent was clearly the stronger singer of the two. Graham did his best to cover his lack of range by affecting some gravelly rock 'n' roll vocal mannerisms but there was no disguising his failure to reach the high notes and his dodgy pitching. He also stood very awkwardly and his right hand strummed along in a rather offputting manner, as if he would far rather be playing than singing.

Calvin let the two of them complete their entire verse and chorus, the first time he had let anyone get that far all morning. When it was over Emma's voice could be heard once more congratulating the singers. A flicker of irritation, perhaps even pain, passed across Calvin's face and once more he cut her short with the pause button.

'What's he like behind the sunnies?' Calvin enquired. 'Nice blind or weird blind?'

'Chelsie?' said Trent quickly.

'Weird blind, I'm afraid,' Chelsie replied, making a point of speaking directly to Calvin. 'I got him to take off the shades, bit distracting to be honest. He's got really deep hollows with half-closed lids set into the skull. I don't know much about blindness and didn't like to ask but I'm not sure if he actually *has* any eyeballs. You couldn't really tell.'

'Doesn't matter, he can stick with the shades. The

Big O never took them off,' Calvin replied. 'This is looking very, very tasty, there is *so* much journey potential here, from nerd to sexy, from friends to lovers, from chaste to horny, from dull, repressed, God-bothering choristers to rock 'n' roll sluts! AND the kid's blind! How good is that? I am *so* loving these two. Next!'

Trent pressed the forward button on his control.

A boy band appeared. 'We're the Four Busketeers and we are in it to win it.'

'No, you're not. Fuck off. Next,' said Calvin.

An overweight housewife with a strong Dorset accent and a lisp.

'Moi name'th Thuthan an' Oim goin' ta thing "Thomething" by George Harrithon.'

'Definitely. Love her for a one-shot Ming,' said Calvin. 'Next.'

Two nerdy sisters with glasses and big hoop earrings.

'Fine,' said Calvin before they could open their mouths. 'Ming montage. Next.'

A boring-looking middle-aged man.

'Hi. I'm Stanley.'

'Why's he here?' Calvin asked.

'He can sing and he's a single dad,' piped up a researcher from the back.

'That's right, chief,' Trent reiterated unnecessarily. 'He can sing and he's a single dad.'

'Does he have a job?'

'No, he's bringing up his kids on benefits.'

'OK, we'll have him. Next!'

A sweet old grannie.

'Not sweet enough. Next.'

A cute, precocious five-year-old kid.

'Not cute and precocious enough. Next.'

A plain-looking girl with a crew cut.

'Hmm, not bad,' Calvin said. 'Tell me about her.'

'Name's Tabitha,' said Trent.

'Lesbian?' Calvin enquired.

'Yes,' said Chelsie. 'The girlfriend's gorgeous, totally gorgeous, a real classic lipstick lezza *and* she strips. Professional pole dancer, don't you love it? The guys want to screw her but she's a lady's lady.'

'The girlfriend, not her?' said Calvin, indicating the rather severe-looking plain Jane on screen.

'No.'

'So why isn't the girlfriend fucking auditioning?'

'Well, she didn't—'

'Will the girlfriend be prepared to feature?'

'Definitely, she was with Tabitha at the audition.'

'Good, make sure she's there. Next.'

The next person to appear on the screen was Shaiana. Glancing at Emma's notes, Trent could see that she had marked her down as a real prospect. *MAJOR CLINGER* was written across her photograph in the turquoise ink of Emma's neat, attractive, feminine hand.

'I think this one's a goer, boss,' said Trent. 'Major Clinger.'

Calvin studied the young woman frozen on the screen.

'Yes, she does look pretty intense, doesn't she?'

Shaiana's thick make-up and severe fringe gave her face a slightly masklike look, as if it might shatter at any moment.

'Certainly wouldn't want to meet her in a dark alley,' said Calvin. 'Right, she's in. Next.'

And so the long day wore on. They plodded through the gruelling process of choosing the finalists and also-rans who would be brought before the three judges, that pre-selected group who would make up the principal 'characters' in the *Chart Throb* story and the ones who, after a lengthy period of 'auditioning', would or would not 'win' a place in the finals. It was of course possible that Calvin would change his mind along the way as characters developed; nonetheless, the decisions he was making in that room would effectively shape the course of the entire series.

This meeting was probably the most important one in the whole development process and yet, as the afternoon progressed, Calvin appeared to be finding it harder and harder to concentrate. He snapped at people unnecessarily, he asked questions twice, even lost his thread mid-sentence, which made him furious. Nobody had ever seen Calvin lose his thread. Nobody had ever seen Calvin distracted. Something was on his mind but of course nobody dared ask what.

Unemployed Girl

The reason for Calvin's deteriorating concentration had sat in Soho Square for almost an hour, quite numb with shock.

After that she decided to go shopping.

She could think of nothing else to do with herself. She was certainly not hungry and she could not face going home to her flat in the middle of the day, that flat from which she had emerged in such a sunny mood only a few hours before and to which she must at some point return, rejected and unemployed.

She decided to walk along Oxford Street and get the tube from Oxford Circus to Harvey Nicks. Who knew when she would next be in town? She was out of work and had been sacked from her last job, so she would scarcely get a glowing reference. What could she do now? Retire to South Wimbledon and try to make ends meet, she supposed. Leave London, which she could probably no longer afford, and try to find work

165

elsewhere? Her first job had been writing features for estate agents' magazines – perhaps she could do that again?

One good thing, she reflected as she stumbled along the crowded pavement, still clutching the useless, empty pink folders that had contained the research notes which Trent had now appropriated, was that whatever idiotic, self-deluded, romantic musings she might have been prey to over Calvin Simms were now exposed as the nonsense they had always been. Calvin was a bastard, she could see that now, he had always been one and yet she had been allowing herself to fall in love with him. Why did she *always* fancy bastards?

At least she would delude herself no longer over him.

There were even moments during that strange day, as she wandered aimlessly through Harvey Nichols and then on down to Harrods, when she experienced sudden inexplicable rushes of elation as if she had suddenly become wild and free. But as the hours progressed those moments became less frequent and the anguish of victimhood began to settle upon her. She found herself replaying her sacking in her mind, wishing she had said this, fantasizing about saying that, feeling abused and a fool. Memories of her days in crisis counselling came back to her, how often had she listened as tearful girls fixated on how *unfair* the whole thing was. Why *them*? Why had they got on to that bus? Walked past that doorway? Agreed to see that boy? Now she herself was the victim, torturing herself for having allowed things to develop as they did, dwelling on how things could so easily have been different.

As the end of the day drew near she began to panic. She did not want to go home yet, it was just too sad, and yet she could not bear to call a friend. She was embarrassed. Eventually people would have to know what had happened: that she had lost her job, her glamorous job, her often jealously resented job. Also that she had lost it at the hands of the man whom all her friends knew she had been developing a crush on. It would all come out in the end. Soon. But not yet.

Just then her mobile rang. The number was withheld and for a moment Emma considered not answering it. She was not in the mood for conversation with a cold caller, but on the other hand life had to go on. Perhaps it would make her feel better to tell some poor wage slave in New Delhi to piss off.

'Hello,' she said warily. 'Emma speaking.'

'Emma. Hi. It's Calvin.'

She dropped the phone. It clattered to the ground and the battery popped out of the back. Scrabbling for it on the floor of the shop, she pushed the battery back in, half hoping that somehow the call would still be connected. Of course it wasn't.

She got up, wondering what to do. What had he wanted? What should she have said? Above all, would he ring again? In a moment she had convinced herself that he wouldn't. He had intended to apologize and grovel and prostrate himself over the phone and now he would never call again.

Then he did. And it came so suddenly and so sure had she been that it would not come that once more she dropped the phone.

This time, however, it fell into her bag, which she had put down on the floor beside her. It was still ringing, somewhere in the recesses among keys, her purse, loose change, crumpled paper currency, tissues, tampons, scraps of paper, half-eaten packets of mints, books of stamps, pens, an electronic organizer that she never used, receipts, an Oyster card and the tangled wires of her iPod headphones. She knew she had just four rings to retrieve it, of which one and a half had already been exhausted. She did what she had to do:

sweeping her bag up from the floor, she took two steps towards a perfume counter and upended it on the glass top. Keys clattered, coins rolled, fluff, dust, sweets and tampons lay about the polished surface. Surprised and angry-looking faces turned towards her. The over-made-up young woman behind the counter glowered and a security guard approached.

'Doctor on call,' Emma stated as she swept up her phone and thumbed the green key. 'Emma speaking.'

'Please don't ring off again,' she heard Calvin say.

'I didn't ring off. I dropped the phone,' she replied as with her free hand she attempted to sweep up the bag debris that littered the counter. 'But I ought to ring off now. What do you want?'

'I want to take you to dinner.'

De-blurring

The moment it had dawned upon Calvin that by sacking the cute senior researcher who was blurring his focus he had not restored his clarity at all but actually blurred it further, he resolved that he must meet her and deal with whatever it was that was disturbing him. Therefore, as suddenly as he had sacked her, he decided that he would have to take her out to dinner.

Calvin called a brief coffee break and retrieved Emma's number from the staff file in his computer.

'I know you're free tonight,' he said, 'because we might have been working through.'

'Thanks to you, I'm free for the rest of my life,' Emma replied.

'Then come to dinner.'

'What is this? What's going on?'

'I want to buy you dinner.'

'I don't want to have dinner. I want my job.'

'Well, perhaps we can talk about that.'

'What do you mean?'

'Over dinner. We can talk about your job if you want.'

'I'm afraid I don't understand. What's going on, Calvin?'

'Nothing's going on.'

'What the *fuck* is going on, Calvin?' she asked angrily. 'Is this some game you like to play with women you employ?'

'Look, Emma, nothing's going on, all right? I do things. I say things. I act on instinct.'

'You sack people.'

'Well, I'm sorry. Let me buy you dinner.'

'No! I don't want dinner and I don't like this conversation at all. I don't like being played with. What's going on?'

'I've just *said* nothing's going on. Stop asking me what's going on,' and Calvin's bossy, commanding tone was already returning. 'Now listen, I'm mid-meeting, Emma. You know how important today is, you've worked on it yourself, damned hard, so I'm not going to continue this conversation until we can speak about it in a more relaxed—'

'You're a married man!'

'I'm not.'

'You *are*. The wedding was in *Hello!*'

'All right, I am, but she's history.'

'Did you sack her too?'

'No, she . . . Look, what the hell has this got to do with my wife?'

'Because you're asking me out to dinner.'

'Yes, dinner. I'm not proposing marriage.'

'Well, what *are* you proposing? What's going on?'

'*Stop asking me what's* . . . Look . . . Emma, please, you know that I have to get back to this bloody meeting. So stop asking me what's going on and say you'll have dinner with me.'

There was a long pause.

'Emma?' Calvin insisted. 'I really have got to get back to my meeting.'

'All right. Yes. But . . .'

He did not allow her time for caveats.

'I'll send a car to your home to pick you up at eight.'

And with that the call ended. Emma stood for a moment staring at her mobile and suddenly she was furious. *Livid*. The bastard! Who did he think he was? She should *never* have agreed. *Why* had she agreed? Why had she not told him to fuck off? And . . . what was she going to wear?

Refocusing

Calvin felt instantly better. For a moment at least he had the best of both worlds. She was not in the room blurring his focus but neither was she blurring his focus by *not* being in the room because he would shortly be seeing her again. Therefore, for the time being he could address his intellect in its entirety to the job in hand.

'Next.'

A 'hilarious' Goth appeared.

'I am a member of the Undead and I'll—'

'Fine, good. Next.'

Another hilarious Goth.

'I come from a galaxy far, far—'

'Pause it. Do we have enough for a Goth montage?' Calvin asked.

'I'm afraid not,' said Trent.

'What if we throw in the Trekkies and the mystics

and make it a weirdo montage?'

'Then yes, definitely. We've got four Elvis re-incarnates and a Patsy Cline.'

'Still no one with the guts to tackle John Lennon, eh?' Calvin said. 'OK, keep him. Next.'

More grannies, more cute kids, more ugly nerds, more chippy thugs who thought they were Eminem, and more fat slappers with amusingly strong regional accents.

'Oim gown t'sing "C'mon Byeby Loit Moy Foyer".'

'Love her,' said Calvin. 'Next.'

A sad, bald near-midget who confessed to being in love with Beryl: 'She's my perfect woman. She's so kind and lovely I don't think my restricted height would be an obstacle. With her I could feel ten feet tall.'

'We keep doing that,' Calvin snapped angrily. 'Come on, Trent! Don't waste my time.'

'I thought perhaps it could be a running theme,' Trent replied bravely.

'What, you mean that Beryl attracts midgets?'

'Yes, it always works so well. You know, what with Beryl's whole sexy mum thing. I mean midgets can be sort of cute, can't they? And they're child-sized men. It sort of subliminally combines sex and mothering. When she hugs them they get lost under her tits, sort of sexing them and suckling them all in one.'

'*Suckling them?* Beryl is a transsexual!'

'Oh, I really think people have got over that now, boss. She's everybody's mum these days.'

'That is fucking sick. I love it. Keep him in for now. Next.'

A strangely dated-looking young couple who looked like they had dropped in from the 1930s: 'We are mad about Noël and Gertie,' the boy said, 'and would like to sing "Someday I'll Find You" from *Bitter Sweet.*'

'Yes. Good for a quickie. Next.'

And so it went on until eventually Trent's supply of Ming, Cling and Bling ran out and it was over.

'That's it, boss. The best we could find. Of course we probably missed a few but I reckon we got the cream. Apart of course from . . .'

Calvin knew to whom he was referring. They all did.

'Yes. Now regarding HRH,' Calvin said, 'obviously it's something of a coup for us at *Chart Throb* that the Prince of Wales has independently applied to test his singing talents and personal mettle against his future subjects and I'm sure we're all terribly honoured and all that, blah blah *blah*. But let us never forget that if, and I say if, this man is chosen to proceed through selection it will also be an *honour for him*! An equal honour, if not a greater one! Yes. Never forget that *we* are number one, not him! We are number one and *he*, my friends, is number *zero*. We at *Chart Throb* are everything that he as future head of state would like to be but isn't. First and foremost we are *popular*! Hugely popular, as popular in fact as he is generally ignored. Also we are *democratic*. We are as democratic as he is oligarchical, elitist, unaccountable and *posh snob snooty*. We are *modern Britain*. He is fuddy-duddy, out of touch, *boring old Britain*. We represent the people, he represents an outmoded upper class which is struggling to find a role for itself in our *meritocratic* society. He has come to us, my friends, because he *needs us*. He wants to reach the people that we reach and show them *who he really is*. Well, so be it! He shall have his chance but on a *level playing field only*. He will receive no special treatment beyond that which meets the minimum requirements for security and the prevention of terrorism. He will be exposed to the public as all our candidates are exposed to the public, for we are judging the *man*, not the position. He will play by our rules. If, for instance, he wins through to the second round but it clashes with him hosting the Commonwealth Games or attending the State Opening of Parliament, then he'd better be here with us singing "Stand By Me" or he will be OUT. Because *we* are what matters to the British public today. WE are the masters! So it's my way or the highway! The Prince of Wales can either shape up or ship out! If he does well then he will have his chance to reach his people. If he comes on all lah-di-dah, posh snob and hoity-toity, and expects special treatment, then he will find himself reduced to a five-second clip in a Minger montage or my name isn't Calvin Simms and we are not the greatest show on television!'

After a brief pause to ensure that he had finished, the room burst into enormous applause and the meeting broke up on a genuine high.

'Trent?' Calvin said, gathering up his papers. 'In my office.'

He looked at his watch: it was already nearly seven o'clock and he wanted to shave.

'Well done, Trent,' he said. 'Good selection, mate.'

'Thanks, boss. Great speech about the royal thing. Love it. *Dig it*. Nobody is bigger than the *Throb*, right? We can love him or shove him.'

'Don't be ridiculous, you idiot. Of course we're not going to shove him. He wants to face a popular vote and he's going to face one. He's going through to the finals.'

'Right. Yes. Of course he is.'

'That's why he has to appear to be treated normally.'

'Yes. Mmmm.'

'Or it'll look rigged.'

'OK. Copy that, boss.'

'He's worth a lot more to us on the show than off and the way to keep him on is to give the public a chance to get to know him and like him. They will never like him if they think he's getting special treatment, will they?'

'No.'

'Because if there's one thing we know about us as a nation it's that we want a royal family with palaces and pomp because *we do it so well*, but we don't want the royal family to get any special treatment.'

'Uhm . . . right. Was there anything else, chief?'

'Yes . . .' Calvin said it casually, as if it had only just occurred to him.

'I want a teenage kid who can't read.'

'OK. Good. Ri-ight,' Trent replied, taken by surprise but trying not to show it.

'Also a victim of domestic violence. Female, obviously, don't go getting me some henpecked wimp or a bruised poof with a boyfriend who likes it rough.'

'No, of course not. Right.'

'Also somebody who is waiting for an operation . . . No, better still, whose *kid* is waiting for an operation.'

'Uhm . . . Fine, chief. Good. Got that. Uhm, are these to be contestants?'

'No, I want them as holiday companions. Of course as contestants. Fucking hell, Trent, I'm in a *hurry*. Trawl back through the envelopes and try and find them and if you can't, find them anyway. Just make sure they're in the mix before the regionals.'

Trent knew better than to argue.

'Right. OK, chief. You got it. A kid who can't read. A female victim of domestic violence and somebody either waiting for an operation or whose kid is waiting for an operation. Any other clues?'

'Well, telegenic of course. Cute if possible, particularly the kid and the battered wife. Clingy but not Mingy, I think. Also it would be better if they can sing a bit but obviously not essential. Right, that's it. Meeting over. Well done. Get on with it. See you for the first audition day.'

And Calvin hurried from the room.

Dinner and an Indecent Proposal

That evening at eight o'clock exactly the bell rang in Emma's little flat. It had been a rush but she was ready. Home by seven, she had settled on a little black number from Kookai with a red lacy fringe at the décolletage, and been left with enough time to do her face and not enough time to worry too much about the evening ahead.

The car Calvin had sent was a Jag, beautifully luxurious, and in it on the back seat she found a single rose with a card attached that said *A rose from a prick*.

The last vestiges of Emma's anger evaporated. He was saying sorry. He hadn't meant it. He'd had a brain-storm, been suffering from a salt deficiency. Something like that. Emma had previously resolved to be tough with Calvin but if he was going to be that contrite then it would be churlish not to forgive him.

They dined in a private upstairs room at the Ivy, which, despite Emma's efforts to be underawed, felt glamorous and exciting. Calvin apologized early on for his brutal behaviour and with due contrition offered Emma her job back plus a raise, which she was pleased to accept. Calvin then insisted that they spoke no further on the matter and instead he regaled her with amusing anecdotes about Rodney and Beryl and the American pop industry. He mentioned his broken marriage briefly but in a light and self-deprecating manner, concluding that two arrogant, manipulative superegos had made a big mistake and in so doing proved once and for all that only opposites attract. Then, when the last of the wine had been drunk and coffee had been served, he asked if she would return with him to his house in Belgravia.

Of course she should have been expecting it but in fact she hadn't been. She was not a particularly vain girl and knowing that Calvin could pick and choose his women at will she had not flattered herself that this dinner might in his view be a means of seduction. At the back of her mind she had thought it might be more of an effort to avoid the possibility of her taking legal action against him for unfair dismissal. After all, the days when mega-rich employers could do whatever they liked with their employees were mercifully past.

'You want me to come home with you?' she said.

'Yes. Absolutely. Now would be great.'

'For coffee?' she enquired weakly, trying to maintain the niceties.

'No. We've had coffee. I want you to stay the night.'

Emma was taken aback. She had not received so blunt a proposal since her drunken first-year nights in the Student Union bar and she did not like it much.

'Calvin, I can't,' she said quickly.

'Emma, please,' said Calvin. 'It really would mean a lot to me.'

'Mean a lot to you? How do you mean, mean a lot to you?'

'Exactly that. I want to sleep with you. It's very important to me.'

'*Important to you?*'

'Yes.'

Now Emma was becoming as angry as she had been surprised.

'God, you're a plain speaker, aren't you, Calvin?'

'Well, I'm sorry if I'm being blunt but it's late, we both have work in the morning and this is important to me.'

'Who I go to bed with is important to me. So no,' Emma said firmly. 'Absolutely not.'

'Why not?'

'What do you mean, why not? Goodness gracious, I never heard such a thing! I don't just sleep with blokes when they ask me to. Particularly when it's practically a bloody order. It isn't me. There has to be . . . I don't know, something more.'

'What? Romance? I can do romance.'

'Clearly you can't.'

'Emma, you *have* to do this for me.'

'No, Calvin, I really don't have to do this for you and I really shan't either.'

If he had waited she might have added something. Something like, maybe next time. That they'd have to see. And if not next time, almost certainly the time after that. Depending on how things developed. Unfortunately Calvin did not give her the chance.

'Well, then,' he said, 'and this is going to sound really wrong but there's no nice way of putting it, you can't have your job back.'

Emma could not believe what she had heard. It was so *blatant*! She had never come across anything like it in her life.

'You're joking, of course.'

'I'm afraid I'm not.'

'You mean you're actually saying to me, straight out, that my getting my job back is dependent on my going to bed with you?'

'Well, it wasn't . . . before.'

'Before I said no?'

'Yes.'

'But it is now?'

'I'm afraid it has to be, Emma. It's about focus, you see. You're blurring my focus. My mind is wandering. Do you have any idea how serious a thing that is at this stage in programme development? I need to get it out of my system. Right now. Tonight. I can't afford to lose another minute of concentration time.'

'So you sacked me just so you could then blackmail me into having sex with you?'

'No, absolutely not, that's not how it happened at all. I sacked you to try to get you out of my focus, so that I could concentrate on the job in hand. But it didn't work.'

'I'm going to the police. This is completely illegal, it's not the tenth century, you know. You're not a baron, you can't just shag your serfs when you feel like it.'

Now it was Calvin's turn to be taken aback. It had already been dawning on him that he had played the situation rather badly but things were suddenly getting out of hand.

'You can't go to the police, Emma,' he said, his manner losing something of its self-assurance. 'I'll deny it, it's your word against mine. I'll say this is your way of getting revenge.'

'I've been recording you. I brought a tape recorder.'

'Emma,' Calvin replied gently, 'you haven't. I always carry a device that lets me know if anybody is recording anything within half a mile of me. You can get them at any of those spy gadget shops.'

'Oh,' said Emma, looking slightly crestfallen.

'Actually that was a lie,' Calvin added. 'I don't have any such device.'

Emma picked up her bag to leave.

'Goodbye, you horrible bastard.'

'Emma?' Calvin said urgently. 'If I could give you your job back without you having to sleep with me I would. I really would. But believe me, I can't. You're just too . . . too *fascinating*.'

'Too *fascinating*?'

'Yes. I keep trying to work and you keep . . . distracting me.'

'And you *sacked* me for that? For being unwittingly distracting?'

'Yes. I'm a busy man. I need to concentrate. If I let you back in I'll probably just get distracted again. I can't afford to have that happen.'

'But it will be all right if you sleep with me?'

'Yes, that's my theory anyway. I think I need to see you naked. If I can just see you naked and have sex with you then all that will be out of the way. I won't be messing up my meetings thinking, what would that girl look like naked, because I'll *know*. My mind won't be wandering off thinking, if I could have sex with her just once . . . because I'll have *done it already*. Do you see? That's why if you won't sleep with me I can't let you have your job back. I have responsibilities, a lot of people's jobs depend on me doing my job right. I have a show to make. I can't allow you to ruin that. In a way I'm as much a victim of this as you.'

Emma could only stare. If nothing else, she now understood a little better how it was that this man had so quickly become such a colossus in the business.

'You really think you can fix anything, don't you?' she said finally. 'Manipulate any story, even your own?'

'Well, don't you think it's a good thing to take responsibility for one's life? To assume control?'

'What I think, Calvin,' Emma said, getting to her feet, 'is that you are going to die a very lonely man.'

Then, refusing to discuss it further, she left the restaurant and went home.

Reality Check

As it was eleven in the morning in Wardour Street it was 3am in LA. Priscilla had been in the club for about an hour and whatever was in the uppers she had bought from the bathroom chick was not doing the trick. She was supposed to be having fun. There was a line outside fifty metres long of people desperate to be where she was and she had walked right past it and been nodded through. She was, after all, Priscilla Blenheim and the last time she had visited the club she had gained them some welcome publicity by bringing with her a camera crew covering her 'spontaneous' night out clubbing despite having been grounded by her two mothers for getting her first boob job.

She had hated those boobs. They were so lame, though when the idea had come up at the story meeting it had sounded fun. Like the whole episode would be about her, instead of the usual thing which was just her whining on the periphery, and she would get to have badass fuck-you space hoppers done live on TV. But then the people at the network said that because she was still a teen they would have to be really small tasteful titties so as not to offend any parents or encourage irresponsible behaviour. Like those pathetic token peaches that preppy girls got done in their first semester away from Mom, which didn't even look like a boob job at all. What was the point of having a boob job that didn't look like a boob job? Priscilla had wanted Pammies, two huge, fuck-off, rock 'n' roll tits with She Devils and butterflies tattooed all over them, but her moms had said no. And despite the fact that the tits were so obviously a sad token effort she'd have to act like she was really scared of what her mom and mom would say.

Now of course she had two enormous balloons straining the confines of her jumper and Beryl had been furious, not least because nothing had been caught on camera. There were no cameras with her now either. Nobody at all, in fact. The friends whom she had come in with, who had breezed in on the coat tails of her celebrity, had all grabbed their passes to the VIP area and evaporated.

Then she noticed a band she had always admired sitting in a booth drinking beers and laughing. They were an indie rock band, not big at all, but they had a small deal and played regularly and were kind of respected. The sort of band she had always liked. She went over to talk to them. It was OK to do that, they were fellow celebrities, it was a special bond.

'Hi,' she said. 'I'm Priscilla.'

'Hey, Priscilla,' said the lead singer.

'I really admire you guys. I think your shit is awesome.'

'Excellent.' There was a brief pause before he added, 'You know, we really used to dig your mom, like when she was your dad.'

Then the bass player shifted up the booth a little and invited Priscilla to sit down.

'Hey,' he said drunkenly, 'if we party with you does that mean we get on the TV? Like you have little cameras following you around, right? Hey, guys! Maybe we should sing our new song and it will get on the TV!'

Priscilla wondered if he was being serious. He wasn't.

'Like those cameras,' he continued. 'You should have one in your bedroom, babe! That would like be huge! Or in the john! We could all watch Blaster Blenheim take a dump, and take a look to see how his cooch construction's going. That would be hot! We have to watch those fucking pigs shit, why not you guys too?'

The bass player's face was close to hers, which seemed to amplify his sneer.

Priscilla had encountered this kind of resentful aggression any number of times and depressingly it always seemed to come from people she admired. She understood it, of course; these guys were musicians trying to struggle up a very greasy pole. They had a tiny independent record deal with no distribution to speak of and the only exposure they could get

181

themselves was by gigging, thrashing out their set night after night in a series of half-empty hellholes before loading out their own gear. She, on the other hand, was a major celebrity with her own TV show and a massive record deal.

And why? Because she was a rock star's step-daughter whose parent had sold her adolescence to the media.

'So anyway,' the bass player said, getting even closer to her, 'how's it all going?'

Priscilla was familiar with this too. They held her in contempt but they wanted to fuck her. Why not, she was cute enough and she was world famous. What was not to fuck?

'Well, you know,' she replied, 'I've been doing stuff. Kind of working on my songs and shit.'

'Your songs?' he asked.

'Yeah. I write songs.'

'You write songs? I didn't know that.'

'Yeah.'

'Hey, guys! The babe writes songs! Did anyone know that?'

But the rest of the band weren't listening. The club was noisy and they were leaving the bass player to it.

''Cos you're a singer, right?' the bass player said, turning back to Priscilla. 'You did an album, didn't you?'

'Yeah.'

There was a pause after this. The album had conspicuously flopped, so there was not much to be said.

'Hey!' The bass player was already drunker than he had been earlier. 'Maybe you should sing with us then we could be famous too! Wouldn't that be cool?'

'You already have a singer.'

'Aw but he's shit and besides he ain't a *babe*.'

Priscilla did not know why but she let him take her to bed. On reflection she concluded that it had been vanity.

182

He had credibility. He had cool. And famous though she was, Priscilla had neither. Not really. Not real cool. Mall rats and suburban metal heads might have thought she was cool but *cool* people didn't, and yet there she was hanging out with one. She knew that he held her in contempt but nobody else in the club did and as she rocked drunkenly on his arm and was photographed at the exit a tiny little piece of his credibility rubbed off on her, just as a smidgeon of her fame attached itself to him. It was a very LA kind of thing.

Around the Couch

Calvin was too angry even to sit on the couch. Instead he paced about the book-lined study, trying not to knock over the objets d'art. In the week since he had sacked and then failed to have sex with Emma, he had been infuriated to discover that removing her from his proximity had not taken her off his mind.

He was *thinking* about her. *All* the time.

And he *hated* himself for it.

This was not Calvin's thing at all. His thing was control. Control in every part of his life and business, that was how he managed to run his various hugely successful enterprises, how he managed to dominate vast sections of the pop and television industries in both Europe and the USA. He did it by being *in control*. By organizing his time and his thinking. How was he supposed to organize his time and his thinking when he found himself *wasting* his time on entirely unbidden thoughts of this bloody woman! He had tried to ignore it, gone out and got drunk on the arms of several of his highly glamorous occasional companions, thus creating a storm of media interest about the state of his marriage, but it had been no good. Emma kept returning to his thoughts and it was driving him mad. He had *things to do*. They were only days away from starting to film the *Chart Throb* auditions, plus there was all his usual workload of record contracts, management deals, court cases, spin-off shows and celebrity editions of his various franchises. And one small ex-employee was getting in his way.

Finally, in desperation, he had done something he had never done before, something he would never even have considered doing a week earlier. He had arranged to see a therapist. He hated himself for it, for he saw it as a sign of shameful intellectual weakness, but there was no one else he could turn to.

'Look,' he said, pacing round the couch upon which he had been invited to sit. 'This really is serious. I need to concentrate, I need to *focus*. You have no idea how hard it is to make television that is as successful as my stuff. I don't *want* to think about this girl, I scarcely know her, and yet she keeps dropping into my head. What the fuck is *wrong* with me?'

The answer was so simple that even a trained therapist was able to work it out.

'You're in love,' he replied after a little thought.

'I can't be.'

'You quite obviously are,' the therapist asserted.

'But I've never been in love before.'

'I thought you had recently got married?'

'What's that got to do with it? I've never been in love before.'

'Well, then I suppose there is a first time for everything.'

'I don't *know* this girl!'

'You don't need to know her. Love isn't logical like that.'

'I could sleep with any number of the most beautiful

184

women on earth. *Why* do I only want to sleep with this one? She's not even the most beautiful! I mean not in an obvious sense anyway.'

'I've told you. You're in love. That's what love is.'

Calvin sat down on the couch for a moment and almost immediately bounced up again.

'I'm absolutely convinced that if I could just sleep with her I'd be over it. It's the *not* having her which is beating me up.'

'Well, you *may* be right.'

'So what do I do?'

'I suppose you have to try to sleep with her.'

'Duh! I *know* that. But I can't. She won't return my calls. I fucked up, you see. And that's another thing that's driving me insane. I *hate* fucking up. It's so not me.'

'How did you fuck up?'

'I sacked her, horribly, abruptly, demeaningly and without just cause. I think that was a mistake.'

'Hmm. Certainly not the usual behaviour of a man in love.'

'Yes, but I didn't know I was in love with her *then*, did I? I just thought she was . . . *distracting*. I'd noticed that I'd been looking at her, thinking about her, *focusing* on her. I had to do something about it so I sacked her. I don't like being distracted. What else could I do? This is all new territory for me.'

'You could have displaced the distraction into a social context.'

'How do you mean?'

'Asked her out for a coffee.'

'I don't have *time* for that shit! I don't *do* that shit. My programmes are franchised in a dozen different countries! I am a colossal *star*. I run a huge record label and rock management company and that's just a *sideline*. I can't be taking bloody girls out for *coffee*!!

185

Are you insane? Do you have *any* idea what my time is worth?'

'So you sacked her to get her out of your way and off your mind?'

'Yes. I acted decisively. That's what I do. I act decisively.'

'But it didn't work?'

'No. By mid-afternoon, in the middle of a *very* intense character development meeting, I might add, I realized that this girl was out of my way but not off my mind. I was thinking about her and *in particular* thinking about what she would look like naked. So I invited her to dinner and asked her to sleep with me.'

'Straight off the bat?'

'Well, we had dinner first.'

'But then you asked her to sleep with you?'

'Yes, I said that she was on my mind and that I needed to sleep with her in order to forget about her.'

'Hmm. You are new to this, aren't you?'

'Look, I know what you're thinking, that I'm a complete asshole . . .'

'No, no, no, no . . . no.'

'But this is serious. I didn't ask for this. I am blameless but I cannot operate properly until I've lanced this boil.'

'Boil?'

'Yes . . . I am fucking *obsessed*.'

'Well.' The therapist put his hands before his face as if in prayer. 'There is no doubt about it, you are suffering from that intense mental imbalance which is popularly known as love. This young woman Emma is affecting your work and I agree with you that you need to develop a personal well-being strategy in order to . . . uhm . . . lance her. My professional opinion is that, by sacking her and then saying that she can only have her job back if she sleeps with you, you have lost her trust.'

186

'I know. I *know*,' Calvin replied, wringing his hands in despair.

'This young lady has come to view you with suspicion.'

'Which is *so* unfair when you consider that I have been completely and absolutely honest with her.'

'That's women for you, I'm afraid,' the therapist sighed. 'However, what you need to do now is to find a way to make her see you differently. Differently from the utterly amoral sexual predator and bully that she must currently consider you to be. She is clearly a young woman of principle. When you made your suggestion she did not for a moment consider it, but neither has she sought to avenge herself on you or exploit your weakness for her in any way.'

'Yes, that's true. I've been expecting a sexual discrimination rap every day for a week.'

'Which would of course be entirely justified.'

'I know that. Don't rub it in.'

'But, for whatever reason, this woman has decided to retire with dignity from the scene and not seek to punish you as she has every legal and indeed moral—'

'Yes, yes, *all right*. I *said* don't rub it in.'

'You are in love with a woman of principle who considers you to be a man utterly without principle. You need to change that.'

'You mean get her to drop her principles?'

'No, you've tried that. I was thinking more of you *acquiring* some principles or at least *appearing* to do so. You need to win her trust. Unless she trusts you she will never sleep with you. She is a boil who will remain unlanced.'

Calvin considered the advice carefully and the more he thought about it, the more it seemed to annoy him.

'I do not have *time* for this!'

Family Trip

Beryl, Priscilla and her twin sister Lisa Marie sat together in the back of the stretch Humvee. Once more they were stuck in traffic on their way out to LAX.

Beryl was returning to Britain to begin recording the new series of *Chart Throb* and Priscilla was having talks with a dildo manufacturer about developing a range of sex toys under her name. Lisa Marie was just going to hang out.

'I might go to Europe and check out Berlin,' she said. 'I hear they have some awesome industrial metal going on, whole bands with just chainsaws and pneumatic drills. If you take the right drugs you actually believe you're on a building site.'

'All that happened before in the late eighties, dork,' Beryl sneered.

'Hey, if Green Day can get a Grammy playing punk rock, nothing's dead.'

'Except my album,' said Priscilla morosely. She had that morning learned that it had been officially remaindered and could now be found in the bargain dump bins alongside the Country compilations and last year's *Chart Throb* finalists.

'Oh, do stop it,' Beryl snapped. 'So the record stiffed. Get over it.'

'The record stiffed,' Lisa Marie echoed. 'Didn't even make the top forty.'

'Shut up, dork. At least I made an album. What did you ever do except eat?' Priscilla snapped back.

'At least I'm good at what I do,' Lisa Marie countered. 'I eat, I get fat, it works. You make an album, all you get is nothing.'

'Behave!' Beryl shouted. 'I cannot put up with you guys bickering for the next fourteen hours.'

'Hey, bickering made us famous, Dad.'

'Mum! You fucking bitch. I am not your dad, I am your other mother!'

'Whatever. Bickering's what me and my sister do. We bicker. Fox Network *pays* us to fucking bicker. It's one of the most popular parts of our show.'

'Nearly as big as the pigs shitting on the floor and Mom's lips getting stuck in doorways,' Lisa Marie added.

'Yes and it pays for your first-class lifestyle, darling. Don't forget that.'

'Oh, come on, *Mom*,' Priscilla sneered. 'You had a squillion dollars anyway from dickhead metal nuts still buying your albums.'

'Whatever,' said Beryl, gathering together her papers. 'Now I'm going to be very, very busy over the next few months with *Chart Throb* so you two need to behave, OK? No drug busts, and *please* steer clear of grunge rock morons you meet in clubs . . .'

'Did you see they're at thirty-two now?' Lisa Marie sneered. 'Congratulations, you can't get on the chart yourself, Priscilla, but the guy who fucked you can!'

'Bitch!'

Priscilla swung a punch at Lisa Marie and caught her hard on the ear which she had recently had pierced right up through the cartilage so it was sore already. Lisa Marie shouted in pain and whacked Priscilla with the magazine she had been holding. Priscilla kicked her, she kicked Priscilla back and suddenly they were wrestling on the floor of the Humvee.

'Stop it, you bloody morons,' Beryl shouted. 'We are working here.'

When order was restored and Lisa Marie banished to the other end of the stretch to watch TV, Priscilla and Beryl compared diaries.

'So we finally got a one-week postponement on *The Blenheims*,' Beryl said. 'We start back in LA with the new lawn-mower episode one week after the *Chart Throb* final in London.'

'That's very tight, Mom.'

'Well, I only need a little lift around the eyes and a few more nerves stitched into my clit.'

'*Please*, I do *not* want to know. That is so gross.'

'I am a *woman* now, Priscilla, I deserve to feel what a woman feels. Anyway the whole thing should only take a morning. That gives me six days to heal. It should be OK. I thought you said your guy was good.'

'He is, all the girls are using him.'

'Did he do those tits?' Lisa Marie called from the other end of the Humvee. 'You want to talk about gross, Priscilla, those are gross. They are *so* dumb! They look like two fucking space hoppers.'

'She's right, you know,' Beryl said, adopting a gentler tone. 'A boob job that radical isn't right for a teenager, Priscilla. You should have them reduced.'

'No way,' Priscilla replied defiantly. 'They empower me as a woman.'

'Oh *please*,' Lisa Marie sneered.

'Shut *up*, bitch! Who asked you? I *like* huge tits. There is more room for tattoos. If you want to talk to someone about reductions, Mom, how about talking to Lisa Marie about her fat fucking gut!'

'I like being fat!' Lisa Marie shouted, defiantly pushing cookies into her mouth.

'Don't do that!' Beryl snapped. 'A little puppy cuddle is fine but . . .'

'*Puppy cuddle!*' Priscilla exploded. 'She's a whale! A fucking *moose*!'

Beryl looked at her other stepdaughter critically.

'Actually, you know, dear, your gut really is getting out of hand. You don't need to stop eating, just get some work done.'

'Mom! I'm seventeen.'

'Well, don't leave it till late like I did. You should

consider getting your appendix knotted now.'

'I'm comfy being porky, Mom.'

'You're a celebrity. It's your duty to be thin. You won't be a teen for ever.'

'Sure she'll be a teen for ever, Mom,' Priscilla said. 'We both will, you saw to that. We're stuck in a *Blenheims* time warp. I'll be eighty and people will still remember me the way I was when I was fourteen.'

All for Love

Emma finally agreed to meet Calvin.

She told her friends it was either that or change her mobile phone number which she was damned if she was going to do because she hated it when other people did that. Her friends all thought she was mad not to meet him anyway: after all, here was this fabulously rich man whom she had already been dreaming about positively *pursuing* her yet she was avoiding him.

'So he sacked you. So what? Now he wants you back and *you* have the control,' Mel and Tom assured her.

'You don't understand,' Emma would reply.

She knew that it was precisely *because* she had been dreaming about him that she should now put him from her mind for ever. He had given her a very clear lesson in just what a dangerous person he was to have feelings for and every atom of her instinct was warning her to avoid him at all costs.

'He's a bastard,' she kept reminding herself and her friends. 'I don't need to invite bastards into my life. He actually admitted that he only wanted to sleep with me in order to be able to forget about me. Like a notch on his fucking bedpost! I don't like men who twist their emotions into exit strategies.'

'Ah *yes*,' her friends would say, nodding wisely. 'Of course.'

And Emma knew they were thinking of her father, which of course they were. The worst thing about having a father whom you both loved and hated and who had walked out on you and your mother was that everybody always thought that everything in your life from that point on which had *anything at all* to do with men was really all about your dad. Which, of course, in some ways it was.

In the end, after ignoring a bombardment of text messages, flowers and bike-delivered notes for almost a week, Emma, who was still as attracted to Calvin as she had ever been, had gathered up her courage and texted back simply, 'OK. When? Where? E.' As an afterthought, she had sent a PS: 'Daytime only.'

The meeting took place over morning coffee at Claridge's Hotel and Calvin leaped straight in with his usual disarming honesty.

'I can't get you off my mind,' he said. 'It's affecting my work. I'm a very, very busy man. I need to deal with this.'

'That's not my problem,' Emma replied, trying to sound tough but secretly pleased.

'It *is* your problem. You're part of the team.'

'You sacked me.'

'And I've offered you your job back. A raise even. I'll promote you.'

'If I sleep with you.'

'*Yes*. If you sleep with me. I've admitted that. You keep bringing it up as if I've committed some terrible moral crime.'

'Which you have.'

'Look, we're going round in circles here. This isn't about just *your* job, a lot of people's lives and livelihoods depend on me having my shit together.'

'Are you saying I have to screw you for the good of the team?'

'Yes! *Exactly*. Is that so wrong? I'm fucking up here. I can't stop thinking about you. That's the truth of it and it's very annoying . . . very inconvenient. It's very . . . painful.'

Emma reddened. She always blushed so easily and so furiously at the slightest hint of emotion. She could feel her face burning and hoped it wouldn't go blotchy.

'Well, you've ruined it, haven't you? Because, if you must know, I had been thinking about you as well and that was sort of painful too.'

Calvin leaped at this sudden chink in Emma's armour.

'But that's *great*,' he said, brightening hugely. 'I had no idea! You *see*, there's so much confusion going on here. We just need to get to know each other better. We could have dinner again and—'

'Calvin, I know what you want. You want to shag me.'

'Yes, yes, *obviously*. Of course I do. You can't punish me for being honest. You're very cute, not my type as it happens but very cute. Why shouldn't I want to shag you? Wanting to shag you isn't a crime. I'm sure lots of men want to shag you. Do you hate them all for it?'

'No, because they're not my boss abusing his position by sacking me unfairly and then demanding sex immediately afterwards in return for re-instatement.'

'Oh, do stop *dwelling* on that. I played it wrong, I admit that, but we have to move on here. Yes, I want to sleep with you, what man wouldn't, but I *like* you too, that's the problem. It's so unlike me to care about anyone very much but . . . I think you're great.'

'You don't know me.'

'I know you a bit and I'd like to have the opportunity to know you more . . .'

193

Emma finished her coffee and began to gather up her things. So much of her wanted to give him a second chance but she knew a great deal about giving men second chances. In the aftermath of her parents' break-up she had watched her mother dole out second chances to her father on an almost weekly basis. Men didn't change, she had learned that. If you took them back, you did it for what they *were*, not for what you wanted them to be. And she did not like what Calvin was.

'I'm sorry, Calvin, but you've blown it. You really have, which is such a shame because I really did like you. But the truth is I know you a lot better than you could ever know me. I've worked for you. I know what you *do*. You're a manipulator; you think you write the stories, *all* the stories, and now you want to write mine. You *use* people. You can't help it; it's the way you were born. It's made you heaps of money and I have to admit it's also very attractive. But no girl should ever be allowed anywhere near you.'

'There's more to me than you think. You have to trust me.'

'After what's happened, Calvin, I'm afraid that would be absolutely impossible.'

'Look, I was having a bad day, I did some stupid things . . .'

'Oh, come *on*, Calvin.'

'All right, how about this?'

There was a long pause. Emma waited.

'You can have your job back,' Calvin said finally. 'No strings attached. Then a bit later on, if you feel like it, maybe . . .'

'I sleep with you.'

'Yes.'

'Just sort of delay it a bit, you mean.'

'Uhm, yes.'

Emma seemed about to rise once more.

194

Calvin added quickly, 'But I won't make it dependent on that.'

Emma stayed seated, toying with her coffee spoon.

Calvin pressed on: 'I'll try . . . I'll try and *win* you. In the coffee breaks. It will be up to you. We'll start again. Come on, that's fair.'

Emma played with the cutlery for a while before looking Calvin in the eye.

'I don't want my old job back.'

'I've told you. No strings. I promise I'll leave you alone.'

'No, I mean it. It's not about you. I don't want it back anyway. Independently of you and your wolfish tendencies.'

'Why on earth wouldn't you want it back?'

'You sacking me gave me a chance to look at everything differently. And now I've had a week to think about things I've come to realize that working on *Chart Throb* was turning me into something I didn't want to be.'

'You were bloody good at your job, our youngest senior.'

'Exactly. Every day I got better at it. I got used to looking at people from a predatory point of view, wondering how we could *use* them, what we could *do* with them. And the funny thing was the more I did it, the more I believed that it was OK to do it. I know you're not a wicked man, Calvin, I just think you've managed to persuade yourself that standards and principles don't count. The end justifies the means. You have all this power, all this influence, all this *talent*, and what do you do with it? You make the most vapid and forgettable entertainment show in history.'

'Is there anything wrong with entertainment being vapid and forgettable?'

'I don't know. No, not really. I mean, it's great telly, I admit it. But also maybe yes. It's corrosive, isn't it? It undermines standards. I mean it used to be possible to be hugely entertaining without being crap as well, look at The Beatles.'

'That was genius, Emma. I have never claimed to be a genius or to be looking for genius. If you judge people by that sort of standard nobody would make anything.'

'Yes, but there were lots of great bands around in the sixties, too many to count. It was almost as if The Beatles were leading by example, as if their example raised everybody's game. Now *you're* the biggest thing. You are the example. People are following you. Your talent has made you powerful. I think that brings with it responsibility.'

'So what do you think I should do about it?'

'I don't know. I'm not the clever one. I just feel . . . you know that term "dumbed down"?'

'Of course. Hear it all the time. Fucking snobbery.'

'Well yes, I expect often it is but whenever they go on about how more kids vote in your shows than in general elections you can't help wondering if there isn't some truth in it. I mean nothing is *about* anything any more, nothing *means* anything. Everything's a laugh, everything's disposable. You're the richest, cleverest man in TV and yet everything you create is gone like a puff of smoke.'

'A good soufflé doesn't last beyond the eating, does that make it any less valid?'

'Not everything in life should be a soufflé, Calvin. For instance, what about the royal thing? What about the Prince of Wales?'

'Keep your voice down, Emma,' Calvin said gently. 'Public place and all that.'

'You're going to make a fool of him.'

'We may allow him to make a fool of himself.'

'Oh, come *on*, Calvin, don't try that one. Don't forget I've been in the team. I'm a professional. You will make a fool of him. He thinks he can find an audience through you. Poor bastard, I can't believe he's so naïve as to think *he* can use *you*. We *know* what will happen. You'll lure him in, select the edits that make him look a complete fool, chew him up and spit him out. That's what you *do*.'

'Look, I didn't come here to talk about the Prince of Wales or the show. I came to talk about you. You and me. My therapist says that I've fallen in love with you . . .'

'Your *therapist*?'

'Yes. I never had one before. See what you've driven me to? That's how serious my feelings are.'

'How romantic.'

'Yes, well, let me assure you that personally I feel a fool even uttering the word "therapist" but there you are. It is what it is and somehow or other I've got to get beyond this. I don't know how or where it will lead but somehow I've got to get this knot out of my stomach and this confusion out of my head . . . Now you won't sleep with me . . .'

'No.'

'And you won't come back to work for me?'

'No.'

'Then tell me what I can do to make you see me at least. Not sleep with me, let's leave that aside, just . . . see me.'

'Do you mean you want to "go out" with me, you want me to be your girlfriend?'

'Yes. I think that's what I'm saying. I want to start again. Forget everything that's happened and just . . . see each other. I don't know. Find out where it leads. I suppose that's what people do, isn't it?'

'Yes, it is, Calvin. But we can't forget what's happened. At least I can't. I just don't trust you.'

'Well, somehow or other you have to find a way to trust me. Think about it. Concentrate. Tell me how. Tell me what I can do to make you trust me.'

Emma sat for a little while in silence. Then a thought struck her. It wasn't an idea that she had come prepared with but suddenly it seemed obvious. 'I'll tell you what you can do,' she said, 'if you really want to prove yourself.'

'Yes?'

'Deselect HRH.'

'Deselect him?'

'Yes, turn him down for further audition. Dump him, don't bring him in. You threw out plenty of others at final selection. Chuck him out too. Do the decent thing. You know he's completely out of his depth. Protect him from making a fool of himself.'

'But . . . but he's already been notified,' Calvin stammered. 'He's been offered an audition.'

'Denotify him. You've read the rules, you wrote them, and the main one is that you can change them at any time. Tell him you've changed your mind.'

'But he's fantastic telly.'

'Exactly. That's the point. Show me you can give something up. Show me you can do something for reasons other than profit, just because it's the right thing to do, something like preventing a middle-aged man from making a mockery of his life's work, degrading his position and all the principles he's stood for and which may even have inspired other people. If you do that, then maybe I could be your girlfriend . . . and . . . well, we'll see how it goes.'

Calvin did not answer for a moment. Instead he poured himself another cup of coffee. It was clear that he was struggling with something. His usual easy smile had gone and the spout of the coffee pot rattled against the edge of his cup as he poured.

Emma saw his hesitation and it made her sad.

'You see,' she said, 'you can't do it, can you? You can't give up a single puppet in your show. Not for me and not, I think, for any girl. Remember what I said to you the last time we had this conversation, Calvin? One day you're going to be a very lonely old man. Goodbye.'

'Not HRH!' Calvin pleaded. 'Ask me to drop any of the others . . .'

'Why should I, what's the difference?'

'I have my reasons . . . Reasons outside the show. Please.'

'No, Calvin. You said you loved me and I asked you to do one thing for me and you won't. You don't need the Prince. Yes, it's an amazing thing to get him but you don't *need* him. You can't get any more successful than you are, and besides people are so punch-drunk with royal and political compromises that nothing surprises anybody much any more. How can the poor bloke's stock get any lower? You'll get one good bunch of headlines out of him then chuck him out. But you won't even give up that, will you? Not even for the woman you say you can't stop thinking about. This really is goodbye, Calvin. Please don't call me again.'

'Wait! No! Hang on, you're wrong,' Calvin said. 'Of course I'll dump him if you want, I'll dump any of them, but I can do better. I can do more for you than that.'

Emma had been halfway out of her chair. She hovered for a moment before resuming her seat for the third time. She raised her brows as if to say 'go on'.

'You say that I was going to use him. Chew him up and spit him out.'

'Well, weren't you?'

'Yes, of course I was. Because we don't deal in ideas or substance. We deal in personalities and disposable emotions. In fact, along the way we've actually made ideas and substance look boring and stupid. Chucking the heir to the throne off our show will be the ultimate proof of that.'

'That's right, which is why I don't want you to have him on in the first place. Surely something should be left that's worthy of respect? If not the man, at least his position.'

'How about this? We don't use him. We let *him* use *us*.'

'What do you mean?'

'I'll tell you what I mean,' said Calvin, suddenly becoming excited. Excited, it seemed, by a fresh idea. 'Not only do I let him on to the show but . . . I let him win?'

Calvin allowed this to hang in the air for a moment before pressing on.

'How about I don't chew him up and spit him out? How about instead we have him back week after week? We give him time to talk. We edit him sympathetically; we bring the public on to his side. We show that he was right to put himself and his ideas and principles on a new and democratic platform, to reach out to his people in a *modern way*. And then I find a way for him to win.'

'The Prince of Wales? The fox-hunting, tax-absorbing, plant-chatting, seed-nibbling, "doesn't know when to shut up" Prince of Wales *win Chart Throb*?'

'Yes. Wouldn't that be proof of me using my skills for something of substance? Preserving something, not destroying it? You're a posh bird, you went to a private school, you respect the monarchy, surely you have to accept that that would be a *good* thing?'

Suddenly it was Emma who was excited.

'I think it would be amazing. It would be a cultural watershed . . . Do you really think you could do it? I mean getting His Royal Highness into the finals of a pop contest would strain credibility enough, but once the public start voting? How could you possibly manipulate that?'

Calvin stared straight into her big blue eyes. He spoke quietly, sincerely. Like a father.

'I don't know. It's a whole new idea for me. I'm acting on impulse here but hey, that's what I like to do . . . busking, improvising, dancing on the edge. When I get given a challenge by someone I admire, I like to double it and then some . . . It would of course be *incredibly* hard, I don't know if I could even *start* to pull it off and I'd certainly be risking the credibility of my show . . . risking my whole career. But I'd do it for . . .'

'For me?' Emma whispered.

'Yes. For you, Emma. If I prove to you that I'm not just in this for myself, if I show the world that our programme has substance, that it's not just a tawdry showbiz money-making machine which is all about phone-line revenues, if I turn the Prince of Wales into the nation's Chart Throb . . .'

'Yes?'

'If I do that, will you sleep with me?'

'Yes.'

Shetland Mist Prepare to Rock Dundee

For a pub that was licensed to provide entertainment for as many as two hundred and fifty punters they really should have put in a dressing room.

'The *toilets*!' Iona exclaimed in disgust to the enormous ginger-haired man who had greeted them in the car park. 'You want us to change in the toilets?'

'I don't care where you fockin' change, darlin', but it's the toilet or on stage which I'm sure would make a lot of fellahs very happy but we don't have a licence for the lewd stuff.'

'But it's the *public* toilets,' Mary, the bass player, protested. 'We can't change in front of the fans!'

The big man just smiled at that. The girls had of course put on their stage gear in the toilets many times in their careers but usually there was at least a staff toilet in which to do it. There was something considerably more demeaning about having to don their little glittery hotpants and boob tubes in front of the crowd before whom they would shortly be appearing.

'It'll take away all our mystery,' Mary lamented.

'Come on,' said Iona. 'Let's do it now before the pub fills up. We certainly won't be bothering with the second cossies so leave them in the van, Billy.'

Billy, Shetland Mist's roadie and sound mixer, had been in the process of pulling the 'second half' trunk from the van. Now he nodded and returned it.

'But if there's no back-stage area, where are we to wait once we've got our gear on?' asked Fleur, the keyboard player. 'I can't sit at the bar with my tummy out, it's bad enough having it out on stage.'

'You have a coat, don't you?' Douglas, the fiddle player, replied.

'No. I thought we'd have a dressing room. It's all very well for you and Jamie. You boys don't even bother to change.'

The girls trooped into the barn of a pub and made their way to the ladies, leaving Billy and the boys to set up the gear on the stacked rostrum which had been erected as a stage.

There was at least a mirror and the floor was moderately clean but it was nonetheless a depressing way to begin an evening's work.

'Let's ring our manager,' said Mary. This comment was greeted with hollow laughs, for their manager was none other than the elusive Rodney Root.

'He doesn't even bother phoning back any more, the bastard,' Iona reflected bitterly. 'I'm off to get a chair to stand on while I take my jeans off, I don't want them touching this floor.'

Iona returned to the main room, where Billy called out from the stage.

'You girls had best keep your trainers on!' he said. 'This stage is just boxes, like a kettle drum. With heels you'll sound like a herd of elephants every time you move.'

Iona nodded. They were used to this. Solid stages were something of a luxury and often the girls were forced to perform in trainers, which looked pretty good with the hotpants but terrible with the gowns. Iona was glad they would not be bothering with the long dresses that evening.

She gathered up a wooden stool from beside one of the tables and headed back into the toilet. Fleur had commandeered the mirror. She always claimed most mirror time because, at nearly forty, she said she needed the most make-up.

'I don't know, Iona,' Fleur said, blowing on her mascara and rubbing it between her hands in an effort to warm it up. 'I'm beginning to think it's time you shopped that bastard to the *News of the World*. Once the show comes back on, I bet you could get a packet for the inside story of how he wooed you, promised to wed you then weed all over you.'

'For the final time, Fleur, it's one thing being made a fool of, it's another telling everyone about it.'

Fleur simply sighed. The girls had spoken many times of how they might avenge themselves on Rodney Root for the way he had promised so much and delivered so little. But Iona refused to buy into it.

'I'm not making myself the tragic victim. I was a grown-up girl and I thought I loved him and I thought he loved me. That's all. What would talking to the papers make me look like? All the *Chart Throb* fans hate us anyway after the last series, when everyone booed us. I'd just look like a sad tart.'

'Oh well. No sense crying about it, eh?' Fleur said,

finally managing to get some movement into her congealed make-up. 'We'll earn three hundred tonight and we've two gigs at the weekend so things could be a sight worse.'

Of course three hundred pounds did not go very far between five band members and a roadie, particularly once travel and dry cleaning and other expenses had been deducted. It was certainly a long way from the dreams of wealth and stardom that they had all indulged in the previous year when embarking on their *Chart Throb* journey. They all had real jobs now but they still loved the music.

'We don't do so badly, do we, girls?' said Mary cheerfully. 'And the pub's providing supper, so get your pants on, Iona, and go and grab some menus. Be sure to bat your eyelids and lean well forward over the bar. If you don't come back with a round of free rum and Cokes you're a disgrace to Scottish rock chicks!'

Just then Iona's mobile phone rang. At that point she was standing on the bar stool with one leg out of her jeans.

'Oh shit. Who's that?' she said, crouching down and trying to pull the phone from her scrunched-up pocket.

By the time she retrieved it she had missed the call and she didn't recognize the number.

Moments later her message service rang.

'Hi, Iona. You don't know me, my name's Chelsie. I'm on *Chart Throb*. Calvin asked me to call . . .'

The Meeting Fails to Start

It was the day before full-scale recording on the new series of *Chart Throb* was to begin. On the morrow the three celebrity judges would 'start' the lengthy process of scouring the country in their obsessive and highly motivated personal quests to discover new talent. The days would be long and draining, and meticulous forward planning was essential. Therefore the entire team had foregathered in the spacious morning room of the summer house at Copton Thorpe Manor, a country house hotel that nestled cosily in a long loop of the M4 motorway some miles north of Newbury. Calvin would brief them fully on how he saw the various storylines developing in the early stages of the 'audition' process. There was an enormous amount to get through and everybody was anxious to be off. Unfortunately the meeting had stalled before it could begin, due to the continuing absence of one of the famous judges.

What was even more frustrating was that it wasn't one of the important ones. It was the one whom nobody gave a shit about.

'Where the fuck is Rodney?' Beryl rasped angrily from a corner of the room. She was still suffering somewhat from further massive treatments of liposuction which she had endured as final preparation for her forthcoming TV appearances, and so, despite the old-fashioned soft furnishings in which Copton Thorpe Manor took such pride, she declined to sit.

'I *said* where the FUCK is Rodney?' she repeated, brutally flexing the muscles of her celebrity by swearing loudly in such ostentatiously genteel surroundings. The prim duty manageress and her smartly dressed staff might redden and purse their lips at such an uncouth display, but Beryl had not got to where she was today by playing by other people's rules. On the contrary, as she was wont to tell people, she was one strong woman (who used to be a man) and she made her own fucking rules and if people didn't like it they could go fuck themselves.

205

'I spoke to him earlier,' Calvin replied soothingly. 'He said he'd be here.' He turned towards a comely production assistant. 'You did tell him we're in the morning room, didn't you, babes?'

The girl's name was Gretel but she was 'babes' to Calvin. Everyone was a 'babe' or a 'darling' or a 'mate' to him. He employed so many people in so many countries that he could not possibly remember anybody's name and had long since given up trying. In fact he had already fallen completely in love with Emma before he knew her name.

'I texted, e'd and slid hard copy under his door, Calvin,' Gretel replied, almost snapping to attention and saluting. She knew that Calvin valued nothing more highly than efficiency. He liked his girls to look and talk like hip, self-assertive, independent young troubleshooters but he liked them to do what they were told.

'What the fuck *is* a morning room anyway?' Beryl enquired, massaging her ass. 'What happens to it in the afternoon? Does it disappear into another fucking dimension?'

'It's a room built and windowed in order to favour the morning sun, dear,' Calvin informed her.

'There! You see why I hate England!' Beryl almost spat. 'They have to build special rooms to make the most of the five minutes of watery piss-poor sunlight that shines on this shithole. In LA we can't get away from the stuff. We build rooms to *avoid* the fucking sun.'

There being no reply to this, nobody attempted one and a silence fell. An uncomfortable silence as it was a very crowded room.

'Where the *fuck* is Rodney?' Beryl asked once more. '*We* came from LA, Calvin. *He* only has to buzz in from London. Stupid twat.'

Rodney Is Not Happy

Rodney was at that moment standing at the hotel reception desk and he was most unhappy.

'So you're saying you have two suites?'

'Yes, sir. The Brunel and the Glenfiddich.'

'Two suites?'

'Yes, sir.'

'And I'm in neither of them?'

'No, sir. You have an executive room.'

'An executive room?'

'Yes, sir, with a view of the artificial lake.'

'Oh well, *that's all right then*,' Rodney spluttered, the icy calm which he had been struggling to maintain utterly deserting him in the face of this damning affront to his status. 'As long as I've got a view of the *artificial lake*.'

Rodney did not need to enquire who was occupying the Brunel and the Glenfiddich suites, he knew the answer as certainly as if he'd made the bookings himself. Beryl Blenheim and Calvin Simms. Of course they would be in the two available suites while he was in an executive room with a view of the lake.

A thought struck him.

'Do the Brunel and Glenfiddich have views of the artificial lake?' he asked, clutching at what in his heart of hearts he knew to be the thinnest of straws.

'Yes, sir, of course.'

'In which case *my* view of it can scarcely be considered a bonus, can it?'

'I don't understand, sir.'

'No, I don't suppose you do. Anyway it doesn't matter,' he said with the same weary sadness which Hamlet might have shown when considering the possibility that his uncle had murdered his father and was shagging his mother. 'Where is the morning room?'

The receptionist explained that the morning room was in the summer house, which was situated in the middle of the golf course.

'It's a buggy ride, sir,' she continued. 'You can drive yourself, which is great fun, or some of our guests prefer to be driven by a qualified member of our hospitality team.'

'A buggy?'

'Yes, a golf buggy. Great fun. Although helmets must be worn.'

'Do you know who I am?'

'Yes, sir. You're Rodney Root.'

'Do you imagine that Rodney Root attends meetings in golf buggies?'

'Well, uhm . . . you could walk, sir. It's about a fifteen-minute stroll. Some of our guests prefer that . . .'

'You think that I *walk* to my meetings, is that it?'

'Well, I . . .'

Rodney banged his hand down on the reception desk in a manner which he imagined appeared commanding and decisive. There had clearly been a *major* cock-up and it was time he took control.

'Is there access by road?'

'By road, sir?'

'Yes, miss, by road. We are all speaking English, aren't we? I presume this summer house is regularly maintained and supplied. I don't imagine all that is done by golf buggy.'

'No, sir. There is road access but it means rejoining the A34 heading north, coming off at the next exit and doubling back. It takes rather longer than . . .'

But Rodney was already heading for the front door, beyond which he knew that the leather-lined comfort and appropriate status of his chauffeur-driven Mercedes was waiting.

Getting On with It

In the morning room Calvin had decided he would have to start.

Beryl was making his skin crawl and it was only the first day. The woman was an obnoxious bully at the best of times and her enormous success in the previous series (which Calvin himself had so carefully engineered) had gone horribly to her head. He had created a monster, a nightmare ego, and the brutalized buttocks and half-finished clitoris were doing nothing to improve her people skills.

Besides which, the atmosphere was becoming oppressive. The great crowd of production staff who had been bussed in from the unit base at the Newbury Ramada had already been sitting about for nearly three quarters of an hour. The coffee had been consumed, the pastries nibbled and the jolly greetings with which the room had earlier buzzed had long since fallen silent. Calvin was captain of a ship becalmed, and although his was a pretty docile crew every minute that ticked by put another tiny dent in his authority. If there was one thing that Calvin liked to be it was decisive, and there was nothing less decisive than hanging around. Everyone was waiting for him and he was waiting for *Rodney*. That was simply outrageous.

And he had been in such a sunny mood at breakfast. He had talked on the phone to Emma for nearly twenty minutes and loved every moment of it.

There could be no doubt now that Emma was his girlfriend.

Certainly she had continued to decline his invitations to return to work but they had seen each other or at least spoken every day since the morning coffee summit. He still needed to win her trust so that she would have sex with him but in the meantime, just as she had previously blurred his vision so frustratingly, she was now having the opposite effect. He was *focused on his goal.* Calvin was going through what was for him the almost entirely novel experience of 'the early stages of a relationship'. Not since his dim and distant youth had he known such a process of personal discovery and deferred gratification. He had always enjoyed both sex and the company of women, but all his adult life he had experienced them only on *his* terms. He had associated with women who were interested in what he had to offer them and who were therefore happy to play entirely by his rules. Emma's refusal to do the same was a new and curiously exhilarating sensation for him, reminding him of the innocence of youth.

It actually made him feel younger.

So far he had only kissed her. *How weird was that?* Usually he had scarcely even kissed them before they were having sex and now he had only kissed her. He had not even pawed her body, he had hardly *seen* any of it. He was planning seaside trips just to get her into a bathing costume. *Weird.* And for the most powerful man in TV, who was accustomed to getting whatever he wanted whenever he wanted it. Very weird. But also fun; strange, exhilarating, utterly unfamiliar fun.

Standing at the head of that crowded meeting room he wanted to talk to her some more. He would have liked to phone her right there and then. But he knew that she was busy in her new job, writing an article about the fledgling café society in East Finchley. And he had an incredibly busy day ahead of him, a day which he could not even begin because he was *waiting for Rodney.*

'All right, let's get started,' he said decisively. 'Rodney can catch up later.'

'I doubt he's caught up on the last fucking series yet,' said Beryl.

Calvin turned to Trent. 'Get on with it.'

Once more Trent took up his favourite position in front of the audiovisual displays.

'Right. So, as you know, team, tomorrow we kick off in Birmingham. We'll be seeing six of our proposed finalists, although two of them, Latiffa, our black girl with attitude, and Bloke, the boring old party band, will be cut into the Manchester show, so, for God's sake, Continuity, can you *please* be careful with Beryl's jackets.'

'We have Beryl in the beige Versace for Manchester day one,' said the head of costume, referring to one of the enormous files which lay before her. 'And the silver sheen Lacroix for Birmingham. Is that right, Penny?'

Sitting nearby was Penny, the continuity girl and hardest-working person in the room after Calvin. She too was surrounded by enormous files.

'Yes, Versace Manchester and Lacroix Birmingham,' Penny agreed.

'Well, I hope you've done a proper deal this time so I get to keep the frocks,' Beryl grumbled from the doorway, reaching for her cigarettes and her phone. 'I'm fucked if I'm showcasing their rags for nothing.'

'So,' said Trent with forced good cheer, 'moving on. We are also recording thirty-seven comic novelties tomorrow.'

'Thirty-seven!! From one town?' Beryl moaned. 'You can't possibly use thirty-seven!'

'Yes, darling,' Calvin chipped in with scarcely disguised impatience. 'But as I have often explained to you before, you can't accumulate if you don't speculate. In order to get a handful of decent comic novelties we have to shoot a shedload and see what works. People clam up, people won't play ball, more often than that people turn out to be utterly boring and neither comic nor novel. This is why we must spread

211

our net wide or we will be left naked in the edit. We *could* do it over two days if you wanted but then, darling, you would have to stay here for a whole twenty-four more hours, something that I know you are not anxious to do.'

'Too fucking right I'm not.'

'In which case, perhaps we can proceed. Trent?'

'Right. We start with Juanita. She's Spanish and has a really funny accent.'

'Oh, my fucking Christ!' Beryl snapped. 'A funny *accent*, is that what we're reduced to?'

'Worked well last year with the amusing Swede,' Trent said soothingly. 'And I think this one might work even better. She's quite pretty and has a nice innocent face with a kind of a blank look about it. So the plan is to get her to sing something very sweet and plaintive like "Feelings" or "Yesterday" and you guys keep cracking up because her accent sounds really funny set against the deep, emotional lyric, but poor Juanita just looks around blankly because she has no idea what you're all laughing at.'

'Oh Christ,' said Beryl.

'And it just gets sillier and sillier because when one of you manages to stop laughing another one starts up and of course that starts the first one off again, and in the end you all really, really, *really* pull yourselves together to give the poor girl a chance but she does like one word, and bang! You're all off again. It will be *so, so* funny. You guys are just *brilliant* at this stuff.'

'I think I just lost the will to live,' said Beryl.

'Good. Loving Juanita,' said Calvin, ignoring Beryl's negativity. 'Next.'

'Katarina,' Trent replied. 'Sweet, pretty. Very amusing Ukrainian accent.'

'Please!' shouted Beryl. '*Another* girl with an amusing accent!'

Calvin was beginning to lose patience. 'Yes.

212

We've got three, we'll do them one after another.'

'Three girls with amusing accents!'

'Beryl! How long have you been doing this show? We won't *use* all fucking three.'

'Unless we do an amusing accent *montage*,' Trent chipped in.

'Yes,' Calvin conceded. 'Unless we do an amusing accent montage. But we'll probably only use the funniest one . . .'

'Gotta be Juanita,' said Trent. 'She seems to have almost no ability to pronounce consonants at all.'

'Whatever. The point is, Beryl, that by shooting three girls we have three chances at getting you and Rodney to fake a vaguely convincing hysterical laugh and even though we only use one girl we can use shots of us laughing at all three and edit together the best bits.'

'Sorry, Calvin,' Penny, the continuity girl, piped up. 'I thought we'd decided that we'd definitely go with a funny accent montage. I have Beryl down for three different jackets for the three funny-voice girls.'

'Yes, that's right,' Costume agreed and once more vast binders were opened up containing notes, drawings, catalogues and swatches of fabric. 'One Beryl cossie for each girl with an amusing accent so we can place them in different towns. Also you and Rodney get green Irish rugby shirts because we have our "virtual" Dublin visit scheduled for St Patrick's Day.'

'Shit, you're right,' Calvin conceded. 'Well done, girls.'

The Irish audition day was dubbed a 'virtual' because the tightness of schedule meant that the three judges would not actually be visiting Dublin, so their 'audition day' there would have to be faked. This would be done by cutting together footage taken when Trent and Emma and the team had done their pre-selection in the city, coupled with shots of the judges

213

taken in Birmingham but with Irish set-dressing. This of course presented a continuity nightmare for Costume, Hair and Make-up, and on this occasion also Props because the St Patrick's Day complication meant that the prop man would have to slip a leprechaun gonk on to the table.

'Either way, Beryl, you have to be there,' said Calvin. 'Now can we please get on? Trent. Skip the other girl with the amusing accent, I think we all understand the process.'

'You got it, chief. Right, so after that we get through as many In and Outs as we can before coffee and then—'

'Ugh,' said Beryl. 'You really don't pay me enough, Calvin.'

Beryl hated the In and Outs. These were the hundred or so people summoned to each of the celebrity judge audition days, who could sing a bit but were neither bad enough nor good enough to be assigned their own character or story. They were there to fill out the holding area (so it wasn't just Mingers and finalists) and to make up the montages of people shrieking 'yes' as they were put through to the second and third rounds, after which point it became possible to concentrate exclusively on the selected characters and stories.

'Do you *really* need me for the In and Outs?' Beryl pleaded.

'Of course we do, for God's sake!' Calvin snapped. 'We can't just have you patronizing the Mingers and flirting with the finalists, can we? I'll admit it is absolutely amazing the extent to which our audience is prepared to suspend its disbelief but there are limits, Beryl! We can't just take the piss. Obviously we need to see the three of us interacting with contestants other than our chosen storylines.'

Beryl shrugged moodily. There were not many

people in the world whom she would countenance ticking her off, but Calvin was one of them. Really it was just him and the man who sucked out her bottom.

'Right,' said Calvin. 'Please carry on, Trent.'

'Well, straight after the first break we set up a Beryl feature with Rodney.'

'Who is not here so we'll have to explain it all again to him.'

'We have to explain everything to him three times whether he's here or not,' said Beryl.

'Trent. Get on with it.'

Trent touched his keyboard and there appeared on the screen a buck-toothed teenage girl and a buck-toothed woman in early middle age who was clearly her mother.

'Vicky Carter and her mum,' said Trent. 'Let's hear from the mum first, shall we?'

Trent pushed the button and on the screen Vicky's mum began to speak.

'She's just mad for it. She really is, I can't hold her back. Always singing, all the show songs. There was never any question of her not going to stage school. Madam here was going to stage school and that was the end of it. "Mum," she said, "I am going to stage school," and that was the end of it! Judy Garland's her hero, and Céline Dion.'

Trent pressed Pause. 'And now the daughter.'

'Mum never pushed me,' Vicky said, leaping into life on the screen. 'She just told me to follow my dream and believe in my dream and that not everyone is lucky enough to have a dream and that you have to have the courage to dream the dream.'

The room watched in some awe as pale, shapeless, buck-toothed Vicky Carter proceeded to murder 'Over The Rainbow', somehow managing to be a semitone flat on every single note except for the last one in each line, when inexplicably she went sharp.

'Wow!' Beryl said. 'She is really quite awesomely pathetic.'

'Isn't she?' said Trent proudly. 'But really quite awesomely convinced that she can sing.'

'How do they *do* that? It's like their ears are on a different planet to their voices!'

'And, of course, we will big her up as she goes in,' said Trent.

'Yes,' Chelsie interjected, having been itching for a chance to jump in since the meeting began. 'I told her mum I thought she was brilliant and that the judges would love her. I said I reckoned she'd make it through to Pop School at least.'

'Yes, thank you, Chelsie,' said Trent impatiently. 'So obviously when you all laugh at her and reject her out of hand she's going to be devastated, and the plan is that Rodney then goes a bit far. You know, makes some smart alec comment . . .'

'Trent!' Calvin snapped. '*What* smart alec comment? This is final planning. We make these decisions *now*!'

'Well, we have it scripted, boss, but I thought we'd let him have a go first. You know he's always talking about his own personal input.'

'Yes, fine. And once he's had his go, what's he actually going to say?'

'We thought, "That was so awful it took my mind off my haemorrhoids,"' said Chelsie quickly.

'Not bad. Not bad. Don't give it to him until we do his close-ups or he'll overrehearse it.'

'I thought this was one of *my* features,' Beryl complained.

'It is,' Trent replied eagerly. 'Because when . . .' He glanced at his notes.

'Vicky,' Chelsie managed to say before he could find the name.

'Yes. Vicky starts to cry . . .'

'She'll do more than cry,' Chelsie added. 'She'll

protest, she's a right cocky little madam, the mum's brainwashed her. She truly believes.'

'Right, so when Vicky cries and protests,' continued Trent, trying not to look too annoyed at his pushy subordinate, 'you, Beryl, leap to her defence, right? We can see you know she's crap but she's brought out your mothering instincts . . .'

'This is good,' said Beryl, pleased. 'You know I want a lot of that this time, Calvin. Lots and lots of "everybody's favourite mum" stuff from Keely, it's one of my strongest features. Half my advertising revenue comes from it.'

'We're on it, Beryl,' said Trent. 'What's Keely's voiceover script here?'

A young man, one of seven scriptwriters present, spoke up from the back of the room.

' "Meanwhile it looks like Rodney has gone too far," ' the writer quoted, ' "and big-hearted supermum Beryl has gone all clucky over Vicky." '

'Good. Excellent,' said Beryl, beaming. 'Loving "big-hearted supermum", more of that, please. Maybe I should have some mugs made up?'

'Glad you like it, Beryl,' said Trent, beaming also. 'So you tell Rodney to stop and he won't, he repeats his haemorrhoids gag and you go and hug Vicky and tell her that she has every right to follow her dream if she wants and Rodney laughs and—'

'I throw the water over him!'

'Yes!' said Trent. 'You throw the water over him.'

'Love it!' said Beryl. 'I'm going out for a fag.'

Sat Nav

Rodney had returned to reception.

'I need the postcode.'

'Pardon, sir?'

'The postcode for the summer house. My driver has to key it into his sat nav.'

'I can give you directions, sir.'

'I don't need your directions, miss, that's why we have sat nav, to eliminate human error.'

'They're very simple.'

'Exactly. Unlike the sat nav in my Merc, which is rather complex and sophisticated and uses the same software as the American military. Could you get a missile through a window in Baghdad?'

'No, sir.'

'Well, the US military can and my sat nav has access to the same satellite information as they have. Not simple. Not human. Incapable of errors. Please give me the postcode immediately.'

'I'll just get you a letterhead, sir.'

The receptionist followed Rodney out into the car park and handed Rodney's driver a comp slip with the information printed on it.

'I don't *believe* this,' Rodney commented.

He was then forced to wait while his driver keyed the postcode into the dashboard computer of the car.

'Route being calculated,' the sat nav voice assured Rodney, and his driver steered the car out of the manor's imposing gates and on to the A34.

'Where possible make a legal U-turn,' the voice added shortly afterwards.

That section of the road was a dual carriageway, so it was not possible to turn immediately. The driver was forced to continue for some miles up the road before the next exit provided an opportunity to turn back.

'Continue on to the next exit,' said the voice.

Rodney tutted impatiently as he watched the hotel pass by on the other side of the carriageway.

'At the next roundabout,' said the sat nav, 'take the third exit.'

'Bollocks!' said the driver as he turned back down the dual carriageway once more.

'Exit left at the slip road. You have arrived at your destination.'

And the driver drove back through the gates of the hotel.

When they had once more arrived, Rodney tore open the door and strode back into reception.

'Miss. Is the postcode for the summer house the same as the one for the hotel itself?' he enquired angrily.

'Yes, sir,' the receptionist replied. 'It's a part of the hotel. It doesn't have its own postal address.'

Rodney knew when he was beaten.

'Where are the fucking golf buggies?'

Summit in the Vestibule

Beryl was smoking in the summer house vestibule when Rodney arrived, hurrying red-faced through the front door.

'Morning, Rodney,' she said. 'Nice of you to join us. Are you late for this series or early for the next one?'

Rodney and Beryl, 'genuinely great mates' according to the *Chart Throb* website, had not laid eyes on each other for nine months and neither of them showed any signs of regretting a moment of their separation.

'Did you arrive here by buggy?' Rodney enquired.

'Rodney, I don't do walking.'

'Yes, but did you come here by golf buggy?'

'No, I got Captain Picard to transport me via the *Enterprise*. Of course I came here by buggy, this place is in the middle of a golf course.'

Rodney relaxed ever so slightly. This assurance that

the indignity of being driven to a highly important meeting in what was little better than an electric shoebox had been visited upon his colleagues as well as him went some way to soothing his offended soul.

'Quite a good service, I thought,' Beryl continued. 'They picked me up at my front door.'

'At your front door?' Dark clouds of suspicion gathered once more in the raw and tender wound that was Rodney Root's ego. 'They drove the buggy along a hotel corridor?'

'No, of course they didn't, you fucking ass. I'm in a chalet.'

It was a hammer blow.

'I thought you were in a suite?'

'I am, the suite is a chalet. Suite? Chalet? So what! Why are we having this fucking conversation?'

'A *detached* chalet?'

'*Yes*, a detached chalet. There's two of them down by the lake.'

'Is Calvin in the other one?'

'I don't fucking know. I suppose so. I think I could hear him on the phone when I was having breakfast on my upstairs balcony.'

'*Upstairs balcony!* Your chalet has *two storeys*?'

'Yes.'

'*And a balcony?*'

'Look, Rodney, I am not going to spend the rest of my life discussing my accommodation with—'

'I'm in a room.'

Rodney was so agitated he could hardly continue. There was a pause, and despite her obvious lack of interest in anything that Rodney might have to say, Beryl finally felt obliged to speak.

'And?' she queried impatiently.

'It is an executive room but it's still a room.'

'Rodney, please. Why would I give a fuck?'

Rodney might have explained that the whole

premise of the *Chart Throb* judging panel was that the three of them were equals. He might have pointed out that he in fact had a contractual guarantee to absolute parity on travel, perks, catering and accommodation. He might have mentioned that he was fed up with being treated like a second-class judge and that they would one day push him too far. But he said none of these things because at that point Beryl's phone rang.

She did not spare Rodney so much as a cursory nod of apology as, curtailing their conversation, she popped open the little diamond-encrusted handset and turned away, leaving him to hover aimlessly for a second or two before slinking into the morning room to join the conference.

'Mom, you fucking bitch!' said Priscilla so loudly into Beryl's phone that the retreating Rodney heard it. 'Did you really invite Helmut to my party?'

'Hello, darling, how is everything? Settling into London, not too jet-lagged?'

'Did you invite Helmut to my fucking party?'

'Helmut's *gorgeous*, darling. He's a babe.'

'My *eighteenth*, Mom! It's like fuck, does *everything* have to be a photo op with you?'

'I like Helmut.'

'He's trash and so are you! You are *not* inviting Helmut the Helmet to my birthday party!'

Helmut had been a finalist in the previous year's series of *Chart Throb*, during which he and Beryl had conducted a famously flirtatious relationship. Helmut had been previously employed as a male stripper, a heroically well-endowed male stripper according to the papers (a piece of information originally leaked by the *Chart Throb* press office). It was hinted that not only was Helmut's penis huge but that it was top heavy, like a sledgehammer, hence his nickname, Helmut the Helmet. Helmut had not won the competition but to Calvin's beautifully acted 'surprise' and 'horror' he had come very close. He had gone on to score a novelty hit covering Peter Gabriel's song 'Sledgehammer' and now presented a cable holiday game show called *Bikini Beach*. Helmut was certainly the only member of the previous year's final twelve who still had a contract pertaining to any area of show business.

'Are you balling him, Mom?' Priscilla asked.

'Don't be disgusting. You're talking to your step-mother! Of course I'm not balling him. Apart from anything else, my vagina isn't finished yet. He's cute, that's all, and he's buff. I like a man with muscles.'

'You are *so gross*. He's like twenty-five and you're like one hundred and I do not want that German fucking sleazoid human penis loser at our party.'

'Well, he's coming. I have a profile to maintain and me and Helmut will make a very sexy photo.'

'*Mom!* This is my fucking party! Mine and Lisa Ma-fucking-rie's.'

'And *I* am your fucking stepmother! And *you* will do what you are fucking told!'

Rodney Joins the Meeting

Rodney had intended that his would be a grand entrance.

Arriving late is not necessarily a bad thing, particularly if you are a senior member of the team and in a position to make your own rules. Everyone would be there, Calvin would no doubt have begun the meeting and all eyes would be on him but he would have to stop when Rodney walked in. Not to admonish him as he would a tardy employee, but to greet him as he must an equal, a *fellow member* of the judging panel.

Calvin would be obliged to welcome him back, introduce him to those new members of the team who did
not know him from the previous series (know him
personally that is, for of course *everybody* knew
Rodney Root as a celebrity). Pretty PAs would offer
him coffee, comely researchers would leap from their
seats in order that he might be given his rightful
position at the centre of the action.

The arrival of Rodney Root on the first day of a new
series of *Chart Throb* was undeniably an *event* and
Calvin would feel obliged to treat it as such.

And indeed he would have done had Calvin been
his usual self. Normally Calvin was happy to take
some small care with Rodney's delicate ego. Not to the
extent of letting him have the best room when only
two were available, of course, but within limits he
tried not to be rude. It did not take much to make
Rodney happy: a curt instruction that Rodney should
be brought coffee, a kindly enquiry as to whether
Rodney would like biscuits and was he satisfied with
his wardrobe selection? These small courtesies Calvin
was happy to show. Most of the time, that is, but not
today. Today Calvin simply pressed on, and since the
king was still holding court no courtier was going to
take their eyes or ears off him for a moment. Certainly
not for Rodney. Rodney might have been a celebrity
judge but no one was under any illusions as to which
end of the panel he hailed from. Nobody moved.
Nobody offered him a coffee, let alone a seat. Nobody
mentioned biscuits. How could they? Calvin was
speaking and that was something no employee of
CALonic TV could afford to ignore. Rodney was forced
to hover by the doorway and wait. The room was too
crowded for him to find a place with any dignity, not
unless people were prepared to take notice of him and
move, which they were not. Every seat was filled,
every arm of every sofa and easy chair had a pert

youthful bottom perched upon it. The edges of the coffee table were likewise occupied and one or two of the youngest and cutest of the girls were even sitting on the floor. Rodney was trapped at the doorway and Calvin had not even said hello. He had nodded, that was all, nodded mid-flow and pressed right on, and there was nothing Rodney could do.

Calvin wanted to get through the pre-coffee-break agenda as quickly as possible so that he could ring Emma. He wanted to find out how she was, what she was doing, what she was thinking. It had, after all, been nearly two hours since their breakfast conversation. There would be so much to talk about, so much that was new and different about her to discuss and to discover. Calvin was therefore pressing ahead. He did not want to have to cancel the morning coffee break or squeeze the lunch hour as he would normally do when he was behind. Normally he hated coffee breaks and he particularly hated lunch hours. Who took an hour for lunch? He personally would be happy to eat a sandwich on the run and take no break at all, but the fucking unions had their rules. Today was different though. Today Calvin was anxious to preserve every precious second of leisure time available to him. Because he wanted to ring Emma.

'Right!' Calvin continued, forcing himself to focus. 'I have scheduling issues here, Trent.'

'Issues, boss?'

'Yes, recapping. We kick off the auditions with the three funny-accent girls, right?'

'Check, chief, although we'll have taken some arrival shots and some moodies prior to that. You know how you wanted to get the three of you walking in all in black ready for a shoot-out, like in a spaghetti western?'

'Yes, yes, yes. But we're talking about the auditions here. We start with the three foreign birds, then

224

we hoover up In and Outs till the first break.'

'Yes, hoping to get through twenty-five or so, and we can pick up more in a separate room from you guys for drop-ins.'

'Then after the break you wanted to kick off with the appalling sixteen-year-old who Rodney disses and Beryl mothers? Right?'

Standing at the door, Rodney grabbed the moment to make his presence felt.

'I like that, Calvin. That's good. Rodney disses the kid, that's great. So you've really been working on my suggestion for a meaner me?'

Calvin scarcely turned towards him.

'Hi, Rodney. Yeah. We love you mean. So . . .' He turned back to Trent. 'Obviously we're going to want to set up a hospitality-room confrontation over this one. Usual stuff, me inspecting the sandwiches while Beryl threatens to walk out and Rodney sulks, right?'

'Of course. We love all that, boss.'

'Plus Rodney's going to be covered in coffee, which brings in hair and make-up issues . . .'

'Plus sound,' said a representative of the sound department. 'We'll need to get his tie mike off him before Beryl chucks the coffee.'

'Excuse me,' Rodney interjected, looking suddenly concerned.

'So that's my scheduling issues right there,' Calvin pressed on.

'Excuse me,' Rodney tried again and was once again ignored.

'Surely we should set this one up *before* the first break so that we can go straight into hospitality and shoot the quarrel over the sandwiches with Rodney already soaking wet?'

'Excuse me . . .' said Rodney.

'That way the crew can take their break without us having to move twice and Rodney can dry out then rather than having to bring in Hair and Make-up for ten minutes of faffing about while we're trying to shoot, plus of course putting his mike back on.'

'Excuse me . . .'

'In a MINUTE, Rodney!' Calvin snapped before turning back to Trent. 'Surely that's got to be the time-effective solution?'

'Well, I suppose it's an option, boss . . . I was thinking of shooting the audition and Rodney's dissing the little Minger straight *after* the break, then holding the story at that point, hoovering up the rest of the morning's Minger quickies, then picking up the second half of the Rodney and Beryl row plus the coffee-throwing just before lunch, then we can move the crew into Hospitality with Rodney dripping wet and shoot the catering confrontation at the top of the break. That gives Rodney plenty of time to dry out over lunch and we can start the afternoon with a couple more comedy calls to Rodney on his mobile because we really need to be getting that story moving . . .'

'Trent?' Penny, the continuity girl, chipped in. 'I'm really unhappy about split stories. I make this point at *every* debrief, split stories are a continuity nightmare.'

'Hear, hear,' said Costume.

'Seconded,' said Make-up.

'Thirded with knobs on,' said Hair.

'Anything can happen,' Penny continued, warming to a topic on which she could speak without pause for hours. 'Remember last year when Rodney got stung on the nose by that wasp when we had just shot the first half of the cute toddler story?'

'Excuse me . . .' said Rodney.

'It was a continuity *nightmare*! One minute he's fine, then what was supposed to be two seconds later he's got a nose the size of an apple. It looked like his nose swelled up *mid-sentence*.'

226

'We did our best,' said Make-up.

'So did we,' said Lighting.

'Never mind his nose,' said Costume. 'What about the Frappuccino he spilt all over his shirt when the wasp stung him? *And* I had him in darks that day. More fool me.'

'Excuse me,' said Rodney.

'Just a MINUTE, Rodney,' Calvin snapped. 'People! We need to focus here. No sense in fighting old battles. We begin recording *tomorrow*! Now, let us proceed towards a decision here. What costume is Rodney wearing immediately pre-lunch?'

Once more massive files were opened and consulted by all relevant departments.

'Well, currently we've scheduled to go to virtual Dublin at the end of the Minger quickies so that we can knock off the Irish Mingers along with the UK ones, which means he'll have changed into his St Paddy's Day rugby shirt. Therefore if we were then to pick up the second half of his row with Beryl we'd have to change him back.'

'Plus,' said Props, 'we'll have to move the leprechaun gonk and lose the shamrock.'

'You see,' said Calvin, 'it just doesn't make sense to split the story.'

'Could we shift the Paddy Mingers to after lunch?' Trent enquired. 'And not go to virtual Dublin till then?'

But the production secretary had admin issues with that.

'They've all done their travel arrangements. The last cheap flight back leaves at two thirty. We'd have to put them up and there's nothing left in the budget for overnights.'

Calvin turned to Trent with a shrug. 'Gotta tell you, Trent, I don't think splitting the story and doing the second half pre-lunch is a goer . . .'

'Excuse me, Calvin?' said Rodney.

'YES, RODNEY! What is it?'

'Did you say . . . Beryl throws the coffee over me?'

'I *think* that's what we've been discussing for the past ten minutes. Yes.'

'I thought we'd agreed.'

'Agreed what?'

'That we wouldn't be bothering with all that this year.'

'All what?'

'The throwing water over Rodney stuff. I thought we'd agreed that the joke's got tired.'

'That's right. We agreed. Throwing water, very tired. So *X Factor*, so *Pop Idol*. Sharon Osbourne, Louis Walsh, they did that. Throwing water is *so* five minutes ago.'

'Exactly, and—' Rodney tried to intervene.

'Which is why we've decided that Beryl should throw coffee.'

'You really think that makes a difference?'

'Oh, absolutely. On *Chart Throb* coffee is the new water. I'm glad you brought it up, Rodders.'

'Oh . . . right. Happy to help.'

There was a moment's silence before Calvin turned back to the group.

'So. It's agreed then, Beryl throws the coffee over Rodney just before the morning break.'

Virtual Carnegie Hall and Other Dreams

Late that afternoon, as Calvin and his team were struggling through the tenth hour of their exhausting pre-production day, one of the subjects of their debate was checking into the Birmingham Holiday Inn.

Most of the selected contestants would be travelling to their 'auditions' early the following morning, but Shaiana lived a long way away and so she had decided to come up the day before and take a room.

After consuming an undressed salad and a Diet Coke from room service, she ate all the chocolate in the minibar and washed down a final upper with the little bottle of red wine. She had plenty of stuff to put her to sleep later but for now she wanted to be awake, to mentally prepare, to centre herself.

Sitting on the end of the bed and assuming a lotus position, she closed her eyes and considered the moment. She wondered how she would view it in years to come. Would she look back fondly and remember how the journey towards her destiny had begun right there, meditating alone in a Holiday Inn? Just her, the electric kettle, the trouser press and a heart bursting with dreams. Would she always have a soft spot for Holiday Inns? Would she think them lucky? Her good luck charm? Perhaps in the future, despite having long since been able to afford presidential suites in five-star hotels, she would still insist in staying at Holiday Inn Expresses before her shows. For it was certain that were she to succeed on *Chart Throb* and be recognized as the significant musical artist she so much wanted to be, then no sold-out gig at Carnegie or the Albert Hall could ever compare in importance to the gig she would play on the morrow.

'The first step on the ladder is the longest stretch,' she said quietly to herself. 'Place your foot upon the rung and progress boldly and without fear.'

Then she hummed quietly for a while, enjoying the feeling of the vibrations within her throat. Smiling to herself, she indulged in fantasy.

'For dreams are the harbingers of reality and what is reality if not a dream?'

She fantasized that one day she would be the 'face' of Holiday Inn. Refusing Revlon and Estée Lauder as beneath her talent, she would nonetheless promote Holiday Inns (donating her fee to the UN Children's Fund) because it had been in a Holiday Inn that it had all begun.

Opening her eyes, Shaiana concentrated on her breathing. Then she got off the bed and stood before the mirror, her hairbrush to her lips. She breathed in deeply and belted out 'The Wind Beneath My Wings'.

Somebody banged on the wall but Shaiana didn't hear them. She was at Carnegie Hall.

Dreams were alive all over the Midlands that night as in two hundred different homes unborn stars hovered in limbo waiting for the morning when, with luck and divine justice, they would explode into a sparkling, brilliant light, a light that would warm and illuminate every aspect of their lives and the lives of those they loved.

The four members of The Four-Z were in church with their mothers. Each of them was praying fervently that this would be the last evening in which they would contemplate a future with almost no prospect of salvation from the grim urban nightmare into which they had been born. A future in which they and the majority of their friends were either unemployed or criminals.

Quasar was stripping for a hen night. He didn't mind the work normally but this bunch were rough as dogs' guts. Quasar was thirty-eight (he admitted to thirty-two) and thought he could remember a time when ladies had still been ladies. When he had started out in the business women had not grabbed at his thong with their long nails and then expected him to humiliate

230

himself for the fivers that occasionally they slipped beneath it. Then it had been *cheeky* (or so he told himself), it had been *fun*. Now it was almost entirely sexual, and some of the women were predatory, as if blaming him for the shitty men they'd have to deal with when they got home.

The Quasar, however, liked to look on the bright side and as the women shrieked and dared each other to touch his penis he told them that they were lucky girls because they were touching the love pump of a future star.

Suki would have *loved* to be stripping – she had always infinitely preferred it to prostitution – but she was forty, which was pushing it for an exotic dancer, besides which her boob job was nearly eleven years old and had recently turned into rather a painful mess. They still looked all right when forced into a push-up bra but naked they were scarred and limp, one hung lower than the other and the implants had hardened, pulling at the skin, so there was now a clear resemblance to a ball in a sock. Suki desperately wanted to get a second job done on them but she was not stupid and understood that it would have to be done properly to avoid serious health complications. For that she needed a lot more money than she was likely to earn working the pavement.

As she leaned across the handbrake of her client's car and undid his fly she was thinking, as she always did, of her audition. Pulling out his dick, she imagined for a moment that it was a microphone and even smiled to herself. Suki knew that it was an impossible dream; on the other hand sometimes they *did* let the strangest people through. That was what was so wonderful about the show, it gave anyone a chance. Who knew? Anything was possible. Perhaps one day soon she really would swap those dicks for a microphone.

*

Iona and her bandmates were eating fish and chips and drinking lager in a Tennant's pub in Glasgow. They had travelled down to the city that evening because Iona had an early flight to catch in the morning.

'Budget Air,' said Iona, eyeing the ticket. 'I remember when that little wanker used to talk to me about private jets.'

'Ugh,' said Douglas. 'Sounds disgusting.'

They all laughed.

'I still feel really weird about this,' said Iona. 'It just seems wrong.'

'We've discussed it over and over again,' said Fleur. 'If you do well then it's good for all of us.'

'And if you do badly it can't get much worse,' Mary chipped in.

'But I've never sung alone in my life,' Iona moaned. 'I'll probably end up just singing the harmonies.'

'As if they'd notice anyway,' Douglas sneered. 'Rodney Root and Beryl "rock chick" Blenheim wouldn't know a tune from a harmony if it bashed them over the head and Calvin doesn't care either way. Come on, Iona, we've been through this, we know how it's done. We know what the game is.'

'I know. I *know*,' said Iona nervously.

'Which is why this is so important for us. You have another chance for yourself *and* the band and this time you know a bit more about it. This time you have to play the game.'

'Oh, I'll do that all right,' said Iona. 'If I can just get through the first round or two, I'll play the game.'

'Chelle from Peroxide treated herself to a bikini wax while her partner Georgie treated herself to a king-sized Mars bar that would remain in her system for just three minutes.

Graham and Millicent sat in Graham's room holding hands and listening to Bob Dylan.

A sixteen-year-old boy called Troy, whose room was full of comics but no books, stood before his mirror singing 'Angels' by Robbie Williams.

A young single mum struggled to arrange a full day's childcare for her sick little boy.

Over dinner in a refuge for victims of domestic violence, a group of women toasted the future success of one of their number in champagne that had previously been reserved for Christmas.

And all over Birmingham, Wolverhampton, Leicester and the whole Black Country, right up to Stoke, down almost to Watford and as far west as the Welsh border, they sang their songs, practised their moves, gargled their Listerine and considered their outfits. Mingers danced, Blingers preened, Clingers confided in friends, talked to God and attended self-assertion workshops. And they all shared the same dream. Every Clinger Blinger, Minger Clinger, Blinger Minger with a bit of Cling and Clinger Minger with a bit of Bling dreamed of stardom. And every one of them wondered . . . what would it be like? What *would* it be like? To be chosen, to win through. To be a star!

A few miles down the M1, Christian Appleyard, winner of the first-ever *Chart Throb* contest, left his Docklands flat for the last time and headed home to his mother's. There was a photographer there to record the event. An ex-number-one artist having his mortgage foreclosed was definitely still news.

The Prince does the King

His Royal Highness had also been summoned to attend the Birmingham audition, in preparation for which he was trying out songs on his long-suffering wife.

'I expect I shall look an absolute *muggins*,' he said.

'Yes, I expect you will,' his wife replied, polishing a riding boot.

'Do you think people will laugh?'

'I certainly would.'

'Well really, dear, I do think you might be more positive about all this. I am trying to save the monarchy, you know.'

'Yes, darling, I know and I'm very proud of you. But it is all rather *droll*, do admit.'

The Prince had been working on 'Burning Love', a song made famous by Elvis Presley. He drew a deep breath and began again.

'It's *hunkah*, darling,' his wife interrupted. 'Not *hunk of*. You're saying *hunk of*, it's *hunkah*.'

'Is it?'

'Yes, definitely.'

'Goodness, I can't say *hunkah*, it's appalling. I've been banging on for *years* about the importance of diction and the need to teach proper grammar in schools. Not that anybody listens, of course. But honestly, if I can't be bothered to take the Queen's English seriously, who can? Children watch this programme, I have a responsibility to *set an example*.'

'Well, all I'm saying is that if you say *hunk of*, not only will you sound silly but it won't scan.'

'Won't it?'

'No, of course it won't,' the duchess said, putting away her brushes and her boot polish. 'Just listen: *hunk of* is two syllables, *hunkah* is one

234

and a bit. It fits, surely you can see that.'

'Well, I suppose so but it does seem an awfully lazy use of English.'

'Have another go and for heaven's sake try to give it some *swing*.'

The Prince of Wales sang the verse and chorus of the song once more, this time being careful to say *hunkah*.

When he had finished, his wife considered for a moment before finally saying, 'I think we need a different song.'

The Prince sighed and poured them both a small glass of Riesling.

'One of the boys suggested something called "Smack My Bitch Up". Ever heard of it?'

Hello, Baby

The man upon whom all the dreams were focused was in his hotel room indulging in a dream of his own.

'Hello, Emma,' he breathed into the telephone, 'what are you wearing?'

'I'm wearing jeans and a T-shirt. I've been at work.'

'Shoes?'

'No. I'm at home now. I've taken my shoes off if you *must* know.'

'What about your socks?'

'Calvin, I thought you were a busy, important man. Don't you have anything more interesting to talk about than my socks?'

'What could be more interesting than your socks? Except your feet?'

'I'm going to hang up in a minute if this conversation doesn't improve.'

'Take off your jeans.'

'Certainly not!'

'Please.'

'No! Absolutely not! I'd feel ridiculous. Why, anyway?'

'Well, because I've asked you to, I suppose.'

There was a pause.

'I'd have to put the phone down.'

'No, keep it in your hand.'

'Oh, for heaven's sake!'

'Hold the phone close to your zip as you undo it. Do it slowly.'

'No!'

'It isn't a lot to ask.'

'In my opinion it is.'

'I think about you all the time.'

'That doesn't mean I'm obliged to let you listen to my zipper.'

'I didn't say you were obliged, I just asked. I don't see why during this lengthy and, I might add, extremely demanding period in which I'm supposed to win your trust I shouldn't be allowed some tenuous sexual connection with you, that's all.'

'And listening to me take off my trousers at a distance of a hundred and twenty miles would help, would it?'

'Yes, as a matter of fact I think it would. Bit pathetic, I know, but that's how much I love you.'

There was a pause and then Calvin heard the tiny, staccato clicking of a zip being pulled.

'There. Happy?' he heard her say.

'Take them off, keep the phone in your hand and take them off. Pull them down over your knickers, right down your legs and over your socks.'

'You take yours off.'

'They are off. I'm in my suite. I've just had a shower, I'm wearing the hotel dressing gown and in a moment I have to go downstairs and have dinner with Rodney and Beryl and all I can think of is you.'

Another pause.

'Well,' said Emma, her voice a cross between defiance and seduction. 'Take off your dressing gown then.'

'Now you're talking.'

Calvin did as he was told.

'It's off,' he said. 'It's on the floor.'

'So you're naked then?'

'Yes and I look fantastic. Totally hot, as they say. Now you take your jeans off.'

Calvin turned the volume on his phone up to full as he strained to listen to the muffled noises of someone disrobing.

'They're off,' Emma told him, returning to the phone. 'And I feel rather silly standing here in my knickers.'

'So you're wearing just knickers, a bra and a T-shirt?'

'Yes, that's right. Knickers lilac. Bra white. T-shirt pale pink before you ask. I suppose you want me to take them off too?'

'No. I want to be there when you do that.'

'If you were here I wouldn't do it.'

'But you will, one day.'

'I might.'

'Will you put the phone into your knickers and rub the mouthpiece against yourself?'

'NO!'

'Please?'

'NO!! Absolutely not! Definitely absolutely not!'

'Why not?'

'Because you're a bloody pervert!'

'What's perverted about that? I want to listen to the rustle of your bush.'

'Don't be *disgusting*!'

'I think that's a nice idea.'

'Well, I'm not doing it.'

'You do *have* a bush, don't you? You haven't done the full wax or anything horrible like that, have you? I hate that. Absolutely *hate* it.'

'Have you seen many bald ones then?'

'Loads. In America all the girls seem to do it, they think it's sexy for some reason. It's all part of this grim juvenilization of society. First grown women started to talk like they were little girls . . .'

'Like Beryl.'

'Yes, like Beryl for instance. Now they all want little girls' twats. It's actually sort of sick when you think about it.'

'Do you get to see a lot of fannies then?'

'Say that again.'

'What?'

'What you just said, it sounded so cute. Please say it again.'

'Don't be pathetic. Answer the question.'

'Yes, in the past I have seen an awful lot of fannies, and, as I say, recently an increasing number of them have been bald, regrettably.'

'And you like a fanny that makes a noise when you rub a telephone on it?'

'Yes.'

'Well, I'm not going to do it. Get one of your other girls to, there must be some who haven't Brazilianed themselves.'

'There are no other girls, Emma. Not any more. And for what it's worth I've never asked any girl to do this before. I've never felt the remotest interest in doing so. You're the only girl who has ever excited me enough that even the thought of listening to the rustle of her pubic hair turns me on. This is all new territory for me.'

There was another pause, then Calvin heard a faint, soft, scratchy sound over the phone. After a little while he heard her voice again.

'Can I stop now?' she said.

'A minute or two longer,' Calvin replied. 'I mean, only if you're happy to. If you don't mind?'

'No,' she said. 'I suppose I don't mind although I do feel ridiculous.'

A few seconds later the faint rustling resumed and it was two or three luxurious minutes before she spoke again.

'Are we done?' she enquired sweetly.

'Yes. We're done,' Calvin gasped. 'You can stop now.'

'Good.'

'That was sort of wonderful.'

'I'm glad, although I didn't actually do it, I'm afraid. I rubbed the phone on the carpet.'

'*Bitch!*'

'I think it's funny.'

'Please say you took your trousers off.'

'Nope.'

'Fuck.'

'Sorry. Will you call me tonight after your dinner?'

'I'm never going to call you again.'

'Please.'

'All right.'

As Calvin dressed, he truly wondered what had happened to him. He had enjoyed sex with Emma more than he could remember enjoying anything in years. And he had not even *had* sex with her. He hadn't even had *telephone* sex with her. He'd had telephone sex with her carpet. And yet still he had loved it. For a man used to being in control it was all most confusing.

Keen to Be Mean

Downstairs Rodney had been waiting for some time.

The three judges had agreed to meet at seven thirty in the hotel bar, so Rodney had been there since seven. Calvin arrived shortly before eight and Beryl, not surprisingly, was nowhere to be seen.

Rodney's ill humour was slightly assuaged by the fact that, unlike earlier in the day, Calvin now seemed disposed to be pleasant.

'Well, something's certainly put a smile on *your* face,' Rodney observed.

'Yes,' said Calvin bluntly but declined to illuminate further.

'Champagne?'

'Of course. But not that crap,' Calvin said, nodding towards the bottle that Rodney had chosen and which he had in fact almost emptied during his hour's wait. 'I'll order something decent.'

'You always were a bit of a wine wanker, weren't you, Calvin?'

The booze was having its effect on Rodney and he was taking a tone with Calvin that he would never have taken when sober. Calvin merely smiled.

'I was wondering,' Rodney continued, hoping to capitalize on his companion's sunny mood, unaware that he was fast deflating it, 'if you'd given any further thought to what we discussed in the restaurant the night before we shot the travelling stuff?'

'What was that then?' Calvin asked without looking up from the wine list.

'Oh, come on, Calvin. We were talking about me being meaner, tougher, wittier this time round, and all I've heard of your plans for me this year is more of that bloody ridiculous business of Beryl throwing stuff over me which I'm quite sure everybody knows is staged.'

'*Are* you, Rodney?'

'Yes, I am.'

'Well, in my view if the British public will accept that the twelve people we annually offer up to them are the best new performers with the most star quality we could find in the *whole of Britain*, then they'll believe anything.'

'Look, Calvin, let's cut to the chase here. I want to be tougher this time and I won't accept anything else. What's more, Beryl's not throwing any coffee over me. All right? I won't have it. I mean it. I won't.'

'Cristal '96,' Calvin said to the wine waiter. After that he said nothing.

'Did you hear what I said, Calvin?'

'Yes, I heard.'

'Good.'

There was a long and uncomfortable silence which once more Calvin forced Rodney to break.

'So we're agreed then? I mean . . . are we?'

Calvin smiled, a weary, long-suffering smile. The champagne arrived and he allowed the waiter to open it and pour two glasses before speaking again.

'Do you really think being tough is your thing, Rodney? I mean we should all play to our strengths, don't you think?'

'I'm tough.'

'Are you?'

'Yes! You should have seen the way I laid into the receptionist this morning when I found out I was in an executive room . . .'

The words tailed away. Rodney had not intended to air this particular grievance. He was not drunk enough to fail to understand that by complaining about his inferior room he could only increase its significance. Rodney had promised himself that he would maintain a dignified silence on the issue but now he had blown it.

'You're not happy with your room, mate?' Calvin enquired, his voice full of sympathy.

'No, no, it's fine. It's fine.'

'So what were you complaining about to the receptionist?'

'Nothing.'

'I'm sorry, I thought you said you'd laid into her?'

'I did.'

'Why?'

For a brief moment Rodney was consumed with an internal struggle. He was not a stupid man nor did he lack human experience. He was well aware that complaining about room status would make him look weak and pathetic, something he already suspected Calvin thought him to be. His intellect informed him that the only sensible course would be for him to make up a broken kettle or an asymmetrical trouser press to explain his confrontation with the receptionist but the righteous anger that burned deep in his soul, fuelled by a thousand real and imagined slights that he had suffered throughout the previous series, plus nearly a whole bottle of champagne, forced him to speak.

'I'm in a room, Calvin. A *room*!'

'Yes?'

'And you and Beryl are in suites. *Houses*, as a matter of fact. You have your own houses *by the lake*.'

'You asked the receptionist what sort of rooms Beryl and I had?'

'Well . . . it just came up. I was asking about my room and . . . yes, it came up.'

'Don't you think that makes everybody look a bit stupid?'

'Uhm, no. Not really. I enquired casually.'

'So this wasn't when you were laying into her?'

'No.'

'That happened at another point in the conversation?'

242

'Uhm, yes, sort of.'

'Would you like my room, Rodney?'

'No, that's not the point . . .'

'You're very welcome to it. I can pop back after dinner and pack my stuff. I've only used a couple of towels and the bed's been remade.'

'No, that's not what I want. That isn't the point I'm making.'

'What do you want? What point are you making?'

'Nothing, I'm . . . Look, we were talking about my image.'

'Rodney. You're a mate. A good mate. We are good mates, aren't we?'

'Yes, I hope so.'

'I value you enormously as a senior member of the *Chart Throb* team and truly respect the contribution you've made. But you have to understand, mate, that there can only be one producer here. You do see that, don't you?'

'Well, of course.'

'I have to follow my instincts for the good of us all. You do understand?'

'Well, yes.'

'I knew you would.' Calvin gave Rodney a little hug. 'Thanks, mate. You're a true friend and a true pro. Look, Beryl's obviously not coming down and to tell the truth I'm knackered. Reckon I'll just get room service. You have the Cristal.'

With that Calvin got up and left, leaving Rodney to drink another bottle of champagne on his own.

The following morning Calvin approached the young woman at reception.

'Miss, were you here on duty yesterday?'

'Yes, I was, sir.'

'When Mr Root made a fuss about having a smaller room than I have?'

'Uhm . . .'

243

'Come on, love, we're mates, we've already had a laugh about it.'

'Well, yes, he did complain about that and at first he refused to use the golf buggy to get to the summer house. I believe he tried to drive there in his limousine, even though the summer house is in the middle of the golf course.'

Calvin laughed out loud and produced a copy of the *Sun* newspaper which he had opened at the Bizarre page.

'Do you see this "gotta story?" phone number? They pay very good money for star titbits. Why not give them a call and tell them all about it? You know, just for a laugh, eh?'

Calvin left the newspaper with the receptionist and, still chuckling, went outside to his car.

An Auditions Day: There's a Kind of Hush

Shaiana, the Quasar, Graham, Millicent, the blokes from Bloke, The Four-Z and Suki were all there, and so were Latiffa and Blossom, and Troy clutching his comic. So were a hundred and fifty or so other hopefuls and the funny old fellow who looked a bit like the Prince of Wales.

They were all sitting in the holding area they had been directed to on arrival.

But where were the rest? It was so quiet. So still.

'I must say I thought there would be *oodles* of us,' said the man who looked like (and indeed was) the Prince of Wales. 'That's how it looks on the television, doesn't it? Or has muggins here got it wrong again? I often do, you know, my boys tease me *endlessly*, the rotters. I do think they're mean.'

The vast Birmingham Bullring Conference and Leisure Centre echoed with emptiness.

Where were the crowds, the vast hordes of hopefuls who could be seen cheering and shouting throughout all the early episodes of *Chart Throb* in an effort to win the attention of the three famous judges?

They were there already, duly recorded and digitized and sitting in the editing computer at the *Chart Throb* production offices, awaiting their moment to cheer once more when cut back into the footage that would be recorded today.

For the time being, however, they were gone and everything was strangely quiet.

An Auditions Day: Priming Vicky

Chelsie began her second day in Birmingham teeing up Vicky, the sixteen-year-old Minger, and her mum, who were destined to trigger a coffee-throwing incident between Rodney and Beryl.

'She's been dreaming of this,' said Mum. 'It's all she talks about. It's her life.'

'I'm not surprised. She's a very talented girl,' said Chelsie, pressing another styrofoam cup of coffee into Vicky's mother's hand. 'She's going to rock their socks.'

'She can't wait for this, it's her dream. It's all she wants.'

'It's my dream,' Vicky confirmed. 'It's all I want.'

'I've talked to her about having other dreams,' Vicky's mum added, as if suddenly concerned that the family might appear a tad single-minded. 'But she won't have it.'

'I won't have it,' Vicky echoed.

'She won't have it at all,' Vicky's mum reiterated. '"It's my dream, Mum," that's what young madam here says and she won't have it any other way. Will you, little Miss Showbiz? You just want to be a star.'

'I just want to be a star,' Vicky assured her mother.

'It's her dream,' Mum reiterated.

'It's my dream,' said Vicky.

'She'll never stop dreaming her dream,' said Mum.

'Nor should she,' Chelsie assured them both. 'Today is Vicky's big chance. A girl like Vicky *should* dream her dream because special is as special does.'

'That is *so* right, Chelsie,' said Mum.

Chelsie was on fire. She needed to be, because while today was most certainly *not* to be Vicky's big chance it was definitely going to be Chelsie's. Having been given temporary promotion on the *Chart Throb* team to the position previously occupied by Emma, she had enhanced her status by securing for Calvin the battered wife he had requested from Trent. Now she was determined to confirm that promotion by delivering the auditionees to her boss in perfect psychological condition to play their roles in the stories allocated to them.

In Vicky's case this required her being convinced against all the physical evidence that she really was the next Judy Garland. Her subsequent disillusionment and humiliation would then provide the catalyst for a major confrontation between Beryl and Rodney, which it was hoped would run throughout the entire episode. Vicky's fall therefore had to be totally convincing.

'You can't fake catharsis,' Calvin was fond of saying.

Chelsie was born to the job. Even before she had joined the *Chart Throb* team she had instinctively understood how the process must work. Her innate cunning and understanding of human nature had told her that the extraordinary cockiness and belligerent self-belief of such ludicrously untalented people must be at least partly tutored. It was simply not possible that the village idiots at whom the nation howled as they assured Calvin that they were the new Justin Timberlake could act as they did without at least *some* prompting. Of course the human material had to be there in the first place, these people had already to be insanely self-deluded — but that was a given since most of them had of course applied for the show of their own volition. It was Chelsie's job to nurture those pathetic delusions until the victims appeared before the judges truly believing that they were going to win. Only then could those precious shots of television gold be gathered, the looks of shock, fury, disbelief, the slowly dawning realization that not only had they failed utterly but that they were being roundly laughed at and insulted by those whom they had fondly imagined would be their saviours.

'You can't fake hubris,' Calvin often remarked. 'First rule of drama. Before the hero falls he must first be exalted.'

While much on *Chart Throb* could be faked, that could not. Both the pride and the fall had to be genuine or it wouldn't work, which was why Chelsie was taking such trouble bigging up Vicky and her mother.

'You know what, babes?' Chelsie said, taking both mother and daughter by the hand. 'I truly believe that if *you* truly believe, that dream of yours just might be about to come true.'

And with a little squeeze of the hands and a group

hug Chelsie was gone, off to school a room full of weeping and shaking Clingers.

An Auditions Day: The Judges Arrive

In another part of the hotel and leisure complex, the three judges were shooting their 'arrival' shots. This required two sets of costume for Beryl since once the shots were edited it was to appear that in their obsessive search for talent the judges had visited the city more than once.

'Meanwhile,' Keely would later be saying in her voiceover, 'the judges have returned to Birmingham. Will they be lucky this time?'

There was also to be a third costume change to cover virtual Dublin.

'I still don't see why we need to construct this whole fucking *Dublin* fiction,' complained Beryl. 'I mean if we can't be fucking bothered to go there why lie about it? Who cares about the Micks anyway?'

'Telephone votes, darling. The Irish are big phoners. We need their revenue. We have to include them and pretty much have to have an Irish act in the finals. It makes a big difference to the money we make on the phones.'

When she had finally been presented with an argument she could understand, Beryl squeezed herself into a new jacket, pinned a shamrock to her lapel and got back into the limousine. Her pet pig was installed on her lap and the massive extra who had been booked to play her intimidating minder was placed by the limo door.

'Do you think people really believe that we're

248

followed about all the time by huge security guards?' Calvin asked Trent. 'I mean that bastard's so fat he wouldn't even fit in the lift with me. If he tried to ward off an assassin he'd have a heart attack. Maybe next series we should get little Japanese ninja bodyguards. That'd look pretty good, wouldn't it?'

'Great thought, boss,' said Trent. 'Duly noted.'

The big fat extra playing the minder opened the car door and Beryl was filmed getting out and bustling self-importantly into the lobby of the building.

'Maybe I should say something cute as I pass the camera,' Beryl suggested. 'Like "Oh God, Fifi's weed in my Cartier handbag and it was a fucking gift from Elton and David" – how about that?'

'Great, Beryl,' Calvin shouted, anxious to get on.

'Uhm . . . I'm afraid you're not mic'd,' said the sound operator nervously. 'We have this down as a mute shot. It's to be dropped into the credits '

'Well, sling the fucking boom in, dickhead!' Beryl snapped. 'I've thought of a line, I am being *spontaneous.*'

'I'm afraid the boom's in the truck, Mrs Blenheim. It'll take ten minutes to—'

'In the fucking *truck!*'

'We have this down as a mute shot. We discussed it yesterday at the meeting . . .'

'And what if I want to be spontaneous? I thought the whole point of me being on this show was because I'm so fucking spontaneous! I have an Emmy for my spontaneity. Have you seen the award-winning *Blenheims* barbecue episode where the pet pig eats the steaks so we barbecue the pig?'

'Uhm . . .'

'I *made that up*! And fortunately when I did make it up no *fucking sound guy* said sorry *I forgot the fucking microphones!*'

'Yes, but at the meeting . . .'

'Have you *any idea* just how fucking spontaneous I can be? I *shit* spontaneity!'

Keely, the comely presenter, had been standing by ready to shoot an opening link. Only the previous evening she had flown home from shooting a travel show in Mustique, so she was tired, but being a genuinely nice person and a team player (ex-girl guide) she was always anxious to help.

'Perhaps I could voice your gag, Beryl,' she suggested helpfully. 'You know . . . "Beryl's in a terrible rush because Fifi's about to wee in her Cartier" . . . Would that help?'

Beryl's face turned cold as stone.

'Are you trying to pinch my joke, Keely?'

'No!'

'It fucking sounds like you're trying to pinch my joke.'

'No! Really, Beryl, I was just trying to . . .'

'Here's a thought, eh, Keely? You stick to looking cute and leave the clever stuff to me, OK?'

Keely looked like she wanted to cry. She could never get used to Beryl's rudeness, it always shocked her as if she was experiencing it for the first time.

The minutes were ticking away. Trent looked at Calvin and then pointed towards his watch. There was most definitely no time for this type of halt in proceedings on a *Chart Throb* audition day and Calvin's was the only authority that Beryl would acknowledge.

'Beryl,' Calvin snapped, 'brilliant though your Fifi pissing gag is, as indeed are *all* the numerous jokes you suggest concerning the incontinence of your menagerie, we are not set up to record sound on this shot. So we will simply have to move on.'

'So much for sponta-fucking-neity,' Beryl said, accepting the inevitable.

Finally able to proceed, the director asked the

script girl what the next shot was and the script girl informed him that it was to be Rodney's arrival.

The limo from which Beryl had emerged was driven away and a new one manoeuvred into its place. Rodney went over to it and with exaggerated casualness walked along its length, appearing to be inspecting its glossy black paintwork. He fooled no one. Everybody had seen him doing exactly the same thing to Beryl's car and they knew that he had been pacing them out to ensure that Beryl had not been given a longer car than him to arrive in.

Once Rodney was satisfied that the car was of a dimension appropriate to his status he took the important-looking briefcase that Props provided him with and got into the back of the car.

'Action!' called the director.

Nothing happened.

'Action!' the director called out once more.

Still nothing. The director approached the parked limo with its smoky black windows.

'Rodney?' He tapped on the window. 'Can you hear me in there?'

The window of the limo descended and Rodney looked out, smiling pleasantly.

'Yes, I can hear you,' he said. 'All good in here. Any notes?'

'Uhm, no. We haven't taken the shot yet.'

'Good, OK. Well, I'm ready.'

'Good. Great. So we'll go, shall we?'

'Fine.'

The window closed once more. The director retreated to his position behind the camera, the shot was marked and once more he cried, 'Action!'

Still nothing happened.

'Action, Rodney!' he called out again.

The window descended for a second time.

'I'm here, I'm ready. I can hear you. I'm waiting.'

Minutes were ticking away. Calvin interjected, 'Well, get out of the fucking car then!'

'I can't. The door isn't open.'

'Of course it isn't open, it's supposed to have just pulled up.'

'Exactly, and then the minder opens it and I get out,' Rodney explained, confident that he was not the one holding up proceedings. 'I'm not the first cue. The minder is the first cue.'

Calvin turned to the director. 'Where's the minder? It's his cue.'

'The minder?'

'Yes. To open Rodney's car door.'

The director looked helplessly towards the continuity girl, who, being made of sterner stuff than he was, decided to state the uncomfortable truth.

'There is no minder,' she said without apology. 'This shot's down as a single on Rodney.'

Rodney was not a large man and he was cramped in the back of a stretch limousine but everybody within fifteen metres felt him bridle.

'*A single on Rodney?*' he almost hissed.

'Yes,' the continuity girl replied fearlessly, then glancing down at her shot list she read out: '*Shot Two. AM. Ext Audition Hall. Loose single. Rodney gets out of car and scurries past camera.*'

'*Scurries?*'

'Yes. You're in a hurry.'

Rodney began to go very red. The make-up department, who were used to this, hovered close by with wet wipes and cold towels at the ready. They knew that if Rodney had a meltdown he would have to go back into the chair for his powder, eyes and lippy to be fixed, at which point Calvin would probably sack everyone.

'Calvin?' Rodney said through clenched teeth, clearly struggling to master his emotions.

'Yes, mate?'

'Beryl has a fat, bald minder who opens her car door and then follows her respectfully and protectively as she strolls into the building. Am I expected to open my *own* door and *scurry* into the building alone?'

'I don't have a minder for my arrival shot, Rodney.'

'Yes, I know that, Calvin, because you drive yourself. *You* arrive commandingly in control at the wheel of your own personalized Rolls. Beryl is met by her security staff and I . . . I . . .'

Once more, Keely, ever kind and cheerful, attempted to pour oil on troubled waters.

'I could run up and grab your door for you, Rodney. I don't mind.'

'You want to get into my shot, Keely?' Rodney replied icily.

'No!' Keely almost shouted, shocked at the spin Rodney was placing on her innocent offer.

'You don't think that what with introducing the show, doing all the links, interviewing the candidates, sending them in to us, hugging the winners, weeping with the losers and top and tailing each ad break, perhaps you might already have *enough fucking shots in this show, Keely*? Without having to muscle your way in on mine?'

'No, really, I—'

'My *arrival* shot no less. One of the very few featured solos I have in the *whole fucking* show.'

'But . . . but . . .' Keely could find no words with which to proclaim her innocence.

'Maybe we could use Beryl's bloke again?' the continuity girl suggested. 'Make him kind of the greeter?'

An angry screech emanated from the quick-change tent where Beryl was slipping out of Dublin and back into Birmingham.

'Fuck right OFF!' she shouted, sticking her head out

253

from between the flaps of the tent. 'He's not having my fucking bloke!'

'Please, Beryl,' shouted Hair and Make-up together. 'Your hair!'

Beryl ignored them.

'What kind of security would that be? "Oh sorry, Beryl, we can't defend you from that mad psycho fan at the moment because we've to go and open a car door for Rodney fucking Root." Oh, do please FUCK OFF!'

Beryl retreated back into her tent with Hair and Make-up hurrying in after her.

'Calvin?' said Trent, once more staring desperately at his watch. 'The *time* . . .'

'Right!' said Calvin decisively. 'Get in the car, Rodney, we'll arrive together.'

Instantly Rodney's face lit up.

'What, you and me in the same car? Like proper mates?' he said, scarcely daring to hope.

'Yes. You can even get out camera side, I'll get out of the far door and walk round behind you.'

'That's fantastic,' Rodney gushed. 'What a great shot. No minders, no security. No faff. Just two tough professionals, colleagues and great mates, arriving to do a job together.'

'That's right, Rodney, get in the car.'

'I've a thought,' said Rodney eagerly. 'How about we're in the middle of some animated discussion as we get out? You know, we could still be talking as we slam the doors and walk into the building together, ignoring everyone, locked in our own high-powered argument stuff . . .'

'No sound, Rodney, we aren't mic'd. Get in the car.'

'But we wouldn't need sound. It'll be mute. We can be talking about anything because the credit music will be playing, we just need to look like we're having a really animated chat, like two tough pros oblivious to—'

'Rodney. Get in the fucking car.'

'Right.'

'And on action, get out of the car again and walk past camera into the building. I'll be right behind you.'

Both men got into the car.

'Action!' they heard the director call.

'Go, Rodney,' said Calvin. 'I'll follow.'

Rodney got out of the car and Calvin watched him through the window as he made his way past camera. After Rodney was well out of shot, Calvin got out himself and called cut.

'Great shot, everybody,' he said before whispering to the continuity girl that she need only mark the first part of the shot to be digitized. Rodney Root would not know until he watched the broadcast that he had in fact got out of his car and scurried up the carpet alone.

An Auditions Day: Priming the Massed Clingers

In a corner of the holding area (a section of a large conference room which had been cordoned off with hessian partitions), Chelsie had gathered together her prospective Clingers for a session of group motivation.

'Now Keely is going to ask you about your DREAM,' Chelsie shouted, in the tone of a sergeant major briefing a group of raw recruits. 'The dream you all share but which is special and unique to each and every one of you. The dream to be a star! What's your dream, people?'

'To be a star!' they all shouted.

'That's right. And it's a *good* dream. A great dream. A dream to be proud of! Keely's going to want to hear that it's your *only* dream. The only dream you've ever had! A dream that you've had since childhood and without which you'd be nothing. *Nothing*, do you hear?'

The assembled Clingers (who included a tense and brooding Shaiana) were about to reply but they were interrupted by the sound of a loud voice singing 'Copacabana' while people clapped along.

Peering out from between the screens to investigate, Chelsie discovered that Gary and Barry had grabbed the opportunity to get a shot of the Quasar doing a limbo-dancing routine with the help of the Peroxide girls, who were holding a mop for him to dance beneath.

'Gary? Barry?' Chelsie snapped. 'What are you doing?'

'Just grabbing a bit more holding area high jinks, Chelsie,' Barry said. 'You know, all the contestants bonding and spontaneously having a laugh together.'

'We got miles of that shit on the crowd day, guys. Calvin will use about ten seconds in the final edit. Today is about *auditions* and I am trying to psych up the contestants, so will you *please* keep it down.'

'Sorry, Chelsie,' said Barry.

'Yeah, sorry,' said Gary.

'I ain't sorry, babes!' grinned Quasar. 'I is *pumped* an' I have to tell you, Chelsie darlin', you look like you could use a little piece of the Quasar yourself, UH!' And with this last syllable Quasar grabbed his crotch and thrust it forward.

'Save it for the judges,' said Chelsie.

'Oh baby, I got plenty of that to spare.'

Chelsie returned to her Clingers.

'Now another thing Keely is going to want to talk to you about,' she shouted, once more turning her headlights on to the assembled rabbits, 'is *just how much you want it!*'

An Auditions Day: When Irish Eyes Are Smiling

In the car park the first coach containing the Irish contestants had arrived from Birmingham International Airport. On arrival in the car park they were all asked to wait on board for the second bus to catch up.

'Won't be a minute,' a cheery PA informed them and indeed it wasn't. It was twenty-five. Eventually a second coach full of Irish auditionees pulled up and Barry, Gary and Keely were summoned to do their bit towards ensuring that the revenue from the Irish phone lines would remain buoyant.

'Right! Top of the morning to you!' shouted Barry once both coaches had disgorged their occupants and the whole group had been assembled in front of a large *Chart Throb* banner decked out in emerald green bunting and Irish tricolours. 'And welcome to our own special *Chart Throb* St Paddy's Day.'

'Yes, that's right!' shouted Gary, who had donned one of those big comedy Irish hats they give away with the Guinness in London on St Patrick's night. 'We are going to pretend it's St Patrick's Day and in order to celebrate we are going to lead you all in a special *Chart Throb* rendition of "When Irish Eyes Are Smiling" but for a laugh we'd like you to say "Calvin's" instead of "Irish", OK? It's like a little *Chart Throb* St Paddy's Day joke from the Irish posse, OK?'

There being no obvious voices of dissent, the cameras were lined up and Barry and Gary counted everyone down and the song began.

' "When Calvin's eyes are smiling," ' they sang.

All went well for the first line as the crowd sang lustily and with an attempt at good humour. After that, unfortunately, it petered out very quickly and it became clear that nobody knew the rest of the words. Some of them vaguely remembered the stuff about the world seeming bright and gay but by the time they got to the bit about hearing the angels sing there was scarcely anyone left singing at all.

'Fuck!' said Barry. 'Calvin really wants this. What are we going to do?'

'I just assumed they'd know it,' wailed Gary.

At this point Chelsie arrived with Keely.

'Haven't you recorded the bloody singalong yet?' she demanded.

'They don't know the words,' Gary explained.

'Go back to the edit truck,' Chelsie commanded one of the runners. 'They have wireless internet. Ask the production secretary to go online, Google the lyrics and bring them back as soon as possible.'

The runner scuttled off.

'Right,' said Chelsie. 'We'll do Keely's bit while we're waiting.'

Keely was given a shamrock and instructed to stand in front of the Irish crowd.

'Well, here we are in Dublin's fair city where the girls are so pretty,' she shouted. 'And this mad crazy lot have prepared a little musical surprise for Calvin!'

'OK,' Chelsie shouted. 'Then we drop in the song once we've recorded it. Now Keely, do your outro.'

'Wow!' Keely shrieked. 'That was *brilliant*. Calvin's eyes will be smiling when he hears that! Well done, everybody! How good was that?'

After which she and Chelsie hurried back into the building, leaving the Irish posse to await the lyrics of their spontaneous gift to Calvin.

An Auditions Day: Mean and Moody

By this time the three judges had recorded their various arrival shots and it was time for some generic footage of the three of them looking tough and moody. Each had been taken back to Costume and Make-up and dressed head to foot in black. Then they were set against a white background and shot looking as grim and hard as possible. Like killers in a spaghetti western.

There were two camera crews at work here, which made the situation more complex than it might otherwise have been for the director. One crew was recording the moody stuff which would form part of the credit sequence and the other crew was filming the process of filming the moody stuff. The director of the first crew, who wanted to concentrate on his shots, had complained about the presence of the second crew.

'You're new to this show, aren't you, mate?' Calvin said.

The director admitted it.

'Well, let me tell you something,' Calvin continued, speaking through the make-up brush that was fluttering around his face. 'We waste *nothing*. Have you any idea just how little usable stuff we might end up getting today? Fuck all, that's how little, and why? Because people are basically boring. *That* is our challenge as makers of "people TV". It is our job to shoot hours of material, days of the stuff, in order to get a few usable seconds of genuine entertainment. My God, *Paris Hilton* is a star. *That's* how low the fucking bar is set! Why do you think that half of each of our shows is just a repeat of the other half? Because usually *half* a show is all we've fucking got! We audition thousands of people and we *still* end up repeating the same shots of about a dozen of them. *Anything* we have that's even remotely good we must repeat over and over again. We'll show it before the break, after the break, during the fucking break. *Chart Throb* is the only show on TV that's repeated three times during its initial run! I'm very proud of that. That is why, if we're going to have a load of shots of the judges looking moody, we should also get a load of shots of us being shot looking moody. Let the audience in on the process because we've fuck all else to show them most of the time.'

After the generic shots had been taken it was time for the three judges to change once more, back into their 'Birmingham One' outfits, and begin the real meat of the day, the thing that had made all three so very famous. It was time to record those familiar scenes of the three of them sitting in fresh, unbiased judgement on whoever might happen to put their heads round the door.

The auditions.

An Auditions Day: Destroying Vicky

The three of them took their seats in the 'audition' room and submitted themselves to the last-minute attentions of Hair and Make-up. Then, as planned, they shot the three foreign girls with the amusing accents, each of whom was laughed at and then rejected and led weeping from the room.

Then they made good progress gunning through twenty or so In and Out fillers, alternating yeses and noes in strict order. Around mid-morning they arrived at Vicky, the first major story of the day.

The girl and her mother were outside with Keely, Chelsie, Trent and the production crew. Trent was just about to begin recording Vicky's pre-show interview when Chelsie spoke up.

'Trent, I think we have make-up issues here. Are you happy with Vicky?'

'She looks all right to me.'

Chelsie did not discuss it further. Instead she went into the audition room and asked if Calvin could possibly join them for a moment. Chelsie had spent the morning dealing with other people's mistakes and Calvin had been a witness to none of it. As far as her own career advancement was concerned, she might as well have been as shit as the rest of the team. But on this occasion she was going to ensure that her light emerged from under the bushel.

Calvin, who was waiting for Beryl's copious paint job to be retouched, joined the party assembled around Vicky and her mother.

'Oh my God!' they said in star-struck unison as the great man emerged. 'We *love* you, Calvin!'

Calvin nodded a greeting and turned to Chelsie.

'Babes?' he enquired. 'What's up?'

Chelsie asked a runner to take the auditionees discreetly aside before explaining herself.

'Trent is happy with Vicky's hair and make-up.'

Trent tried to take command.

'Look, I didn't say—'

Calvin cut him short.

'What's your point, babes?'

'Yes, *babes* . . .' said Make-up rather aggressively. 'What's your point?'

'My point is, look at her,' said Chelsie. 'She's been fully made up, slap, powder, they've done her hair, *covered her pimples*, for God's sake.'

'Well, yes, she's a featured story, isn't she?' said Make-up.

'*Yes*, she's a featured story but have you *read* your character notes?' Chelsie snapped. 'You've made her up as a Blinger and she's a Minger.'

'No, Chelsie,' Make-up protested. 'She's a Blinger.'

'Look at your *notes*! What is the point of me and the continuity team writing them if nobody ever reads them? She's a Blinger personality but *physically* and *talent-wise* she's a Minger. That's the point of the story. She's a classic Ming Bling! She thinks she's great and she's just about to find out that she's not. That's why we've set her up! So that Rodney can brutalize her and Beryl can go all mumsy and defensive. But for Beryl's mumsiness to work, the girl's got to look pathetic. Deluded, naïve, totally out of her depth, and here's you lot trying to make her look like Rita Hayworth.'

'We just—'

'Surely the crapper she looks, the sillier and sadder her pretensions become. *We need her acne!* It's her best feature!'

Keely asked if she could be excused from the conversation at this point.

'Sorry, I just can't hear this. I've been to drama school,' she explained, 'and as an artist I feel strongly that I have to *believe* in my performance. Honesty is the first rule of acting, I think Olivier said that, or Pacino, and if I'm to convincingly interview Vicky as Bling I simply cannot be a part of a conversation in which the entire production team condemn her as Ming.'

Keely then stood apart while Chelsie referred everybody to the character notes.

'We've got our key quote down here, that this girl thinks she could be *a better mover than Britney and a better singer than Céline*. Surely this has

262

got to be a no make-up, greasy hair and spots job?'

Calvin looked over Chelsie's shoulder at Vicky. Then he looked at his watch: seconds were, as always, ticking away. On the other hand, if they were going to do it they had to do it properly.

'Chelsie's right,' he said, turning to Make-up. 'No slap, greasy hair, and if there's time accentuate the acne.'

With that, Calvin returned to the audition room leaving Chelsie a very unpopular victor.

'You didn't have to go running to Calvin,' said Trent.

'I asked you what you thought,' Chelsie replied. 'You said you were happy with her.'

Hair and Make-up removed their previous efforts from Vicky's face and hair. 'You're so young, dear,' they assured her and her mother. 'You don't *need* make-up. Calvin wants to accentuate your youth and freshness. Might as well, eh? It doesn't last for ever, does it?'

Then it was time for Keely to record her 'before' interview.

'Bet you're really nervous, aren't you?' said Keely once the cameras were rolling.

'Well . . .' the mother answered. 'She would be nervous but she's worked so hard and everyone she knows thinks she's a real talent. She really believes she's ready for this.'

Keely glanced down at her notes.

'Are you going to be a star, Vicky?' she asked.

'Yes,' said Vicky, 'I'm going to be a star.'

'It's her dream,' her mother added.

'Then you go, girl!' said Keely, giving Vicky a hug.

Vicky then made her way through the hessian-backed door which separated Conference Room B in the Bullring Complex from Conference Room A, its adjoining, slightly larger twin.

After Vicky had left, Trent directed Keely and Vicky's mum to 'listen' at the door as if they could hear what was going on within, which in fact of course they couldn't.

Inside the Cumbrian Room the auditions had finally begun.

'Hello, hello,' Beryl shouted out as Vicky emerged and presented herself. 'Who are you then?'

'I'm Vicky.'

'Vicky!' Beryl gushed as if the name alone was evidence of something special. 'Vicky, Vicky, *Vicky*, you're so young! You're a *baby*!'

'I'm sixteen, Beryl.'

'Oooooooh,' croaked Beryl, contorting her stiffly Botoxed features into a drippingly mumsy expression as if she'd just been presented with her own newborn infant. 'Sweet *sixteen*! My little girls are only seventeen. God, I miss them. As a mum I really miss them. You could be their kid sister. You're a *baby*! God, I miss my kids.'

Sitting next to Beryl, Calvin smiled. For all that he loathed her, he could not deny that she was quite brilliant at her job. A real find, in a class of her own. Beryl was a star independent of him, booking her had been a stroke of genius and it was worth putting up with her for that.

Rodney was fidgeting. Only twenty seconds into recording and it was obvious that Rodney was already worrying that Beryl was hogging the limelight.

'Yes, Vicky's very young,' he said, trying to make his presence felt. 'But can she sing?'

'Of course you can sing, can't you, Vicky?' Beryl cooed. 'Just you ignore him.'

'I will ignore him, Beryl, because I can sing and I'm going to prove it to you.'

'You go, girl. Just you go. Own that song.'

If ever there was a cue for a song this was it, and by rights Vicky should have sung at this point. There were after all a hundred more people in the holding area and once the show was edited it would appear that there was a crowd of at least a thousand outside. The judges had already spent an entirely disproportionate amount of time on this one unimpressive-looking girl who could no more be a pop star than a heavyweight boxer. If this had been a genuine audition the judges could not possibly have spent more than a moment with Vicky. But this was not a genuine audition, this was *entertainment*, and most of the people waiting outside in the holding area were merely fillers. Vicky was a *story* and the groundwork had to be laid.

'So who do you admire, Vicky?' Calvin asked, paying out the rope with which Vicky was expected to hang herself.

'I really like Britney and Céline Dion,' Vicky replied.

'Good choices,' Rodney said, nodding wisely as if this represented encouraging evidence of Vicky's critical and intellectual faculties. 'Great artists, both of them. Those are very good choices for role modelling.'

'Do you think you could ever be like them?' Calvin enquired, paying out a little more rope.

'I think I could be bigger than them, Calvin.'

Chelsie had prepared the girl well. Vainly self-deluded though she was, she would never have been quite so aggressively arrogant in front of three famous people had Chelsie not assured her that this was what the judges *loved to hear*. 'They really respect confidence,' Chelsie had said, 'so totally big yourself up.'

Having heard her big herself up, Calvin pulled an expression which indicated that he was surprised and by no means convinced that Vicky *would* be bigger than Britney and Céline, but that he would reserve judgement until Vicky had had the chance to show what she could do.

'All right, Vicky, what are you going to sing for us?'

'I'm going to sing "Hit Me Baby One More Time" by Britney Spears.'

'Good choice,' said Rodney, nodding wisely. 'That is a great choice of song. Clever choice.'

'You go, girl!' Beryl said.

It was of course appalling, as the research notes had promised it would be. Utterly excruciating, both flat and sharp, loud and quiet (during the sexy croaky 'oh baby baby' bit which Calvin instantly noted down for inclusion in the DVD) and devoid of any entertainment value whatsoever beyond that of the freak show. Yet despite the fact that it was a car crash from the first note Calvin let Vicky sing her entire number. Despite the fact that there were numerous better singers waiting in the holding area, despite the fact that most of the original applicants were better singers, Vicky was allowed to sing the whole of 'Hit Me Baby One More Time' and occupy a full fifteen minutes of the judges' time during their single day in Birmingham. Vicky might not have been much of a singer but she was very good telly.

As the girl sang, each judge, aware that they were being covered by a solo camera from behind Vicky, ran through their 'amusing' faces. Calvin did his wide-eyed 'I can't quite believe this' look and Rodney did his smug smirk. Beryl's was best of all and she didn't even have to try. She was famous for her dead-eyed stare of blank shock and incomprehension, a brilliant mix of both witty and tender which was in fact merely the result of the drastically reduced mobility left in her features after the brutal regime of Botox and surgery that she had put them through.

When the song was finally over Vicky stood nervously awaiting judgement, still unaware of what had been planned for her.

'Vicky?' said Calvin finally. 'That was . . .' He paused for what seemed an age while the girl stood trembling with anticipation. 'Awful.'

Vicky didn't quite seem to understand.

'Wh . . . wh . . . what do you mean?'

'What do I mean? What do I *mean*?' Calvin asked. 'I mean it was terrible, pathetic, just awful, hopeless.'

The girl was clearly stunned, as well she might have been. Nothing had remotely prepared her for so negative a reaction, let alone such a brutal one.

'Hit me, baby?' said Rodney, using a line he had been working on throughout Vicky's entire performance. 'I wanted to *hit you*. The only good thing I can think of to say about it is that it took my mind off my haemorrhoids.'

Beryl slammed the table.

'Hey, Rodney, that is out of order. She's *sixteen!*'

'I don't care if she's six hundred, she'll never be able to sing. The girl's a joke, don't give her false hope. She needs to go and work in a shop.'

Calvin was quietly impressed. He had worked so hard on Rodney's cuddly side on the previous series that he had not quite realized the man's talent for spite. Perhaps he *should* get some meaner storylines.

'Hey!' Beryl snapped. 'That's enough, mister! Yes, it was a little . . . inadequate, but she's *sixteen!*'

'And she's talentless.'

'Don't you listen to them, Vicky!' said Beryl, finally including the traumatized girl in the conversation. 'You have a dream, that's a *good* thing.'

Vicky could only stare, clearly still trying to understand what was happening to her, trying not to cry.

'If Vicky's dreaming then she needs to wake up,' said Rodney with a grin. 'Because her dream is our nightmare.'

Again Calvin was surprised at Rodney's natural talent.

'That's *enough*!' shouted Beryl, also playing her part beautifully. 'She's *sixteen*. You are out of order,

Rodney. Totally out of order! I did not sign up for this. This is not what I do. You've crossed the line, Rodney. Don't you listen to him, girl.'

'Right,' said Calvin, suddenly going all decisive and professional. 'What's the verdict? Rodney?'

'Are you joking? No. No. No. Sixteen noes. One for each year that this girl has not been able to sing.'

'Beryl?'

Beryl gulped, paused and gulped again. She allowed her lips to tighten. She stared long and hard at Vicky, forcing her eyelids wide open so that a film of water began to appear on her eyes. She looked down, she looked up again. She played with her pencil. There was a universe of sadness and regret written across her face. Meanwhile Vicky stood and quivered.

'Oh God . . .' said Beryl. 'I can't do this.'

Calvin turned to the traumatized girl.

'Vicky?' he said gently, seductively. 'Tell Beryl how much you want it, how hard you've worked, how good you really are. It's your last chance, *appeal* to her.'

'*Please, Beryl,*' Vicky responded. 'Please. I want this so much. I've worked so hard. I'm good, I know I'm good. Please. I'm begging you.'

'Oh, don't *do* this to me, Vicky,' Beryl pleaded back, apparently on the verge of tears.

'I need an answer, Beryl,' Calvin prompted.

'It's . . . it's . . . it's . . .'

There was a ridiculously long lip-quivering pause.

'It's a no, Vicky. For the talent it's a no. But not for the dream! It's a big, big, big yes, yes, yes for the dream. But it's a no to the talent. I'm so, so sorry, babe. You don't deserve this. You're *sixteen.*'

'And it's a no from me,' said Calvin brutally. 'Goodbye.'

Vicky began to cry. Beryl jumped up, went round the table and, grabbing Vicky, gave her a hug.

'You know what, babes?' she whispered, gently

escorting her from the room as if to save her from further humiliation. 'You don't need this, you don't have to take this. You enjoy your dream, girl. You own it. You own that dream.'

As Beryl reached the doorway she turned and glared at Calvin and Rodney, the mother hen with every feather fluffed out as she protected a defenceless chick.

'She's *sixteen*!'

Outside the audition area, Keely was waiting with Vicky's mum and a camera crew.

'How did it go? How did it go?' Keely asked anxiously, almost convincing even herself that she didn't know.

The look on Beryl's face said it all.

'Look after her, she's been hurt,' Beryl said before leaving Keely to play the second act of the drama with the girl and her mum.

'*Babes,*' said Keely, 'What *happened*?'

'They laughed at me!' Vicky choked, a camera barely two inches from her face. 'They said I was a joke, that I should work in a shop.'

The mum was genuinely stunned. She had always tried to be aware of the possibility of rejection but that her daughter could be so brutally humiliated and dismissed had not even occurred to her.

'Come here, babes,' said Keely, hugging Vicky. 'Don't you worry about what they said. Don't think about it. Forget it. *What did they say?*'

'Rodney said I was like haemorrhoids, that if I lived to be six hundred I wouldn't be able to sing.'

'He didn't! What a horrible man! Well, never mind, babes. It's over now.'

But Chelsie, hovering nearby and waiting to whisk both Vicky and her mum off to the Bite Back Box for a further dose of knife-twisting, knew that it was far from over. The scenes currently being filmed would be played over and over again for months to come. In trailers, in the show, in the repeats, on the support channels and finally on the spin-off DVDs. Every single person Vicky and her mum knew would witness their humiliation time and time again. Their laughable delusions would eventually come to be known verbatim by everyone at Vicky's stage school, everyone at Vicky's mum's work.

Beryl had been right. Vicky needed to enjoy her dream. She was going to pay a high price for it.

While Chelsie took Vicky to the Bite Back Box, back in the auditions room Trent and a crew were recording Beryl's return.

'And . . . Action!' he shouted.

Beryl stormed back into the room, her face like thunder.

'She was *sixteen*, Rodney!'

'She's old enough to know better.'

'You bullied her! You demeaned her! I didn't buy into this. I did not sign up for this! We're dealing with a kid's dreams here!'

'Yes, and like I said, our nightmare.'

It was hardly a convincing row, pretty wooden in fact, but cut up and with music it would just about serve.

'Try and be a bit more angry, Beryl,' Calvin directed. 'Tell him to apologize.'

'I think you should go and apologize to her and her mother,' Beryl duly shouted. 'Give her a hug and tell her you're sorry.'

'I have nothing to apologize for. You're being ridiculous,' Rodney replied.

'Be tougher, Rodney,' Calvin interjected. 'Say it again but say she's being pathetic and stupid.'

'OK . . .' Rodney collected himself. 'Can you give me the cue again, Beryl?'

'Fuck off! What do you think this is, *Hamlet*? My

270

line was perfect, just fucking do yours.'

'It helps me get into it if I have a cue.'

'And do I care?'

'Oh, go on, Beryl,' Calvin snapped. 'Just give him the fucking cue!'

With ill-disguised resentment Beryl repeated her line. 'Apologize! Give her a hug and tell her you're sorry.'

'I have nothing to apologize for,' Rodney shouted, rather unconvincingly. 'You're being pathetic and stupid.'

'Right,' said Beryl, jumping up, 'have some of your own medicine!'

She grabbed her glass.

'Cut!' shouted Trent. 'Don't throw it! Don't throw the water!'

Beryl put the glass down.

'Lots to do this morning,' Trent said. 'Can't have Rodney wet yet. We'll pick up the coffee-throwing as we go into the first break. Right. More Mingers.'

Three More Mingers

Outside, Chelsie had returned from the Bite Back Box where she'd had mixed fortunes with Vicky and her mum. Vicky, too upset and confused to speak, had given nothing more but with only minimum prompting her mum had produced one classic bite.

'Just you wait, Calvin Simms,' she spat at the camera. 'My Vicky will be a star and then you're going to have to eat it!'

That was good enough for Chelsie. There was a long morning ahead and so, with only the most perfunctory farewell, she left mother and daughter to slink off to contemplate the ruination of their dreams while she returned to the holding area. There, while Keely had her make-up retouched (Vicky's tears had streaked it slightly), Chelsie began to tee up the first Minger quickie of the morning.

'Can I have Damian, please?' Chelsie shouted.

Damian was a youth of twenty-two, a veterinary student. He had been selected as a featured quickie because he had buck teeth. Spectacularly buck teeth, the sort of teeth normally seen only in a horse, in fact the sort of teeth normally seen only in a horse with buck teeth. Damian was short-sighted too, spectacularly short-sighted. Damian's vision began to blur a mere inch and a half beyond the bridge of his nose. In fact, had Damian's optician and Damian's dentist ever met they might have had an interesting conversation about which reached further beyond Damian's face, his eyesight or his teeth.

When Damian had been pre-selected by Emma on the previous *Chart Throb* visit to Birmingham he had been wearing glasses, thick glasses, glasses with the sort of glass they use in the windows of Tiffany's. Glasses that would stop a bullet. Everyone had loved the glasses almost as much as the teeth.

Chelsie was concerned to see that Damian was not wearing his glasses now.

'Not wearing your bins, babes?' Chelsie cooed.

'Uhm, no.'

'*Loved* those bins, babes,' Chelsie added.

'Really?' Damian replied, surprised.

'Oh *yeah*. Buddy Holly meets Elvis Costello meets Thelma from *Scooby-Doo*,' Chelsie assured him. 'Gotta respect your bins.'

'Actually I thought I'd probably wear my contact lenses when I perform,' Damian replied.

'Bad move, babes!' Chelsie protested. '*So not loving it*. Glasses are *fierce*, babes. Gotta remember the geek factor. Very hip. Very now. Nerd is the new hunk.'

'Is it?' Damian enquired eagerly. 'I didn't know that.'

'They make you look vulnerable, babes,' Chelsie continued. 'Beryl *loves* the vulnerable boys and you know how soppy Rodney can be.'

'You think I should wear my glasses then?'

'*Duh!*' Chelsie urged. 'It's a slam dunk. Of *course* you should wear your glasses!'

And so Damian was ushered before the famous judging panel wearing his glasses. Staring myopically through lenses that grotesquely magnified his eyes, he parted his enormous teeth and announced that he would like to sing 'Everything Is Beautiful'.

The song had been Chelsie's suggestion.

'Something upbeat but also soulful, babes,' she had assured him, by which she had meant that this highly dubious thesis would have a particular comic resonance when coming from ugly little Damian.

Damian couldn't sing at all. Calvin knew he couldn't sing because he'd watched Damian's video during the final selection. Nonetheless Calvin assumed an expression of stunned incredulity as if taken utterly by surprise. Then just as Damian reached the third line Calvin called a halt.

'Thank you!' he shouted. 'It's a no. Goodbye.'

Now it was Damian's turn to be stunned. He knew the way *Chart Throb* worked, he had watched the show, the contestants sang their whole song. They got a moment to argue their case. They received constructive criticism. Then all three judges were called upon to vote.

'But can't I—' he began.

But Damian did *not* know how the show worked. He did not realize the pre-assessment of him had been that he had no potential Cling or Bling at all, he was pure Ming. He would not plead pathetically and he was too sensible a lad to be persuaded to claim to be the new Justin Timberlake. The only interesting things about him were his teeth and his glasses. These had been duly committed to camera and would later be included in a two-second bite as part of a Minger montage. *Chart Throb* was done with Damian.

As if from nowhere, a security man (a real one, not one of the enormous bald extras who featured in the show) suddenly appeared in the company of a pretty junior PA. The good and the bad cops then marched Damian directly from the room.

'Next up is Doreen,' Trent said. 'Chelsie's got her all bigged up and ready.'

Trent had noticed Calvin's clear approval of Chelsie's performance and he was far too clever to try and kick against that particular shit. Much better to go with the flow and try to colonize Chelsie's ascendancy as if it had in fact been him who had nurtured it.

'Which one is Doreen again?' Beryl enquired with weary martyrdom, as if she was a saint to put herself through the gruelling process of making television.

'Tic Toc,' Trent informed her.

Tic Toc was *Chart Throb* slang for Toothless Old Crone.

'Oh God,' Beryl lamented. 'Is she a smack head?'

'Didn't like to ask.'

Doreen, a terrifying social casualty, skeletal, toothless, ancient long before her time and with a distinct aroma of urine about her, was duly brought before the judges. The fleshless quality of her cadaverous frame was emphasized by the fact that her minidress had a heart-shaped hole cut in the front revealing the grey, dry skin of her stomach and the deep, hollow navel. Doreen had arrived wearing a leather jacket but Chelsie had assured her that she would be so much prettier with it off. Doreen's cheeks were sunken into her toothless mouth and her dyed black hair had been falling out in chunks. What was left of it hung greasily from a centre parting, framing the face of a woman who looked sixty but wasn't.

'How old are you, Doreen?' Calvin asked.

He knew the answer, but he wanted to hear her say it.

'I'm forty-three, Calvin,' Doreen said, at which Calvin pulled his stunned mullet expression. He then proceeded to engage Doreen in a brief discussion about her ambitions to be a singer, which, had it been broadcast in full, would have revealed her to be a damaged, hopelessly inadequate, almost certainly drug-addicted borderline mental case who had lived an appalling life of deprivation and abuse. However, the two or three bites that would emerge from the edit just made her look like a mad, nasty, arrogant old bat.

'I'm a singer, Calvin. I reckon I can show them little girlies it's experience that counts . . . I got glamour I have, I've turned heads. Just let me show you what I got to offer . . .'

Then Calvin invited her to sing. They gave her three lines of 'Amazing Grace' and then let her have it.

'If you were the only contestant in the competition you'd lose,' said Calvin.

'You might get work at Hallowe'en,' said Rodney.

'Have you thought about investing in a hair weave?' said Beryl with croaky-voiced sincerity, for it was her special talent to be able to look both sympathetic and contemptuous all at once.

In the depths of Doreen's malfunctioning brain a tiny light bulb lit up and in a rare moment of clarity she suddenly recognized something which would have been blindingly obvious to her, had she had all her faculties. She'd been had.

'That fucking woman told me my hair looked lovely!' she suddenly screamed, pointing at Chelsie, who had poked her head round the partition. 'She told me you like the natural look!'

Chelsie was very grateful to have confirmation of

275

her grooming process delivered to Calvin straight from the horse's mouth.

'I wanted to keep me hat on,' Doreen protested.

But further discussion was superfluous. Doreen's story was done. The good and bad cops appeared and she, like Damian, was ushered quickly from the room.

'Next up, Madge, another oldie,' Trent informed them.

'Please not another ex-crack whore,' Beryl pleaded.

'No, a Moby.'

Moby was *Chart Throb* slang for Mad Old Bat.

Calvin featured a couple of Mobies every year, frail but feisty grannies who wanted to sing 'proper songs'. They were good telly and they helped support the outrageous fiction that *Chart Throb*, unlike other talent shows, was genuinely oblivious to age.

'Hello, hello,' said Madge, hobbling in on her Zimmer frame. She had wanted to leave her coat and handbag outside but Chelsie had assured her that it would look great if she had all her bits and pieces with her.

'Hello, Madge,' said Calvin, assuming his expression of bemused tolerance.

'Hello, darling!' shouted Beryl, pulling the cloyingly protective face that she reserved for babies and Mobies.

Rodney grinned with what he imagined was a wry twinkle.

Once again an inordinate amount of the judges' time was allocated to a person who had no more chance of being a Chart Throb than an actual corpse would have done but who would provide, when suitably edited, a minute or so of good telly.

'I just think it's time to give us old 'uns a go,' Madge was coaxed to say. 'Do you mind if I play my ukulele? I can dance, too, you know. A lot of chaps think I have very fine ankles.'

Then in a sweetly quivering voice Madge sang 'Daisy, Daisy'. It sounded suitably grannie-ish, as if it was a song from her youth, although it had in fact been an oldie when Madge's own grannie was young. When it was over Rodney and Beryl voted to put her through, which was how the notes Trent had given them suggested they should vote. Calvin looked suitably stunned at their decision even though it was he who had given the instructions. The three then briefly 'debated' their 'choice'.

'You honestly think Madge could be a Chart Throb?' Calvin asked.

'Yes. Yes, I do,' said Rodney. 'I think she has something.'

'You think Madge could cut it live? In a studio?' Calvin insisted.

'You're being ageist,' Beryl claimed. 'What is the point of us having no age restriction if you dismiss someone like Madge?'

When Calvin felt the pantomime had gone on long enough he called a vote and at two to one Madge was through to the next round. Calvin then helped her from the room, carrying her bag and coat. Outside, Madge was hugged by Keely while Calvin assumed his long-suffering look.

There followed in quick succession a whole host of Minger quickies, one-shot wonders whose ambition was pitiable enough to raise a laugh but who were not sufficiently interesting or insane to get a story to themselves. Shouters, screamers, midgets, beanpoles, porkers, baldies, speccies and goofies. Nutters in fancy dress, half-naked Druid couples, axe-wielding Vikings and Bacofoil-clad aliens. All were paraded in quick succession before an amusingly astonished judging panel before being just as quickly ejected.

Finally it was time to chuck the coffee over Rodney.

Resignation

'This is all wrong!' shouted Beryl. 'I did NOT sign on for this. You know what, Rodney, you're a great mate and I love you big time but you have just walked right through the edge of my envelope!'

They had retreated to the hospitality area to shoot the final part of the Vicky story. Beryl ranted and raved while Rodney, dripping wet, fondled a vol-au-vent nervously.

'I just didn't think she'd cut it in our business,' he whined.

'She's *sixteen*, Rodney. The girl was *sixteen*!'

Behind her, Calvin was studying the sandwiches. Beryl rounded on him.

'You know what, Calvin?' she said. 'I've had it, I didn't buy into this, this is NOT what I signed up for. I'm out of here, that's me done. Someone get me my fucking car! I'm going home. I love you both but I think you're both horrible. I'm done!!!'

And with that Beryl swept out of the room.

'Cut!' shouted Chelsie before either Trent or the director had had a chance to.

Beryl swept straight back into the room.

'Any good?' she enquired. 'You can bleep the "fucking", can't you? I'm not doing it again whatever you say, that was the third take and I have a shitload of calls to make.'

'No, Beryl,' Calvin assured her, 'that was very, very good.'

Beryl then gathered up her phone and retreated to the make-up area.

'OK, we're done on that sequence,' Trent called out. 'We take fifteen and when we come back we'll pick up Rodney apologizing to Beryl and her agreeing to stay.'

With that the crew began to lay down their

278

equipment and Calvin too took up his phone.

'Hang on!' Rodney said firmly. 'Hang on, hang on, hang *on*! What about our discussion, Calvin? Beryl leaves and we then have a blokey chat about how she gets too emotional and how it's unprofessional and eventually for the good of the show I volunteer to try and coax her back.'

'Not doing it, Rodney,' Calvin explained. 'No time. The item's getting top heavy. Our chat's been binned.'

Calvin was heading for the door.

'HANG ON!!' and this time Rodney shouted. 'What do you mean, "top heavy"? It's top heavy all right. Top heavy with Beryl! All we have is Beryl being mumsy, Beryl chucking coffee over ME, Beryl being all moral and righteous and Beryl walking out on the show. What exactly do I do?'

'You apologize to her. We'll shoot it after the break.'

'EXACTLY. I apologize to BERYL! It's her item again. What is it with you and this woman, Calvin?'

'Beryl's a mum, Rodney. It's good telly.'

'She's a transsexual stepmum!'

'People love all that. She's lived, she's suffered. Now we have only eight minutes left on the break, mate, I suggest you grab a cup of tea and get your make-up redone, you're covered in coffee.'

'How about this, Calvin?' said Rodney, red with rage. 'How about instead of Beryl *pretending* to resign, how about I *actually* resign? How would that be?'

Calvin thought for a moment then turned to Trent.

'Trent,' he said, 'we need to cover this. This is gold. Real rage beats fake rage every time. I'll pay the overtime, get the cameras back up to speed.'

Everyone in the room put down their coffee cups and took up their equipment. Once more Calvin turned to Rodney.

'Rodney, mate, I know you're pissed off but you are under contract so if you really are going to resign I'm going to have to ask you to hold for a couple of minutes while we get the cameras lined up.'

Rodney looked about him like a cornered animal.

'You're . . . you're joking of course,' he said, trying to smile.

'Are you?' said Calvin, smiling back.

'Yes . . . yes, of course I'm joking.'

'Good,' said Calvin finally before standing the crew down once more.

'Seven minutes on the break,' Chelsie cried out, then, 'Crew A with me please to the gents loo to shoot Planet Mars putting his make-up on.'

Words of Love

Calvin was finally able to grab a moment to put a call through to Emma. Standing discreetly in the corridor, he pressed autodial and found a frisson of pleasure even in the appearance of her name on the screen.

'We just shot that spotty stage-school girl and her mum,' Calvin said. 'Do you remember them?'

'Yes,' Emma replied. 'You weren't too hard on her, were you?'

'No, no. Not really. But come on, Emma, it's a game, they all know what they're buying into.'

'I suppose so,' Emma replied doubtfully.

'Don't go *too* soft on me, Em,' Calvin said. 'I'm doing what you want over HRH but I still have to make a show, you know.'

'Yes, I know,' he heard her say. 'And I suppose you do make some dreams come true, don't you?'

'Of course I do. That Quasar bloke's going to get a meal ticket for life. Lots of them do.'

'Yes.'

280

'What stuns me is the way people buy into the whole "we love Beryl" thing. The woman is so evidently a lying, self-obsessed, bullying bitch. I've seen her diss Mingers this morning like you wouldn't *believe*. We had this half-dead skeleton of a crack whore in and Beryl asked her if she'd thought of a hair weave! You can't get much meaner than that, but five minutes later she's pretending to give a shit about some sixteen-year-old human zit with attitude and we all *believe* her. The woman's a genius. A fucking genius.'

'Everybody hates her on the team, you know.'

'You *amaze me!*' Calvin grinned. 'Guess what, Rodney just threatened to resign again!'

'You *amaze me!*' Emma laughed back. 'Did you let him?'

'Of course. Told him I wanted to film it.'

Emma laughed. 'You know, Calvin, I think that's why people like you. I think deep down they understand that you *know* this whole thing is a joke. That you are actually enjoying the pantomime as much as the audience.'

'Do *you* like me, Emma?'

'You know I like you, Calvin. If you hadn't been such a prick I'd be there with you now.'

'But I'm making back the ground, aren't I? Slowly?'

'Yes. Slowly. Just don't forget your promise.'

'I think about it every day, Emma. It's going to be hard but I will save the future King from himself.'

'I can't believe how confident you are . . . Confidence is attractive.'

'I'm in love with you, Emma.'

'I have to go.'

'Are you in love with me?'

'I . . . I'm trying to take things easy. Control my emotions.'

'I've controlled absolutely every aspect of my life for

years. Falling in love with you was the one thing I couldn't control and yet it's the one thing that makes me happy and excited. You should try losing control.'

'I'm not like you, Calvin. I'm the opposite. You need to loosen up, I don't. *Not* being in control has always been my problem. I need to be in control now.'

'But why?'

'Because, Calvin, that day when you sacked me and tried to fuck me . . .'

'Oh, not *that* again.'

'Yes, *that* again.'

'I've said I'm sorry.'

'And I've no doubt you are, Calvin, because you showed me something of your true self that day and I am in no doubt that if I'd slept with you that night and taken my job back you wouldn't be in love with me now. It's because you *can't* have me that you care so much. You just love a challenge, Calvin. You can't resist one.'

'Will you ever love me?'

'When I can trust you. Look, I have to go, I'm in Sainsbury's. Will you ring me later?'

'Of course.'

'Bye.'

Calvin turned off his phone, both frustrated and thrilled. He knew that she was right. He did love a challenge. He *had* to get that girl.

Troy Learns to Read

Chelsie was back in the holding area where her next shoot was scheduled. This was one that Calvin had scripted himself but which he did not wish to attend.

'Uhm, Your Royal Highness?' Chelsie said.

The Prince of Wales looked up from the book he had been reading.

'Eh, what? Oh hello. How *are you*? Just boning up on my crop rotation. Smallholdings are an absolute *nightmare* to farm, do you agree? At least I always think they are. Perhaps I'm *mad*, a lot of people seem to think so, but I keep *banging on* just the same. Not that anybody listens but I do think it's *important*, don't you?'

'This is Troy.'

The cameras Chelsie had brought with her began to close in as the sixteen-year-old youth stepped forward, still holding his comic.

'Hello. *Hello*. Troy, is it?' the Prince said, jumping up. 'How *are* you? What's that? A *comic*, I see. Well *done*. Is it good? I know some of them are *awfully* cleverly done. How *are* you?'

'I read comics because I can't read very well,' Troy replied in a rather wooden manner, as if these were words he had been told to say.

'Goodness! Really? Well, you know, we do positively *heaps* of work on *the literacy issue* in my charity. We run *homework* clubs, you know. I do believe *very strongly* that we can't simply leave young people *behind*. We *have* to find a way to include them. Of course I *bang on about it* all the time, but I don't suppose anybody *listens* very much, do you?'

A few feet away Keely edged into the shot and whispered a piece to camera as if she were listening in on a genuinely spontaneous encounter.

'Meanwhile in the holding area,' she whispered, 'Troy has got chatting to the Prince of Wales. Like most people here, the penny hasn't dropped for Troy that he's speaking to the heir to the throne. Everybody else thinks he's a lookalike but I don't even think Troy thinks that. The royal family are simply not on his radar at all.'

The Prince was still politely chatting with Troy, who had sat down next to him and was showing the Prince his comic.

'Goodness, *Batman*,' the Prince was saying. 'Is it very exciting?'

'I don't know,' Troy replied. 'I can't read it.'

'I *see*,' said the Prince. 'It's all Greek to Troy, eh?'

The Prince laughed as if he had made a joke but Troy had clearly not followed it.

'It's frustrating,' said Troy, offering the Prince his comic.

The two serious-looking men sitting nearby stirred for a moment.

'Oh, don't *fuss* so!' the Prince admonished them, taking Troy's comic. 'Goodness, *Deep in the Bat cave the Dark Knight sits brooding* – how thrilling!'

For a moment the Prince and the youth sat together and pored over *Batman*.

At a discreet distance, the cameras rolled.

Congratulations, You're Through: Quasar and The Four-Z

After lunch, which Calvin and Beryl spent on the phone and Rodney spent pretending to be on the phone, the second half of the day began with the drudgery of setting up those characters who it had been decided would proceed through to the Pop School stage of the contest and also in some cases on to the finals.

The Quasar was up first, doing everything that was expected of him. He walked in wearing a skin-tight string vest and announced that he was already a superstar and it remained only for the three judges to alert the world.

Calvin pretended to hate him, as planned.

Beryl asked him if his muscles were real, as planned.

The Quasar played up to it all beautifully as the selectors had assumed he would. They had expected him to offer Beryl a squeeze test so that she could make up her own mind, and he did. They had not expected him to ask if she'd like to squeeze his love muscle to see if that was real too, but regrettably (since it was that rare thing on *Chart Throb*, a moment of genuine comedy) it would not make the final cut of a family show.

The Quasar was voted through as planned. Calvin had long since decided that the Quasar (who, although no singer, was a genuinely amusing and personable Blinger) would make it all the way to the finals.

Next came The Four-Z, who did a not-bad four-part a cappella harmony of 'Three Times A Lady' in which no fewer than three parts were in tune most of the time. They were voted through in a unanimous orgy of dewy-eyed enthusiasm, as if The Commodores themselves had turned up for an audition.

'You know what?' said Calvin, going all professional and serious. 'It is rare to encounter such innate musical talent in people so young. You *owned* that song. You boys are genuine stars and you have huge recording careers ahead of you.'

'You know what?' said Beryl, half mother, half sex kitten. 'You guys just blew me away. I'm a rock chick from way back and I know that that is one tough song to nail, but you know what? You guys owned it.'

'You know what?' said Rodney. 'I honestly think you sang it better than Lionel Richie did, you took that song and you know what? You owned it.'

The boys left the room weeping tears of joy.

'You know what?' said Calvin testily, after they had left. 'We can't *all* say "you know what" so can you please refer to the phrase distribution chart which is included in each morning's briefing notes?'

Calvin was referring to the system he had developed in the face of the plethora of judging-panel shows that had emerged since *Pop Idol* and *X Factor*. Phrases which had arisen in those early days – 'you know what?', 'you owned that song', 'you could sell a lot of records', 'you rock big time', 'the dream's over', 'the song was just too big for you', 'I loved you *so* much but it's a no from me' – had soon become the staple audition language for all panels and it had been necessary to ration them.

Outside the audition room The Four-Z didn't care what language had been used to put them through, they were too busy leaping about with Keely and collectively thanking God for taking them one very big step closer to moving out of hell.

Congratulations, You're Through: Graham and Millicent

The next auditionees were Graham and Millicent.

'Hi. I'm Millicent,' said Millicent, leading Graham in.

'I'm Graham,' said Graham.

'And together we're Graham and Millicent.'

Millicent announced that they would like to sing 'Bright Eyes' (which had been suggested to them by Chelsie, although the idea had come from Calvin).

'Good song,' said Calvin, looking serious. 'Good choice.'

Beryl, who had been discreetly pulling at the hairs

on the inside of her nose in preparation, wept real tears as they began.

Millicent sang well and Graham sang badly. Not, however, according to Calvin, who as usual was not inclined to let the facts get in the way of a good story, particularly one that he had written himself.

'You know what?' Calvin said, once more playing the role of the straight-talking perfectionist. 'For a double act that was a great solo performance.'

The two young people stood in silent confusion, waiting for Calvin to explain himself.

'Millicent?' Calvin enquired. 'What do you think you bring to this act?'

'Well, I . . .'

'I'll tell you,' said Calvin. 'Currently, nothing. Graham has a voice and you don't, it's as simple as that. He's a singer, you're a passenger, Millicent, and I think you know it too. He's carrying you, Millicent. No, he isn't carrying you, you're not that good. He's *dragging* you, Millicent. Right now Graham is *dragging* you along. How do you feel about that, Millicent? Is that what you want? To be dragged? You must be aware that you're holding him back.'

Millicent did not reply. By the look on her face she would have had more chance of replying if Calvin had punched her in the stomach. She was clearly sick with horror.

'How do you feel, Graham?' Calvin asked. 'You're a singer, you're singing with someone who can't sing. It's screwing up your act. How do you feel?'

Graham could not find words either. The two young people, young lovers, simply stood and stared like witnesses to a tragedy. Which, in a way, they were.

'Right!' snapped Calvin, going all businesslike. 'I'm going to put you through because of Graham and only because of Graham, it's as simple as that. Rodney?'

'I agree,' said Rodney, who knew what was expected

of him. 'Graham has the voice. He's the talent.'

'Beryl?' Calvin snapped again.

'Yes,' croaked Beryl, picking up her cue from Calvin. 'I'm going to say yes but only because of Graham and his beautiful rock 'n' roll voice. You are *so* sexy, Graham, and that *voice*!'

'All right,' said Calvin, playing it tough. 'You're through. You get another shot and all I can say is this, Millicent: you had better work, young lady. You had better work like you've never worked before. You had better work and learn and grow and grow and learn and work because it's down to you, young lady. You are what is standing in Graham's way, his career is in your hands and if you don't get your act together you will bring this boy down.'

With that Graham and Millicent were escorted, shaking, from the room.

'God, you're good,' said Beryl after they had left. 'That was brilliant.'

'The problem surely,' said Rodney, 'is that in fact she's the singer, not him.'

'Yes, yes, I *know* she's the better singer, Rodney! For God's sake, this is our third series together, haven't you worked it out yet? These people are whatever we *say* they are, however we *edit* them to be. If we look at this little blind chap with his phlegmy, throaty, crappy little voice and say that he has the voice of a young James Brown then the voice of a young James Brown is what he's got. God knows, I've lost count of the times Beryl has told some saggy-boobed barmaid who's covered "My Heart Will Go On" that actually she preferred her version to Céline's. Sometimes even I cringe. How many times do I have to tell you, *the singing doesn't matter*! *Please* try to remember.'

Outside the audition room Keely met Graham and Millicent, breathless with anticipation.

'Did you make it? Are you through?' she asked.

'Yes, we're through,' Millicent said before bursting into tears.

'Babes, babes, *babes*,' said Keely. *'Babes!'*

Keely hugged Millicent and Millicent told Keely what had happened. 'I'll drop out now!' she protested. 'I would *never* stand in Graham's way. Calvin might as well have said that I don't want Graham to succeed without me.'

Watching from behind the camera which was hovering inches from Millicent's distraught face, Chelsie noted down the time code. That last sentence, if taken out of context, was dynamite. *I don't want Graham to succeed without me.* If ever a girl was condemned from her own mouth . . . That sentence played before, after and if possible during the commercial breaks would hang that little goody two-shoes choirgirl high.

Congratulations, You're Through to the Next Round: Bloke

Next came Bloke, a weddings and parties rock 'n' roll band. Four pleasant-faced lads in their early thirties who humbly explained that they had paid their rockin' dues up and down the M1 and the M6 (just them and their battered old guitars) and they reckoned that this was their last chance at the big time.

'This is our last best shot, Calvin,' explained one Bloke.

'We came here to rock,' another Bloke added. 'And that's what we're going to do.'

'So hey, why don't we quit talking,' said the first Bloke, 'and do this thing!'

Beryl whooped, Calvin smiled and Bloke sang 'Stand By Me' in gut-wrenching, throat-tearing four-part harmony, by the end of which their faces were so contorted with pain and emotion that they might easily have been enduring a hedgehog enema rather than singing a song.

When it was over, Beryl was the first to speak.

'Guys,' she said, 'that was awesome. You know me, I'm just a rock chick from way back and all I can say is you *rock*! You *rock*, GUYS! You *owned* that song. It was awesome.'

'That is a tough song too,' Rodney added, trying to look intelligent and hard to please. ' "Stand By Me" is a very tough song to cover. That is not an easy song at all. It's a tough song, but you owned it.'

Rodney was sitting in the middle seat, having temporarily assumed the role of team leader. Occasionally he and Beryl were instructed to do so as part of Calvin's effort to create the illusion of equality between the judges.

'I'm putting you guys through,' Rodney said. 'Beryl?'

'Yes!' Beryl agreed. 'Yes, yes, yes, the guys rock.'

'Calvin?' asked Rodney, absolutely loving his moment in the middle.

'I hated it,' said Calvin.

Beryl and Rodney howled in protest and then the three of them went through the exhausting motions of playing out their fictional conflict.

'You've gone mad, Calvin!' Beryl protested woodenly. 'Behave! What are you like? I don't *believe you*. Behave!'

'That was a very tough song,' Rodney added, and if Beryl's performance had been wooden Rodney's was hewn from solid mahogany. 'I think you owe these fellas an apology.'

'Just because you wouldn't personally have the range to cover a song like that, Rodney, does not make it a tough song,' Calvin quipped. 'I thought the guys were boring.'

In fact Calvin was not in a position to consider Bloke's performance either boring or otherwise because he had been standing in the corner speaking to America on his mobile while they were performing.

'Sorry, guys,' said Calvin, 'but I've seen a hundred bands like you paying their dues in every down-and-dirty rock pub in the country.'

Bloke in fact played mainly hotels and party halls and Calvin would not have entered a down-and-dirty rock pub if Britney Spears had been on stage going down on Madonna, but it sounded good. Tough and professional.

'Yeah, Calvin,' one of the Blokes replied. 'Maybe you're right, maybe there are a lot of guys like us out there paying their rock 'n' roll dues. And maybe we're playing for them.'

'Yes!' shrieked Beryl. 'YES! *Good* answer! You go, guys.'

'Well said!' Rodney nodded.

Calvin, his face a picture of honest good humour, pretended to be swayed.

'Yes, Beryl's right, that was a good answer,' he conceded. 'I like your attitude. Maybe you guys are as good as you think you are. Damn it, maybe I should take a risk . . .'

Once more Calvin paused, as if wrestling with every ounce of his instinct and his intellect.

'This is a life-changing moment for you guys,' he said, stringing it out. 'If I make a mistake and you can't cut it, I'm going to look a fool.'

'Hey, we won't let you down, Calvin,' said one of the Blokes.

'You'd better not. OK. You're through.'

Congratulations, You're Through to the Next Round: Iona

Iona had been having an uncomfortable time in the holding area. Unlike the Prince of Wales, she had been recognized by all the other contestants in the room, who had witnessed the humiliation that had been dealt out to her and her bandmates the previous year. They had also all seen Rodney Root publicly declare his affection for Iona and predict that Shetland Mist would become enormous stars. They were also aware that this prediction had been followed by an entire absence of stardom, enormous or otherwise.

'I can't believe you're back here having another go,' one of the girls sitting nearby said.

'So you've dumped the band then, Iona?' another remarked. 'I think that's a shame.'

Iona could not tell them that she had in fact been invited to reapply. This was one of the *Chart Throb* rules by which she must abide and which, as Chelsie had reminded her when she had called, could change at any time.

Eventually a researcher arrived with Keely and a camera team.

'Just look who I've found lurking in the holding area,' Keely shouted at the camera, feigning surprise. 'Yay, it's Iona, out of Shetland Mist from last year!!! How cool is that? Come and say hello, missus.'

Iona made her way forward.

'Hello!' said Keely. 'Fantastic to see you, girlfriend. So you've come back for another bash, eh?'

'Yes, that's right, Keely. I'm starting right from the bottom again,' Iona explained.

'But without the rest of the band?'

'Well, you know, I miss them heaps, Keely, but we

292

all talked about it and we reckoned there was no point just repeating what we did last time, so . . . well, here I am.'

'Yay, babes! Go, girl! How cool is that?' Keely gushed. 'Now it's no secret to anyone that you and our very own pop Svengali, Rodney Root, were an item way back last year. He was a big fan as I recall.'

'That's right, Keely, he was a very big fan.'

'So you're looking forward to seeing him again?'

'Oh yes,' said Iona, her pale eyes narrowing. 'I'm looking forward to seeing Rodney Root again.'

'No time like the present, missus! Let's do this thing!'

Keely and Iona, accompanied by the camera team, made their way towards the audition room.

For a moment Rodney had been enjoying himself. He always loved the times when he got to sit in the middle and he had almost forgotten about what Calvin had planned for him. Therefore the look of shock and horror on his face when Iona entered the room was entirely genuine.

'Hi, Iona!' shrieked Beryl, as if surprised. 'You came back! Good on you, girl, for having the sheer freakin' balls to get back into the ring and face us again. That takes guts. *I like that.* You go, girl!'

'Hello, Iona,' said Calvin, smiling. Then, turning to Rodney, 'Just look who's turned up for another shot at the title, Mr Root.'

It is never easy to bump into ex-girlfriends, particularly ex-girlfriends whom one has let down in public and been avoiding ever since. It's even harder when doing so in front of television cameras. Rodney conspicuously failed to rise to the occasion.

'Uhgh . . . uhm . . . right. Yes,' he said.

Calvin had Rodney covered from every angle. As the master creator of fictional drama he knew that nothing beat the real thing, and ever since Rodney had

293

dumped Iona the previous year he had been planning this moment and looking forward keenly to exploiting Rodney's genuine discomfort.

'Hello, Iona,' Rodney said eventually, his voice weak.

'Hello, Rodney,' Iona replied sweetly but with a tinge of wistful sadness. 'Haven't seen you in a while.'

'That's right, no. Absolutely. No band with you today then?'

'No, Rodney,' Iona replied. 'We had to call it a day. We never did hit the big time, *as you know*, and you can't wait for ever, can you?'

'No, that's right,' said Rodney, swallowing hard. 'You can't.'

'Wait for *you*, she means!' Beryl shrieked while Rodney squirmed. 'We all remember what you said last year, mate! It's about time one of the acts you promised a career to turned up again and chucked it in your face. You're always doing it.'

'Yes, Rodney,' Calvin added. 'You mentioned apologies a moment ago. I rather think you owe Iona one. After all, you did promise that Shetland Mist would be stars.'

'Yes, well, I thought that the band had talent,' Rodney stammered. 'I still do, of course.'

'But not enough for you to get them a deal?' Beryl pointed out.

Suddenly Rodney saw red and for a brief moment the worm turned.

'Well, I'd rather see them fail *before* they got a deal than have the embarrassment of public failure afterwards like your precious daughter Priscilla, Beryl! How *is* her album doing, by the way?'

For a moment Beryl was stunned, unable to believe that Rodney had dared to diss her family. *Her family*. That thing to which she was publicly known to be utterly and slavishly devoted. Was he not aware that she was the world's greatest mum?

'What the FUCK did you say?' Beryl shouted.

'You heard what I said,' Rodney replied, but he was already losing his nerve.

'Yes, I did, mate. And I shan't forget it either.' Beryl turned to Calvin. 'You won't keep it in, will you?' she enquired. 'What this *cunt* just said?'

'No, of course not,' Calvin replied. 'Certainly not. I doubt it. Probably wouldn't work anyway. We'll see. I mean I'll have to *look* at it, we look at everything, but I doubt we'll use it. Probably not anyway.'

Calvin glanced at Chelsie, who gave a tiny nod to indicate that the time code had been noted.

'Well, let me tell you now, Calvin,' Beryl said, continuing to speak across Rodney as if he was not there. 'If this little shit *ever* disses my daughter again, or *any* member of my family, I walk. Got it? You can do without him but you can't do without me. So remember that.'

There was another pause while Calvin stared back at Beryl, like her, entirely ignoring Rodney. Calvin smiled but it was a cold smile.

'You know I'd *hate* to lose you, darling,' he said with the tiniest touch of menace. 'But in the long run these decisions are mine. I have told you, Beryl, I *doubt* we'll use it.'

Leaving Beryl to fume impotently, Calvin turned to Rodney, smiling pleasantly.

'Rodney,' he said, 'we can't leave Iona standing here all day, she's here for an audition. You're in the middle, get on with it.'

Ignoring Beryl, who continued to smoulder, Rodney made an effort to pull himself together.

'Right, Iona. What are you going to sing for us today?'

'I'd like to sing "You Raise Me Up" by Westlife.'

'Off you go then, babes.'

Iona sang the song very sweetly, her pretty green

eyes even growing wet with tears as she got to the big bit. When it was over Beryl and Calvin applauded with some enthusiasm.

'Go, girl!' shouted Beryl. 'You *owned* that song!'

'Yes. Congratulations,' said Calvin, who seemed to have scarcely been listening, perhaps still preoccupied with the growing tension between his fellow judges and how best to exploit it. 'You've come a long way since last year.'

'Yes, yes,' Beryl agreed before giving Iona her vote on the grounds that she had obviously listened carefully to all her comments. 'I really feel you've taken on board everything we said last year. I told you to go away and to learn and grow, and that's exactly what you've done.'

Calvin agreed and put her through also.

'Rodney?' he asked.

Rodney knew what was expected of him, he had read the script. His eyes made one last appeal to Calvin but Calvin simply tapped the relevant page with his pencil.

'No need for my vote,' Rodney said, with forced jollity. 'Iona already has your votes, she's through to the next round anyway.'

Calvin was having none of it.

'Rodney,' he said quietly, 'what's your vote?'

Rodney had no choice. For all the pretence about independent celebrity judges, he was an employee of CALonic TV, a creature of Calvin's, every ounce of fame and status that he had he owed to Calvin. He did what he was told.

'I'm sorry, Iona,' he stammered. 'I just don't think you can cut it without the band. I don't think you're good enough. It's a "no" from me.'

It was a truly terrific moment of television. Even the senior members of the crew who had known what was coming gulped at the cruelty and the audacity of it. As for the runners and the juniors who were not in on the script loop, they simply gasped. It was incredible: Rodney Root, Iona's great public champion of the previous year, the ex-boyfriend who had promised her the world, was knocking her back in the first round. It was amazing, incredible. Everybody knew that they were present at a watershed moment in popular culture, like the moon landings or Kennedy's assassination or the first shag on *Big Brother*.

Understandably the person in the room who was most taken aback was Iona herself. Clearly, whatever she had expected from Rodney, it wasn't this. The camera, which had crept up to within an inch of her soul, captured the stunned pain of a woman utterly betrayed.

'Well, Rodney,' she said icily, 'funny thing that. I was good enough for you before, wasn't I? In public and in private.'

Without another word she turned and left the room.

Watch Out, She's Mad

Calvin announced a five-minute break. It wasn't that there was time to spare but he just *had* to ring Emma. Clearing the camera team out of the hospitality room where they had been hoovering up the vol-au-vents, he lit a cigarette and prepared to luxuriate in the music of her voice.

'You didn't make him reject her?' Emma gasped when Calvin had explained the exquisite tension and embarrassment of Iona's confrontation with Rodney.

'Of course I did and I'm going to bring her back round after round and make him do it again and it's going to get better and better.'

'Fictional drama's fine but real drama's TV gold, eh?' Emma quoted.

'Of course. Can't beat the real thing.'

'He should have stood up to you though, he really should. I mean his ex-*girlfriend*, that is pathetic.'

'Third judge syndrome. They *are* pathetic. It's their job.'

'Speaking of drama,' Emma said, changing the subject, 'have you seen that girl Shaiana yet?'

'No. She's in the batch up next. Why do you ask?'

'I don't know. Nothing, I suppose.'

But Calvin was not having that. He knew Emma was a terrific researcher, her instincts had never let her down, and if she chose to enquire about one of the thousands of names that she had processed in the long months of pre-production he wanted to know why.

'Come on,' he insisted. 'Why do you ask?'

'Well, it's just I've never forgotten her,' Emma replied quietly. 'I say not forgotten, I *had* forgotten her but she sort of came back to me. I remember her application form, *I am me*, and the way she wanted it so much.'

'They all want it so much.'

'Of course, I know that, but this girl wrote it *twice*. On her form. I've never seen that before.'

'Emma, you've seen them written in blood. Didn't you tell me you got one in spunk last year?'

'I don't think it actually *was* spunk. I think it was flour and water glue meant to *look* like spunk.'

'Well whatever, it isn't as if you haven't seen enough weirdos.'

'Of course. All the same, I think Shaiana is in a bit of a different class. I remember her selection day in Birmingham. She was so *desperate*. So *intense*. Like she really, really had something to prove, *to herself*.'

'That's how I like them, Emma. The more they

298

believe, the harder they cling and Clingers are great TV.'

'All the same, don't let her near Hair and Costume, they have a lot of scissors. What story did you end up assigning her? You're not putting her in the final, are you?'

'No. We'll drop her after Pop School. Usual thing, taunt her to improve then tell her she hasn't.'

'I think you should drop her sooner. I think you should drop her now.'

'Which is exactly why I'm not going to.'

'What do you mean?'

'Emma, you were brilliant at your job. If you didn't have morals and a conscience you could have ended up a junior partner in CALonic . . .'

'No, thank you.'

'And if you think some saddo is so on the edge that I should avoid them, then that means we have a classic Clinger on our hands which I have a public duty to milk for all she's worth.'

'I'm telling you, Calvin, she's too intense. There's too much going on there.'

'There is *never* too much going on for me, Emma. I *love* it, you know that. Don't worry, these people don't scare me. Never have. Never will. Look, I've got to go. We're miles behind. Love you, Emma. Love you lots.'

'*Might* love you. Bye.'

As Calvin put away his phone he glanced up and realized he was being watched. It was Shaiana. He recognized her immediately. She had wandered up from the holding area. Perhaps to go to the ladies, or perhaps just to stare.

'Hello there,' said Calvin, looking her up and down. 'Be with you in a minute.'

She looked ordinary enough to him. Bit of a Goth. Too much make-up perhaps, and wearing an entirely

299

inappropriate bustier because she had no bust to speak of. Just one more dull nobody to be made briefly interesting in the edit. Calvin could not see what Emma was going on about. Perhaps for once her instincts had failed her?

Just Doing It for the Kids

The Prince entered the audition room, leaving his two detectives hovering in the wings. Calvin had not informed his two colleagues of the Prince of Wales's decision to try his luck on *Chart Throb*. As always, he preferred real drama and genuine reactions to those that had to be faked and he was curious to see how Beryl and Rodney would respond.

'Oh my *God*!' Beryl exclaimed. 'That's brilliant! You look exactly like him!'

'Extraordinary,' Rodney agreed. 'Can you do the voice?'

The Prince seemed rather taken aback at this and was clearly not sure what they meant. He therefore politely ignored it, as he was so often forced to do when confronted by gawping strangers who babbled nonsense at him.

'*Hello!* How *are* you? Are you *well*?' he said.

Beryl and Rodney cheered.

'That's *fantastic*,' Beryl exclaimed.

'Amazing. Can you do anybody else?' Rodney enquired, after which there was a brief and slightly uncomfortable silence, the Prince still having no idea what they were talking about.

'Are you the judges?' he said finally, years of experience of making small talk kicking in. '*Well done*. I do think that must be an awfully difficult job. Is it *hard*? I *bet* it's hard. Poor *you*.'

'This bloke's amazing,' Rodney said, turning to Calvin, who smiled and indicated that he wanted Rodney to lead the interview.

'So, tell us a bit about yourself,' Rodney asked the Prince. 'Who are you?'

'I'm the Prince of Wales, for my *sins*,' the Prince replied, at which Beryl shrieked with laughter.

'Brilliant!' she said.

'I *see*,' Rodney replied. 'And how should we refer to you?'

'Well,' the Prince replied, '*Your Royal Highness* is customary but really *sir* will be absolutely fine. No really, I do think too much formality can *get in the way* sometimes, don't you?'

'All right then . . . sir. What brings you here?'

'Well, do you know, I've come here to *learn*,' the Prince explained. 'A great many people seem to see *muggins here* as a bit of an *old fogey*. And who knows, perhaps they're right, perhaps I have lost touch with young people but, unlike *some*, I refuse to *rail against* them, condemning their culture as *empty* and *worthless* while knowing nothing whatsoever about it. That's why I'm here to *learn*. To learn about this vibrant, new, impatient generation, and also about *myself*. Because if I don't know myself then how can I expect people to *know me* and I suppose I'm vain enough to hope that some day they might.'

As the Prince spoke, the cameras focused on the faces of the judges and it was clear that for Beryl and Rodney the shocking reality was beginning to dawn. Calvin, playing his part beautifully, also allowed his jaw to drop open as it became more and more obvious that this was no lookalike.

'Excuse me?' Beryl said when the Prince had finished speaking. '*Are* you the Prince of Wales?'

'Yes. Didn't I *say*? Goodness gracious, I'd forget my own *head* if it wasn't *screwed on*!'

'The *actual* Prince of Wales?' Beryl continued.

'Yes, *absolutely*, Knight of this, Companion of that. All a lot of nonsense really, although I do think that some tradition is *important*, don't you? Otherwise in pursuit of the *ephemeral* we lose sight of the *eternal*. We disenfranchise the next generation from their own *history*. We have no right to do that, surely? We have to pass on the means by which people in future times can understand their own past. *History matters*. Don't you agree? Or am I just *banging on*? I do that, you know.'

When the Prince had finished once more there was a pause. Even Beryl was stunned into silence.

'Uhm, well, sir,' Calvin said, 'what would you like to sing for us?'

'I should like to sing "Rockin' All Over The World" by Status Quo,' the Prince replied.

'Good choice,' said Rodney, as if on autopilot. 'That is a great choice of song.'

'That's rock*in*', not rock*ing*,' the Prince added. 'The "g" is silent. Sacrificed for dramatic effect and in order to make the lyric *swing*. I do think that's acceptable, don't you? Proper English does matter but one must avoid being *overly rigid*. Do you agree?'

The three judges indicated that they most certainly did agree and the Prince duly performed the old Quo classic. When he had finished, the three judges applauded enthusiastically.

'Your Royal Highness,' said Calvin, putting on his serious face.

'Please, *do* call me *sir*,' the Prince interrupted. 'Really, honestly, a simple sir is absolutely *fine*.'

'Well then, sir,' Calvin continued, once more assuming his serious voice. 'I am very pleasantly surprised. When I realized that it really was you wanting to audition for us, quite frankly I was horrified.'

A flicker of confusion passed across the Prince's face. Clearly Calvin had not made him a party to the fact that he intended to deny any foreknowledge of the royal appearance. Calvin pressed on quickly before the Prince could point out that Calvin had in fact invited him to audition.

'We are constantly presented with an image of you as an out-of-touch, aloof, effete, snobbish, obsessive, interfering old bore.'

'I know. I *know*,' the Prince lamented. 'It *is* dispiriting, isn't it?'

'I never believed any of those nasty rumours for a *moment*, sir,' Beryl cooed. 'You've done *so much* for understanding and tolerance. Between races, religions . . . gender preferences. Why, I believe it would now be possible for a transsexual to be made a Dame of the British Empire.'

'Shut up, Beryl,' Calvin snapped.

'I'm just saying!'

'Well, don't. Sir,' Calvin said, once more turning to the Prince. 'We all know the dreadful things they say about you. But *Chart Throb* is a level playing field. We don't respect rank but we don't condemn it either. Everyone who comes here is judged absolutely on their merit. Anyone can be a star . . .'

'*Well done you*,' the Prince interrupted. 'I *do* think that's commendable. It's exactly the *ethos* I try to promote with my Trust. We always say that no matter how desperate or difficult the circumstances into which a young person may have fallen, it is our job to help them *rise above all that* and unlock the natural potential that is in us all.'

Calvin smiled. 'And no less so for you, sir. You too have a right to be taken on your merits. I'm going to put you through.'

'*Really?* Oh, you *are* kind.'

'Me too,' Beryl said quickly. 'You *owned* that song, sir.'

'Yes,' hastened Rodney. 'Covering the Quo is not easy. But you owned it, sir.'

The Prince was then led from the audition room. Outside he found a breathless Keely waiting to ask how His Royal Highness had done.

'Well, do you know, I rather think they *liked it*,' he replied. 'Heaven knows why. I expect I was *awful* but I did my best and of course it is an awfully good tune.'

'So you're through to Pop School?' Keely squealed.

'Well, that's what they *said*.'

The Prince did not jump up and down screaming in the time-honoured manner of contestants who were put through to the next round, so Keely jumped up and down for him.

'Yay!' she said. 'That is *so* fierce! Hot or what! How cool is that?'

After which the Prince and his two detectives hurried back to London to attend a service of remembrance at St Paul's Cathedral for the victims of the most recent tsunami.

Congratulations, You're Through: Latiffa and Suki

After His Royal Highness came Latiffa, the pre-assigned BAT or Black girl with ATtitude. Calvin always liked to include one of these in his shows, and sometimes also a WOMBAT, or White girl Obviously Masquerading as a Black girl with ATtitude – which was even funnier, there being nothing more amusing than pale girls from Essex strutting about, clicking their fingers, calling themselves hos and generally giving the impression that they were brought up with Eminem on Eight Mile.

Latiffa strutted into the room as if she was auditioning to join a Destiny's Child tribute band. She was an uber-girlfriend with the kind of aggressive self-confidence that the Wehrmacht must have had on the morning they invaded Russia, and of course the same potential for disaster. American in all but nationality, Latiffa was not inclined to conceal her light under a bushel.

'I'm da best!' she proclaimed loudly. 'So forget da rest. I is sexy and I is a strong woman and I got claws so you better watch out. Nobody wants this like I want it so everybody had better get outa my way because Latiffa's comin' through!'

Time was short so it had been decided to rush her audition. She was given just enough time to be wholly irritating, which was her assigned role in the chemistry of the final group that Calvin was assembling. She sang 'Nasty Boys' by Janet Jackson and Calvin let her do three lines before informing her that she was through to the next round. He did not even bother to consult his fellow judges. He was not intending to feature Latiffa much until the later stages of the competition, lest the grating quality of her all-consuming self-confidence peak too soon. A flash or two was all that would appear in the first two or three shows.

After Latiffa came Suki, the surgically inflated stripper-turned-prostitute whom Trent had tried to dismiss straight out of the envelope and whom Emma had only included in the Bling pile on a sympathetic whim. But the same thing that had caught Emma's eye had later caught Calvin's. Trent had offered her up in pre-selection as an In and Out, good for a quick shot and a giggle: 'Imagine this sucked-out, dried-up old whore thinking she could ever be a pop star' was the idea. But when he stared at her video there had been something so all-encompassing about Suki's neediness that Calvin found it almost attractive. She was so fascinatingly vulnerable. The classic bird on a wire. Still attractive (just) but literally with only months, maybe even weeks left before she turned irreversibly into a horrifying cartoon of a Disgusting Old Slapper or DOSser. Something in Calvin's instincts had alerted him to the possibility that Suki would be good telly. Many men would lust after her because her vulnerability made her seem attainable and many women would sympathize with her as someone who stood on the edge of an abyss. She could even sing a bit, which was always preferable in a prospective finalist.

A couple of years earlier, when *Chart Throb* had first been screened, a figure like Suki with her ridiculous breasts and hungry eyes would only ever have been considered as a peripheral quickie. But expectations had changed. Women like Suki were becoming the norm. The alpha versions of the type stood on every catwalk, and *OK!* and *Hello!* regularly featured cartoon women cradling new babies that were smaller than their grossly inflated breasts.

'What are you going to sing for us, Suki?' Calvin enquired.

'Well, Calvin,' Suki replied, 'I think you're the sexiest man on TV so I'd like to sing "Hopelessly Devoted To You" from *Grease*.'

Calvin gave his little boy grin.

Beryl said, 'Oh *please!*'

Rodney said, 'Good song, that is a good choice of song. But tough.'

'Before I start,' said Suki, 'I just want you to know that I really, really want this, I mean really. I want it so much. It's my dream.'

Peroxide Meet Their Nemesis

While Suki lived out her dream in front of Calvin, Beryl and Rodney, Chelsie had returned to the holding area to spend a last few moments with Peroxide.

Georgie and 'Chelle were sitting where they had been sitting for most of the day. On the floor, backs to the wall, cramped close together, surrounded by styrofoam cups, holding each other very tight. They held each other partly because they were cold – almost immediately on arrival they had changed into their costumes, which were little more than knickers and bras – but also they clung to each other because they were so excited. Holding on to each other was pretty much the only way that they could actually keep still. Seldom had two teenage girls been at such a pitch of excitement. They were almost too excited to breathe.

They felt different to the other fifty or so remaining contestants scattered about the room; at least they thought they did because they really thought they had a chance.

Chelsie thought so too.

'Come on, girls,' she cooed. 'Calvin's *got* to put you through. I mean why else would they ask you back like this? They know you're good. They know they made a mistake last year. You remember the protests in the press and all that? I honestly think that Calvin was embarrassed by how much people *loved* you guys.'

Georgie and 'Chelle needed little encouragement to believe that this was indeed to be their year. Analysing it endlessly in the preceding weeks, they had concluded that barring some unforeseen disaster like an attack of tonsillitis they *had* to be good for at least a few rounds. Although trying hard to avoid over-confidence, they could not help feeling that they would not be at risk until the Pop School stage at least. After all, their early rejection the previous year *had* been a major *Chart Throb* scandal, the papers *had* all howled in dismay. Calvin *had* specifically asked them back to try again this year (not that they were allowed to divulge this fact).

One thing was certain, the judges were not going to repeat what had happened last time.

Chelsie crouched down in front of the girls and held out her arms for a final hug. Three-way hugs are never easy, particularly when the instigator is hovering above the two other participants who are sitting on the floor, but Chelsie was an accomplished air-kisser and she managed to gather the two young women in for a brief bonding moment. As Georgie leaned towards her, Chelsie was conscious of two things: an overwhelming smell of toothpaste and mouthwash and also how much more skinny she had become even since the selection day in Birmingham. The bra Georgie was wearing was tiny and yet not tiny enough for Georgie to fill it. As Georgie leaned in and the cups fell forward they revealed entirely the shocking state of the girl's breasts. They were really nothing more than big hard cold nipples, pathetically oversized for the little flaps of skin (like small balloons prior to inflation) to which they were attached. She looked starved.

'Come on, girls,' said Chelsie, 'let's go and rock their asses!'

The three of them joined Keely outside the audition area. Keely was utterly thrilled to see them.

'GIRLS!' she screamed. 'BABES! You look *fantastic*!' Keely then turned to address the camera that was hovering just behind her. 'Look who's here! It's last year's megababes, Peroxide! We *love* these girls. *SO* brave to give it another bash. Yay!'

There followed the usual conversation regarding the

dream and how entirely and absolutely the girls wanted it, and then Georgie and 'Chelle entered the arena.

All three judges convincingly feigned surprise and delight to see Peroxide.

'How are you *doing*, girls?' beamed Beryl. 'You look *great!*'

Beryl even got up and went round her desk to give each girl a hug. Once the reunion celebration was over, Calvin put on his serious face and called the meeting to order.

'So, girls,' he asked, 'why did you come back?'

'Well, Calvin,' 'Chelle replied, 'we were really gutted to lose out last time and we really, really believe in ourselves and think that we deserve another chance.'

Calvin nodded wisely. 'Well,' he said, 'that shows considerable character, Michelle. I like that. I am always looking to see character in the people who come to see us because ours is a tough business and to cut it live you need character.'

'Georgie,' said Rodney, 'we liked you last year, you know that, you sailed through the first round and made a big impact. Then you lost it in the second round. What do you think you can do differently this year?'

'We've worked so hard,' said Georgie, her voice a little huskier than it had been because of the stomach acids with which her throat was regularly drenched.

'We've grown,' 'Chelle added. 'We've worked so hard and we've learned and we've grown. We've taken on board all the things you said to us last year and we've really, really thought about them and worked hard and tried to grow.'

Beryl stared at the two girls through moist eyes, as if it were her own daughters who were showing such grit and such character.

'In that case, babes,' Beryl said, her croaky little girl voice dripping with love, 'you deserve a second chance. If you've listened and you've worked hard and you've grown, then you deserve this. This is your moment. You own it, girls. Just you own it.'

'Thank you, Beryl,' 'Chelle replied humbly. 'We will.'

'We all want this for you, girls,' Rodney added, he too working his eyes into a convincingly dewy mistiness. 'You took some hard knocks last year and coming back here now shows real guts. It's up to you now, girls, the dream is back and all you have to do is grab it and own it. Own the dream.'

'OK,' said Calvin, once more doing his businesslike bit, as if to remind the world that they were hardbitten pop professionals who would not let sentiment cloud their judgement. 'What are you going to sing for us?'

'We're going to sing "Dancing Queen" by Abba, Calvin.'

'Good choice,' said Rodney, nodding wisely.

'Off you go, girls,' said Calvin.

They sang it quite well, in tune and with the simple harmony intact. They executed the little seventies-style dance moves that they had worked out with some aplomb and the flourish at the end had genuine charm. On balance, being a year older they were slightly better than they had been the year before, and considerably better than at least three of the acts who had made it to the previous year's finals.

And so they stood, flushed and breathing hard. Two dreamers in their underwear. Virgins waiting to be sacrificed.

Calvin let the silence sit a while. He looked down, he looked up, sucked his pencil, he threw his body backwards against the chair and stared at the ceiling.

'Girls,' he said, 'I am *so, so* disappointed.'

Another pause. 'Chelle tried hard to nod wisely as if she was still prepared to learn and to grow. Georgie began to shake.

'You know what?' Calvin continued. 'I really, really wanted you to be good. You showed talent last year and I was absolutely ready to give you the benefit of the doubt. But you know what? You've lost your innocence. You're trying to *look* like pop stars instead of *being* pop stars. I'm sorry, girls. It was terrible, like two drunk bridesmaids at a wedding.'

'No!' Beryl protested. 'Calvin, behave!'

'Really, Calvin,' Rodney chimed in, 'I didn't think the girls were that bad. Yes, it was a massive disappointment but the costumes were great and—'

'OK, Rodney, bottom line. Sentiment aside. Ours is a tough game. What's your vote?'

Now it was Rodney's turn for a dramatic pause. He stared at the two near-naked teenagers as if he would have traded his life to put them through.

'Please . . .' 'Chelle quivered. 'We've worked so hard . . .'

'This industry's tough,' Rodney replied, feeling Michelle's pain. 'I just don't think you're tough enough to cut it.'

'We are, we are! We're strong! We're strong women. We've grown. Please . . . *Please.*'

'Girls, I'm sorry,' Rodney said, staring at them man- fully. 'Last year you showed promise but we didn't think you could cut it, this year you've proved that we were right. In a way you should see that as a positive thing. You have closure.'

'Yes or no, Rodney?' Calvin snapped.

And despite the fact that it was already abundantly clear that it was a no from Rodney, he went for yet another pause, a pause so long that even though he had just told them they had failed entirely it was almost possible for the girls to believe Rodney might be contemplating a yes.

'It's a no from me,' he finally concluded.

'Beryl?' Calvin asked.

Beryl could not speak. Her lip was quivering (within the icy constraints of the Botox that filled it) and her eyes were brimming with tears. All she could do, for that moment at least, was stare.

It was in fact 'Chelle who found words first.

'Please, Beryl,' she said. 'This means everything to us. Please.'

'Don't,' Beryl stammered. 'Don't say that. Don't *do* this to me.'

'It's our dream, Beryl. *Please.*'

'Calvin!' Beryl snapped. 'Why have you put me in this position? Why are you doing this to me?'

'Because you have to make a choice, Beryl. That's your job,' Calvin replied calmly.

'Well, I don't *want* this job! I don't *want* to destroy people's dreams. This shouldn't be what it's about.'

'I need your vote.'

'Please, Beryl!' begged Michelle.

Once more a pause. Once more the two near-naked girls were forced to stand, shaking, pleading, crying, as time crawled towards the foregone conclusion.

'Oh *God*,' Beryl wailed. 'I *wanted* it to be good. I *so* wanted it to be good. I love you girls, you're strong women, you've grown but . . . I'm sorry, girls.' Her voice was that of a six-year-old who smoked forty fags a day. 'I think you're going to have to find yourselves another dream.'

Yet again, despite the fact that Beryl had clearly pronounced her judgement, Calvin managed to string matters out one more time.

'I need an answer, Beryl,' he said. 'Is it a yes or a no?'

Once more the pause. One final plea from Michelle.

'Please, Beryl. We'll do anything.'

312

One final plea from Beryl.

'Don't *do* this to me, Calvin.'

One final opportunity for Calvin to pretend to be the clear-headed professional unaffected by the maelstrom of emotion around him.

'I need an answer, Beryl.'

'I'm so sorry, girls,' Beryl said. 'It's a no from me.'

'And it's a no from me too,' said Calvin bluntly. 'Thanks for coming to see us, girls.'

They couldn't move. They simply could not move. Every fibre of the two young women's beings was struggling to comprehend the shocking, stunning reality that it was over *already*. That they had failed to progress through a *single round* of the judging. That they had done *even worse* than last time. This was the genius of Calvin Simms. Anybody could have seen the drama in having the girls back, bigging them up through the early stages and *then* dropping them. But to drop them *instantly*, to claim that their performances the previous year had actually represented their *peak*, that was truly electric drama.

Georgie cracked first, the tears exploding suddenly and with force. 'Chelle only began to weep after Beryl had rushed round the table to hug them.

'Come here!' Beryl shouted. 'Come here, girls. You know what? You don't need this, you're better than this. Let me give you a hug.'

As Beryl began to usher the girls from the room, Costume and Make-up hovered close, Wet Wipes poised, ready to clean the girls' snot from Beryl's shoulder pads.

When the devastated girls had gone and Beryl had returned to her seat, the judges made ready to shoot their impromptu 'discussion'. This supposed eavesdropping on the judges' private thoughts followed each of the staged auditions and was supposed to lend an air of care and consideration to the proceedings.

'Everybody happy?' called Trent. 'Ready with what you're going to say?'

The three judges indicated that they were.

'Can you huddle a bit closer together?' Trent asked. 'It looks so much more honest and intimate.'

The judges reluctantly shuffled their seats a little closer. Calvin even laid a hand on Rodney's shoulder.

'Action!' cried Trent.

'What a disappointment,' Calvin said. 'I had real hopes for them.'

'Pretty girls and very nice,' Beryl added, 'but they just can't cut it.'

'Look,' said Rodney, 'they had a whole year to get better and they didn't. Ours is a tough game.'

'I admire them for coming back and having another shot though,' said Calvin, his serious face firmly fixed. 'That took a lot of guts and at least now they know.'

'It's better in the end this way,' said Beryl croakily. 'They'll learn, they'll heal, they'll grow.'

'Or shrink in the case of the little one. Fuck me, she's got thin,' said Calvin, indicating to Trent that he felt they had had enough eavesdropping chat.

'Great,' Trent called out. 'Rodney, we were a tiny bit unclear with you. Can we take your line again.'

Rodney collected himself, thrilled to get a single shot.

'Look,' Rodney repeated, 'they had a whole year to get better and they didn't. Ours is a tough game.'

Trent was happy with the second take.

'Calvin,' he called out, 'since we're set up can we knock off some funny drop-ins?'

'Got to do them some time,' Calvin replied wearily.

'Right,' said Trent. 'We'll start with Beryl.'

The principal camera closed in on her.

'Good, so blank stare to start with . . . bit of open-mouthed amazement . . . comical horror, you've just

314

seen a *real* Minger . . . Could you shake your head in disbelief?'

Beryl went through her gamut of amusingly stunned faces.

'Thanks, Beryl, that's you done,' said Trent. 'Right, Rodney, could you give us your bent-mouthed bemusement? People *love* that one . . . As if Calvin's asked you to pass judgement on a *total Minger* and you are just lost for words . . . Lovely. That is *so* funny.'

Chelsie Delivers Shaiana

The sound of Peroxide wailing could be heard up and down the corridors of the leisure complex.

'We just wanted it *so much*.'

In the holding area everyone knew how Peroxide felt. They all wanted it and every single one of them believed that they wanted it the most. Particularly Shaiana, who had sat all day in a series of yoga positions awaiting her moment, waiting to put her foot on the first step of the ladder to Carnegie Hall.

When the deeply ambitious senior researcher walked her from the holding area towards the audition room, she kept up a constant, urgent, half-whispered mantra of intense encouragement. Not encouragement to sing but to cling, to impress upon the judges just how heartfelt was her desire to win.

'You *know* they love sincerity, Shaiana,' Chelsie whispered. 'They *love* it and you give *major* sincerity. You are *so not* insincere. Never forget that being a Chart Throb is about *so much more* than having a great voice. To survive in this business you have to be able to cut it emotionally and to do that you have to *want it*, babes! And you *do* want this, don't you, babes? You really, really want it.'

'Yes,' said Shaiana through pursed lips, speaking almost perfunctorily as if conserving her energies, like a boxer before a fight, not wanting to release an iota of her pent-up tension until the time came to unleash its full force.

'Then *tell* them, girl!' Chelsie breathed. 'You go in there and tell them what you *feel*, what you *believe*. Tell them it's your dream, tell them you'll die if you fail, tell them that nothing in this universe or the next could compare with your need to do what it is that you have to do, and that is to sing a verse and chorus of "The Wind Beneath My Wings" like you never sang it before, babes, like it was the last song on earth. Like you were the last singer, babes. Like *God* was listening. Like God was *singing through you*, babes.'

Further Frustrations

Calvin could scarcely believe it. Emma had agreed to spend the night with him in a hotel but only in *separate rooms*. It was extraordinary, he was forty-two years old, he was worth hundreds of millions, he was arguably the most powerful man in show business, he wasn't even bad-looking and yet he and his girlfriend were going to sleep in *separate rooms*.

He hated it. But much, much more than that, he loved it.

He was finding the process of *courting*, of deferred gratification, intensely exciting, partly of course because he loved a challenge but also for the way this new experience of denial had so invigoratingly sharpened and focused his interest in sex. It had been *years*, decades even, since he had *craved* a woman, since his entire physical being had homed in specifically on one individual in this way, to the point where he was uninterested in the idea of sex with anyone else. Calvin was clever enough to understand that this exaggerated desire was very much a result of the fact that he was being denied what he wanted, but that did not decrease the intensity of his need. He *liked* the fact that Emma was standing up to him, teasing him. He admired her for it and he was grateful to her for reawakening things in him that he had forgotten even existed.

When the auditions day in Birmingham had finally ended, Calvin had scarcely bothered to say goodbye before hurrying off to phone Emma from the privacy of his car.

'I am *so* knackered,' he said. 'I think we saw over seventy people today.'

'*Seventy people*,' Emma replied sarcastically. 'So only about two thousand days to go then and you'll have seen all ninety-five thousand of them.'

'Look, I have to see you, Emma. Sorry but I do. I'm on my way to the Cliveden House Hotel, do you know it?'

'I know *of* it. The scandal place.'

'Oh, for God's sake, that was over forty years ago. It's just a lovely hotel now. All the luxuries. I've sent a car for you, will you get in it?'

'What, now?'

'Now-ish,' Calvin replied. 'I've only just ordered it so you've probably got half an hour to pack a toothbrush. It's Saturday tomorrow so I presume you're free.'

'Well, I'm not working if that's what you mean. I do have a life.'

'Oh, never mind about all that. I'm supposed to be editing, but I can do a lot of it on my computer once

317

they've digitized the tapes. You could go to the spa and have your toenails done.'

'I don't much like all that pampering stuff,' Emma lied.

'All women like the pampering stuff.'

'Calvin, you don't know anything about women.'

'Then forget the spa. Bring a book.'

It was then that Emma said she would consent to come but only on the strict understanding that she would have her own room.

'Of course. *Obviously*,' Calvin replied. 'Don't you think I know the rules of this bloody game we're playing by now? Bring something smart for dinner, it's all a bit posh.'

When he had said goodbye to Emma he called Cliveden for the second time.

'Yes, I'd like a second room please.'

They both arrived at the hotel around nine and retired to their separate (but adjoining) suites to change for a late dinner.

'Can you hear me?' Calvin called through the dividing door.

'Yes I can,' Emma cried back. 'Stay where you are, I'm changing.'

'Will you tell me what you're wearing?'

'You'll see in a minute.'

'No. What you're wearing underneath.'

'Calvin, you are beginning to sound ever so slightly like a horrible little pervert.'

'I can't help it. I've never had to hang around like this. It isn't normal.'

'Well, I'm not discussing my knickers with you so please don't raise the subject again.'

Calvin tied his tie and wondered. Nothing in his adult life had prepared him for this kind of frustration. Either she really was as sweet as she seemed or else she was a brilliant manipulator who made his wife look like Sooty. Either way he found her irresistible.

Over dinner Emma asked Calvin about the show.

'Did you dump Peroxide?' she asked.

'Yes. They sang quite sweetly but in the end . . .'

'In the end their pain was better telly than their joy.'

'Em, they can't all win. It's a lottery, I believe anyone who fills in a form is aware of that. God knows, people are so media-savvy these days, it's like everyone's a TV producer. Look at *Big Brother*, just a few series in and the whole nature of the programme changed. Those kids went on that show *knowing* how it was done and what was going to happen to them. The first lot were taken completely by surprise.'

'You think Peroxide understood the process?'

'Not entirely, obviously, but they had to understand that there were winners and losers.'

'Did you notice how thin the younger one's got?'

'Yes, I did actually, and that's another reason I was glad I'd planned their story the way I did. That girl's a casualty, the last thing she needs is to become part of an industry that feeds on casualties . . .'

'That's a very convenient argument, Calvin, considering you've just fed on her.'

'I'm serious. She's clearly vulnerable to eating disorders, imagine what she'd be like if she had a record deal. Doing a 24/7 promotional schedule, three photoshoots a day and a Nazi stylist at every one of them. You know what happens to young women in pop these days, it isn't enough just to be able to sing. That little girl would have been chewed up and spat out in no time.'

'Isn't that exactly what's happened to her?'

'Hey, Emma, come on. Just because I've fallen in love with you doesn't mean you get to put that shit on me. I make TV. I'm not Mother Teresa but I'm not Jack the Ripper either. Besides which, you worked on one and a half series of the show, so where do you get off?'

'That's true, obviously. I just wonder whether we should be going a little deeper into what we do. Considering the damage done.'

'We can't. Who can? Life isn't fair, as my mum used to say. The whole world is heaving with rejection and injustice and disappointment and unfairness. It seems to be how we want it. People had a go at equality and fair play, socialism and all that bollocks, and it didn't work. Nobody was interested. People want the dream, they don't want equality, they want fairy tales. We *like* a cruel world. For every kid that's heard of Marx, *a thousand* have heard of Paris fucking Hilton, *ten thousand* in fact. Just think about that. Those two girls in Peroxide are a part of society that wants to *be Paris Hilton*. There has to be a downside to that and, sadly for them, for a brief moment they're it.'

Emma sipped her wine.

'I think that's why people find you so attractive, Calvin,' she said finally. 'You're a bastard but you're an honest one.'

'I don't think I'm a bastard. I told you, my business is fairy tales, it's what people want. Proper fairy tales – the originals were full of abuse, disappointment, cruelty and betrayal. That's what made them compelling, that's what made the happy ending so sweet. The point is only Cinderella gets to go to the ball, there's only ever one prince to marry and everyone else can fuck off. That's what makes the story good, it's what makes *Chart Throb* so good. If we went around being nice, nobody would watch.'

Stepmother and Child Reunion

At about the same time that coffee was being served to Calvin and Emma, Beryl Blenheim and her daughter Priscilla were being ushered to their table at Nobu restaurant in London. The object of all eyes, Beryl simply adored this kind of thing. What few lines remained on her face positively shrieked self-satisfaction as she paraded grandly through the tables, confident in the knowledge that absolutely *everyone* knew who she was and was whispering about her to their companions. It did not matter that much of what was whispered would no doubt be jealous and negative, they were still whispering about *her*, while she knew nothing of them, cared less and quite frankly, at the end of the day, did not give a fuck whether they lived or died.

Priscilla was smiling too. This was less common; usually when out and about with her mother she sulked and pouted, perhaps unable to forget the fact that she was infinitely the less celebrated of the two. Famous, yes, but really only as a conduit to her stepmother. In terms of celebrity the umbilical cord remained uncut.

On this evening, however, she seemed in a sunnier mood. Perhaps coming to Britain, where her spectacular failure as a recording artist had passed with little comment, she felt less exposed.

'I think maybe soon I'll be ready to make another album, Mom,' she said over the dim sum.

'Jesus, Priscilla, you just fucking made one, what's the rush?'

'I want to express myself artistically.'

'Didn't you do that getting those enormous boobs which I *still* can't get used to?'

'No, really. I think that first album failed because it

was kind of about somebody making a record just because they could. Like "Hey, I'm a teenage celebrity, I guess I'd better make a record," if you know what I'm saying.'

'I got you a fucking good deal, young lady.'

'I'm not talking about the deal, Mom! I'm talking about the record. I think I need to be taking a look at myself and asking what *I* want to sing and how *I* want to sing it, not what I think the public want to hear.'

'Well, let's face it, darling, the public didn't want to hear anything at all, did they?'

'Because I was *lying* to them, Mom! If I want to make a good record I need to be honest with the public and that starts with being honest with myself, which starts with believing in myself. In my dream.'

'Oh, do fuck off, Priscilla, I'm not on *Chart Throb* now.'

Visions of Shaiana

Calvin had suggested that coffee be served in his suite and Emma had consented. As they left the dining room together and ascended the magnificent, thickly carpeted stairway she felt nervous. Not because she feared that he would pounce but because she feared that if he did, she might succumb.

The conversation over dinner had of course eventually turned to sex.

'You know I think you're attractive,' Emma had admitted.

'But you don't want to sleep with me?'

'Of course I want to sleep with you and it's not out of any prudishness that I won't. The simple truth is that I don't trust you. You're an amoral manipulator . . .'

'Amoral but not immoral?' Calvin enquired. 'I suppose that's something.'

'No, not immoral, I don't think so anyway. I don't think that you go out of your way to do harm or to abuse people. On the other hand I don't think you go to any great efforts to avoid it either.'

'Hmm. I'm not sure that's fair, you know. I do *try* to be kind when I can and I'm pleasant to people. I don't throw my weight around too much, do I?'

'Let's say not as much as some.'

'And I most certainly do try to avoid abusing people . . .'

'Peroxide?'

'What I do on *Chart Throb* . . . what *we* did until quite recently . . . is not abuse, or if it is, in my view it's entirely consensual. I don't think that I am any more morally compromised than the people who compete or more particularly the people who watch the show.'

'I think that your *understanding* of the process makes you more compromised. Because you *know* better, you should *do* better. It's the old public hanging debate, isn't it? Does the fact that people would go to an execution justify mounting them as entertainment? I mean, if popular support provides moral justification then you've got Hitler vindicated right there.'

'I *knew* you'd fucking get it round to Hitler. Every time I have one of these conversations somebody brings up Hitler. Well, personally I think that most people can see the difference between making *Chart Throb* and invading Poland.'

They both laughed.

'Anyway,' Calvin added, 'I thought we were talking about you sleeping with me.'

'We can *talk* about it all you like,' Emma replied.

'In my suite?'

'If you like. It won't make any difference.'

So Calvin asked for coffee and cognac to be brought to his suite and together they went upstairs.

As the door closed behind her, Emma hesitated. It was all so luxuriously comfortable. Dangerously so. A couch and two beautiful antique armchairs were set around a delicate-looking coffee table. Through a set of open double doors the bed could be seen with the sheets all folded back for the night.

'Do you know,' said Calvin, 'if we were to begin to kiss now we should have to stop in five minutes when the coffee arrives. I doubt much harm could come to us in five minutes. What do you think?'

'No. I don't suppose so.'

Emma stepped forward and allowed herself to be enfolded in an embrace. Together they stumbled across the carpet and, narrowly avoiding a disastrous, shin-denting collision with the coffee table, collapsed on to the couch. After a little while, however, a certain self-consciousness began to pervade the proceedings.

'We're waiting for the coffee now, aren't we?' said Calvin.

'Yes, I suppose it's inevitable given what you said.'

'Yes, silly of me,' Calvin said, disengaging himself. 'It seemed a clever line at the time but now we're kind of in limbo, aren't we?'

'Oh well, it was fun anyway.'

'Yes.'

The coffee took nearly twenty minutes, which were passed in slightly awkward small talk like that which takes place once the taxi has been ordered.

'I could have made love to you in this time,' said Calvin, looking at his watch.

'No, you couldn't,' Emma replied.

'I meant in terms of time, not opportunity.'

'So did I. If we ever do get round to it you're not getting away with a fifteen-minute thank you ma'am or I'll ask for my money back.'

Eventually the coffee arrived and almost immediately thereafter a dispatch rider from London, bringing the digitized disks of those episodes from the day's proceedings worthy of review.

'I shall have to get into this lot first thing,' Calvin said, 'but there's a pool and loads of stuff to do. Unless you fancy giving me a hand? You always were brilliant in the edit. No need for a contract, I could pay you cash.'

'No thanks, Calvin. I'm starting to like you again but I don't think I really like the you that makes *Chart Throb*, or the me for that matter. I'm not going back to all that.'

'Fair enough. Then will you come to bed with me instead?'

'No.'

'Bollocks.' Calvin got up. 'In that case I suppose I shall have to go to bed alone. Long day today, long day tomorrow.'

'Will you show me Shaiana?'

'What?'

'That's the only bit of today I want to see. That girl Shaiana. The uberClinger.'

'Still scared of her?'

'I don't know. Not really. I mean, God knows, we've seen off enough intense weirdos on this show but . . . Well, she just sort of *sticks* in my mind. Something's wrong there. I don't know why I think it but I do.'

Calvin opened the box full of disks and, having checked the time codes against the annotated script that Penny (Continuity) had pressed into his hand at the end of the day, he slipped a DVD into his computer.

'Not interested in HRH then?' he enquired as he typed in the code. 'I thought he was the key to our relationship.'

'I am interested in him but, I don't know, having

opted out I sort of want to *stay* out really. I don't want to interfere, I don't think it's fair. After all, you do have a job to do and I've made it complicated enough as it is. But this girl, Shaiana, I don't know why . . . It's got nothing to do with the show or a professional interest, I genuinely worry about her.'

'About her?'

'Well, about her and, if I'm honest, about you.'

'What, you think she's going to do a John Lennon on me?'

There, it was said. The silent fear that all very famous people share.

'It could happen.'

'And don't think it doesn't occur to me. Particularly in America. Over *sixty million* votes were cast for the last winner over there. Even presuming each caller phoned ten times, that's still *six million people* who give a very large fuck about a bloke who I have dissed utterly. Sometimes I wonder if among all those millions of psycho fans there won't be one of them who thinks it's time that nasty old Calvin faced his own judgement day . . .'

'Or one of the contestants themselves.'

'Yes. Absolutely. But what can you do? I'm still more likely to get randomly mugged in Knightsbridge or knocked over by a car or catch bird flu or contract a superbug while having my ingrown toenails done. Life's too short, say I. Besides I don't like the idea of allowing myself to be intimidated. Fuck 'em.'

'Tough guy, huh?'

'Oh yes, I hope so. Very tough. Here we are . . .' A frozen image of Shaiana appeared on the screen. 'This is her bit with Keely.'

Calvin pressed Play on the screen and Keely leaped into life with her usual energy.

'And this is Shaiana!!' Keely shouted. 'She is *one hot babe*. Yay! Are you ready to rock, babes?'

'Yes, Keely, I am ready to rock,' Shaiana replied, steadily and clearly, as if testifying to a faith. 'This is my one time. This is my one moment.'

'Yay!' shouted Keely. 'You grab it, girl! You *own* it.'

'I'm going to grab it, Keely. I'm going to own it. I'm going to *eat* it.'

Emma leaned forward and pressed the space bar, thus pausing the recording.

'Eat it?' she said. '*Eat it?* Never heard that one before. They're all going to own it but they don't usually want to eat it. That's scary.'

'Why?' Calvin replied. 'So she wants to eat it, sounds fair enough to me.'

Calvin pressed Play. Keely spoke again.

'And you've come here on your own, babes,' she said. 'What's that about? Focus? No distractions? Or is it that your family and mates aren't down with what you're about and just don't get you?'

Emma smiled. Keely was good. Much underestimated in fact. People tended to think of her as just a chirpy lovely who gave good sympathy and knew how to squeal with delight, but actually she was so much better than that.

'I remember noting the family thing down myself,' Emma said, having once more pressed Pause. 'How Shaiana seems to be very alone. But I remember Chelsie saying she wasn't going to push it. Amazing how Keely's picked up on it anyway.'

'Yes. We love Keely,' Calvin agreed, 'although I think you could do her job even better. You're prettier too.'

Emma blushed and pressed Play once more.

'Yeah, Keely,' said Shaiana, 'that's right. They're not down with me at all. They don't really understand what I want. What I *need*. What I can do. That's one of the reasons I'm here. To show them. To *make* them understand. Them and everybody else who's ever laughed at me.'

After a little further small talk Shaiana was ushered through the door. There was a tape stop and then once more she appeared, this time in the audition room facing the judges. The sequence had not yet been edited and all that could be seen was the single mid-close-up shot of Shaiana. However, the voices of the judges could easily be heard off camera.

'Hello, hello. Who are you?' Beryl could be heard saying.

'I'm Shaiana, Beryl, and I'm here to rock your world.'

'Right on! You go, girl. You look *gorgeous*.'

'Thank you, Beryl,' Shaiana replied.

'She doesn't,' Calvin interjected. 'I've never *seen* so much make-up, like a mask. Some of these girls are their own worst enemies.'

'Shhh,' Emma said.

'I'm really nervous,' Shaiana was saying.

'Don't be, babes,' Beryl cooed. 'We're all friends here and you look *hot*.'

'Before we start, Shaiana,' Calvin chipped in, 'tell us a little about how much you want this.'

'Calvin, I want it so much.'

'They all want it, Shaiana. How much is so much?'

'Well,' Shaiana replied, having paused for a moment's thought, 'I think I'd be prepared to die for it, Calvin. I really do. I think that if I could do a deal with God so that all my dreams came true and everybody believed in me as me and didn't laugh at me any more and they all said, "Yes, Shaiana, you do have talent, your own talent, and you *can* sing," then I wouldn't mind if I died straight after.'

'Wow,' said Calvin and even though he was off camera anyone listening who had seen *Chart Throb* even once would know that he was nodding in his amusingly bemused way, astounded at the intensity of the people who seemed so randomly to appear before him. 'You really do want it, don't you?'

'Like I said, Calvin. I want it so much I could die.'

Emma pressed Pause.

'Or kill. That's the flip side of her coin. She scares me.'

'Oh, come on, Emma. The only person this woman is ever going to damage is herself. She's a grade A, twenty-four-carat victim. Anyone can see that.'

'Yes, well, worms do turn and who knows, one day when she's thinking about how much she'd like to die because she never got to prove anything to anyone, she may suddenly think, hang on, why should it be *me* that has to die? How about that bastard who chucked me off *Chart Throb*?'

Calvin laughed. 'Are you in league with this woman, Emma? What are you trying to persuade me to do, make her win? I thought you wanted the Prince of Wales to win?'

Emma shrugged. 'I don't know. I don't know what would be best to do with her. Chuck her off, keep her on, either way the die's cast. You're stuck with her.'

The suite was lit only by a crimson-draped standard lamp that stood in a far corner, shedding a subdued light which before had seemed romantic but which had suddenly become rather gloomy.

Emma pressed Play once more.

'All right, Shaiana,' Calvin's voice could be heard saying, 'what would you like to sing for us?'

'I'd like to sing "The Wind Beneath My Wings" by Bette Midler,' Shaiana replied.

Now Rodney's voice could be heard intruding for the first time.

'Good choice. That is a great song and Bette is a fine artist. Well done, that is a very good song to choose.'

Then Shaiana took a deep breath and began her song. Had the judges been looking for pain and emotion alone she would assuredly already have won. Shaiana made Bloke's tear-drenched, face-crunched, fist-punching rendition of 'Stand By Me' look perfunctory and dismissive. This was a woman who clearly believed that every single syllable of a lyric was a fresh opportunity to revisit a lifetime of pain and rejection. Her small breasts heaved, her knuckles turned white, her chin lifted ever higher as if (following Chelsie's advice) she wanted to make absolutely sure that God was listening. Shaiana was clearly a woman who saw her voice as a sledgehammer whose job it was to deliver the notes blow by blow until the audience had been bludgeoned into submission. Like so many contestants before her, she had watched great singers and listened to them and had drawn the conclusion that the key lay in trying to emulate everything about her heroes all at once and at all times throughout the entire song.

She was, however, in tune.

When it was over, once more Emma pressed Pause.

'She really isn't too bad, is she? With a bit of help to calm down, she could certainly carry a song.'

'Ah but so many people can,' said Calvin. 'And besides, as you know, it's—'

'Not about the singing,' Emma completed his sentence. 'Yes, I know, and one of the best things about not working for you any more is not having to listen to you say that every five minutes of the day.'

'Well, I'm right, aren't I?' said Calvin. 'Anyway, have you had enough or do you want to hear what we said?'

'I want to hear. I hope you didn't lay it on too thick.'

'No, actually we didn't,' Calvin replied. 'She's a Challenge and Chuck, remember.'

Challenge and Chuck was the process, much favoured on *Chart Throb*, of suggesting to a contestant that they must go away and work harder and attempt to grow and when the contestant returned (claiming to have worked *so* hard and grown) informing them that they had failed to do so and chucking them out.

'What will you do,' Emma enquired, 'if ever anyone asks you what you actually *mean* when you tell them to go away and work hard and learn and grow?'

'Edit it out,' Calvin replied, pressing Play once more.

'Shaiana,' Calvin's voice could be heard off screen, 'you confuse me.'

There was a pause while the camera crept in slowly towards Shaiana's quivering, heavily caked face.

'You have a voice,' Calvin said, finally. 'It's not a *terrible* voice. I doubt it's a very good one either but it isn't terrible. The question is can it improve?'

Shaiana leaped at the bait like a starving fish.

'Yes. Yes it can, Calvin. It can. You see I want this so much, I'll do anything, I'll work, I'll work so hard. I'll learn and I'll grow . . .'

'You really do want this, don't you, darling?' Beryl could be heard croaking in her little girl voice.

'Yes! Yes, Beryl, I really, really do want it.'

'I can see that it's your dream, isn't it, darling?'

'Yes! Yes, it is!'

'Well, it's a good thing to have a dream. But for dreams to come true you have to really, really want them to. You have to believe so very much.'

'I do, Beryl! I do! I swear I do! My dream is all I have.'

'I know, darling, I know,' Beryl said with the voice of a nurse comforting a terminally ill patient.

'All right,' Calvin could be heard saying in his businesslike voice. 'Here's what I think. You go away now, Shaiana, and you work, right? You work hard, you learn and you grow . . .'

'And believe in your dream,' Beryl could be heard interrupting.

'And you come back and see us and we'll see how you've got on, OK? Because right now you don't have it, OK? That's clear, but you might have it and whether you can find it is up to you. On that basis I'll put you through. Beryl?'

'If Shaiana can believe in herself and in her dream . . .'

'I can. I *can. I can,*' Shaiana pleaded.

'Then yes. I say yes, darling. For your dream. I'll put you through.'

'In that case,' Calvin could be heard saying, 'you're through to the next—'

Suddenly Rodney's voice could be heard. 'Yes, and me too, Shaiana. My vote is yes too.'

'Oh yeah. Sorry, Rodney,' Calvin said. 'What was your vote?'

'I say yes,' Rodney said.

'You're through,' said Calvin.

Shaiana wept. She leaped up and down. She mentioned God. She fell to her knees.

'Thank you! Thank you, thank you, *thank you*!' she screamed. 'I won't let you down, I promise. Yay! Yes! Yes! YAY! *THANK YOU!* I love you, Calvin! I love you, Beryl! I love you, Rodney! Yay! Thank you! I'm going to rock your world!'

'Come on, darling.' Beryl could be heard just before she walked into shot. 'Lots of work for you to do.'

A shaking and almost hysterically happy Shaiana was then led from the room and into the arms of Keely, who was waiting to join in the tear-filled catharsis of celebration.

Emma pressed Pause.

'If she's that crazy when you challenge her, how crazy will she be when you chuck her?'

'Very. They all are. What makes her so different?'

'I'm telling you, Calvin,' Emma said, looking very serious, 'she *is* different, that one, there's a different level of intensity. I've seen it before in real victims. People who have been damaged. They're not right and their weakness makes them strong, in a vicious, hysterical kind of way. You know, like jilted wives who cut up their husband's suits then set fire to the family home.'

'Good, good, *good*. That's what we want. Bunny-boilers.'

'As long as it isn't your bunny she boils.'

'Emma, I've told you. I have a very, very firm rule, and that is not to be scared of contestants. Ever. That way leads to madness. My job is to pursue the passion in people. To massage their dreams and expose their needs. If I allow myself to be intimidated by those passions or needs then I'll no longer be able to pursue them. Shaiana does not scare me.'

The Cute Kid

For the first three days of the following week the judges repeated the process that they had gone through in Birmingham in London, Manchester and Glasgow. All in all, they sat in 'judgement' to a greater or lesser degree on around three hundred people, an exhausting series of In and Outs punctuated by specials and of course the designated finalists.

There was the by now obligatory amusing four-year-old who was allowed to 'audition' despite the minimum legal age for entry being sixteen. At the story meeting it had been planned that this year Calvin would at first refuse to see the lad on the grounds that it was pointless but under heavy mumsy pressure from Beryl he would reluctantly agree.

'And rock 'n' roll supermum Beryl is not going to let young Lance have his heart broken by big bad Calvin,' Keely would say.

And so, even though he was ineligible for

consideration the cute little poppet in an England shirt and with an adorable Scouse accent ended up filling nearly three minutes of screen time in the final edit.

'Lance, you're so scrummy I want to eat you,' Beryl said in her gooiest manner.

'You may want to eat him but we can't put him through,' Calvin gently reminded her in his firm but amused voice.

'Why? He's so-o-o cute. I'm a mum and I love him, all mums will love him. Why not give him a chance?'

'Because it's illegal, Beryl.'

'I don't play by the rules, I'm a rock chick from way back, don't forget. Don't talk to me about rules. I'm a mum and mums have to break rules just to get through. I've had it hard, these have not been easy years, I know all about breakin' rules.'

'Beryl, he can't enter the competition.'

And so the comical banter went on until the last treacly drop had been milked from the original concept and the boy finally went on his way.

Afterwards, when the 'eavesdropping' moment had been shot . . .

'I can't *believe* you wanted to put that kid through, Beryl.'

'But he was so *cute*.'

Rodney experienced a rare moment of doubt.

'Do you truly believe that people won't realize we set that up?'

'Obviously, Rodney, or I wouldn't have shot it,' Calvin replied tartly.

'But we've spent over fifteen minutes on him! On our *one day* in Manchester. Surely somebody's going to do the maths!'

'Nobody ever does the maths, Rodney.'

Pop School

Eventually the series of regional heats came to a close and it was time for the *Chart Throb* team to sift and edit all the material that they had collected and prepare for Pop School.

Pop School was the part of the process where those selected at the initial auditions attended an intensive residential training course where they were supposedly given lessons in the art of being a pop star by the three highly experienced judges. It was at this point that the judges were supposed to assume a more supportive and educative role in the development of the fledgling talents that they had chosen. The idea was that, having unearthed the raw material, they would now use their enormous music industry expertise to mould pop stars from it.

A number of factors stood in the way of their achieving this or, indeed, of Pop School being in any sense an educational process. The first factor among these was that, with the possible exception of Calvin, none of the judges was remotely qualified to train anyone in any aspect of the performing arts except, by example, that of naked self-advertisement.

Another factor which would have prevented the judges from developing and moulding any talent even if they had had the skills to do so was that they were not actually there during the developing and moulding (such as it was). Although the Pop School process lasted three days, the judges attended only the last of these, the one on which the 'judging' took place.

Shaiana, like all the other contestants, had gone home after her first audition, having been told to prepare a new song to present at Pop School. She was informed that she would then be given some training and advice on how to sing her chosen song before being required to deliver it in a 'live concert' setting, meaning that she would be singing on an actual stage instead of in a hotel conference room. The stage in question was meant to represent a tough club and therefore provide the contestants with an introduction to the hard but essential business of 'paying your dues', 'working the clubs', 'getting your act together and taking it out on the road'.

'This,' as Keely would announce breathlessly at the beginning of the Pop School edition of the show, 'is where it gets real. *This* is where the going gets tough and the tough had better get going because today our gang of wannabe stars will get their first taste of the "road", as Calvin, Beryl and Rodney put them through their paces to see if they can handle the rough, tough side of rock 'n' roll that every star must learn to conquer on their way to the top.'

The rough, tough 'club' in question was the spanking new, pale pine, two-hundred-seat auditorium of a large private school that had been rented for the purpose. Originally the *Chart Throb* art department had hoped to dress the stage and front stalls in a club-like manner. They had brought large quantities of black paint, some threadbare glittery drapes, various old rock posters and great crates of empty bottles pinched from a recycling bin. They also hoped to remove the front three rows of seats since brand new, luxuriously padded seats with comfy armrests did not look very rock 'n' roll. Sadly for the art department, however, the school administrator had firmly ruled out any adornment to the stage or auditorium since term was about to begin again and the Lower School were to start rehearsal for their production of *Joseph and His Amazing Technicolor Dreamcoat* and they could not countenance any disruption.

On hearing this, Calvin had thrown a hissy fit and announced that he would simply buy the fucking school but he was informed that it was not for sale.

Shaiana arrived on the morning of the first day with a song in her heart and 'loose dance clothes' in her overnight bag, ready to give her all to the Pop School process. There were about seventy other contestants involved and they had all been billeted in a nearby Travelodge. Shaiana was to share a room with a pretty, delicate-looking girl called Cindy, who, like Shaiana, wanted it so much.

Having checked into their accommodation, the crowd of hopefuls were all bussed up to the school and assembled in the gym for their 'training' to begin. This process was in many ways very similar to their initial selection day in Birmingham, in that it consisted of a great deal of hanging around punctuated by a series of heavily staged 'spontaneous moments'.

Shaiana and Cindy sat cross-legged on the floor in their tracky pants and tops while at the piano the middle-aged man who looked like the Prince of Wales was filmed being 'schooled' in the vocal arts. This consisted of a deliberately eccentric-looking fellow in plus fours and with long dyed hair running through a piano scale which the Prince then attempted to sing.

'That was rubbish,' shouted the long-haired man.

'I know, I *know*,' the Prince lamented. 'I'm making an absolute *pig's ear* of it, aren't I?'

'Do it again!' the eccentric pop coach shouted.

'Righty-ho.'

The Prince was about to do it again when Chelsie intervened to explain that this would not be necessary as they already had their shot.

His Royal Highness sat down and busied himself with some state papers. The camera angle was changed and Chelsie instructed the girl with the blind lad to lead him towards the piano. After they had arrived at the piano, Chelsie called cut.

'Thank you, Millicent. Thank you, Graham. That's all we need for now.'

'Don't you want us to sing?' Millicent enquired.

'Plenty of time for that, darling,' Chelsie replied. 'Just wanted a walking shot for now.'

Shaiana herself was then summoned to the piano and His Royal Highness was asked to take her place in the group of bodies who were populating the back of the shot. 'And can you all please *try* and look interested,' Chelsie shouted. 'Haven't you seen the show? This is intensive training, you're all being put through your paces, those of you sitting about must focus on whoever it is that we are filming. Pretend you're in *Fame* or *A Chorus Line*, for God's sake. Right now you look like you're in *The Night of the Living Dead*.'

Shaiana was placed in a position near the piano and asked to sing something.

'Sing what?' she asked.

'Doesn't matter, love,' Chelsie snapped. 'It's a mute shot, we'll be dropping it in in slow motion when you tell Keely how hard you've worked.'

'But what about the pianist, surely he needs to be playing the same song?'

'I've just *told* you, darling, it's a mute shot. Besides which he's in deep soft focus. As long as his fucking arms are moving we're happy. Now sing!'

Shaiana began to sing as the cameras prowled about her.

'Look more soulful, Shaiana,' Chelsie called out. 'Clench your fists, look like you're in pain . . . Good. Got that. Cut.'

Next The Four-Z were filmed privately rehearsing and then allowing themselves a mutually supportive group hug.

'Can you do some high fives with each other?' Chelsie called out from behind the camera. 'That's a black thing, isn't it?'

The Four-Z agreed that it was indeed a black thing and hugged and high-fived as hard as they could.

'Now how about a prayer?' called Chelsie. 'Could you stand in a circle and bow your heads in silent prayer for me?'

Again The Four-Z obliged.

'Finally turn to the camera and tell us that it's hard work but you're working hard and learning and growing and that you want to make the judges proud.'

Michael, the leader of The Four-Z, stepped forward.

'This is hard work but we are working hard and we know that we will learn and grow and hopefully make the judges proud.'

And so the long day wore on.

Groups of contestants were brought forward and taught a rudimentary dance step, not so that they could learn it but so that they could be filmed learning it.

'Where does it go from here?' one of the girls enquired after mastering the three steps and a clap that they had been taught.

'It doesn't,' the choreographer explained. 'That's all we need.'

During the 'dance class' Shaiana noticed that one by one contestants were being taken off to be filmed sitting in the stairwell. First the blokes from Bloke, then a middle-aged man who had introduced himself as Stanley and then a middle-aged blonde woman with enormous false tits.

'What's going on in the stairwell?' Shaiana asked one of the blokes from Bloke during a short coffee break.

'Nothing,' he replied. 'We just had to sit there and look tense and thoughtful.'

'Tense and thoughtful?'

'That's what they said.'

The Quasar was standing nearby and joined the conversation.

'I reckon you is well in, geeza,' he said. 'You is goin' all the *way*, man.'

'Why do you say that?'

'Ain't you seen the show?' the Quasar asked, sounding most surprised. 'They was filming your *moment of doubt*, guy! Like when you has crept away from the madness and is wondering if you is *ever* gonna be a star. They always has shots like that but I don't fink I ever saw no moment of doubt for anyone who wasn't in the final.'

'You really think so?' the bloke from Bloke enquired hopefully.

'That's for sure, geeza. I'm tellin' you that if they was to shoot me looking all moody and sad in the stairwell I would be *well* chuffed, cos it means that they is going to feature you.'

'But they didn't shoot you like that.'

'No, man, but I ain't worried because they knows that the Quasar does not *do* self-doubt.'

Sure enough, straight after the coffee break the Quasar was called forward for his own personal 'moment'. This consisted of his breakdancing in front of a group of other contestants who were all required to clap and look delighted to be a part of things.

For two days the contestants were marshalled between dance moments and piano moments. Occasionally some vague effort was made to suggest a genuine interest in their work but mainly it was to gather more shots of the process.

Cindy, Shaiana's new friend, was filmed massaging her feet as if having danced herself to exhaustion. Iona was filmed on her mobile phone, supposedly speaking to her ex-bandmates.

'Yeah, I'm at Pop School,' she said, as instructed. 'I'm going back to basics, relearning my craft. Sure it's

340

hard but if I'm serious about a solo career it's what I have to do.'

'Tell them you miss them,' Chelsie prompted.

'Oh, I miss you guys so much,' Iona dutifully parroted. 'Have a wee dram of whisky for me.'

'Brilliant,' said Chelsie, well satisfied.

'I'm a little worried that we could see that the phone wasn't on,' the cameraman interjected. 'Iona had the display turned towards us.'

'Nah. It'll never read,' Chelsie replied, anxious to get on with the day. 'All right,' she called out, 'I need Troy.'

Troy was given a copy of *Harry Potter*.

'I can't read it,' he replied. 'Not all the words anyway.'

'We know,' said Chelsie. 'What I want you to do is find a word you don't know and go and ask that posh bloke if he can tell you what it means.'

'Why?'

'Because I'm asking you to, Troy, that's why, and because Calvin asked me to ask you. Don't you want to make Calvin happy?'

The boy most certainly did want to make Calvin happy; that was the sole ambition of pretty much everybody in the room. Troy therefore dutifully walked over to the posh bloke.

'Excuse me,' he said.

'*Hello*, young man,' the Prince of Wales replied. 'How *are* you? Are you well? What have you got there? *Harry Potter*? How marvellous. I *do* think they're good, don't you?'

'Can you tell me what this word means?'

The Prince took out his reading glasses and studied the book.

'Hmm. Ahh. Well, do you know I'm not sure,' he said. '*Quidditch*. Hmm, actually I rather think that might be a *made-up* word. It's a game in the stories, isn't it? It sounds rather like Latin but I don't think it *is*.'

The youth shrugged and, having nothing more to say, wandered off.

'Cut,' said Chelsie. 'Lovely.'

'Eh? What?' said the Prince.

'That's fine, sir,' Chelsie shouted. 'Everything's fine.'

And the Prince returned to his study of the latest estimate of declining fish stocks in the North Sea.

Towards the end of the second day, Calvin finally put in an appearance but only to film a little special of his own.

'OK, people,' he shouted to the assembled contestants, who had been draped artfully about the school gym as if interrupted amid strenuous rehearsals. Some sat on the floor in tracky pants and vests, towels draped round their shoulders, some stood round the piano, others clung to the climbing bars attached to the wall and performed what they imagined to be stretching exercises. 'You've all worked damned hard,' Calvin continued, 'and tomorrow we find out what you've learned and whether you can cut it in a live rock 'n' roll gig. The drinks are on me!'

Everybody cheered and cheered.

When it was over the cameraman confessed that he was not happy. He had intended to sweep across the delighted, grateful faces before spinning round to take in Calvin's indulgent fatherly grin, but he had tripped on a cable and there had been a nasty bump in the shot.

'Can we do it again?'

'I suppose we'll have to,' Calvin said with impatient ill grace. And they did.

'The drinks are on me!' Calvin shouted for a second time.

And once more they cheered and cheered.

Pop School: Cindy and Shaiana

Rodney and Beryl arrived the following morning. Beryl, grumpy and hungover, had been awarded yet another Mum of the Year title, this time at the UK Retail Traders' Federation 'Inspiration' Awards Gala. Rodney, on the other hand, was fresh and rested after a week at a celebrity golf tournament in County Sligo as the special guest of the Western Irish Plumbers' Guild.

When Calvin joined them, all three judges swept into the school theatre and the Pop School stage of the audition process began.

The first half of the morning was given over to further hoovering up of the In and Outs where once more, as in Birmingham, half the contestants were destined to be rejected while the other half would be thrillingly 'put through'. These fortunate ones would proceed to the next round, All Back to My Place, before the chosen few went on to the actual finals.

Shaiana and Cindy sat waiting for their turn in yet another holding area, watching as in quick succession one hopeful after another was collected from the little group around them, only to be returned shortly afterwards either tear-stained and distraught or leaping about with hysterical joy.

Keely's reaction was pretty much the same either way.

'Babes!' she said. 'Babes, babes, *babes.*'

Finally Cindy got her turn.

'You rock, girlfriend,' Shaiana said to her as the slight, pretty girl bade her farewell, although clearly Shaiana's mind was elsewhere.

Cindy approached Keely expecting to be ushered perfunctorily into the auditorium just as the twenty or so previous auditionees had been, but in fact Keely held her back, seeming inclined to chat.

'You OK, babes?' Keely said, her voice full of concern. 'Cos I know you're like really, really, really delicate and sensitive and you're *so lovely*.'

'Uhm, yeah, I'm OK, Keely,' Cindy replied, slightly taken aback. 'Bit nervous, of course.'

'BABES!' Keely almost wailed. 'Babes, babes, *babes*! I *know*. Of COURSE you're nervous. It's really, really tough. Just you do your best, girl.'

Cindy did not know it but against her name in the day's production schedule had been written the words 'Weepy-looking Clinger. Looks delicate. Reject and MTT.' MTT was *Chart Throb* code for Milk The Tears.

As Cindy disappeared into the wings she could hear Keely addressing the camera behind her.

'Bless!' said Keely. 'Oh *bless*!'

'Hello, Cindy!' called Beryl as Cindy walked on to the stage. 'Welcome to Pop School. This is where it gets tough, you know. Are you ready for that?'

'Yes. Yes I am, Beryl,' Cindy assured her in a clear, confident voice.

And indeed she was, she was at least as psychologically and emotionally prepared for pop stardom as most of the other contenders present that day. She wanted it desperately, would do anything for it and, what's more, she could sing better than most of them too. But that didn't matter: what mattered was that she *looked* delicate and vulnerable, so that was what she was going to be.

'You look so *fragile*, darling,' said Beryl. 'Are you *sure* you want to do this? It's a tough, tough game you're getting into.'

'Yes, I definitely want to do it, Beryl. I'm tough.'

'I'm sure you are, dear,' said Beryl, as if addressing a little girl who had announced that she wanted to be as brave as her daddy, 'but I'm not sure you're tough enough.'

'What are you going to sing for us, Cindy?' Calvin asked.

Cindy announced that she would like to sing 'Eternal Flame' by The Bangles.

'Good choice,' Rodney remarked, putting on his intelligent face. 'That is a great song to choose.'

'Off you go then,' said Calvin.

'And don't you be nervous or scared,' Beryl added in her most cloying baby voice.

When Cindy had sung her song, Beryl asked her once more if she thought she was tough enough for the big bad world of pop. Cindy assured her that she was but Beryl replied that as a rock chick from way back and as a mother, she wasn't at all sure. Calvin and Rodney went further. They conceded that Cindy was pretty and had sung well, but they just did not believe she had the *hunger*, the *guts*, the *toughness* to 'cut it live'. The fact that 'cutting it live' in their world normally consisted of miming to backing tracks while surrounded by trained dancers did not concern them. The fact that they had never met Cindy and couldn't possibly know anything about her personality did not worry them either. They were adamant in their 'expert' opinion that Cindy was not tough enough to cut it live, and every time she assured them that she was, they said that in their opinion she wasn't, until eventually, after fully six minutes of taunting, Cindy finally burst into tears and Beryl was able to rush over and hug her out of the room.

'Fuck,' said Calvin as she left the stage, 'I didn't think that girl was *ever* going to cry. Maybe we should get the Clinger MTTs to chop a few onions before they come on.'

Beryl handed Cindy over to Keely, who hugged her also, and Shaiana, who was waiting to be summoned next, would have liked to hug Cindy too. She was sorry that Cindy had been rejected – it would have been fun to stay on the journey with her – but there was no time for regrets or sentiment now. No time, indeed, for anything but herself because this was her moment and she *wanted it so much*.

'This is my one moment in time,' she told Keely when Cindy had finally been ushered from the scene. '*I want this so much*.'

It was now that Shaiana shed the famous once and future tear. The tear which, unlike her actual performance, was destined to be such a special feature of the Pop School edition of the show.

'You go, girl,' Keely said and Shaiana went.

'Hello again, Shaiana,' yelped Beryl from behind the wall of water bottles that stood on the white-cloth-covered trestle table.

'Hello, Shaiana,' said soft-spoken Rodney to her left, staring at her unblinkingly. Rodney believed he had nice eyes. He felt that they projected empathy.

Calvin, on Beryl's right, said nothing, preferring to stare down at his note pad and play with his pen.

'Have you been working hard?' Beryl enquired.

'Oh Beryl, I have been working *so hard*.'

'You really want this, don't you, babes?'

'Oh Beryl, I want it *so much*.'

'Then you go, girl,' said Beryl.

'I just want to say before I start that I've really tried to think about all the things Calvin said because this is my dream and I'm going to rock your arse, Calvin!'

Calvin smiled, a smile which seemed to say that his arse was ready and willing to be rocked but that nonetheless it was not an easy arse to rock. Particularly if the person attempting to rock it was a no-talent saddo.

'Yay! Big it up, babes!' Beryl yelped in that curious hybrid dialect which is Californian white brat meets US urban black all wrapped up in a hint of Swindon. 'You go, girlfriend!'

'I'm going to, Beryl, because I believe God put everybody on earth for a reason and the reason he put me here was—'

'Shaiana,' Calvin interrupted, looking up for the first time since she had entered the room, 'just sing your song.'

'I just want you all to know that I've worked so—'

'They've all worked hard, Shaiana. Sing your song.'

For a moment it looked as if Shaiana would start to cry again.

The camera operators who stood to her right and left edged a step closer, like fielders at a sticky wicket in anticipation of a slow bowl. Outside in the car park the director and vision mixer, hunched inside their mobile control box, stopped their conversation and the script girl made ready to note down the time code.

Beryl got Shaiana through it.

'You be strong, girl,' she said. 'Just you be strong. And you go.'

Shaiana nodded solemnly and began.

When it was over Shaiana stared briefly at the stage beneath her feet, her chest heaving as if the strong emotions which the song had wrung from her were only now departing her body. Like rings in a disturbed rock pool, they were radiating from her centre and rippling outwards, visible in her clenched fists and quivering lips.

'That was completely . . .' Calvin paused lengthily for effect – 'ordinary.'

Shaiana looked like she had been punched.

Beryl leaped to her defence.

'Calvin, behave!' she exclaimed. 'She's worked so hard!'

'Shaiana, you're what I call an almost act,' Calvin continued. 'You're almost pretty, you can almost move a bit and you can almost sing. You've even almost got a personality but I'm afraid rock 'n' roll's a tough business and "almost" just doesn't cut it live. Never did, never will.'

Shaiana's lip began to quiver. Tears were springing into her eyes.

Beryl put on her mumsiest voice.

'You really want this, don't you, babes?'

'Oh Beryl, I want it so much. It's all I've ever wanted, it's my dream.'

'Well, *good on you* for following that dream, girl.'

'All right,' said Calvin decisively, 'what's the verdict? Is she going through to All Back to My Place or does the dream end here? Rodney?'

'I'm afraid it's a no from me, Shaiana.'

'Beryl?' Calvin asked.

Beryl did her long agonized thing, staring at Shaiana with the deepest concern. Her face was set in the look of stony Botoxed immobility that she habitually assumed to show empathy. To anyone who knew the show at all it was obvious which way she was going, there was so much pain and sorrow in her eyes. It was her 'I love you but you're crap, fuck off' face.

'I'm sorry, Shaiana, but the dream ends here. You just can't sing well enough. You'll never be a star.'

'And it's a no from me,' said Calvin. 'Thank you, Shaiana.'

Shaiana just stared. She didn't cry, she didn't plead, she just stood and stared.

'Thank you, Shaiana,' Calvin repeated. 'You can go now.'

'Where?' Shaiana enquired, still not moving.

'Where what?'

'Where am I supposed to go?' Shaiana asked, her voice suddenly like a voice from the grave, deep and disturbing. 'I didn't make any plans beyond now.'

'Well, I'm afraid that's not our problem, darling.'

'I told you, if I can't do this there isn't anything else for me to do.'

348

'Shaiana, goodbye.'

'Don't you understand? *God made me* for this purpose. Who are you to contradict the word of God?'

'You have to go now, Shaiana. We have a lot of people to see, all of whom believe in themselves as much as you do.'

'I told you, I have nowhere to go. I had only planned my life up to this point.'

'That is not our problem.'

'I think it is.'

'No, it isn't. Goodbye.'

'Yes it *is*, you fucking *cunts!*'

At this point two security men who had been edging ever closer appeared suddenly on either side of Shaiana.

'All right!' Shaiana screamed. 'But you haven't heard the last of me, Calvin fucking Simms, or you, Rodney, or Beryl fucking Blenheim.'

Shaiana turned on her heel and ran from the stage. As she passed through the holding area she nearly knocked down Graham, who was standing with Millicent waiting to be called.

'Get out of my fucking way, you prick!!' Shaiana screamed. 'Can't you fucking look where you're going?'

'He's blind!' Millicent shouted.

'Like that's *my* problem,' Shaiana replied and then she was gone.

Pop School: Graham and Millicent

Graham and Millicent were feeling a little emotional themselves.

They had spent the morning shooting 'specials'.

First they had been taken to a small nearby bistro where, despite the fact that it was before 10am, they were placed at a table for two set for dinner and asked to chink wine glasses. After less than ten minutes in the bistro they went outside and were filmed walking through a field of poppies hand in hand. Finally they returned to the school gym, where footage was taken of the two of them at the piano, Graham playing and Millicent singing. The shots were grabbed quickly because the crew were working without the complication of sound.

'These are mute shots,' Chelsie explained, 'to be dropped in to illustrate your interview. They'll probably run in slow mo while you talk about your love.'

'Love?' Graham asked.

'Yes, you do love each other, don't you?'

'Well, I . . .' Graham replied.

'Isn't that our private business?' Millicent added.

'Girlfriend,' Chelsie reminded her firmly, 'if you have any interest in making it in pop you had better understand that nothing is your private business any more.'

Next came the interview itself. In the school grounds the locations department had found a picturesque little bridge over a babbling stream. The interview was much more demanding than the specials, and it took Chelsie half an hour of coaxing and tutoring before she was sure she had got the sound bites she needed. She had of course planned the segment meticulously in advance, as she knew that doing the job properly on the ground saved many hours later in the edit.

When she finally pieced the interview together it ran exactly as it had done in her script:

Opening shot. Keely addressing the camera.

KEELY: 'Meanwhile, our two young lovers, Graham

and Millicent, have had lots to deal with.'
Wide shot. Graham and Millicent are revealed standing together on the bridge.
MILLICENT: 'It has been hard for us.'
Close shot on Millicent staring down at the water.
MILLICENT: 'After what the judges said about my singing.'
Slow motion flashback (Birmingham footage). Millicent's face as she's told she is holding Graham back.
MILLICENT VOICEOVER (*over flashback*): 'But we believe in ourselves and I've worked really, really hard to improve.'
Two shot. Graham and Millicent at Pop School rehearsal piano.
Wide shot of the two of them on the bridge. Graham speaks.
GRAHAM: 'It really hasn't been easy.'
Slow motion two shot. Graham and Millicent at Pop School rehearsal piano. Millicent at piano, clearly disappointed in herself. Graham feels his way towards her and hugs her supportively.
GRAHAM VOICEOVER: 'But we're there for each other.'
Mid two shot. Once more the couple are revealed on the bridge, now with their arms round each other.
MILLICENT: 'One thing's for sure, this whole thing has made us stronger.'
GRAHAM: 'It's brought us together and nothing's going to tear us apart.'
Long shot of bridge. Fade out.

After the filming, Graham and Millicent had been returned to the holding area to await their turn to 'audition'. It finally came after Shaiana's dramatic exit from the competition.

After the usual love fest with Keely they were

ushered into the presence of the judges, Millicent leading Graham by the hand as she had been instructed to do.

'Hi, Graham. Hi, Millicent!!' Beryl squawked. 'Welcome to Pop School!'

'What are you going to sing for us?' Calvin enquired.

'We're going to sing "The First Time Ever I Saw Your Face",' Graham replied.

Knowing that this would be the reply, Beryl had quickly tugged at the hair on the inside of her nose again to make her eyes water.

'Graham, I salute you,' she said through her tears. 'For a young man with seeing issues and ocular challenges to choose such a very beautiful and poignantly ironic song is brave beyond brave.'

'Yes,' agreed Rodney, ' "The First Time Ever I Saw Your Face" is a great song, tough to sing but a great choice.'

Graham and Millicent held hands and sang their song together. As predicted in the very first assessment notes that Emma had written, Millicent sang sweetly and Graham sang poorly, and once more his free hand could be seen desperately strumming the guitar that he wished he was holding.

When it was over the three judges sat for a moment in silent, awestruck respect. The inside of Beryl's nose was now completely bald and her face was streaked with crocodile tears.

'Mister,' she said finally, 'Mister, I salute you. You rock – my – world.'

'Yes, it was an incredible performance,' Rodney interjected. 'You're going to sell a lot of records, my friend.'

'You actually made me believe that you *could* see that girl's face,' Beryl pressed on. 'Which, considering we all know you can't because you are so tragically blind and unsighted, is simply so poignant and ironic it isn't funny. You are a star, mister. A great big shining blind star.'

'Yes,' Calvin agreed. 'Graham shows enormous potential as a rock vocalist of great range and passion. He still had some pitching issues in his upper range . . .'

'*Calvin!* Please!' Beryl exclaimed in horror. 'The boy is *blind.*'

'And he deserves the respect of not being judged on that fact, Beryl,' Calvin replied firmly. 'We will consider him on his singing merit and his singing merit alone. The fact that he has overcome *enormous* hurdles to be singing *at all* is entirely irrelevant. I see Graham as a singer, *not* as a blind singer, and if he had come to us today as a *solo* singer, as far as I'm concerned he'd be through with a bullet and a serious prospect to win. But he didn't come here as a solo singer. Did he, *Millicent*?'

The cameras focused on the quaking girl like the rifles of a firing squad.

'No,' Calvin continued, 'he came here with you.'

Millicent could only gape in horror, her mouth open, her lower jaw almost hitting her collar bone. But no words came. Her tongue lay exposed and motionless, like a big, fat, dead fish, its tip resting on her lower front teeth. She looked as if she might never speak again.

Graham did his best.

'We came here together, Calvin. We are Graham and Millicent.'

'And I fear it's beginning to look very much as if you will be leaving together,' Calvin said.

'No!' Beryl exclaimed.

'Calvin, the boy could sell a lot of records,' Rodney added.

'With old Mildew hanging round his neck?' Calvin asked.

'Well no, obviously,' Rodney conceded, aware of his duties as a judge. 'Clearly she's the passenger.'

'Passenger! It's like Roy Orbison had teamed up with a checkout chick from Tesco's.'

'Except I'm sure some checkout chicks can sing,' Beryl added.

They were speaking now as if neither Graham nor Millicent were present.

'How do you feel, Millicent,' Beryl asked, 'to be the weight that's dragging Graham down?'

What colour there had been in Millicent's pale features had now completely drained away. Even her tongue had turned from pink to grey. The two young friends stood there motionless, powerless beneath the assault. The knuckles of their clasped hands were white with tension, shaking with it.

'OK, here's how it is,' said Calvin, once more the cool professional. 'We challenged you to improve, Millicent, and so far you have failed woefully.'

'We said go away and grow, not go away and *shrink*,' Rodney added, clearly delighted with the line.

'But if we send you home as by rights we should, Millicent, we lose Graham. And that I am not minded to do.'

'We can't lose Graham!' Beryl exclaimed. 'He's a babe!'

'So in my view we have to give you another chance. One more and one more only. Go away, Millicent, and work. Work and learn and learn and work and grow. Will you do that, Millicent? Will you try to lift your game to justify this blind boy's touching faith in you?'

But still the grey/pink mullet that lay in the saliva pit of Millicent's lower jaw could not be stirred. No words came. Not even the suspicion of words. Just tears, suddenly and in a flood, big silent tears.

'Millicent!!' Beryl gasped. 'You are being given another chance here! You've been given another

354

chance when you should be going home. That's not something to bloody cry about! I've seen kids during my charity work who have *nothing to eat*. That's something to cry about! You should be crying tears of joy. Now go home, work, learn, pull yourself together and *raise your game!*'

Running through the holding area in tears, Millicent bumped into the Prince of Wales, who was deep in concerned conversation with a young mother and child. Chelsie was discreetly committing the encounter to camera.

'Mind out where you're fucking going!' Chelsie shouted as Millicent ran from the room.

'I say, no!' the Prince exclaimed. 'Really, *please*. There is a young child here. That kind of language is all very well on the rugger field or in the smoking room but it has no place among children.'

'Sorry,' said Chelsie.

'I'm quite serious. How can we possibly expect children to achieve acceptable standards of *civilized* behaviour if we *adults* fail to *set standards*?'

'Yes. You're right. I'm sorry.'

'I know I *bang on* about it all the time and of course I doubt anybody *listens*. But really, it starts with casual profanity and ends with crack cocaine.'

'Yes. You're right. I'm very sorry, sir,' Chelsie insisted.

'Good. We'll say no more about it, eh?' and once more the Prince turned to the young mother.

'I'm so sorry we were interrupted,' he said. 'You were telling me about your little boy?'

'I was telling you about my little Sam here, how he's waiting for an operation.'

With the cameras still rolling, Keely walked back into shot.

'Excuse me, sir,' she said, 'we need you for your audition.'

'Oh bother,' the Prince replied, adding, to the young mother, 'Look, I have to go and *strut my funky stuff*, as my boys say, but I shall get someone to find out who to write to about your problem. Some *ghastly quango* or NHS *pen pusher*, I imagine. Personally I think they should stop counting the teaspoons and *employ more nurses*. But that's just *my opinion*, and I don't suppose any *politician* is going to listen to muggins here. I shall keep *banging on* regardless, it's all I can do. Who'd be a prince, eh? In the meantime I shall certainly try to find somebody to write to about young Samuel here.'

'Samson.'

'Really? As in Judges, chapters thirteen to sixteen?'

'No, as in the World Wrestling Federation.'

'Goodness! How *fascinating*.'

'Cut!' said Chelsie. 'Fucking perfect. I mean . . . great.'

Pop School: Iona

The Quasar was through. Suki the prostitute was through. Bloke were through. Stanley, the single dad who was just doing it for his kid, was through. Tabitha the lesbian was through, having turned up and been filmed wandering hand in hand with her glamorous girlfriend in the same field of poppies that had provided the backdrop for Graham and Millicent's romantic tryst. The Four-Z were through and had paid fulsome tribute to the Lord Jesus Christ for the crucial part he had played in their success so far.

The Prince of Wales was also through, having delivered a spirited rendition of 'The British Grenadiers' before he was whisked off to open a Whole Earth centre in Cornwall and deliver a speech on the importance of teaching history at Exeter University. The news of the Prince's entry into *Chart Throb* was not yet in the public domain since the early programmes had still to be broadcast. The confidentiality agreement that all entrants signed would have kept the news from leaking out had it been necessary to invoke it, but the truth was that those contestants who had noticed the Prince at all continued to believe him to be a lookalike. Even the young mother whom he had offered to try to help set no store by his promise.

'He's been playing it so long,' she assured Keely, 'I reckon he thinks he *is* the blooming Prince.'

The comment was of course time-code-noted for inclusion in the final edit.

As the Prince hurried away with his detectives and his equerry in tow, Iona was finally summoned for her audition.

She looked very nice and she sang very well. As an experienced semi-professional who had been through the entire audition process the year before, she had the edge and it showed.

'I should like to sing "A Woman's Heart",' she explained.

'That's a good song,' Rodney said, almost by instinct. '"A Woman's Heart" is a great song to choose.'

Iona turned and stared at Rodney for a moment but she did not comment. Instead she looked away and sang her song in a pleasant, clear voice with what appeared to be genuine emotion.

When it was over Beryl was once more misty-eyed. While not actually crying – she had used up the last of her reachable nose hair on Graham – she was obviously moved.

'Iona,' she said, 'you *owned* that song.'

'Thank you, Beryl,' Iona replied sweetly. 'Coming from you that means a lot because I know you've had your doubts about me in the past.'

'Not today, Iona. Not today,' Beryl replied firmly. 'I'm a woman and a mum and I know all about the pain in a woman's heart, particularly because, as you know, for quite some time my woman's heart beat in a man's body and you can't get much more painful than that, and let me tell you now, you were so emotional it wasn't funny.'

'Yes, Iona,' Calvin agreed, 'I thought that was a very fine performance indeed. Clearly as a woman you understand heartache. You've been through rejection and disappointment and you've used it to grow. Don't you think so, Rodney?'

Calvin, Beryl and Iona all turned to look at the hapless Rodney. There was a long pause before Rodney turned to Calvin and whispered *sotto voce*, 'Please, Calvin . . .'

'What did you think, Rodney?' Calvin replied firmly.

Rodney's face grew resigned. It seemed he knew his duty and he would do it, excruciatingly embarrassing though it might be.

'I . . . I . . . just don't think you've grown since last year, Iona.' Sweat was breaking out on his forehead. 'You know that I loved you and your band last year and I went to a lot of trouble to say so, but I have to be honest here. I just don't think you've grown.'

'Really, Rodney?' Iona replied, remaining calm but with her eyes flashing furiously. 'That's so strange considering how much "nurturing" I received from you after the last series ended. As I recall, for a while there you were *most appreciative* of what I had to offer.'

Calvin grinned broadly, not bothering to conceal his enjoyment of Rodney's predicament.

'I am simply taking a professional view here, Iona,' Rodney blustered. 'I like you, you know that, and I did my very best to encourage you after you were eliminated last year . . .'

' "Encourage", Rodney? Is that what it's called? Actually, as I recall, it was you who needed the encouragement, particularly when you'd had a few drinks and couldn't *rise* to the occasion, so to speak.'

Rodney's jaw dropped, Beryl shrieked with cruel laughter and Calvin decided that for the time being enough was enough.

'So,' he said, 'it's a yes from me. Beryl?'

'Oh definitely. A yes from me.'

'And Rodney?'

Rodney squirmed as he had never squirmed before, withering under the fierce, steady gaze of the woman he had used and was now expected to betray.

'Please, Calvin,' he whimpered, 'she's through anyway on your two votes.'

'Rodney, the people want to know what *your* opinion is. I need an answer and I *think* you know what it is.'

Rodney had no choice. Calvin was the boss. Getting the job on *Chart Throb* had changed Rodney's life completely, transformed him from a middle-ranking nobody into a major television personality, the sort of person who received regular invitations to corporate golfing trips. He could not give that up. He simply couldn't. Besides, how much more could she embarrass him than she had already done?

'I'm sorry, Iona. I just don't think you can cut it alone.'

Iona stood still for a moment, staring hard at Rodney.

'Well now,' she said, 'in that case I shall just have to try harder to find a way of making an impression on you. Shan't I, Rodney?'

All Back to My Place:
Graham and Millicent

Calvin finally ended Millicent's agony during the last round before the finals. In the part of the show called All Back to My Place, each judge supposedly took a group of semi-finalists into their own home for a period of intense training and 'nurturing'. The reality was that the time the contestants spent in the judges' homes was exactly as long as it took for them to perform their song and be informed whether they had made it through to the finals or not.

In fairness it had originally been thought that some genuine nurturing might take place at this stage of the competition but as the reality of having to actually *interact* with twelve desperate star-struck strangers in *their own homes* sank in, the judges had all quickly downsized the level of commitment that they were prepared to make to the show.

'Do you really think,' Beryl gasped, speaking for all three of them (including Calvin, whose idea it had been), 'that I'm going to have a dozen desperate fucking nobodies who've crawled out from under some little English stone traipsing round my beautiful home and using my toilets? These are the sort of people I've worked all my life to *leave behind*! The people I have gated security to keep a-fucking-way! These are the people who ask for fucking autographs while I'm trying to sneak in to see my surgeon. I *hate* these fucking people. I'll greet them at the front door but they're not to come in. You can take them round the back and they can perform down by the pool. If they need the toilet they can use the one the gardeners use. They are absolutely *not* to set foot in the house, do you hear me?'

The home that Beryl's group were to be allowed to knock on the front door of was at least her mansion in Los Angeles. Calvin was not prepared even to go as far as Beryl; he did not volunteer the use of any of the homes he actually lived in. The 'place' where his 'nurture group' were to be permitted to gasp briefly in envious awe was a holiday spread in Morocco that he'd bought as an investment. As in Beryl's case, nobody was to be allowed in the house.

'They can perform on the patio,' Calvin said, 'and change in the gym.'

'Can they have a quick dip in the pool?' Trent enquired, desperate to gain some usable footage to maintain the fiction that the judges were extending some sort of hospitality. 'Beryl won't allow that.'

'All right but make sure they shower first. Make fucking sure they've turned in their cameras and mobiles before they get within a mile of the gate.'

Rodney was happy to have his group inside his home but this did not solve Trent's problem because, rather embarrassingly, Rodney's home was an unremarkable flat in Battersea. Keely always did her best to big it up in the voiceovers.

'And the group that Rodney is to nurture,' she shouted ecstatically, 'are to be whisked off to his luxury penthouse apartment overlooking the romantic River Thames in Good Old London Town.'

But no matter how she put it, Rodney's home simply wasn't a Hollywood mansion, nor was it a huge holiday spread in Morocco. It was still a flat in Battersea.

The shooting for this part of the contest was always the most complex for the production team because of the travel and accommodation arrangements. The selected contestants had to be transported to one of the three nurturing locations, accommodated in the cheapest nearby motel, shot in various travelogue-style

361

set-ups to prove that they really *were* there ('I can't believe it, I'm on Sunset Boulevard and I'm from Leeds'), and filmed wandering round the luxury grounds of Calvin's and Beryl's places, though not Rodney's ('I've always believed in my dream but seeing all this just makes me want to dream it even more').

Then there were the 'auditions' themselves, which meant shooting twelve different numbers in each of three separate and problematic locations in which technicians had to remove their shoes and sign gagging orders before being allowed to look for a power socket. Then everybody had to be got home again. The return journeys were further complicated by the necessity to film the failed contestants staring tearfully out of the aeroplane window, contemplating how they were going to inform their poverty-stricken families back home that the long-dreamed-of fame and fortune were not about to materialize.

The long tease that Calvin had perpetrated upon Graham and Millicent finally ended beside Calvin's swimming pool. They had just sung 'Don't Go Breaking My Heart', the old Elton John and Kiki Dee hit. As before, Millicent had effectively held the tune and Graham had resorted to gravel-voiced rock posturing to cover his shortcomings. As before, Calvin turned black to white without a scintilla of shame.

'Millicent,' he said, 'the way you sang that song broke *my* heart, dear.'

He let that hang for a lengthy moment as once more Millicent's jaw fell open, revealing her fat, pale, familiar tongue.

'I'm afraid the game's up. Graham can't carry you any longer, *I* can't carry you any longer. I have given you every chance to work and to learn and to grow—'

'I *have* worked,' Millicent blurted, for once finding a voice.

'But you haven't learned and you haven't grown.'

'People say I'm good!'

'What people, Millicent? People who produce records? People who make pop shows? I don't think so, dear. The truth is that you are appalling and you had absolutely no business getting as far as you have done on a serious musical talent show such as this one. We all know why you're here. You're here because of your partnership with the saintly and endlessly patient Graham. We wanted to keep him so we kept you but we can't do that any more, Millicent. Like I say, this is a serious talent show. I am *very* serious about the music. The music is *all* that matters. I don't care about *characters*, about personalities or anybody's false hopes and dreams. I am interested in the *singing*, nothing more, nothing less, and *you can't sing*, dear. Sorry, but them's the facts. And because of you I'm sending you both home. Graham, Millicent. Goodbye.'

Millicent took Graham's hand and together they walked away to conduct their tear-drenched post-rejection interview.

Meanwhile Calvin instructed Trent to film him wandering up and down beside the pool looking torn and confused.

'Torn and confused, boss?' Trent repeated.

'Yes. Stick the camera on the other side of the pool, clear everybody out of the shot and get a nice big wide shot of me alone, torn, confused and with the weight of pop's future upon my shoulders.'

'On it, boss,' Trent said. 'It's all good.'

The camera was set and Calvin (who had ruffled his hair into a mop of anguished concentration) wandered about in the shot looking splendid and alone. He threw his arms skywards as if appealing to God for guidance, he sat on a sunlounger with his head in his hands as if deep in tortured concentration. He took up his phone and, without bothering to call a number, playacted a torn and troubled consultation with a mythical adviser.

'I just don't *know*,' he said into the dead receiver. 'I *can't* let the guy go, he's too good! But we can't give her any more chances. The chick just can't cut it . . . She's taken the rope and she's hung herself . . . I guess I don't have any choice.'

Calvin put away his phone and called 'Cut!' Then he instructed Chelsie to bring back Graham without Millicent.

'Take a crew,' he added. 'Make sure you cover the moment when you tell them that I want to see Graham alone.'

'I'll take two,' Chelsie volunteered with enthusiasm. 'Leave one covering Millicent while she waits.'

'Good girl.'

And so the pantomime was created. Graham and Millicent had been sitting quietly together on the coach that was to take all the contestants back to the airport at the conclusion of the final 'audition'. There had been much wailing and keening on the coach as the louder personalities who had been rejected lamented their lot. There was cheering too and singing, high fives and punching of the air from the ones who had got through. Only Graham and Millicent were silent. Sitting together, holding hands, they concentrated only on each other.

'I'm happy really,' Graham had said, finally breaking the silence. 'I don't think I could have handled another round of them treating you that way.'

'God, they've been shitty,' Millicent agreed.

'Yes, but it's obvious why, isn't it? The drama of it all. I'm not stupid, Milly, I study music, I know which one of us is the better singer. The *only* singer, in fact, and it's you. We both know that. I'm an instrumentalist.'

'Do you *really* think that though?' Millicent pleaded. 'I mean I always did think I could sing but honestly they've made me lose faith in myself. He *is* Calvin Simms after all.'

'Come on, Milly. You know I can't sing.'

'But you are a real musical talent. Maybe they've spotted that. Maybe that's what they're going on about.'

'Well, we'll never know now, will we? Because it's over and I'm glad because what I really wanted to say to you, Milly, and I've been waiting till we got chucked out before I said it, was—'

At that point Chelsie burst on to the bus with her camera teams.

'Graham,' she said, 'Calvin wants to see you . . . alone.'

Graham gripped Millicent's hand. It was obvious what this summons might mean, the only thing it could mean.

'Why?' Graham asked. 'He's chucked us out. It's over, isn't it?'

'He wants to see you.'

Millicent squeezed Graham's hand in return.

'You go,' she said. 'See what he wants.'

And so Graham was taken from the bus and brought once more before Calvin.

'Mate,' Calvin said, 'here's how it is. Your journey should not end here. This is where it should be beginning.'

'How do you mean? I thought it *had* ended.'

'I can change the rules at any time, Graham, and I'm prepared to do that now. I'll let you through to the finals but only if you go it alone. You have to drop Millicent.'

'But she's a much better singer than me,' Graham protested. 'You may not know it but it's obvious to me.'

'Maybe she is a better singer, Graham, but that doesn't make her a great singer and it doesn't make her a Chart Throb. You, on the other hand, are a real musical talent. You write songs, I hear you are a fine instrumentalist. In the finals you'll be able to play. You can't pass up this opportunity.'

As Graham wrestled with his conscience the cameras crept in ever closer, feeding on his anguish.

'She said that if you ever tried to split us up she wouldn't do it. That she would never leave me.'

'Why would she want to leave you, Graham? You're the talent.'

Graham clearly did not know what to say.

'I've been watching you two, you know,' Calvin said. 'You're pretty fond of each other, aren't you?'

'Yes, yes, we are.'

'Then I guess she knows how talented you are, mate. And what a crime it would be if that great talent was never tested before the public. Do you *really* think she would want to stand in your way?'

Of course in the end Graham agreed to continue in the competition alone and he was sent back to the bus, along with Chelsie and a camera team, to explain the news to Millicent.

Calvin chose the opportunity of a brief pause in the proceedings to call Emma and bring her up to speed.

'How are you going to get round the fact that Millicent was actually the one who could sing?' she enquired.

'Plenty of dancers and very heavy backing tapes like we always do. But I don't think he'll be in the finals long. He doesn't really have a story now that we've got rid of Millicent. I mean, like you say, if he could sing it would be different.'

All Back to My Place: HRH

Sitting right at the back of the queue of auditionees due to face Calvin in Morocco were His Royal Highness and Bree, the young battered wife whom Chelsie had discovered in the women's refuge.

Calvin had kept Bree at a very low profile until this point, nodding her through as an In and Out in the early stages, but now the moment had come for her to play her part.

His Royal Highness had been forced to arrive late at Calvin's holiday home because of an invitation to take tea with the Moroccan royal family.

'I'm afraid I simply can't be on Moroccan soil without paying my respects,' he had explained to the anguished production secretary, who had been forced to change his call time. 'It's not just a matter of *etiquette*, it's also *simply good manners*. Which I *do* think are important. Don't you?'

When the Prince did arrive, Calvin had him placed at the end of the queue beside Bree. Calvin knew very well that when thrust into anybody's company the Prince's instincts would lead him to enquire who and how they were. A lifetime of brief encounters with complete strangers would ensure that His Royal Highness would not simply ignore the woman he was sitting next to.

'How do you *do*,' he began. 'Are you *well*? Isn't it fearfully hot? I have an umbrella in my case – would you like to borrow it to ward off the sun?'

Bree declined the offer, saying that she was very happy to soak up as much sun as she could get, there not being a lot of it in Birmingham.

'Yes, I suppose you're *right*,' the Prince agreed. 'But really, please do be careful. You know, the carcinogenic properties of sunlight have only recently been *fully revealed*. Particularly with this awful business of *ozone* depletion, which *I* for one have been *banging on about* for years. Won't you at least take a squirt of my Factor 30 for the tip of your nose? My wife insists I positively *slap it on.*'

Bree accepted a small blob of sunscreen from the royal tube and dabbed it on her nose.

'You don't half look like the Prince of Wales,' she said. 'I suppose everybody says that to you.'

'Well, they have done quite a lot around here,' the Prince conceded. 'Normally it rather *goes without saying*, but here of course everybody seems to think I'm a lookalike. Ironic really because I can tell you there have been many occasions over the last few years when I've wished I *was* a lookalike.'

Bree smiled sympathetically, clearly thinking the old boy slightly mad.

'I think he's all right as it happens,' she said.

'Who?'

'The Prince of Wales,' Bree said. 'I once went on an outward bound thing done by his Trust.'

'Goodness. How splendid!' the Prince said, brightening enormously. 'Did you enjoy it? I do hope so, it's really made a difference to so many young people's lives. That's something I'm enormously proud of, you know.'

'It was great. We had a real laugh. I'd never been in the country before.'

'And did you *learn* something, do you think? Independence? Self-reliance? I do think those qualities are *so important.*'

'Well,' Bree replied, 'perhaps I might have done but in the end I don't suppose I can have, really.'

'Goodness. Why is that?' the Prince enquired.

With little further prompting Bree told her tale. It was a long afternoon and there were no other distractions. She told how she had fallen into an abusive relationship, how her violent partner had beaten her and how time and again she had taken him back in the classic cycle of abuse.

'You know the old phrase,' she said. 'If he hits you once, shame on him, if you let him hit you twice, shame on you. Easy to say, of course.'

The Prince had listened sympathetically, murmuring expressions of concern which Bree seemed to appreciate, and all of which the cameras were recording at a discreet distance.

'Well, do you know, I really do think it's a matter of self-respect,' the Prince said finally. 'You have to convince yourself that you don't have to be a victim. It's not *preordained*. You have the means to stop it simply by *believing* that you can.'

'I know,' Bree lamented. 'It's just sometimes so hard to stand up for yourself.'

'Don't I *know it*?' the Prince exclaimed. 'But one simply *has to try*. What song have you chosen to sing?'

'"Stand By Your Man",' Bree answered. 'I like Country.'

'Oh heavens!' the Prince exclaimed. 'I know that one. The cook sometimes plays it. Goodness, you mustn't sing that! It's a victim's song. Even *muggins* here can see that. You need something empowering and self-assertive.'

'Like what?'

'Oh, I don't know, like "Men Of Harlech", or "The Battle Hymn Of The Republic".'

'I don't know them.'

'Well, do you know "Sisters Are Doing It For Themselves" by the Eurythmics? Terribly stirring. They did it at a concert thing we organized. I *do* admire David and Annie and they've been *so* helpful with my charity work over the years.'

'You really think I should change my song?'

'Absolutely. If you're going to start standing up for

369

yourself now's as good a time as any. I know that's why *I'm* here. Look, we're right at the back of the queue, you've got ages to practise. I'll go through it with you if you like. I had been meaning to write a letter to the Dalai Lama about the nature of *faith* but I expect he can wait. He's such a *calm* fellow. So *centred*.'

Hell Hath No Fury

After the All Back to My Place recordings there was a hiatus in the *Chart Throb* schedule to allow time for the footage to be edited and for the completed shows, which were already being broadcast, to catch up with the recording process.

During this brief respite before the ten-week haul of weekly live finals began, Rodney had returned to London and it was there, while killing time playing indoor golf in his office, that he received the news from his secretary that Iona was once more on the line. In the past Rodney had of course been in the habit of avoiding Iona's calls, but that was before the new series of *Chart Throb* began to air. Once the Birmingham audition episode had been broadcast his attitude to his ex-girlfriend changed considerably.

Iona's performance of 'You Raise Me Up', Rodney's dismissive comments about it and Iona's explosive retort had been big news.

'*I was good enough for you before, wasn't I? In public and in private.*'

The press had been full of it and 'in public and in private' had become very much the catchphrase of the week. The Iona/Rodney scandal had been the main story of the series so far, Calvin having decided to hold back the Prince of Wales's first appearance until the last of the regional audition shows.

The truth was that Rodney had rather relished his sudden notoriety, enjoying the exposure that Iona's comment had brought him. For once he was the most talked-about judge, and not for being drenched in coffee either but for apparently having bedded a beautiful and talented young girl and then publicly scorned her. Certainly most of the press comment on him (particularly from female columnists) had been negative but there was no denying that Rodney was looking a lot sexier and a lot tougher than he had ever looked on the show before. He much preferred being a brutal love rat to a boring wimp.

'OK, I'll take the call,' said Rodney self-importantly. 'Put her through on the conference facility, I want to keep practising my putts.'

Rodney was actually delighted that Iona had called him. He had been intending to call her to announce that circumstances might shortly bring him to Scotland, and he had even cancelled an attractive little freebie opening a boat show in Hull to clear his diary. Suddenly Rodney wanted to see Iona, he was attracted to her again, the fact that she was all over the papers being routinely described as 'ravishing' was very sexy to him. She was no longer a has-been, last year's contender, last year's relationship; now she was 'news'. His and her names linked together had always got Rodney more coverage than his alone did and he had been teasing himself with the idea of taking Iona back. They would be a hot couple all over again, front page news once more. And of course she *was* ravishing, he remembered that now, now that the papers were saying it.

'Hello, Iona!' he shouted happily, striking his golf ball with a flourish. 'I see that you and I are in the papers together. Can't be bad, can it? No such thing as bad publicity, as they say.'

'Shut your face, you smug little weasel, and listen to me,' the familiar voice replied.

Rodney was momentarily taken aback. He had been feeling so cheerful that he had allowed himself to forget that as far as Iona was concerned he had viciously and inexplicably demeaned her on national television.

'Now, now, Iona,' he said. 'Hold on a minute. I know I said you couldn't sing but that was just for the drama. A bit of fun. I knew Calvin and Beryl were putting you through so I thought I'd vote against expectations – you know, just to stir things up a bit. And look, it's worked, hasn't it? We *are* the news.'

'I *said* listen to me, you little shit,' Iona replied.

'Now look here, Iona, you can't take that tone with me,' Rodney said, his own tone hardening. If she was going to be unpleasant then she would soon find out that he could give as good as he got.

'Can't I?' Iona snapped. 'Well, perhaps I can take it with the papers then. When I tell them my story.'

'What story? Everybody knows the truth about our affair. We never denied it.'

'Everyone knows the truth, Rodney,' Iona replied, 'but wait till I tell them the fiction.'

'What do you mean?'

'Mary was under age at the time, you bloody animal.'

Iona was referring to Shetland Mist's bass player, who had indeed been a schoolgirl at the time of the previous series, a factor that had brought the group some small publicity.

'What!' Rodney's blood ran cold. He actually staggered a little. 'I never . . .'

'I know you didn't, although my guess is you'd have *liked* to.'

'Rubbish! What do you mean? I sent her one or two presents, that's all . . .'

'She was fifteen, Rodney, she had to get a special

dispensation to appear on the show. How's it going to sound when she says you tried to touch her up?'

'My God! I didn't! You wouldn't . . . !'

'You know where I live, Rodney, although you refused to ever visit my home when we were an item. Not good enough for you, was it? You never even met my family. Well, you'll meet them now. Come tomorrow, come alone and remember, you'll be searched so no recording equipment.'

With that the phone rang off, leaving Rodney to instruct his secretary to book him a flight to Glasgow for the following morning. She had already reserved a seat for him in anticipation of his going to Scotland. Rodney had hoped that the trip would be made under happier circumstances.

Iona lived with her family about an hour's drive from the city in a big old ramshackle farmhouse near the village of Dumgoyne. When Rodney arrived he was horribly uncomfortable to discover that quite a crowd had assembled to discuss whatever Iona had in mind for him, and as he sat down at the big kitchen table opposite his ex-girlfriend he could see behind her all the members of Shetland Mist, plus Iona's brothers and sisters and her parents. Her father, who had been working on his tractor, still held a heavy spanner in his hand. The last time Rodney had seen Shetland Mist he had been Iona's boyfriend and manager to the group; since then he had dumped them and cut himself off from their lives altogether. Now he was back and they were staring at him with ill-concealed contempt.

'So here's the point, Rodney,' said Iona. 'You've betrayed me in bed and you've betrayed me on TV and now it's payback time.'

'What are you going to do?'

'I'm going to announce on television that you told me you loved me and you promised to marry me while

373

all the time you were trying to molest Mary, and she'll swear you did it and the others will swear that she told them about it at the time. Everyone will believe us. Let's face it, you look like a fucking pervert anyway.'

'Iona!' her mother snapped. 'There is no call for language.'

'You wouldn't,' Rodney stammered.

'We would. Unless . . .'

'Unless what?'

Iona let him sweat for a moment.

'You *do* offer to marry me. Live on air.'

'What!'

'The moment I get voted off, you say there's something you want to say and you propose to me. It's as simple as that. We get married. You keep out of my way for three fucking years and then I divorce you and take half your fortune.'

Rodney sat and sucked his lip. Clearly his mind was racing, trying to work out the parameters.

'If you want money, why get married at all? Why not just blackmail me now?'

'Because you'd go to the police and the proof of the plot would be in my bank account. No, Rodney. We'll be married legitimately and I shall take your money legitimately. It's either that or I ask Calvin if I can bring my bass player on to the show because she has something to say. Knowing Calvin, I reckon he'd *love* it. He must be sick of you by now anyway and what a brilliant way to get rid of you.'

Royal Coup

'Way-ll, Calvin,' Dakota purred over the telephone, 'Ah do dee*clare* that when Ah saw the papers thiz mohnin' Ah wuz almos' sorra for you.'

Dakota had rung up to gloat. She could never have imagined when she first nominated the Prince of Wales as her ringer the level of derision that would fall upon the royal head once the news of his candidacy got out. The morning after his first audition was broadcast (once CALonic TV had issued a statement assuring the world that the man in question was no lookalike but the genuine heir to the throne) the press had indulged in an orgy of withering contempt. From the *Chart Nob!* headline in the *Sun* to the more considered *Ill-judged tilt at populism leaves Prince laughing stock* in the *Telegraph*, the media were unanimous in their assessment that this was the last gasp of a man and an institution that had lost all relevance in the modern world.

'Yes, well,' Calvin replied, 'we shall see, eh?'

'Yays, Calvin. We shayll.'

'We're all over the morning news,' Calvin said.

'Ah *know*. Ain it wunnerful? Ah must aidmit Ah nevah eemagined thay-et ma lil' challenge would make for such pop'lah *viewin'*. Ah guess all of this is *massivla* increasin' the value of ma property.'

'It isn't yours yet, darling,' Calvin replied. 'It's all still to play for.'

'Huh!' Dakota snorted. 'You *weesh*. Even you ain' clever'nuff ta turn this one aroun'.'

'Sorry,' Calvin said, 'another call. Got to go.'

So saying, Calvin abruptly ended his conversation with his estranged wife bocause he could see that Emma was on the other line and he never let anything get in the way of a conversation with Emma.

She was as upset as Dakota had been thrilled.

'It's backfired on us,' Emma lamented. 'I thought you showed him really sympathetically but it hasn't done any good. They're out to get him and that's that. They'd already made their minds up the moment he appeared and it doesn't matter what he says, they'll just ignore it and bash him anyway. I never should have let you try and do this for me. I should have made you chuck him out.'

'It's early days, Em, early days,' Calvin comforted her. 'No need to panic yet.'

'I think you should re-edit next week's show and drop him before any more damage is done.'

'How can we? We've put him through all the way to the finals.'

'Oh, come on, Calvin, this is me you're talking to. Just show him singing a line of his song then drop in any old shot of the three of you saying no and the job's done. You've reversed your decisions in the edit before.'

'Yes, but I made you a promise, darling, and I intend to keep it. I'm not going to throw in the towel in the first round. I knew it would be tough at the start so this is no surprise.'

'You really think you can turn it round?'

'Well, I'd like to try . . . for you.'

'I know you've done your best, Calvin, I won't hold you to this.'

'No, I mean it, Emma. I made a promise. This is for you.'

'Really, just for me?'

'Only for you.'

When Emma had rung off Calvin turned on the television and Sky Plussed the news headlines. The Prince of Wales was still top story. A spokeswoman was pictured outside the Prince's modest town house.

'His Royal Highness is not at liberty to comment on his *Chart Throb* candidacy as he is governed by the strict rules of the competition, which preclude any auditionee from discussing any aspect of the process whatsoever. He has, however, authorized me to make a brief statement on his behalf to the effect that he is proud of what he has achieved in the competition so far and he is enjoying shaking his booty and strutting his funky stuff enormously.'

Calvin laughed out loud. Good on you, mate, that's telling them.

Tragedy and Farce

As in previous years, the show proved itself an enormous success from the start. Of course the royal patronage helped but there was no doubt that Calvin would have produced a winner anyway. As before, the nation gloried in the hilarious succession of Mingers, Clingers and Blingers who were paraded before them each week. Everybody loved the show. Everybody, that is, except the Mingers, Clingers and Blingers themselves, who, having been present at their own auditions, no doubt imagined they had some idea as to how they might look on TV. Like many people who have been passed through an edit, they were to find out they were wrong.

It is said that history happens twice, once as tragedy and then again as farce, and in many ways this was true of the numerous rejected *Chart Throb* contestants. Their failure to progress beyond the first stage of the competition and the cruel dashing of their dreams had at the time been a personal and private tragedy. Now it was being repeated as public farce.

They could not believe how stupid they had been made to look. This had been their big moment and, despite their lack of success, they had been proud of their efforts and were secretly looking forward to their appearance on television. Of course they had all watched the show and seen the brutal treatment handed out to all the deluded sad acts who had preceded them, but none had ever imagined that such a thing could happen to them. Now, as their friends and acquaintances howled with laughter at their pathetic posturing, they were getting a brutal lesson in the 'reality' of reality television. Mingers who had fond memories of the sympathetic chat they'd had with Keely after their rejection were stunned to see that chat reduced to a ten-second clip of them claiming to be bigger than Elvis and better than John Lennon. Blingers who could recall the moment when they had been complimented on the impressive strength of their vocal delivery were shocked to find but a single grim shriek of that vocal remaining, featuring for two seconds in a montage taking the piss out of shouters and screamers. A Welsh girl who sang in a gravelly manner that she hoped made her sound like Bonnie Tyler had given a lengthy Bite Back Box interview afterwards in her normal voice, but at the very end of it, almost, it seemed, as an afterthought, she had been persuaded to put on her gravelly voice and say, 'I am one funky rock momma and you suck big time, Calvin Simms.' Inevitably this moment and this alone had ended up being broadcast.

Of course, according to Chelsie, these people were the lucky ones, the ones that had actually *made it on to television*. And it was certainly true that, for every person screaming at their television that their brilliant song had been cut down to one word and they had been made to look a complete dickhead, there were a hundred others saying, 'I can't believe it, they didn't show me at all! And I hung around all day! The researcher said I was *brilliant*!'

Then there were those contestants like Vicky and her mother or Peroxide or Millicent of Graham and Millicent to whom a disproportionate amount of screen time had been devoted. Invariably, in these

378

cases the people involved ended up wishing they had been overlooked altogether, for they were forced to learn that fame is *not* always good.

Vicky and her mum had been looking forward to the broadcast. Despite the brutality of their rejection, in the weeks since then they had persuaded themselves that they would come out of it all right. After all, Vicky had sung her song in full and, according to Keely, she had sung it very well. Also both Vicky and her mum had been given ample opportunity to argue their case afterwards, explaining fully why they thought that the judges had been not only wrong but rude.

'We fought our corner,' Mum announced proudly as she handed round the nibbles to the large gathering of friends, fellow pupils and parents from Vicky's stage school who had assembled at the family home for the broadcast. All these people knew that Vicky had been rejected in the first round but they were completely unprepared for the brutal manner in which the *Chart Throb* team had edited her self-delusions.

They all cheered as Vicky appeared on the television, sitting in the holding area with her mum, but the cheers quickly died as through braced teeth set in her cruelly exposed, brightly lit, spotty face she began boasting about her dream. There were even one or two tuts when Vicky's mum was heard loudly asserting that Vicky was undoubtedly the best in her school.

'I never said *that*,' Vicky's mum protested, although in this case the camera hadn't lied.

Then suddenly Vicky was in the audition room, murdering 'Hit Me Baby One More Time' in front of the judges, who gurned and groaned and sniggered and placed their heads in their hands throughout the song, which was played in its entirety. Vicky's friends watched, stunned, as the judges then ridiculed the panic-stricken creature who stood before them, wet-eyed and shaking. Even Beryl's pitying sympathy

379

seemed to be saying nothing more than 'Yes, she's utter shit, but she's only sixteen.'

Teacups remained on saucers and nibbles froze in hands as Vicky's guests watched her weeping in Keely's arms and indulging in an orgy of sadly deluded self-justification, a delusion finally capped by her mother shouting at the camera in the Bite Back Box that at least Vicky still had the courage to dream the dream.

After this, for a moment Vicky and her mother dared to hope that the nightmare might be over, but then they heard Keely saying, 'And still to come, the judges fight over Vicky's spectacular failure.'

Vicky and her mum had of course been entirely unaware that Vicky's appalling inadequacy was to feature as a running story throughout the whole show, with Beryl and Rodney fighting heatedly over the proper manner in which to reject such a wretchedly untalented child.

'She was worse than my haemorrhoids,' Rodney repeated.

'I know she was worse than your haemorrhoids, Rodney,' Beryl replied fiercely, 'but she's *only sixteen.*'

These conversations were of course illustrated with endlessly repeated clips of Vicky murdering her song, and at the end of the programme Keely mentioned that if viewers wanted to see more of Vicky's performance they need only turn to the cable channel round-up show *Little Chart Throbber*.

'Or why not click on the website and download the Spotty Vicky screen saver?'

Georgie of Peroxide was fortunate in that she did not see her stunning early rejection from the show for having failed to grow and learn from the lessons of the previous year. She was unfortunate, however, in that the reason she missed it was because she was lying unconscious in a hospital bed, having almost succeeded in starving herself to death. 'Chelle, the other member of the group, was made of sterner stuff and watched the show in the pub with friends. She got impossibly drunk and was arrested after hurling a bottle of beer at the screen. This incident proved to be a massive blessing in disguise as far as 'Chelle was concerned, because the papers picked up on it and the following week she was interviewed in several of the cheaper celebrity magazines, making the cover of one with the headline quote, *I'm no lesbian but I would definitely snog Madonna to further my musical career.*

Of the numerous 'stories' that featured in the early broadcasts of the show, Millicent probably suffered the most because she was a 'runner', appearing in three different episodes, her first audition, the Pop School edition and All Back to My Place. Each week her humiliation was absolute as she was portrayed as a hopeless, talentless millstone, selfishly dragging down the innocent Graham. The little looks, grimaces and tears that were edited into gaps in the judges' comments made her seem self-obsessed and spiteful, as if she was abusing Graham's trust and patience. The clear implication was that she should herself have volunteered to leave rather than taking advantage of the judges' reluctant kindness.

People began to shout unpleasant things at her in the street.

'Why don't you fuck off and let Graham get on with it?' they would say, not realizing that the episodes had been recorded weeks before and that Millicent had long since left the programme.

'Don't worry, I'm gone next week,' she would reply feebly.

'And about time!' they would shout back. 'You're ruining that poor blind boy's big break.'

This humiliation was made all the worse by the fact

that by now Millicent had fallen hopelessly in love with the man whose life she was popularly believed to be wrecking, but she was unable to speak to him. Graham, as a finalist, had now been well and truly gathered into the *Chart Throb* bosom and was living in communal accommodation in London with the rest of the finalists, rehearsing for the first of the live shows.

Man of the People

One person who had cause to take some satisfaction from the early broadcasts was the Prince of Wales. Initially condemned as a hideous embarrassment, he had, in a surprisingly short time, begun to find himself growing in the public esteem. His befriending of the lad Troy and apparent selfless devotion in attempting to teach him to read had definitely played well, a development that surprised nobody more than it did His Royal Highness himself.

'Do you know, I had no idea that I *was* teaching that boy to read,' he said to Calvin in a puzzled tone.

'Really, sir?' Calvin replied with a faint air of surprise.

'Yes. Really. And yet when I watch it on the television it certainly *looks* as if I'm teaching him to read. In fact a number of prominent educators have written to congratulate me for highlighting the problem of illiteracy among young urban males.'

'Well, isn't that nice?'

'Mmm. Yes. Except, as I say, I had no idea I *was* teaching the boy to read. In fact, I rather think I wasn't.'

'Well, for me your contribution is more in the way of lending a general air of encouragement,' Calvin replied. 'Just you being there is a big help for him.'

'Hmm,' the Prince replied dubiously. 'I must say it certainly looks in the edit as if I really *am* teaching him to read.'

'Does it?'

'Yes, it does. All those lingering shots of me and the lad poring over that *Harry Potter* book of his.'

'Very sweet, I thought. Touching.'

'We only did that once, you know.'

'Really?'

'But I noticed the same shot appeared in two different programmes.'

'Not the *same* shot, sir. Different angle.'

'And then there's that young lady, Keely, *banging on* about it too.'

'Does she bang on?'

'Well, last week she actually *said* that I was helping Troy with his reading.'

'Well, you did help him, sir. I recall it distinctly.'

'One word, Mr Simms. *Quidditch.*'

'But surely it's all about example and inspiration, sir? Isn't that exactly what your Trust is supposed to do? It's no good spoon-feeding these kids. All you can do is lead by example.'

Despite Calvin's honeyed words, the Prince did not seem entirely convinced.

'I say, Mr Simms, you're not cheating, are you? I mean if I am to progress in this competition I only want to do it on *merit*. If I can't win by strutting my funky stuff and shaking my booty down to the ground then I certainly don't wish to win by manipulation and deceit.'

'Excuse me, sir,' Calvin answered firmly, 'but it is not possible to cheat in *Chart Throb* because, as you will remember from the form *you signed*, the producers are entitled to change the rules at any time. We don't break rules, we rewrite them, which is an

383

entirely different thing and perfectly legitimate.'

'I *suppose* you're right,' the Prince said dubiously. 'But then there's also that young mother with the sick child.'

'Well, you did get your office to write to her NHS Trust about the waiting list for the boy's operation, didn't you, sir?'

'Yes, I *did* but I certainly didn't intend it to be broadcast. I had no idea you were even *filming* it. *Or* that business with the poor woman who'd been violently abused by her *swine* of a partner. Those were private conversations.'

'Please, sir, do read the form you signed. Nothing is private on *Chart Throb*. Everything you say and do during the process belongs to us to use as we see fit. But really, sir, please think about it. You wanted us to show the *real you*. In the world of television sometimes the only way to show the truth is by *lying*. You *are* the sort of person who cares a great deal about literacy but I can't have you *banging on* about it, can I?'

'Gosh, no! Heaven forbid. I'm sure it would be terribly dull.'

'Exactly. Therefore, in order to represent you honestly but in succinct televisual terms, I have to edit *boldly*. I have to *tell the story*. The fact is that by pure good fortune you *happen* to have stumbled upon an illiterate kid, a desperate mum with a sick child and a battered wife. It's just *pure chance*. As to the editing, I suggest that you leave that to me and concentrate on learning the lyrics to "My Way".'

The Eve of the Finals

The finals of *Chart Throb* consisted of a drawn-out series of shows which were no longer the result of carefully edited pre-recorded material but live broadcasts in which all the finalists would perform. Each week the public would vote for their favourites and then the two contestants who had received the least votes would have to perform their song again. After that the judges would decide which one of them would be rejected. It was an agonizingly slow process which many (including Calvin) knew to be nothing like as entertaining as the earlier stages of the show.

'It's an inherent design fault,' he would regularly moan. 'The show's only really good at the start of the series. We kick off with hundreds of dickheads who can't sing, can't dance and can't form a coherent sentence, then we narrow them down to twelve bog-standard pub singers you could hear on any cruise ship or in any hotel lounge, then we finally decide on one complete nobody who everybody will have forgotten about in a fortnight! It's structurally flawed. What we need to do is to find a way to play the programme backwards! *Start* with the nobody, then fan out across the country looking for all the dickheads! We could have a fantastic final at Wembley Stadium with thousands of idiots all singing "You Are The Wind Beneath My Wings".'

On the eve of the first final, Calvin, Trent and Chelsie stood reviewing a chart they had made with photographs and brief descriptions of the twelve finalists:

Tabitha: Dull dungarees lezza but has sexy girlfriend.
Suki: Balloon-boobed, fat-lipped, tragicomic prostitute.

Bloke: Bricklayers with guitars. Semi-pro club act. Dull but worthy.

Graham: Blind. Can't sing.

Blossom: Fat momma. Big laugh. 'Just a cleaner'. Can sing.

The Four-Z: Cute. Christian. Good hard luck story. Can sing.

Troy: Can sing a bit. Can't read a lot.

Iona: Good voice. Rodney used to fuck her.

Stanley: Hero single dad. NOTE: Kids not particularly cute.

Latiffa: Black girl with attitude.

The Quasar: Best Blinger in years. Can't sing but doesn't care and nor do we.

The Prince of Wales: Heir to the throne.

'So, boss,' Trent enquired, 'how do you want to play this?'

'Well, for a start I want to take the focus off HRH for a few weeks. We've performed miracles creating a more sympathetic image for him . . . and, by the way, well done, Chelsie, on that battered bird. Top research there. Cute, vulnerable, her and his nibs rehearsing "Sisters Are Doing It For Themselves" together was a watershed moment in TV history.'

'Thanks, chief,' Chelsie replied, while Trent tried hard not to scowl.

'But the public bore easily,' Calvin continued. 'A little goes a long way in terms of audience manipulation and I think we need to bury the Prince as deeply as possible in the pack for a few weeks and concentrate on other stories.'

'You want to keep him for the final, boss?' said Trent, clumsily stating the obvious in order to re-enter the conversation and instantly regretting it.

'No, Trent,' Calvin snapped with angry sarcasm. 'Why on earth would I want to do that? The heir to the throne in a *Chart Throb* final? Sounds boring to me, let's chuck him out. OF COURSE I WANT HIM IN THE FINAL, YOU FUCKING IDIOT!!'

'Yeah, right, absolutely, boss,' Trent spluttered. 'I'm just working it through in my mind here. Yes, of course we want to keep him for the final but I think taking the focus off him is going to be tough. I mean he's the Prince of Wales, after all, singing and dancing week after week in a series of live studio talent shows, how can we possibly bury that?'

'How, Trent? How?' Calvin replied. 'More to the point, how long have you worked on this show?'

'I'm just saying that—'

'We bury it by pointing the cameras at somebody else, of course. We control the cameras, we control the shots and we control the vision mixing. Have you forgotten that the rules of this show were specifically designed in order to leave absolutely nothing to chance? We give him short songs, we play half his performance on the audience and on shots of other contestants, we shoot him from the knees down if we feel like it and, most of all, we big up other stories.'

'I hope you're right, boss,' Trent replied, desperately trying to back out of the corner in which he had placed himself while still appearing to maintain just enough dignity and individuality to justify his role on the show. Calvin might be a fairly ruthless leader but he did not pay his senior researchers for abject servility. 'The finals are a tricky time, the public does crazy things and I'd hate to lose him early on.'

Trent was speaking without thinking. Unfortunately for him, Calvin was listening while thinking.

'Trent,' he said, almost gently, 'I'm sorry, mate, but you're going to have to swap jobs with Chelsie.'

'What!' Trent stuttered.

'No, I'm serious,' Calvin insisted. 'If you want to stay on *Chart Throb* you have to accept a more junior position. I can't have my number two wasting my time talking complete bollocks, like some naïve punter.'

'But—'

'Trent. Think about it. It's one thing having the *public* believe that because the finalists are subjected to a weekly vote the competition is beyond the manipulation of the judges, but it's quite another having my senior researcher being that stupid.'

Trent hung his head. 'Sorry, chief. You're right.'

Solemnly he vacated the chair closest to Calvin and went to sit beyond Chelsie, placing her between him and his boss.

'Thanks, Trent,' said Chelsie, assuming her new authority with consummate ease. 'I think we'll build a great working partnership.'

'It always amazes me,' Calvin said, speaking as if to cover Trent's discomfort, 'that the only thing the public ever suspects is that the vote is rigged, when the vote is the *one thing* in the entire process which is absolutely genuine. Why would I try and rig the vote? I *never* try and rig the vote. It's so *obvious* that I don't *need* to rig the vote in order to control the process.'

This was Calvin's great secret, although it should never have been a secret since all the evidence was entirely public and no effort was ever made to cover it up. Calvin had been astonished at Dakota's naïvety in not spotting it when they made their bet. He had been equally surprised but also enchanted by Emma's failure to understand it when he offered to ensure the Prince's eventual triumph. Both women had been intimately connected to the *Chart Throb* system, they surely should have been able to see that there was only *one point* in the whole process when Calvin could possibly lose control and that was in the *very final show*. The rules stated that each week the two least popular figures in the poll would be identified and then the judges would decide which of them would leave. This meant that, as long as Calvin controlled the judges, which he most certainly did, then he would always be able to control the final choice and ensure he did not lose anybody he didn't wish to lose. For this reason, he normally instructed his colleagues to keep in the least popular person because unpopular contestants were far more interesting than popular ones and controversy was always good telly.

'They sit at home screaming at the TV, saying how *could* you keep that talentless fuck in the show! Don't they understand that is exactly *why* we keep him in? The more frustrated and angry the viewers are, the bigger the show gets.'

His Royal Highness was in fact completely safe up until the very last show. That was the one and only time in the entire process when the public genuinely made the decision, and even then they did so only on the evidence Calvin gave them. Up until that point, the only possibility of upset was if Beryl or Rodney refused to follow the script and this was never going to happen, for they owed Calvin everything.

Calvin's challenge was not to get the Prince of Wales into the final three, but to do so without losing the trust or loyalty of the *Chart Throb* audience. When he made his bet with Dakota he had committed himself to maintaining the show's popularity, which meant that he could never be *seen* to manipulate the audience. His job therefore was to create a figure each week whom he could credibly dump, to allow HRH to be voted into the final three.

Week One

At the week one production meeting Calvin announced that it would be Tabitha, the lesbian with the glamorous girlfriend, who would leave the show first. He turned to Beryl, who had been designated as Tabitha's 'nurturer'.

'I want you to tell her to sing Marvin Gaye's "Sexual Healing".'

Beryl roared with laughter. She could see which way this was going.

'Oh *yes*! From a paid-up card-carrying muff-muncher! Brilliant! That is so gross.'

'It certainly will be by the time we've staged it,' Calvin replied and turned to the director and vision mixer.

'We'll put her girlfriend in the front row and we'll shoot it so Tabitha is singing it directly to her.'

'*Love it!*' the director replied. 'Lots of close-ups and long, lingering looks.'

'Exactly,' Calvin replied, 'and crotch-grabbing.'

Calvin turned to the choreographer.

'I want you to stage it all hips and thrusting crotch, I want Tabitha grabbing her muff like she's got cystitis. OK?'

'I will if you insist, Calvin,' the choreographer replied. 'But I warn you, Tabitha is no dancer. She's built like a brick shithouse and she's got the rhythm of a dog on heat.'

'You think I hadn't noticed? It'll look horrible.'

'It certainly will. Do you want me to get her to wiggle her tongue during the instrumental?'

Calvin thought about this for a moment.

'OK, but keep it vaguely pre-watershed. Just tell her to lick her lips a bit, I don't want it protruding and, like I say, make sure she rubs her twat like she was Michael Jackson.'

'Will do.'

Next Calvin turned to the costume department.

'What have you dressed her in?'

'A beautiful dark trouser suit with a silver

pinstripe,' Costume replied. 'Slims her down a bit and hides her legs. Her tits are really all we've got to work with so we'll open up her shirt a few buttons and lead with the cleavage. Accessories-wise I thought maybe a homburg hat and—'

'Wrong,' Calvin interrupted, 'wrong, wrong, *wrong*. Give her a boiler suit and a T-shirt with *ALL MEN ARE RAPISTS* written on it.'

'Do you think she'll wear it?'

'She will wear what we fucking well tell her to. They are all under contract.'

Chelsie and Trent were tasked to brief Tabitha on what was being planned for her and to ensure that she did her bit towards her own destruction. Theoretically it should have been Beryl doing this job because in the fiction of the programme Tabitha was one of the acts Beryl was supposed to be 'nurturing'. The reality was that all three judges had long since given up even *pretending* that they had anything to do with the contestants prior to their actual performances. The researchers and producers did all the interacting, occasionally sending flowers and messages on the judges' behalf and always being sure to remind the contestants to thank the judges for these small gestures live on air.

It was the 'nurturing' fiction that amused Beryl most. She loved it. It made her feel invulnerable, like she could get away with anything.

'People actually *believe* this shit!' she would say to her friends in the States, shrieking with laughter at the very idea. 'They believe I go down to the fucking rehearsal rooms each day and hold my contestants' fucking hands! It's incredible. I am proud to say that there has never been a single fucking shot of me working with any of these assholes, not on their routines, not on their songs and not on their emotional well-being, and yet *still* people believe that I'm some kind

391

of mother hen! It's wonderful. Incredible. One day I swear I shall turn to that camera and tell the viewers what a bunch of fucking morons the contestants really are. But I love them, of course. They're my people.'

Love them or hate them, Beryl most certainly was not prepared to do any work with them and so it was Chelsie and Trent who, together with some junior researchers, travelled up to the block of service flats in Kilburn where the contestants were being housed and briefed Tabitha on what was expected of her.

It took a bit of selling.

'*All Men Are Rapists*,' Tabitha said dubiously. 'You think people will like that?'

'Well, not *all* the people,' Chelsie conceded, 'but at this stage of the competition with all twelve acts still in it you need to develop a *niche* vote.'

'But "Sexual Healing"? Isn't that a bit graphic?'

'Absolutely. There's nothing better than a bit of graphic sapphic. Trust me. You have to paint with broad strokes on this show. You only get a couple of minutes to make an impact. Now about the intro clip, what do you want to say?'

Chelsie was referring to the video package that preceded each finalist's performance, in which they were filmed against a black backdrop looking moody with wind in their hair, while they recounted their fears and hopes in voiceover.

'Well,' Tabitha replied, 'I thought I'd talk about how I'm dead nervous and that I've worked really hard because I really, really want to be a singer.'

Chelsie frowned.

'Hmm, I think it would have *much* more impact if you were to talk about how you wished that you and your girlfriend had a daughter who you could dedicate the song to and how you believe that IVF for single-parent lesbians should be available free by right on the

392

NHS and you should be allowed to choose the sex so you don't get a boy because . . .'

'All men are rapists?' Tabitha enquired.

'Exactly. People will love you for having strong principles.'

Tabitha did what she was told to do and was rewarded with a cacophony of booing from the studio audience. Barry and Gary had made it clear in their warm-up that the audience were to feel free to express themselves as loudly as they wished and that booing was acceptable.

Before the telephone votes had been counted it was obvious that Tabitha would be one of the two who were up for rejection.

Encouraged by Keely, the judges indulged in a few moments of clunking, mahogany-hewn banter.

'How could you have given her that song?' Rodney spluttered.

'It's a great song,' Beryl replied. 'It's a Marvin Gaye song.'

'Yes, and it should have been left to Marvin Gaye. The song was too big for her.'

'Yes, Tabitha,' Beryl conceded in her cooing, croaky, trying-to-be-nice voice, 'I'm afraid that the song was just too big for you.'

Tabitha was up against Latiffa for rejection but there was never any doubt about who would be going home.

'Tabs babes,' Keely said, 'is there anything you would like to say to the judges?'

'Well, I wasn't really happy with the choice of song—'

'The song was great, lady,' Calvin interrupted. 'It was just too big for you.'

Tabitha might have liked to add that she wasn't happy with her choice of costume either but sadly her time was up.

Week Two

Having dispensed with Tabitha in an orgy of press hatred in week one, the following week Calvin targeted Latiffa, the wannabe Tina Turner of the group. Previously Calvin had been careful to edit Latiffa's character in a favourable light, making her self-confidence seem positive and strong and her belief in her own sexiness larger than life and sassy. Now he turned all his guns against her, using song choice, costume and pre-performance profile to transform her instantly into a noisy, irritating, loud-mouthed, self-deluded show-off. He gave her 'Simply The Best' to sing and pitched it in Tina Turner's original key, which was way too high for Latiffa. They dressed her in the sort of micro skirt that Tina had worn in the eighties and for which you required legs that had seen a lot fewer kebabs than Latiffa had, and they recorded a profile in which she was coaxed into sounding like an arrogant, self-serving bore.

'Last week I didn't feel I showed half of what I can be . . . Now the gloves are off and the viewers are going to get to see the real me . . . Calvin said he thought I hit a couple of bad notes – out of order, that really hurt . . . It's been a tough week for me but I am a strong woman and I will be strong . . . So bring it on, Calvin, because this girl is Simply the Best.'

Not surprisingly Latiffa's arrogance did not play well against her strained, shrill performance. Calvin was brutal.

'I just don't think you have a place in this competition,' he said, neglecting to explain why in that case she had been chosen to be a finalist.

Beryl damned with faint praise.

'I love you, Latiffa, you know that, but I just think the song was too big for you.'

Calvin hammered the last nail into Latiffa's coffin by instructing Rodney to give her his full support.

'Latiffa,' Rodney said dutifully, 'you had strength, you had power, you're sexy, you're sassy, you sang it better than Tina Turner and I believe that you could be an even bigger star.'

Latiffa inevitably ended up in the bottom two of the public vote and Calvin and Beryl voted her off, with Rodney still protesting that she was a huge talent who should and would get a recording deal immediately.

The other feature of the second week was the surprising success of Bloke, the rough-diamond geezer band who claimed to have 'paid their dues'. Calvin ensured that both Beryl and Rodney greeted Bloke's performance of U2's 'I Still Haven't Found What I'm Looking For' as if Bono and The Edge themselves had been performing it.

'I love you boys,' said Rodney. 'That was fabulous, totally rock 'n' roll. You deserve to have huge careers in the recording industry. No more clubs for you. No more paying your dues. You are going to be as big as U2.'

'I looooooove you guys,' Beryl added in her sexiest croak. 'You are so *hot*! You know what? You *owned* that stage. I'm a rock chick from way back and I *loved* it.'

Even Calvin was supportive.

'You know what?' he said, doing his surprised but honest act. 'You guys were *really good*. I honestly didn't think you had it in you. But now I think you could go all the way and win this thing.'

Calvin treated Bloke this way because he knew from analysis of the phone votes that they were not at all popular with the TV audience, having polled third from last in the first week.

'It's no good acts going out without a fight, without a bit of *drama*,' he would berate the team. 'They can't just be shit then slope off. Greek tragedy rules! If the gods are going to destroy someone they must first exalt them. And we are the fucking gods.'

As he had planned, Calvin had kept the Prince as low on the radar as possible. His Royal Highness had been allowed to dress himself, which meant his appearing in tweed jackets and good stout brogues, which had been incongruous but endearing. He had been given innocuous but sympathetic material to sing – 'Raindrops Keep Falling On My Head' in week one and 'Mr Cellophane' from *Chicago* in week two – and he had recorded only the briefest personal video package from the fireside of his town house.

'I only hope I don't make an absolute *muggins* of myself,' he said in week one. 'My boys have teased me endlessly.'

'I just feel enormously *privileged* to be a part of it all,' he added in week two. 'I'm quite sure I'm the *least* deserving singer here.'

The result was that the public had quickly come to accept the Prince's presence on the show and while many commentators continued to bemoan the massive damage that he was doing to his position, others, particularly the popular press, were starting to enjoy it, even noting that the Prince was the first *Chart Throb* candidate ever to consider the possibility that they might not be the best.

Is self-effacement the new bling? they mused.

Week Three

In week three Chelsie and Trent travelled up to Kilburn and instructed Bloke to sing an Elvis medley: 'Heartbreak Hotel', 'All Shook Up', 'American Trilogy', 'In The Ghetto' and 'Rock-A-Hula Baby'.

'It's a medley,' Chelsie explained. 'Five songs.'

' "American Trilogy" is already a medley,' one Bloke pointed out dubiously, 'so that's seven songs.'

'If you insist,' Chelsie said. 'I'm not into old man music myself.'

'Seven songs in three minutes?' another Bloke remarked. 'It's going to be hard to get into the soul of it.'

'This is all about range, guys,' Trent insisted, 'demonstrating range.'

In fact it was all about hubris, one of Calvin's favourite tools of the trade.

'If you want to alienate an act from the audience, give them the King,' Calvin explained as he laid out his plans at the week three research meeting. 'Covering the King represents hubris set to music. It's the biggest, most famous, most immediately recognizable voice in rock 'n' roll and anyone singing his songs invites instant and damning comparison. It is virtually impossible for an act to survive covering Elvis at this stage of the competition and I can tell you now, a bunch of hod carriers from Stockport certainly aren't going to.'

Bloke were therefore tasked by their 'nurturer' (Rodney, represented by Chelsie and Trent) to cover seven disparate Elvis tracks in their allotted three minutes. And as if the grim comparison with the most successful and influential solo entertainer of all time was not clear enough, the unfortunate club singers were given Vegas Elvis jumpsuits to wear.

'Wouldn't jeans and black shirts be better?' the lead Bloke enquired. 'We look good in jeans and black shirts.'

Chelsie assured them that the producers knew best and jumpsuits it was.

On the night the band were greeted by a cacophony of cheers as they entered the stage. Gary and Barry put in an extra-special effort during the ad break that preceded Bloke's performance and by the time their moment came the crazily whipped-up crowd could probably have been persuaded to elect Bloke dictators and follow them in an invasion of Poland.

'I'd like to introduce some really good blokes,' Rodney said, in his role as 'nurturer'. 'They've done their time, they've paid their dues, they've taken the knocks. Now their moment has come. I am very proud to introduce the future chart sensations, *Bloke*!'

Bloke did not enter immediately. First came their pre-performance video package in which they grimaced solemnly and spoke with anguish about their long, long struggle in rock 'n' roll.

'We've paid our dues,' said one.

'We've done our time,' said another.

Together they stood, with a grim wall at their backs, staring into the wind machine like warriors about to take up their swords in the defence of freedom and the weak.

'This is our moment,' one of them said.

'Our one moment in time,' said the bloke next to him.

'This is our moment,' the first repeated.

'Our one moment in time,' the other bloke said again.

Chelsie had only been able to persuade two of the four men to say these things but Calvin had got round that by playing both quotes twice.

'We deserve this. It's ours and we're gonna grab it with all eight hands,' Bloke said together. 'Tonight belongs to Bloke.'

Not surprisingly, this carefully edited, excruciating display of arrogance further alienated an already deeply unenthusiastic public. It looked particularly grim as it followed the Prince of Wales's customarily apologetic statements.

'I expect I shall be absolutely awful *again* and will

be smartly chucked out *on my ear*, which is probably no more than I *deserve* and a great relief for everybody.'

Bloke walked on in their rhinestone jumpsuits to the previously orchestrated cheers and attacked their medley with gusto, but without quite the charisma that Elvis Presley had brought to the songs.

When, as Calvin had planned, they entered the lowest two (alongside Suki) he was merciless.

'Well, lads. It was truly, horribly, disgustingly, cringe-makingly awful,' he said.

'Calvin!' Rodney protested.

'No, Rodney, it was!' Calvin replied. 'And the truth is, Rodney, that you are massively to blame. The boys aren't great but they aren't as bad as that . . .'

'I admit that the song was too big for them . . .' Rodney spluttered.

'*The* song!' Calvin replied, aghast. 'There were seven songs there, mate, and they were *all* too big for them.'

Beryl agreed.

'Boys,' she croaked in the voice she fondly believed the nation adored her for, 'you know I love you big time and I think you're so sexy it's not funny, but the song was too big for you, the *songs* were too big for you. You can't cover the King.'

Finally Keely invited Rodney, as 'nurturing' judge, to comment.

'Boys, I thought you were quite brilliant. You're true stars. Superstars even, and whatever happens here tonight you have huge recording careers ahead of you. You four could be the new U2.'

What happened was that Bloke were voted off and returned instantly to obscurity.

Emma and Shaiana

With Calvin so heavily engaged in the weekly turn-around of live shows, Emma found herself with time on her hands. Of course she had her work and her friends but what she really wanted was to be with Calvin, and in his absence she found herself dwelling on the show. In particular her thoughts turned increasingly to Shaiana. Calvin had virtually forgotten the girl by this time; she was just one of hundreds of disappointed people who had figured briefly in the *Chart Throb* process before disappearing for ever. But Emma could not forget her. In fact she was thinking about her more and more.

Calvin had been forced to heavily edit the footage of Shaiana being ejected from Pop School. The wounded girl's reaction had been too angry and passionate even by *Chart Throb* standards and she had of course used the word 'cunt', which remained the final linguistic taboo on television. Emma, however, had asked to see all the footage and had found it most disturbing. After watching it a number of times she had not surprisingly found that she couldn't get the vicious, spiteful outburst out of her head.

'I have nowhere to go. I had only planned my life up to this point.'

Emma had clearly been wrong in her initial assessment of Shaiana. She had marked her down only as a victim but it was clear now that she was capable of being an aggressor too. Her victimhood had empowered her.

'Don't you understand? *God made me* for this purpose,' Shaiana said on the tape that Emma could not resist watching. 'Who are you to contradict the word of God?'

Emma knew enough about psychotics to be aware

that knowing God's will was a popular motivation among murderous lunatics and that anyone claiming to get their orders directly from the Almighty was deeply suspect.

'You haven't heard the last of me, Calvin fucking Simms.'

Week Four

In week four Calvin turned his attention to Stanley, the plucky single dad.

Up until that point the judges had spoken of Stanley only in the most ecstatic tones, bigging him up as a new Sinatra or Dean Martin. In week one Stanley had sung 'Ain't That A Kick In The Head', in week two 'Mack The Knife' and in week three 'It Was A Very Good Year'. It was generally *Chart Throb* policy to give anyone over thirty-five songs dating from the 1950s and early sixties, in much the same way as they gave the feisty old grannies songs from the Edwardian era.

Stanley's week three performance had been a huge success, every bit as popular as Bloke's Elvis Presley medley had been a public disaster. Costume had dressed Stanley in a tux and a casually draped bow tie. The music department had given him a gaggle of gorgeous violinists all turned out in their obligatory little black dresses. The director had lit the stage with a romantic moodiness (in stark contrast to Bloke's brash Vegas-style staging) and the vision mixer had cut as often as possible to shots of Beryl looking utterly entranced, hovering ecstatically halfway between tears and lust. It all worked beautifully and as this thirty-eight-year-old sang 'It Was A Very Good Year', that famous song of mature reflection, it was almost possible to believe that he had indeed lived a long and varied life filled with excitement and romance, played out across the dreamscape of a mid-twentieth-century America.

As the song drew to its conclusion, Stanley stepped down off the stage. His children had been carefully arranged in the front row and he sang the last verse of 'It Was A Very Good Year' to his youngest as he dandled her on his knee. The message was clear: no matter how many dusty highways a lone troubadour might have to tread, kids made it all worthwhile.

The studio exploded with wild cheering. Keely had trouble calling the audience to order sufficiently to get on with the serious business of judges' comments. Calvin professed himself enchanted, informing Stanley that he had owned the song. Rodney agreed, adding that in his professional view Stanley might just be the finest crooner in the history of recorded music and that he could confidently expect to be playing the Royal Albert Hall some time soon.

Beryl left her seat and joined Stanley and his children, grabbing him round the neck and kissing him.

'As a mum,' she shouted, 'as a woman and as an old rock chick from way back, I know the real thing when I see it, and Stanley . . . you are it. You are the man. You are manly, Stanley, and don't let anyone ever tell you different because you are so talented and sexy it isn't funny.'

Then Beryl, as ever unable to suppress her deeply vulgar side and considering herself so suffused with the common touch as to be invulnerable to bad taste, turned to the camera and positively shouted.

'Hey, are you watching out there, Stanley's ex? Whoever the hell you are! How does it feel to know that you have lost this hero? This giant of a man? You blew it, babes, and you know it because *every* woman wants him now, babes! I know I do. I know I'd like to give him one! Never mind "a very good year", how about a very good shag!'

'Thank you, Beryl!' Calvin called quickly, pressing his private panic button which alerted the vision mixer to cut away from whoever was on screen immediately. Despite the fact that this device had occasionally been used in other circumstances, it was generally known as the Beryl Button.

'Yes. Thank you very much for that, Beryl,' Calvin continued. 'We are a *family* programme, remember.'

'I say what I feel, Calvin,' said Beryl. 'It's how I was reared. It's what I teach my kids. It's the only way I know.'

Eventually Beryl was persuaded to return to her seat and Stanley was unanimously voted the hit of the show and a real contender to win.

In week four he was instructed to sing 'Firestarter' by the Prodigy. He was dressed in pantomime retro-punk style and surrounded by gurning, half-naked female dancers who were choreographed to rub their crotches on him at every opportunity, thus dramatically puncturing the image of quiet maturity and fatherly sophistication that had been building over the previous weeks.

'I had been meaning to give him a longer run,' Calvin explained to his team at the weekly production meeting, 'but we'll never top last week, so it's a perfect moment to dump him. The website will go crazy. We need a bit of extra controversy to keep the heat off HRH. Besides, I can't risk Beryl going mad like that again. Asking a man to shag her in front of his five-year-old child, ridiculous.'

'Particularly since we all know they haven't finished building her fanny yet,' Chelsie added.

Besides the entirely unsuitable song and the tastelessly oversexualized production, Stanley was to be

further handicapped in week four by his pre-performance video package in which he was persuaded to
evoke the image of his children so often that it went
beyond the point of being bearable even to an
audience generally anaesthetized to any amount of
cloying sentiment.

'I'm doing this for my kids . . . for my little girl . . .
and for my little boy . . . My little boy and girl are
everything to me . . . that's why I'm doing it . . . for
them, my little boy and girl . . . That's all that matters
to me . . . I don't care about myself . . . It's all about my
little girl and my little boy.'

After this Stanley performed his song, at the conclusion of which Beryl, misjudging the mood of the
studio, insisted on leaving the judges' panel and
giving Stanley a huge tear-drenched hug.

'That comes from a mum to a dad,' she said. 'You
owned that song, Stanley. I could see that you were
singing "Firestarter" for your kids.'

Beryl made this gesture of her own volition. Calvin
had not even briefed her on his intention of manoeuv-
ring against Stanley that week. He was confident that
the moment parenthood was mentioned, Beryl, unable
to resist drawing the focus to her own celebrated
mother status, would ignore all other factors and once
more wallow in a mawkish swamp of crocodile tears
and false sentiment. She did not let him down.

Stanley's performance of 'Firestarter', coupled with
Beryl's efforts at parental solidarity, ensured that he
received one of the two lowest votes of the week, so
he could then be safely ejected from the competition.

'I love you, Stanley, big time, you *know* that,' said
Beryl. 'You rock so much it isn't funny. And as a mum
I recognize a dad . . . but I'm sorry, it's time to go
home.'

Week Five

In week five Suki, the surgically enhanced sex worker, was sent home. Calvin knew that she would go at some point and had been happy to wait until the moment arose organically.

'It won't be long,' he predicted, 'before some pimp or trick comes out of the woodwork and the Sundays do her over.' It had taken a little longer than Calvin had expected because the Suki who emerged each week from the hair and make-up department to sing country songs about long-suffering women did not look a bit like the Suki who had recently been working the kerbs of Birmingham's pick-up areas. It was not in fact until she herself began to hint at her past in her increasingly confessional pre-performance videos that the pennies began to drop. When they did they tumbled like an avalanche, with any number of unpleasant figures coming forward to sell their tales of marathon sex romps with the briefly famous Suki.

While many were sympathetic to Suki's recent employment as a prostitute, *Chart Throb* was a pre-watershed family show and the general mood on the websites and of those who wrote to the newspapers began to turn against a woman who had presented herself as an 'ex-glamour girl' and who now turned out to be a not very ex purveyor of kerbside blow jobs. Calvin ensured Suki's fate with his instructions to Costume, Hair and Make-up.

'I want the true Suki to shine through. We are, after all, a people show, a *real* people show. Suki is a real woman. A woman with a *lived-in* feel . . .'

'Well, she's certainly been rented and occupied a few times,' the various departments muttered as they went about undoing the excellent cover-up job they had achieved in previous weeks. They did not

405

like doing it, it went against every instinct they had, but when Suki appeared on stage for week five suddenly looking her age and in a dress sufficiently revealing to expose the tragic inadequacies of the cheap cosmetic surgery she had undergone, Calvin got his wish.

The song she had been given was 'Je Ne Regrette Rien', which quite apart from being beyond her musically was either a lie or else represented self-delusion that had crossed the line into mental instability. From her irregularly Botoxed lips and sagging, asymmetrical breast implants to her knobbly, bony, tottering legs, inelegantly revealed in an inappropriate microskirt designed for teenagers, from her sprayed-on tan, bolted-on cheekbone enhancements and overbleached hair to the string of street pimps queuing up to make a few days' drug money discussing her modus operandi (*The Bus Stop Was Her Brothel*), Suki clearly had a great deal to regret, considerably more than Edith Piaf ever had.

Of course Calvin could have turned all this to Suki's favour.

'Television truth is presentation and editing,' he said in Hospitality after Suki had been voted off the programme. 'I did think about playing her as a strong, streetsmart lady who had used her body and male sexuality to empower herself.'

In the end, however, Calvin had other fish to fry.

Searching for Shaiana

Emma could sit still no longer. She decided that she had to find Shaiana. Her friends Tom and Mel assured her that she was obsessing unnecessarily and Calvin too, when they had a moment together, was entirely unmoved by her fears.

'I've told you, darling,' he said, 'nutters are our business, you must *never* let them get to you.'

Emma herself recognized that her paranoia was basically self-constructed and also self-perpetuating, in that the more she worried, the more worried she became, but that did not make her feelings any less real. She was scared of Shaiana, she simply couldn't help it.

'I thought *she* was the victim,' Emma told Calvin, 'but it turns out I am. I can't get her out of my mind. I have to put a stop to this.'

'All right then,' Calvin said. 'Go and spy on her if you must. She'll be working in a shop somewhere. They all are.'

Shaiana had claimed that she had nowhere to go. Emma decided to find out exactly what she had meant by that and was disturbed to discover that in fact Shaiana appeared to have gone nowhere. Having run weeping from Pop School, she seemed to have disappeared.

Emma went to the offices of CALonic TV and asked a mate to look out Shaiana's original entry form. Within a few minutes Emma found herself once more staring at the bold, childish hand that had initially caught her eye during the envelope-opening stage of the competition.

I want it so much. I want it so much . . . I am me.

Shaiana had, as required, supplied an address and a mobile telephone number. First Emma tried the number. She had no idea what she would say if Shaiana answered but in fact the number turned out to be unobtainable. There was no landline number given, but that was not in itself suspicious as some of Emma's friends had begun to rely solely on their mobiles to keep in touch.

Emma decided that she must visit the address Shaiana had given, which was in South Kensington. Once more Emma did not know what she intended to do when she met Shaiana but had decided she would worry about that if and when she did meet her.

The address turned out to be that of a small and rather expensive private hotel. They remembered Shaiana, who had stayed for a week some months previously, but they had not seen her since.

'Except on *Chart Throb*,' said the lady behind the desk. 'We were so surprised when she turned up on that. Shouldn't have been really because she did nothing but sing in her room, had to stop her doing it at night. I thought she was rather good actually. Don't think Calvin should have chucked her off.'

Week Six

They were halfway through the contest by this time so Calvin had had ample opportunity to study the public's weekly voting patterns in detail and hence knew exactly the levels of popularity that each contestant was enjoying. This was an element of the *Chart Throb* grand strategy that even Chelsie, with her instinctive understanding of the dark arts of reality television, had been only vaguely conscious of.

'The secret truth of all these voting shows,' Calvin explained gleefully to her while Trent went out to Starbucks to get the coffees, 'is *not even a secret*. Like absolutely every other aspect of our manipulation process, it's glaringly obvious to anyone who wishes to see it but—'

'Nobody does wish to see it,' Chelsie interrupted, quoting one of her boss's favourite maxims.

'Exactly.'

'Because it would spoil the fun.'

'Correcto-mundo, lady. But if they *did* want to spoil the fun they might easily reflect that the producers of every single voting show from *Big Brother* to *Shagging on Thin Ice with the Stars* get to see and to analyse every single vote that is cast every single week throughout the entire series . . .'

'And so can manipulate their coverage accordingly?'

'Of course!' Calvin was almost hugging himself with the fun of it. 'Imagine if the political parties in a general election were able to see inside the minds of each individual voter at seven-day intervals throughout a three-month campaign! It's what they dream of! It's what market research and opinion polls desperately try to emulate but of course never can. A genuine window into the mind of the voter. If Labour or the Tories could truly gauge the popular reaction to every single policy launch, every speech and every personality throughout their campaigns, they could cut their cloth accordingly, bigging up the ideas that played well, burying the people who alienated the public.'

'Of course! And we have that information.' Chelsie was as excited as Calvin.

Calvin always kept the data that he was given a closely guarded secret, so nobody on the team was ever in the loop as to how much power that knowledge gave him. Now Calvin was revealing his trump card.

'I always love it when Keely reads out the voting results each week and says "in no particular order". Because I'm sitting there thinking *I know the order*. The nation thinks it's anybody's race, that anybody could win, but from *day one* I know who's a hero and who's a zero.'

'And then you change it?'

'Exactly. Whereas a politician would use the

information to massage his popular policies, I tend to use it to *redistribute* popularity. If somebody is getting too big early on I'll edit against them to calm things down because the last thing we want is a runaway winner. Where's the jeopardy in that?'

'Nowhere! Thanks, Trent.'

Trent had just returned with the cardboard tray of coffees.

'Yeah, thanks, Trent,' Calvin said absent-mindedly.

'No worries, boss. Yo,' Trent replied. 'I got muffins.'

Calvin, carried away with his own cleverness, ignored the proffered bag.

'And without jeopardy, Chelsie, there is no show.'

There followed the usual Starbucks hiatus while everybody discovered that they had the wrong cups and that having ordered a skinny caramel latte they were drinking a chocolate fudge frappé.

'You're supposed to get them to write it on the side of the cups, Trent,' Chelsie said.

'Duly noted.' If Trent was mortified at his reduced status he was covering it well.

'Right,' said Calvin, having finally located his double-shot iced mocha with vanilla syrup. 'This week Blossom goes.'

'Thank God for that,' Chelsie exclaimed. 'If I have to listen to that fucking laugh one more time . . .'

'You're not the only person who finds her irritating,' said Calvin. 'Look at this.'

And so saying, Calvin showed his two senior researchers the voting information that made his life so easy. Blossom, it turned out, had never risen above fourth least liked out of twelve in the public's esteem. This would have surprised the public because through weeks one to five she had been represented on the screen as a national favourite, an irrepressible momma with her huge 'infectious' laugh, her enormous frame and her constantly reiterated backstory of

410

being 'only a cleaner who had entered on a whim'.

'I can't believe it!' Blossom would exclaim each week, shaking with laughter when Keely invited her to comment. 'This is all mad, but I'm livin' it and lovin' it and dreamin' it and I'm here to show the world that ladies of size and of a certain age can still rock!'

Blossom was only thirty-three but, as in the case of Stanley, to be in one's thirties represented venerable maturity in *Chart Throb* years and Blossom had been groomed to appear as an empowering figure of mature womanhood in a world of itsy-bitsy poppets. She had been given Aretha Franklin and Irma Thomas songs to sing as if she was an ageing soul diva.

'I LOVE you, Blossom,' Beryl would shriek at her every week. 'You are a strong woman and being a strong woman I recognize a strong woman and I love you so much it isn't funny. You are big, you are bold, you are strong and you are a woman! As a woman myself, who is strong and who has struggled privately with weight issues in the past, I so LOVE you for being a woman of size! You go, girl! Just you go!'

'Blossom,' Rodney would agree, applying his famous twinkling charm, 'your voice is as big as your personality and as infectious as your wonderful laugh. I love you. Everybody loves you. You are a strong woman of size and a true star. Just listen to the public. They love you big time. We all love you big time.'

But Calvin, who read the voting chart each week, knew that the public only loved Blossom little time, and sometimes not even that much. It was therefore an easy matter to drop her in week six.

'Any special instructions, boss?' Trent enquired. 'Shall we give her a punk rock song to sing or put her in hot pants?'

'No need, Trent,' Calvin replied. 'Just tell her to keep on laughing.'

Week Seven

Calvin and Chelsie were staring at the wall on which hung the profiles of the remaining finalists and those who had been deleted.

~~Tabitha: Dull dungarees lezza but has sexy girlfriend.~~
~~Suki: Balloon-boobed, fat-lipped, tragicomic prostitute.~~
~~Bloke: Bricklayers with guitars. Semi-pro club act. Dull but worthy.~~
Graham: Blind. Can't sing.
~~Blossom: Fat momma. Big laugh. 'Just a cleaner'. Can sing.~~
The Four-Z: Cute. Christian. Good hard luck story. Can sing.
Troy: Can sing a bit. Can't read a lot.
Iona: Good voice. Rodney used to fuck her.
~~Stanley: Hero single dad. NOTE: Kids not particularly cute.~~
~~Latiffa: Black girl with attitude.~~
The Quasar: Best Blinger in years. Can't sing but doesn't care and nor do we.
The Prince of Wales: Heir to the throne.

'So what next?' Calvin mused.

He was coming to confide more and more in Chelsie each day. He discussed with her the thoughts he would have liked to share with Emma but which he could not reveal without showing himself to be that thing which Emma feared most, a man whom she could not trust.

'This is where I have to be careful,' Calvin said. 'The single and only point in the whole series where I'm vulnerable to losing control of the process is in the final episode, the episode where only three candidates remain.'

'Well, yes,' Chelsie agreed, 'but does it matter by

then? At that point we've either done our job properly and had a hit series with a must-see final which is the television event of the week or we haven't. Either the nation's tuning in riveted or we've fucked up. Why would you care who actually wins? You've always told us that record sales are becoming irrelevant these days. All you're really producing is next year's Christian Appleyard.'

'Yes, that's true,' Calvin conceded. 'Normally I don't mind who wins the final and I'm happy to leave it as a clean fight with the three remaining contestants playing to their strengths. But this year I have a designated winner.'

'HRH?' Chelsie enquired.

'Yes,' said Calvin, smiling. 'I suppose it's obvious.'

Although Calvin was of course not going to reveal the nature of the deal he had struck with Dakota or the promise he had made to Emma, he was perfectly relaxed about Chelsie knowing something of his agenda. She was after all bound by the same gagging contract that every employee signed alongside the contestants and as to his motives, well, for the heir to the throne to win a TV talent show was still something of a coup, even in an age where people had become entirely familiar with celebrity in every possible compromise and contortion.

'Who knows?' Calvin said. 'I might get a peerage.'

'I'm afraid he doesn't get to give them out any more,' Chelsie pointed out. 'The government sells them.'

'Well anyway, I still fancy him to win,' said Calvin. 'Thanks, Trent.'

Trent had just entered with a pile of boxes from Pizza Express.

'So what's your plan, Calvin?' Chelsie enquired, not bothering to bring Trent up to speed on the conversation. 'If it's a free vote without the judges getting the final call how can you ensure your man comes through?'

'Yeah? Right,' said Trent, attempting to look as if he knew what they were talking about.

'Well, to ensure a particular candidate wins at the final stage,' Calvin explained, 'we have to make the two other candidates who reach the final with him less popular than he is. Therefore our job is to ensure that the most popular candidates are dropped *before* it gets to that point. If you want someone special to win in the final then you have to do your manipulating *before* it.'

'Damn! They forgot the dough balls,' said Trent, who had been distributing pizzas and salads. 'Do you want me to run back?'

Calvin ignored the interruption, leaving Trent hovering helplessly at the door.

'We know from reading the percentages of the telephone votes who are the big threats to HRH. There's Troy, The Four-Z and Graham. Troy's a good singer and he's young, which of course is attractive . . .'

'And illiterate, which also plays very well,' Chelsie added.

'Yes,' Calvin conceded. 'I put the whole reading thing in to big up the Prince but it's a double-edged sword because it works well for the lad too.'

'The Four-Z are going over pretty big too, aren't they?' Chelsie mused, studying the voting chart.

'Yes, well, they're actually very good, particularly the lead singer,' Calvin admitted.

'And of course Graham's got the blind thing going for him,' said Chelsie, 'plus even if he can't sing he's a brilliant guitar player. It looks like the two we need to go through to the final with HRH are Iona and the Quasar.'

'That's exactly how I read it,' Calvin said approvingly.

'Me too,' Trent added from the door.

'So who do we dump first?' Chelsie enquired.

'Who do you think?' Calvin asked.

'Well, boss—' said Trent eagerly but Calvin was having none of it.

'Trent,' he said firmly, 'I'm asking Chelsie.'

'From the chart it looks as though The Four-Z have the edge. They're definitely the most popular act and getting more so each week, so they're the most dangerous to HRH. Clearly we should tackle them first. That way, if we can't bring them down in a week, we still have some time to spare.'

'Chelsie,' Calvin said gently, 'we can always bring them down if we want to.'

The Four-Z were indeed hugely popular but their popularity was based principally on their leader, Michael Harley, who had obvious musical talent and huge personal charm. What Lionel Richie was to The Commodores, Michael Harley was to The Four-Z.

'All we need to do is rebalance the band,' said Calvin.

Calvin therefore sent Trent to inform the group that Michael's prominence was becoming a problem with the public.

'It looks egotistical, like you're hogging it, mate.'

Michael was devastated. He was very much a team player so he was horrified that anyone might suggest he was being selfish.

'What should we do?' he asked.

'You stand at the back and let the other three have a go. Particularly Jo-Jo,' Trent said, naming the least popular of the other boys. 'Rodney loves him. He's convinced that the public want to see more of him.'

The members of The Four-Z were surprised to hear this, not least Jo-Jo himself, who had always considered he was a bit of a lucky passenger. On the other hand if Rodney, their 'nurturing' judge, was saying that Jo-Jo should come forward then that was enough for them. Rodney was a music *expert*, the boy band Svengali, popmaster extraordinaire, as

Keely never tired of saying in her introductions.

'OK,' said Michael, 'whatever it takes. What song do you think we should sing?'

' "Cop Killa" by Public Enemy,' Trent replied.

The group were again a little taken aback at the choice that had been made for them. They were all good church-going boys and their musical tastes were very middle of the road. Soul was about as funky as they got and they had certainly never considered covering any Hip Hop or Gangsta rap. Trent, however, assured them that Rodney was convinced it was time for The Four-Z to branch out, to get more contemporary.

'He thinks you need to get more black,' Trent explained.

'But we've always sort of tried to be for everyone,' Michael said. 'We don't believe in defining people by racial group.'

'Ah, you see, there you go,' said Trent. '*Big mistake.* Chucking away votes. There's a vast audience out there that is totally unrepresented.'

'You mean Hip Hop and Gangsta rap fans?'

'Exactly.'

'But aren't they unrepresented because they don't watch the programme?'

'That's the point, isn't it? If you can draw them in then you unlock a huge constituency.'

The band were understandably dubious but had no choice other than to perform the song assigned to them. Having been greeted with the hugest cheer of the night, they proceeded to shock and alienate everybody by doing a Gangsta rap led by Jo-Jo, with Michael standing at the back scarcely participating. It did not go well. There were even one or two boos.

There followed the customary manufactured post-show 'quarrel' between the judges, in which Rodney was roundly condemned for having let down his act so entirely.

'I cannot *believe* you let them sing that song, Rodney!' Calvin sneered. 'It was appalling, and you should get your head tested.'

'The boys wanted to be more contemporary,' Rodney replied, dutifully sticking to his brief.

'You mean the boys were happy with that song?'

'Yes, of course.'

The astonishment on the band's faces at this point was not covered by the cameras.

'I believe in allowing my acts to grow, Calvin, to make mistakes,' Rodney continued.

'Well, they certainly made one tonight.'

Calvin had also ensured that the other acts did their very best that week. Knowing that The Four-Z were the biggest threat, he was leaving nothing to chance.

The Quasar, whose chirpy optimism and unashamed self-belief had originally been deeply irritating, was starting to become mildly attractive. Wearing only tight shorts and cowboy boots, he did a version of Right Said Fred's 'I'm Too Sexy' which the judges pronounced 'wildly entertaining'.

'Quasar,' Rodney gushed, 'that was sheer brilliance. You owned the song, you owned the stage, the audience loved you, you deserve to be a big, big, big star and I know that you will be.'

'Quasar,' said Beryl, but so dripping was her voice with gruesomely flirtatious, croaky, mumsy, kitten-like sexiness even in that one word that Calvin moved the process instantly on, fearing that she was about to refer to her soon-to-be-completed female sexual organs and the welcome mat that would always be laid out for the Quasar.

Iona, who had been gaining ground each week because Rodney (on Calvin's insistence) continued to insult her, sang 'Amazing Grace'. She did this accompanied only by flute and acoustic guitar. This was an old *Chart Throb* trick to impress the punters, and it did.

'That was an incredibly brave decision, Iona,' Beryl cooed. 'You stripped it all back, you let your voice do the talking and you *owned that song*. You sung like only a Scotswoman can sing and I can say that because I love the Scots and I'm a woman.'

Troy sang 'Angels', a song which rarely failed for anyone. Despite the fact that Troy knew the song backwards, having sung it a thousand times, Calvin suggested that he might like to take a lyric sheet on with him. Calvin had the director inform Troy that all the camera angles had been changed (due to safety regulations) and that Troy should refer to his lyric sheet at the end of each line in order to find the number of the camera he should sing the next line to. The result was that Troy spent the whole song staring at the sheet, desperately trying to work out which camera he was supposed to look at.

'Ladies and gentlemen,' Calvin explained solemnly afterwards, 'Troy wanted to do that song but he did not know the words. He therefore decided with incredible bravery that he would attempt to *read* them despite the fact that he cannot actually read. Troy, I salute you, for that alone you should win this contest.'

Next Graham did 'I Can See Clearly Now', which made Beryl cry.

'For a boy who is blind, unsighted and cannot see to sing a song that is actually about being *able* to see showed so much incredible bravery and courage it wasn't funny,' she croaked. 'I salute you, babes. You owned that song.'

Finally the Prince of Wales took everyone by surprise by singing 'Do Ye Ken John Peel?' 'I should like to dedicate this song to all the foxhounds that have had to be put down since the hunting ban was introduced. People think it's a song about love of killing foxes but really it's a song about love of the *countryside* and I do think that's important, don't you?'

People didn't. It was the first major own goal for the Prince of Wales and one that landed him in the bottom two of the popular vote alongside The Four-Z. This was exactly as Calvin had intended. He did not want the process of favouring the Prince to become too obvious and he had judged that 'Do Ye Ken John Peel?' with an introductory video package sympathetic to hunting would provoke sufficient negativity to place HRH's rapidly growing popularity briefly in doubt.

'If there's one thing I know about the British public,' Calvin said with confidence, 'it's that they don't like cruelty to foxes. They hate it, they loathe it, they strongly disapprove of it. They don't mind a twenty-piece bucket of KFC with a couple of Big Macs on the side and a nice big sausage made of mechanically recovered meat to follow, and they don't mind the last cod in the western hemisphere being coated in batter and stuck in a deep-fat fryer, but they cannot and will not abide a couple of hundred posh snob snooties chasing a fox.'

Therefore the Prince faced The Four-Z in the sing-off at the end of the show. Once more Jo-Jo fronted up 'Cop Killa' and HRH sang 'Do Ye Ken John Peel?' and most observers judged that the fox killer got slightly more boos than the Cop Killa. However, the decision was down to the judges and during the final advertising break before the vote Calvin took Beryl into the hospitality room and instructed her to vote for the Prince.

'You want me to vote for a fucking fox-hunter!' she replied, absently sucking down a couple of oysters followed by two cocktail sausages and a mini Yorkshire pudding with roast beef.

'Yes,' Calvin replied. 'Rodney is nurturing The Four-Z so he can't and I want the Prince to stay in.'

'Why? He's a posh snob fox-murderer!' Beryl replied, pulling a bit of gristle from her teeth. 'I'm a mum, I'm one of the people, I'm the people's mum, for fuck's sake! I can't vote for a fox-killer.'

'And I am the producer of this show and I'm telling you to vote for the Prince.'

'I won't do it!' Beryl shouted, and a piece of half-chewed rare roast beef landed on Calvin's jacket. 'I'm not voting for a fucking murderer. I'm an ambassador for PETA, for fuck's sake! Anyway it's fucking absurd, how can we possibly vote through an ageing fucking ponce against four gorgeous boys?'

'Who have just sung "Cop Killa".'

'I don't care. I won't do it. I'm not voting for the Prince.'

'If you don't do what I tell you, Beryl,' Calvin said firmly, 'you'll be gone from this show before the credits are finished.'

'You wouldn't do it. You need me.'

'I would and I don't. I will not have my authority on this programme challenged, not by you, not by anybody. You will vote for who I tell you to or you will fuck off, Beryl.'

'What about my integrity?'

'Beryl, darling,' Calvin said quietly through a big, broad, icy smile, '*Chart Throb* made you a proper star, it turned you from a novelty act on *The Blenheims* into a genuine cast-iron mainstream celebrity. Three times National Mum of the Year. Do you really want to throw that away over your integrity? Try to remember that you don't *have* any integrity.'

Beryl nodded.

'Oh, all fucking right,' she said.

In the end the choice of song that Calvin had forced upon the boy band made it perfectly plausible for Beryl to vote as she did.

'Look, I'm no fan of fox-hunting,' she said, 'people know that about me, but boys,' and suddenly her eyes were brimming with sorrow, 'I love you big time so much it isn't funny, you *know* that. But how can I vote for you? It would be a vote against the British police force, it would be a vote for crime, it would be a smack in the face to every widow and orphan who has lost a hero in the line of duty. I'm sorry, boys, but killing cops is wrong even in the world of pop music.'

And so quite suddenly The Four-Z were rejected.

For a day or two or even a week afterwards Michael and his friends imagined that the dream might not yet be over. After all, how many times had the expert judges solemnly pronounced that they were stars? That they had huge recording careers ahead of them? That they were better than The Commodores? A new Jackson Five. Surely the 'record contract' that Rodney had regularly stated should by rights be theirs must now be forthcoming? Surely it had not all been unmitigated bullshit?

But it was. The world was full of good-looking lads who could sing and they were just four more of them (three not counting Jo-Jo). The pompous promises made on *Chart Throb* were valid for exactly as long as it took to utter them and so The Four-Z returned to the lives they had hoped to leave behind for ever.

Weeks Eight and Nine

Troy went out in week eight in a vote-off with HRH, who was still suffering from the hunting controversy of the previous week. Calvin manoeuvred Troy to the bottom of the pack by simply repeating the device of staging Troy's song as if the lad was attempting to read the lyrics. The public had loved this manoeuvre the first time round but when Troy did the same thing again they reacted negatively to what appeared to be a clumsy attempt to manipulate their sympathy.

Calvin knew that Graham would prove a much tougher job to bring down. Graham had risen to a height of popularity second only to The Four-Z during the early live rounds and if he were allowed to get through to the final he would prove difficult to control. Week nine was therefore Calvin's last chance to deal with him.

'We need to turn people against him,' he explained to Chelsie and Trent, 'and the best way to do that is to stitch him up in the pre-show profile.'

'How about using the fact that he dropped Millicent so easily?' Chelsie suggested.

'Good girl!' said Calvin. 'Exactly what I was thinking. We need to make him look selfish, uncaring and mean.'

'Do you think we can do that to a blind boy?' Trent enquired dubiously.

'Of course we can,' Calvin replied. 'All the best villains in literature were disabled, look at Long John Silver.'

Trent was dispatched to the rehearsal room with a camera crew and ordered to manipulate Graham into incriminating himself. However, he returned disappointed.

'He really likes the chick,' Trent explained. 'In fact it's pretty clear he's in love with her. What's more, he knows he's no singer either. I couldn't twist him round at all.'

'Let's look at the tape.'

Sitting in an edit suite, Calvin, Trent and Chelsie watched the tape of the interview.

'I don't like to think of Millicent not being here with me,' Graham had said. 'If I'm honest, I truly believe she's got the better voice, which makes me feel like a sad, selfish no-talent, like I don't care about anybody but myself. Sometimes I just hate myself and don't even want to win. I love Millicent and I always will.

She's always been my friend and respected me and not patronized me or treated me differently because I'm blind.'

'You see?' said Trent. 'The bloke just won't play ball.'

'I think he will,' said Chelsie.

'What, you think you can get him to diss his girlfriend?'

'Of course I can.'

For a moment something of Trent's old self-assertiveness returned.

'Well, go and interview him then, babes. See how far you get.'

'I don't need to interview him,' Chelsie said, 'you already did.'

'Oh, come on, Chelsie! You think you can get a Frankenbite out of that?'

Chelsie smiled, took up the typed transcript of Graham's interview and began to cross things out:

I don't like ~~to think of~~ Millicent ~~not being here with me. If I'm honest,~~ I truly believe she's ~~got the better voice, which makes me feel like~~ a sad, selfish no-talent, ~~like~~ I don't care about anybody but myself. ~~Sometimes~~ I just ~~hate myself and don't even~~ want to win. ~~I love Millicent~~ and I ~~always~~ will. ~~She's always been my friend and respected me and not patronized me or treated me differently~~ because I'm blind.

When she had finished she showed the result to Calvin and Trent.

'You are *good*,' Calvin said, smiling approvingly.

Trent bent with the wind once more.

'Yeah, superb effort,' he conceded. 'Do you really think we can smooth it out?'

Chelsie did not bother to reply. Instead she turned to the editing machine and with expert fingers began cutting up Graham's interview. In time-honoured *Chart*

Throb Frankenbite style she used cross-fades and jumpcuts and different camera angles, all stitched together with moody music and distant traffic noises to cover the cuts. The end result made Graham sound convincingly if nervously conversational, the constant cuts and changes of angle lending the pieces a painful urgency.

Calvin was extremely impressed.

'That, Chelsie,' he said, 'is a textbook Frankenbite. I intend to use that in my tutorials. Watch and learn, Trent.'

'I'm on it, chief.'

'How about we invite Millicent to be in the audience for the show?' Chelsie suggested.

'Brilliant,' said Calvin, 'just fucking brilliant. Trent . . .'

'Already on it, boss,' said Trent, picking up the phone.

Millicent was duly invited to attend the live broadcast of week nine, having of course received no warning of the content of Graham's brutally edited interview. The hovering cameras captured every moment of her devastation and humiliation.

'*I don't like Millicent,*' Graham appeared to be saying. '*I truly believe she's a sad, selfish no-talent. I don't care about anybody but myself. I just want to win and I will because I'm blind.*'

Millicent was crying by the time Graham appeared on stage (oblivious of the upset he had caused) and she continued to cry throughout the first half of Graham's chirpily ill-judged performance of Kylie Minogue's 'I Should Be So Lucky', after which, unable to take any more *lucky, lucky, luckys*, Millicent ran weeping from the studio.

Graham plummeted to the bottom of the telephone vote and was duly rejected by the judges in a unanimous and popular decision.

The Final, Part One

Emma accompanied Calvin to the grand final and had her first taste of what it was like to be seen out on the arm of the world's biggest television star. It was the first time they had acknowledged their relationship in public. Emma had been reluctant at first to go with him but so confident was Calvin of ensuring the Prince's victory that he insisted on her presence on this night of nights and even held her hand as they navigated the red carpet through the flickers of lightning produced by an army of flash photographers.

Calvin had not, of course, shared his confidence about the Prince's final triumph with Emma. The whole point about his promise to her was that it was supposed to represent a sacrifice on his part, a near-impossible job that he had only undertaken to prove his love and commitment and trustworthiness. He therefore did not wish Emma to imagine it was going to be easy.

'Things have gone well so far,' he said, looking noble and serious, 'but now comes the hard part. Quasar and Iona are both hugely popular figures and have been well ahead of HRH up until now.'

This was not true, in fact the opposite was the case. Apart from when he had sung 'Do Ye Ken John Peel?' the Prince had always had the edge on the two other remaining finalists. However, Calvin certainly wasn't going to tell that to Emma, who was becoming increasingly wide-eyed with admiration for the steady, confident manner in which Calvin was carrying out his love task.

'I can't believe you're doing this for me,' Emma said as they got out of their limousine together.

'For no one else, my darling,' said Calvin. 'If the Prince of Wales wins tonight and emerges the hero

425

of a new youth constituency, he has you to thank for it.'

Calvin almost believed it himself. Despite the fact that he had intended the Prince to win from the very start, long before Emma had raised the issue, there was no doubt that victory in his wager with Dakota now meant less to him than victory in his campaign to win Emma's trust and hence her love. She had become an obsession.

'I love you, Calvin,' Emma whispered in his ear as they walked up the carpet between the screaming fans, and her smile was radiant.

Then she saw Shaiana.

Emma almost cried out. The face staring at her was like a mask, not screaming and shouting but grim and silent among the noisy crowd. Shaiana had managed to position herself right at the front and there she stood, oblivious to the hysteria and the forest of hands around her waving pens and scraps of paper.

Just standing and staring.

Emma could see that Shaiana had seen her too and for a moment their eyes met. Shaiana's expression did not change at all. Then Emma saw that Shaiana was looking beyond her, towards Calvin and behind him to Beryl.

Then Calvin pulled at Emma's hand and a moment later she was inside the television studio, her happy mood utterly crushed.

'Calvin, she's out there,' Emma gasped.

'Who? What's wrong? You look sick.'

'I am sick. It's her. That woman. Shaiana.'

For a moment Calvin struggled to remember.

'Oh, *her*,' he said eventually. 'So what?'

'What do you mean, so what? She's out there.'

'So she's come to the final, who cares?'

'But . . . but . . .'

'But what?' Calvin said, putting his arm round her, which provoked another fusillade of flash

426

photos. 'Do you think she's going to shoot me?'

'Well, she might.'

'Emma. I've told you before, one thing I am never going to do is to start getting scared of fans or contestants. That way lies madness. Fuck her. Fuck the lot of them. Fuck everybody except us.'

'Supposing she comes in?'

'If she's out there now she won't be coming in. All the ticketing has been done and the doors are closed, the only people getting in now are us and the star guests. Now come on, this is your night. As far as I'm concerned, all this is for you.'

Allowing herself to be at least partly comforted, Emma followed Calvin into the vast arena where the final was to be held. The place was packed with thousands of fans whom Gary and Barry had spent the previous hour whipping up into a frenzy. The atmosphere was intoxicating and if Emma hadn't known better she might almost have imagined that she was present at the final of a real talent contest.

They made their way into the VIP area, where Beryl was being loud and obnoxious as usual. The whole Blenheim family had turned up but Beryl and Priscilla had had another quarrel and it seemed her daughter had stormed off to the bar.

'She's supposed to be here to support me!' Beryl fumed to her wife, Serenity. 'We're a fucking family, we fucking support each other.'

'She is here, darling,' Serenity mumbled through her vast lips.

'Visibly here! On fucking camera,' Beryl barked. 'There's no fucking point her being here if she isn't *seen* to be here. She might as well *not* fucking be here.'

'I'd go to the bar and look for her,' said Lisa Marie sulkily, 'but I'm through with booze and my counsellor says I can't trust myself in that environment yet.'

The Blenheims were not the only clan who had

turned up to offer support to their representative. Iona's family were also present, along with the other members of Shetland Mist.

'I love that girl,' Beryl commented, 'the way she's making Rodney's life a misery. Oh my God, look, she's going over to talk to the cunt.'

It was true. A frisson shivered across the whole room as Iona made her way through the crowd to where Rodney was standing with his long-suffering secretary. The 'feud' between Iona and Rodney had been one of the media talking points throughout the entire series and this was the first time the two ex-lovers had spoken in Hospitality in all the ten weeks.

'Good evening, Rodney,' said Iona.

The secretary grabbed the opportunity to disappear.

'Hello there, Iona,' Rodney replied. 'You look lovely.'

'You haven't forgotten, have you?'

'No. No, I haven't forgotten.'

'I hope not, because little Mary's standing just over there. Innocent and virginal, she looks. What a shame if she was to rain on anyone's parade.'

Rodney assured Iona once more that he hadn't forgotten his commitment. Then he went over to Calvin and insisted on drawing him aside, away from Emma.

'Well, what is it?' Calvin enquired with little grace.

'I've something to tell you, Calvin, something I think you'll be pleased about,' Rodney replied.

'Spit it out then,' said Calvin.

'I'd like you to factor in a bit of extra space for me tonight, mate . . .'

'Look, Rodney,' Calvin said testily, not bothering to pretend to be polite. 'This fucking show is not about you, all right? Besides which you are about as mean and as witty as jelly babies and quite frankly I am getting pretty bored with your constant efforts to—'

'I'm going to ask Iona to marry me. I'd like to do it live on the show.'

This was definitely not something Calvin could ignore.

'Are you serious?' he asked.

'Very,' said Rodney, beaming at having stopped Calvin in his tracks. 'How's that for a bit of top telly, eh? You've got to admit that's genuine drama.'

'Well, yes, it might very well be,' Calvin conceded. 'What's brought this on, Rodney? Is she blackmailing you?'

The smile disappeared instantly from Rodney's face. 'How did you know?' he spluttered.

'I didn't,' said Calvin. 'It was a joke. But I do now. What's going on?'

'She wants to get her own back for the way I dumped her last year. She wants me to propose live on air and then marry her so that afterwards she can divorce me for half my cash.'

'Good on her! I always knew that girl had guts. And you're going to play ball?'

'Yes, I'm going to marry her.'

'Wow. She certainly dropped your bollocks in a vice, didn't she?'

'Well, you know, the truth is I've sort of fallen back in love with her . . .'

'You're in love with Iona?'

'Yes, yes I am. You know, she's been so good on the show and what with me and her having our weekly tiffs on air it's sort of been like flirting and she *is* very beautiful, of course.'

'If you say so.'

'I do say so. I'm beginning to think I was a fool for ever letting her go in the first place. So I'm going to turn the tables on her. She thinks I hate her but once the show's over and we get married I'll show her a different side of me.'

'Supposing she won't give you the chance?'

'Well, if she wants her money she'll have to. No

divorce court will rule against me for a sham marriage so she'll have to go through with it properly . . .'

'You mean consummate it, you dirty bastard.'

'Well, that certainly, but I mean go through with it in every way. We'll need to share a home and live in it together and I reckon once she gets a taste of being Mrs Rodney Root she's going to start to like it. We'll be a hot couple. She's a *Chart Throb* finalist now, not a failure. I'm a big man in the industry . . .'

Calvin roared with laughter.

'What is it?' Rodney asked, laughing too, trying to gag along with a joke he did not get.

'It's you, mate, it's you,' Calvin said. 'You are so transparent. She's famous again and in the papers so you fancy her again. That is so pathetic.'

'No!' Rodney exclaimed. 'I just happen to . . .'

'Rodney, face it, you and her are a story, that's what you're in love with. You're twice as famous when your name is linked with hers.'

'Calvin, I really do love her.'

'I'm sure you think you do, mate, but all you actually love is yourself. Well, good luck to you anyway, I always enjoy a wedding and you're right, a proposal on air will make great telly. So like I say, you go for it. And when her star fades and you're not in the papers any more and you suddenly realize that you don't love her, just like last time, you can announce your divorce at the start of the next series. We might even bring Iona on to sing "D-I-V-O-R-C-E".'

Calvin turned to go back to Emma.

'Just one other thing, Calvin,' Rodney said. 'Will you be my best man?'

Calvin merely smiled, and moments later the floor manager began shouting that everybody must take their seats.

The final was about to begin.

All the previous acts had reassembled for a last brief taste of celebrity. One by one, Keely introduced them: Latiffa, Suki, Bloke, Stanley, Blossom, The Four-Z, Tabitha, Troy and Graham. Troy was cheered but Graham was booed. Millicent's devastation had been serialized in the *News of the World* and the crowd had switched their allegiance.

Calvin was loving it.

'Incredible, the power of this show,' he shouted to Emma over the din. 'Only *Chart Throb* could get a mob to boo a blind man.'

'Please, Calvin, don't,' Emma shouted back. 'I was just starting to like you.'

Emma was beginning to enjoy herself again too, drunk with the adrenalin of the event, once more finding Calvin's immense confidence and casual cynicism attractive.

Then she saw Shaiana.

She was there, as before standing motionless among a crowd of fans who had been allowed all the way to the front in order to give the final the appearance of a live rock gig.

'Calvin, she's there again,' Emma almost shrieked.

Calvin turned round.

'Don't look! Don't look! She'll see us looking!' Emma insisted.

'Calm down, Em,' Calvin said. 'I've told you these people do not bother me. Never have. She must have wangled herself a ticket, that's all. They're clever, these psycho fans.'

'She's not a fan, she's an ex-contestant, and she said that you hadn't seen the last of her.'

'Which, thanks to you, darling, I haven't. I wouldn't even have noticed otherwise.'

'Yes, well, maybe this is the John Lennon moment. Maybe I've just saved your life.'

For an instant a flicker of concern showed on

Calvin's face but almost immediately he pulled himself together.

'For God's sake, Emma, can we be a little less hysterical about this?' he said.

'What if she's got a gun?'

'Everybody's searched on entry these days. She hasn't got a gun.'

'You said she couldn't get in but she has.'

'All right, all right, I'll ask Security to keep an eye on her. You must *not* let this woman spoil our night.'

Emma promised that she would do her best and retreated to the celebrity guest enclosure, so named despite the fact that as far as Emma could see none of the people sitting in it were actually celebrities. Calvin joined Beryl and Rodney backstage so that they could make their entrance like emperors coming down to the Roman circus to sit in judgement on those who were about to die, and the final had began.

The Quasar opened proceedings with a tuneless but surprisingly entertaining rendition of the classic Black Lace holiday hit 'Agadoo'. The Quasar had by now begun to distance himself from his strippergram past and was pitching himself as basically a children's entertainer.

'Ah ain' stupid,' he informed the Prince of Wales backstage. 'Sex gods come an' go, ri'? Ye kna wha Ahm sayin'? But kids' entertainers work for evah! Look at the Krankees, man, they *cleaned* it. Twenty year from now nobody gone wan' see ma booty but Ahm still gone be good fo' Buttons in panto! Check it out, geeza!'

'That sounds extremely sensible, Mr Quasar,' the Prince had replied.

The Quasar was followed by Iona, sticking to the sweet Scottish girl theme with 'The Skye Boat Song', which went down extremely well. At the end of it Calvin and Beryl heaped their usual praise.

'You know what? You owned that song.'

And then Keely turned to Rodney for his comments. There were laughs, cheers and boos at this because by now it had become something of a *Chart Throb* ritual that Rodney would damn Iona as much as his two colleagues had praised her. Tonight, however, he threw caution to the winds and went off script. Avoiding looking at Calvin, whom he knew he was disobeying, he launched into a carefully prepared speech.

'Iona,' he said, 'I have something to say now that I know will surprise our viewers but that I hope may not surprise you so much. The whole world knows that for this entire series I have been very, very hard on you, I've said things that have hurt you and that perhaps you thought you did not deserve. Do you want to know why I did that? Do you, Iona?'

'Because you're an idiot, Rodney?' Calvin said in a steely tone as if warning him to be very careful.

'I did it because I respect you, Iona. I wanted to put you on your mettle, to test you, to make you prove to the world just how tough you could be, just how fine an artist you are. Everybody knows that last year I supported you wholeheartedly so if I'd just done so again nobody would have taken any notice. They would have thought I was saying it out of guilt and my praise would have been meaningless. By dissing you as I have, I've enabled you to show the world you don't need anybody but yourself. That was a brilliant performance, Iona. 'The Skye Boat Song' is a tough song to own but you owned it, Iona. You've owned every song you've ever sung.'

There was a brief silence in the studio before it erupted into cheers and applause.

'Is there anything you would like to say to Rodney, Iona?' Keely asked.

Iona appeared to have tears in her eyes.

'Thank you,' she said. 'Thank you for that, Rodney.'

Next there was an advertising break, during which

Rodney seized the opportunity to apologize to Calvin. He was so scared he could scarcely look him in the eye.

'I'm sorry, mate,' he said. 'I just couldn't stick to the script today, not with what I have to say later.'

'Well, you know that normally I would consider going off script a sacking offence, Rodney,' Calvin said sternly.

'I know, I know.'

'But I must say it was a surprisingly clever effort. I didn't think you had it in you and as it happens I'm happy for you to start supporting Iona now because I don't want her to win and the quickest way to alienate a performer is usually to have you support them.'

'Thanks, Calvin. You're a mate.'

After the break it was the turn of the Prince of Wales. The show was going out on the Saturday night before Remembrance Sunday and in a fit of inspiration Calvin had decreed that HRH should sing 'Where Have All The Flowers Gone', dedicating it to 'our brave soldiers, the ordinary lads and lasses who pay the price for the vainglorious folly of old men like me'. It was a masterstroke, and the studio erupted.

'Your Royal Highness,' gushed Beryl, 'you owned that song so big time it wasn't funny and that's coming from a mum.'

'Your Royal Highness,' Rodney raved, his eyes wet with tears, 'you are a true star and you have a big recording career ahead of you.'

'Your Royal Highness,' said Calvin, putting on his sensible and honest face, 'when you came into this competition quite frankly I didn't rate your chances. I was wrong. You've worked hard. You've listened to the judges' comments, you've learned and you've grown and you know what? I think you could go all the way.'

'Your Royal Highness,' said Keely, 'great comments from all three judges there. Is there anything you would like to say in reply?'

'Well, they *are* kind, Keely, aren't they?' the Prince replied. 'I'm sure I don't deserve a word of it but *thank you!*'

During the next advertising break, Emma managed to grab hold of Calvin when he was briefly able to leave the judging platform.

'Oh Calvin,' she said and there were tears in her eyes, 'that was brilliant. Just perfect. I really do think you're doing something wonderful and empowering here. Something amazing. I mean isn't it incredible that the only programme in Britain that is actually attempting to show the next head of state in a positive and thoughtful light is *Chart Throb*. It's actually quite noble. You should be very proud.'

'Oh, I am.'

'And I'm proud too because I'm the one who made you do it.'

'Yes, you are, darling.'

With that, he put his arms round her and kissed her in full view of the audience, which of course earned a huge cheer.

'Easy, tiger. You haven't won yet,' said Emma, but she was clearly thrilled.

There being so few contestants remaining, each one of them was expected to sing twice. Calvin had ensured that the Quasar's second effort did him no favours. The ex-stripper's whole appeal was based on his exuberance and an amiably oafish lack of talent, so Calvin's suggestion that he cover Sondheim's sensitive torch song of sadness and regret, 'Send In The Clowns', was certainly a mistake. The Quasar had of course recognized this himself.

'That song is boring, geeza,' he had complained to Trent when given his instructions. But, like everybody else, he was bound by the watertight contract he had signed and must do as he was told.

Iona fared better, despite Calvin's efforts at sabotage.

She had won the nation's heart as the sweet-voiced country girl and so Calvin had decreed that she be given The Sex Pistols' 'Anarchy In The UK' to perform in her last appearance in the hope that this would alienate her mumsy fan base. In fact she played it kookily and with a sense of humour, proving that she could rock, and the song was well received. Calvin was not overly concerned, however, for he knew he had an ace up his sleeve.

When Keely brought on the Prince of Wales for his second performance, Calvin announced that before the Prince sang he felt it was his duty to pay tribute to the courage that the heir to the throne had shown by facing his critics and coming on the show at all.

'And more than that, Your Highness,' he said, 'I want to thank you for the way you have nurtured and cared for all the contestants throughout this whole process.'

'Oh *pish*,' the Prince mumbled, clearly rather embarrassed.

'No, it's true. You have been like a father figure to us all and, although so much that you have done must remain unreported as I know you would wish it, I do want to say that little Sam has now got a date for his bone marrow transplant and I believe that to have been as a result of the advice his mother received from your office, which incidentally strikes me as the way community leaders *ought* to behave in this country but rarely do . . .'

Calvin was forced to stop briefly for applause that for once Gary and Barry did not have to grind out of the audience.

'I should also like to say,' Calvin continued, 'that Bree, the victim of domestic violence whom viewers may have seen His Royal Highness counselling in an earlier show, is now in secure accommodation and has found, let us hope, some modicum of peace.'

In the control booth Chelsie was stunned and thrilled at Calvin's audacity.

'He means she's back in the refuge that I found her in,' she gasped.

Meanwhile, in the studio, in a last, brilliant piece of theatre Calvin summoned Troy up on to the stage.

'And finally,' Calvin said, 'I think somebody wants to wish you luck.'

Troy, who had been well rehearsed and knew which side his bread was buttered, threw his arms round the Prince before announcing to the audience that he now had a reading age of eight! The crowd cheered and cheered, imagining that this was a mighty leap forward for the lad and the result of royal reading lessons. Emma too shouted and clapped until her voice hurt, as unaware as everyone except Calvin and Chelsie that Troy had had a reading age of eight when he had first entered the competition.

After that the Prince scarcely needed to sing at all, but his performance of 'The Greatest Love Of All', delivered in his pleasant light baritone, was rapturously received. Keely could scarcely calm the audience down enough to ask for the judges' comments. Beryl spoke first and she had clearly managed to overcome any moral objections she might previously have harboured regarding blood sports.

'You know what, Your Royal Highness?' said Beryl. 'You are so sexy, sensitive and gorgeous it isn't funny. I *love* older men. I'd like to . . . I want to . . . I wish I could ooooohhh.' Beryl was momentarily lost for words so instead she stuck her tongue out and wiggled it about. 'If I wasn't a faithful wife and working mum,' she said, recovering herself somewhat, 'then watch out, mister! In fact if you fancy a threesome with me and Serenity then get yourself over to our place big time because you were utterly fantastic. You owned that stage. You owned that song. You know what? You went out there and you rocked my world.'

Rodney was equally effusive.

'You know what?' he said. 'You went out there and you owned it tonight. The audience love you, you're a natural entertainer. I think you have a big recording career ahead of you.'

Calvin, realizing that his job was done and not wishing to gild the lily, confined himself to a few words of simple praise and Keely announced that the voting lines were now open.

There now followed a half-hour's pause in the programme while the news was broadcast and the phone voting was conducted. Calvin and Emma retired to Hospitality, leaving Gary and Barry to maintain the audience at a fever pitch of anticipation. Emma looked hard for Shaiana as she and Calvin left the main auditorium but she was lost in the crowd.

'Forget her,' said Calvin. 'I've told you, worrying about these people is a sickness. You simply cannot let it get to you.'

The hospitality room, although large, was crowded and unpleasant. Every reality TV star and member of the wrong end of a boy band seemed to have pitched up and the noise was horrible. On top of that, Beryl and Priscilla Blenheim had finally found each other and neither of them seemed very pleased about it.

'I am not selling my accessories through you,' Priscilla was shouting. 'They are my dildos, I designed them . . .'

'Ha!' Beryl snapped back.

'Well, I was fucking *there* when they *were* designed, which shows I fucking care about what I put my fucking name to. Unlike *you*, Mom, fucking whoring yourself to every fucking supermarket chain in Britain.'

Serenity tried to intervene but as she'd had a drink she found it impossible to manoeuvre her lips with sufficient dexterity to make herself understood.

'Shut up, Serenity, you're pissed, which is not a good look for a recovering alcoholic!' Beryl shouted. 'Now have you got all the arrangements made for tomorrow, Priscilla?'

'Yes, Mom! How many times!'

'And you're sure this guy's good? We start *The Blenheims* in one week and I do not want to be on TV with two black eyes and a throbbing twat.'

'Mom, a few jabs of Botox, a coupla stitches round the eyes, a fold or two of new labium – what's to heal?'

The Final, Part Two

'In third place,' said Keely, relishing the enormous pause that had become something of a trademark for her, 'it's the Quasar!!'

The Quasar took the microphone and screeched, thrust forward his pelvis and performed his trademark drop split, then he thanked God, Jesus Christ, his mum and dad, his fans, Baby Jesus and all the children of the world, and committed his life to the ideal of happiness and the spreading of it, particularly, he hoped, to children.

'I will now announce the performer that the public have voted as this year's runner-up,' Keely proclaimed in her most portentous tone, and then after a long pause, she added, 'after the break.'

This was an old *Chart Throb* trick to keep the audience in suspense a little longer, but by now the judges at least knew who the runner-up was and Rodney in particular could not wait for her name to be announced. As the minutes ticked by, he fidgeted like a nervous schoolboy. It was a very long break, and as this was the peak moment of the most popular show on television, advertising space was at a premium. In the studio Gary and Barry were screaming themselves hoarse in their efforts to keep the crowd in a frenzy of excitement.

Eventually the broadcast began again and after another outrageous series of pauses finally the moment arrived.

'The runner-up is . . . Iona!'

There were cheers and tears. Iona's family were pictured in the front row jumping up and down and screaming and crying. Iona was crying too as she also thanked God before going on to pay tribute to old bandmates without whom nothing would have been possible and expressed the hope that this result might draw a line under the difficult experience that she and the other members of Shetland Mist had had the previous year.

When Iona had finished speaking, Keely stepped forward once more.

'Which means that this year's Chart Throb is—'

'One moment, Keely,' Rodney shouted from the judges' table. 'I have something to say.'

'I'm sorry, Rodney,' Keely replied, 'but—'

'I must speak!' Rodney insisted. 'Calvin, can I speak?'

Glancing at his fellow judge, Calvin was content to nod benignly.

'Keep it brief, mate,' he said.

'Thank you. Iona,' said Rodney, turning towards her and Keely.

'Yes, Rodney,' she answered with a radiant smile.

'Iona, first of all, congratulations on a stunning achievement. You've performed brilliantly, you've come second, you deserve it, you are a big star and are going to sell a lot of records.'

'That's kind, Rodney,' Iona said.

'But life is not only pop music and I have something

personal to say. You and I have had our ups and downs in the past but the truth is in my heart I have always loved you. You're beautiful, you're talented, you have a lovely family and you're a lovely Scottish girl. I would like you to do me the honour of agreeing to be my wife. What do you say, darling? How about you and me try and make a go of it?'

This shock development produced a stunned silence in the room. Calvin broke it.

'Rodney!' he exclaimed. 'You sly dog. Good work, my son.'

There was nervous laughter. All eyes were fixed on Iona, waiting for her reply.

Keely, always the professional, said, 'Iona, I'm going to have to hurry you. I must have an answer.'

Iona smiled and blew Rodney a little kiss.

'Ladies and gentlemen,' she said, 'Rodney Root is asking me to marry him because I have blackmailed him into it.'

There was a huge gasp. Rodney's jaw dropped open.

'You all know that last year he and I had an affair, something I have always regretted because he's a repulsive little man and he didn't deserve me . . .'

Another gasp and a roar of cruel laughter from Beryl. Rodney turned to Calvin, desperation written across his every feature.

'Calvin!' he appealed. 'Move on. Please move on!'

'No way!' Beryl shrieked.

'Sorry, Rodney,' Calvin agreed, declining to conclude one of the TV coups of the decade. 'You've had your say, now let Iona have hers.'

'You all just heard this man say he loves me,' Iona continued. 'He told me he loved me then too and he promised my band a recording contract. He never got us that contract and when the novelty of bedding me wore off he dropped me and from that day onwards refused to answer my calls . . .'

'Calvin, please!' Rodney pleaded but Calvin merely shrugged as if to indicate that matters had passed beyond his control. Clearly he was still not minded to intervene on what was going to be one of the most talked-about TV events ever.

'Anyway, as you know, I came back on *Chart Throb* without my band and Rodney's been a pig to me from that day to this. Recently, however, I turned the tables on him: I told him that our teenage bass player was ready to swear he'd molested her unless he proposed to me on air. I said I wanted to take him for half his money. It was a bit of a sad trick to play but then he's a bit of a sad bloke, isn't he? So here we are and here's my answer, Rodney: no, nay and never. Not in a billion years. What, link myself publicly with a spineless swine like you? As if! I don't want your money, never did. I set you up simply so that I could humiliate you on *Chart Throb* the way you humiliated me. I'm done now, Keely. Thanks for waiting, Your Royal Highness, I do appreciate it.'

The Prince of Wales had of course been hovering on the periphery awaiting his victory announcement.

'That's quite all right,' he said. 'Don't mind me.'

The entire arena had been eerily silent throughout Iona's extraordinary speech. It now erupted into a crescendo of cheering and shouting. Rodney, who if nothing else had some survival instincts, resisted the urge to turn and run and instead assumed a wry grin, as if to say that the joke was on him and that he could take it. When the shouting finally died down he said, 'Full marks for honesty, Iona. I still think you're a great talent, a true star and you're going to sell a lot of records.'

It wasn't a bad effort but Iona was having none of it.

'Fuck off, Rodney,' she said.

'Oh, I say!' the Prince protested, 'No, *really* please. There are children watching.'

The studio erupted once more into cheers and a chant was fast developing as more and more people began shouting, 'Fuck off, Rodney!'

Keely rose to the occasion.

'And with the Quasar and Iona out of the race,' she said, showing the kind of steely professionalism that had made her a dead cert to host the following year's Brit Awards, 'this year's Chart Throb is His Royal Highness, the Prince of Wales!'

After the cheering had once more subsided Keely enquired whether the Prince would like to say anything.

'Oh, I don't suppose anybody wants to hear *muggins* here *banging on*,' he replied.

All the nine other finalists then joined the Prince, Iona and the Quasar on stage and together they sang 'We Are The World'.

Emma ran forward from the celebrity enclosure and threw her arms round Calvin. 'You know what?' she said. 'I love you. Big time.'

She Wanted It So Much

Consciousness returned slowly to Beryl and it was a moment or two before she recalled who or where she was.

'That you, Mom?' a half-familiar voice asked. Familiar but muffled, very muffled. 'I can see your hand twitching. Are you coming round?'

The voice was that of Priscilla, her daughter. And Beryl was in bed.

'Five minutes, that guy took. Ten tops. Can you believe it?' the muffled voice continued. 'And he charged eight thousand. That's sterling, Mom, not

443

dollars. Eight thousand *pounds*. Lisa Marie said a sack over your head would have been a lot cheaper.'

Beryl remembered now. She'd had a bit of work done, that was it. They had done the final of the show, the Prince of Wales had won and then she'd gone straight to the Porchester Clinic to have a bit of work done.

'Oh my God,' she said.

'What?' she heard Priscilla reply.

'Rodney proposing to Iona! I just remembered. Oh – my – fucking – God!'

'Wasn't that incredible? The best. I mean it was just fantastic. The papers have gone crazy, some of them have put it ahead of that Prince of Wales guy.'

'I'll bet they have. Well, Rodney always wanted more press coverage, now he's got it and I hope he's satisfied.'

'They're all saying Calvin's going to have to drop him from the judging panel.'

'Speak up, will you. You're all muffled.'

'That's because the top of your head is bandaged. I said Calvin's going to drop Rodney from the show.'

'Hallelujah! Can you imagine what it's like having to sit next to that little shit? When can I get these bandages off?'

'He said we could take them off any time after eleven. It's ten thirty now.'

'And more to the point, where the fuck am I?'

'Home.'

'LA?'

'No, dickbrain. The London house. It's the morning after you finished *Chart Throb*. Don't you remember? You checked into the clinic straight after the show and they did it at six this morning. Then I collected you and brought you here. This is all your idea, Mom, trying to squeeze in a quick bit of cosmo before we start the new season.'

444

'All right, all right. I remember, and don't call your mother a dickbrain.'

'Well, don't talk like one and you're not my mom.'

'I am your mum, Priscilla, and I'll talk however I like since I have just emerged from an anaesthetic.'

'How do you feel, by the way?'

'Pretty woozy . . . my arms and legs are numb.'

'Yeah, he said you'd feel that. You have to rest.'

'Fine by me. I'm fucking knackered. I've just finished ten weeks of paying for our lifestyle, young lady. Jesus, it gets harder each year.'

'Great show though. Last night was awesome. Except I got stuck with that weird chick for a while.'

'What weird chick?'

'You know, the weird chick that got chucked off at Pop School.'

'Darling, they're all weird. How do you expect me to remember them?'

'You were really nice to her, you told her to learn and grow.'

'I'm nice to all of them, Priscilla, it's my thing. I'm a mum.'

'The one with the tear. You know, they trailed her for weeks.'

'Oh, *her*. Shaiana. Fucking lunatic.'

'You got that right. She was scary.'

'When?'

'Last night. I just told you.'

'She was there?'

'Yes! Aren't you listening? She came right up to me and started talking.'

'She shouldn't have been there.'

'Well, she was and she sure is mad at you guys. Particularly Calvin.'

'God, I hate it when they get angry and righteous. Who the *fuck* do they think they are? Like the world owes them a living. Fuck them. So they have a fucking

445

dream. Everybody has a dream. What makes them so special?'

'You told her she could sing.'

'Yes and then we told her she couldn't. Haven't they watched the show? That's what we *do*.'

'And could she sing? I thought she could sing.'

'And what the fuck would you know, Priscilla? Of course she couldn't fucking sing.'

Emma opened her eyes slowly. For a moment she wondered where she was. But only for a moment, then with an overwhelming sense of happiness she realized that she was in Calvin's bed and that they had made love all night.

She was alone but she could hear the shower running. She was glad actually to have just this moment to collect herself, to stretch out and luxuriate in the wonderfulness of being her. To squirm and yawn and lose herself within the biggest bed and beneath the biggest, softest duvet she had ever experienced.

It had all worked out so well. He loved her, he had said he loved her and he had proved it with his love-making. He had fought to win her trust and he had won. She was his and she wanted nothing more than to remain his for ever.

Then the telephone rang.

Inside the shower Calvin did not hear it ring. He was lost in the cascading water and the guilty turmoil of his thoughts. He no longer loved her. The boil had been lanced and he no longer loved her. He could not believe how quickly his heart had turned. He had loved her utterly the evening before, as he took her home and then to bed. He had continued to love her utterly for at least half the night and had truly believed in all those hours that he had found his soulmate, the perfect sweet girl who was so different from all the others he had known before. But then around four o'clock in the morning, as she had dozed and he had lain awake smoking a cigarette, he had begun to wonder whether he did love her and after she had woken up and they had made love once more he began to realize that he didn't. By the time he got up to have his shower he was certain. The boil had been lanced, the conquest made and he no longer loved her. She had been a challenge, a project. He had won and now it was over.

Emma did not answer the phone. It was Calvin's phone and not her business, so she let it ring until the answerphone kicked in.

'Good morning, Mr Simms,' said that soft, familiar, old-fashioned voice. 'It's the Prince of Wales here.'

The light was becoming brighter. The noise of scissors cutting through fabric was suddenly surprisingly loud in Beryl's ears.

'How do you feel?' she heard Priscilla say.

'My eyes are OK, I think, but I can't move my arms.'

'They were restrained so you wouldn't pull at your bandage while you were asleep. I'll get to them in a moment.'

The light was very bright now even though Beryl's eyes were still shut. It was shining through the lids.

'Fuck,' Beryl exclaimed. 'Dim the lights, babes.'

Beryl felt the light darkening beyond her lids and nervously she tried opening her eyes again.

'You know, I really don't think you should have told her she could sing if you thought she couldn't.'

'What?'

'And if you thought she *could* sing then you should have put her through.'

The bandages were gone from Beryl's ears now and she could hear more clearly. Her daughter's voice had changed.

447

'What are you talking about?' said Beryl, peering into the shadows, wanting to rub her eyes but unable to do so as her arms were restrained.

'Shaiana.'

'Who?'

'Me.'

'Well, goodness gracious,' the voice said, 'you did it and I must say it has been the most tremendous *fun*. I'll admit that when you first approached me all those months ago I had no idea how much I would enjoy the whole thing and of course, as you predicted, it has increased my popularity enormously, which is most *gratifying*. I realize that one shouldn't court public favour but nonetheless it really is *nice* to be *liked* for once. I've been offered my own chat show, you know, and a record deal of all things. Quite extraordinary, I feel like *Val Doonican*. There's even been a suggestion from the *Big Brother* people that they put hidden cameras into Buck House and follow us all about for a bit. I had to tell them that I did *not* think Her Majesty would think much of *that* idea. Anyway, thank you once again for your faith in me and, more importantly, your support for the ancient institution which it is my honour to embody. Anyway must dash, there are reporters climbing over the wall and crushing my petunias. So all the very best and, as we pop stars say, it's been real.'

Scarcely had the Prince rung off when the telephone rang again. As Emma lay waiting for the answering machine to click on once more, she tried to grasp the meaning of what she had just heard. Calvin had been lying; he had known about the Prince being a contestant from the beginning. It was he who had suggested it. But why? If he truly was a monarchist as the Prince had said, why lie about it to her? She was a monarchist herself.

The answer wasn't long in coming. It followed

on immediately from Calvin's outgoing message.

'Way'll, Calvin,' said a female voice that reeked of the Mississippi, 'Ah guess you wern. Ah confess Ah never draimt y'could make that dull old fossil inta a Chart Threrb. So way'll dern. Maybe you rilly are as good as you think you are. Now, ais you know, Ah aim a Serthern werman an' Ah always tra t'be a werman of ma werd. But historeh has taught us Dixie Belles ta also take a practical view an' hence Ah merst declare our lil' bet null an' void. Ah shall see ya in tha deevorce court, Calvin. Bye-bye now.'

As Emma lay listening to this, her skin cold despite the rich duvet that enveloped her, she was thinking of her father. When he had left the family home he had left his daughter nothing but a lesson, a lesson in men. Once more it seemed that Emma had failed to learn it. Once more she had trusted a man.

More fool her.

She got up and dressed herself quickly. Despite the turmoil in her mind she found space to feel foolish, as many a girl had done before her, putting on a crumpled evening gown in the cold light of morning.

Emma had reached the bedroom door when Calvin emerged from the bathroom. For a moment she thought she might keep on running, for she was fully dressed and he was wrapped in only a towel. There was nothing he could have done to stop her. Instead she turned to face him.

'The Prince of Wales called,' she said, 'and your wife. They both left you messages. I heard them.'

Calvin's face showed that he understood immediately what this meant.

'Ah' was all he could say.

'I suppose I should thank you,' Emma said, attempting a bitter little smile and failing. 'I really do believe that I'll now be spared the trouble of ever trusting a man again.'

*

The room was still in deep shadow but Beryl could now see that the woman standing at the foot of her bed was not her daughter.

'You fucking witch,' Shaiana shouted, 'you told me I could sing and then you said I couldn't!'

Now Beryl recognized the voice. The penny, which had been teetering on the edge of the abyss, suddenly dropped and Beryl knew that she had been catapulted into the ultimate celebrity nightmare, the thing that those in the public eye feared most: she was caught in the clutches of a psycho fan.

'Where am I?' Beryl stammered.

'Never mind where you are, witch. Just you worry about what's going to happen to you.'

'How did you . . . ?'

'How did I get you here? Hey, I may not be able to sing but it seems I can act, *can't I, Mom*!' and with these last words Shaiana added the brattish half-Californian whine of Priscilla Blenheim.

'Shit!' Beryl exclaimed.

'Dark glasses, a bit of a sulk, those enormous new tits she had done. There really isn't much to your overprivileged little bitch of a daughter, is there? I stuck two footballs up my jumper, put on a pink wig and picked you up from the Porchester with no questions asked. Of course it did help to have these.'

Shaiana stepped up to Beryl and waved something before her face. Beryl's eyes had become more accustomed to the light now and she thought she could make out a driver's licence, a Californian driver's licence.

'That's right,' Shaiana crowed. 'Photo ID, a driver's licence – an *American* driver's licence. Guess who it belongs to?'

'No!' Beryl gasped.

'Yes! That's right. Priscilla. Your precious step-daughter.'

Flinging down the driver's licence on to Beryl's helpless body, Shaiana pulled out a mobile phone, a phone of the very smartest and most expensive kind.

'Amazing phone, this,' Shaiana said. 'Took me hours to work out how to use it. It even has a voice recorder. Just listen to this.'

Shaiana pressed a button and Beryl gasped and nearly choked as she heard the voice of her stepdaughter, desperate and afraid.

'Mom, Mom! Please!' came the voice from the little machine. 'I'm scared, Mom. She has me, she hit me, I think she drugged me . . . I'm tied up . . . I don't know where I am. Please, Mom, give her what she wants. Do what she says. Please. *Please!'*

Shaiana turned off the phone.

'I hadn't meant to hit her,' she said, 'not then anyway, but then I thought how much me hitting her would hurt you and I couldn't help myself.'

'You have to stop this now, Shaiana,' Beryl said, attempting to sound calm and motherly, 'while you still can before you ruin things for yourself for ever . . .'

'Weren't you *listening*, Beryl?' Shaiana replied. 'Didn't you hear what I told you when I did my last audition? Didn't you listen? I told you that I had no plans beyond the show. I told you that when it was over I had nothing. I *told* you that, Beryl. So don't talk to me about ruining my life, it's been ruined, you ruined it already. You told me to dream the dream and then you took that dream away . . .'

'Not me, not me!' Beryl spluttered. 'Calvin did it.'

'No, *you* did it, Beryl, because at least Calvin was honest about me from the start.'

'Well, Rodney then . . .'

'Oh, come on, Beryl! Even I know that *nobody* gives

451

a fuck about Rodney. But *you*. You gave me hope. You told me to dream the dream.'

'Shaiana, please, listen to me, we tell them all that! Don't you understand? You took it all too seriously. *Chart Throb* is an *entertainment* show. It's not about the singers. It's not about talent. It's a people show, it's just a laugh . . .'

'Yes, and the laugh's on us. The dreamers!'

'But of course it is, Shaiana, how could it be anything else? We're a prime-time entertainment show, you *have* to remember that. We aren't *serious*. If you're serious about becoming a singer, Shaiana, go and audition for LIPA or some other stage school. I can write to the principal for you if you like.'

'You told me to dream the dream.'

'I know I did and I'm sorry, Shaiana, but *Chart Throb* isn't about fulfilling your dreams. Calvin doesn't care about your dreams, he doesn't care about you at all. Do you know what he calls you? Mingers, Clingers and Blingers, that's what. We all do. I'm sorry but it's true. I don't *know* whether you can sing or not. I don't *care*. You put your faith in the wrong people, Shaiana. Don't trust us, and don't believe in us. Let me go and I'll try to help you find people you can trust. Please.' Beryl struggled to free her arms from the straps that bound them to the bed. 'What have you done with Priscilla?' she stuttered. 'You mustn't hurt her.'

'What would you care about Priscilla, you avaricious old witch?' Shaiana snapped. 'You fucked up her life as badly as you've fucked up mine.'

'What!'

'You used her! You used your whole family. Come on. Who came out of *The Blenheims* as top dog, eh? You. You and you alone. Priscilla and Lisa Marie just looked like the sullen, sulky, fame-fucked fuckwits that they are, and Serenity looks what she is, which is semi-brain-damaged! And then there's you! Good

452

old Beryl Blenheim, the rock chick, the ubermum!'

'I made Priscilla famous.'

'Famous for what? For nothing. For swearing? For whining? Not famous enough to sell any albums, that's for sure. Jesus Christ! Lisa Marie and me were in *drug rehab* before we got the fucking vote! I was in the *National Enquirer* talking about my drug hell while you were selling my fucking life to Fox TV!'

For a moment Beryl didn't notice.

'Whose idea was that fucking show, Mom?'

She noticed now.

'Mom?'

'Not mine or Lisa Marie's, we were kids.'

'What are you talking about?'

'Not my real mum's either, she's so screwed up she doesn't know what day it is. But there's always been one fully functioning brain in our family, hasn't there? One clear head, and that's good old Mom's . . .'

'Stop it! Stop pretending to be Priscilla. I'm not your mother. You're just a fucked-up crazy woman. You have nothing to do with me or Priscilla . . .'

The girl strode across the room and flicked the light switch.

'Oh, come on, Mom!' she snapped. 'Didn't you work it out yet?'

Beryl lay blinking in the light.

'Work what out, you mad bitch? Let me go!'

'*I'm fucking Priscilla.*'

'You are not! You are a crazy woman and you need help. Where is my daughter?'

'I told you, right here, *Mom*.'

'Stop calling me Mum!'

'Gladly! Fine. Fantastic. That's great news. You never were my mom anyway.'

'And stop this bloody madness.'

'Mom, you're not *listening*. You didn't listen when I was Shaiana and you're not listening now I'm Priscilla.'

'You are *not* Priscilla. You are Shaiana!'

'Yes, I am Shaiana and I am also Priscilla. Priscilla is Shaiana and Shaiana is Priscilla. We're the same fucking person. It's been me from the start.'

Beryl opened her mouth to exclaim once more but no words came. Suddenly the second penny dropped.

'Good,' said Priscilla. 'Do you get it now?'

Priscilla pulled at her hair, removing the wig with which she had disguised her own pink locks.

'You can't be,' Beryl stuttered, but she already knew that she could be.

'Of course I can,' Priscilla replied. 'A wig, a bit of make-up. Pretending to get a grotesque boob job. I never had one, by the way, that was part of distancing me from Shaiana. Originally I was going to give her the fake boobs but I thought it might constrict my chest movement when I sang. I don't know why I bothered with a disguise anyway, you scarcely looked at me when I auditioned. You were never going to spot me in a million years. The only person you care about on that show is you!'

'I am *so* fucking angry with you, Priscilla,' Beryl shouted in fury.

'Oh no! How will I bear it?' Priscilla sneered back.

'You really have been Shaiana all along?'

'Yes, I keep telling you. I made her up.'

'But for God's sake, why? You're Priscilla Blenheim, why go on fucking *Chart Throb*?'

'Why? Why do you think? To see if you really thought I could sing!'

'What?'

'I have put out an album, Mom, and it has failed utterly. But you let me. You *managed me*. Good old Beryl Blenheim, the rock god from way back, thought I was worth an album deal. At least you believed in me, I always hung on to that, but then I started to wonder. Maybe I truly was just a nobody, somebody who

454

happened to be famous because her stepmother put *cameras in her fucking bedroom* and broadcast her adolescence on Cable TV . . .'

'Everybody has cameras in their bedroom these days, Priscilla! Everybody's life is on TV. So what? Enjoy! Jessica Simpson filmed her marriage, Britney filmed her pregnancy, Tommy Lee filmed his education, the Osbournes filmed themselves sitting on a *couch*, for God's sake, and *still* they had three hit seasons! The entire nation is queuing up to get on *Big Brother* and be filmed 24/7! What I gave you is what *everybody wants* . . .'

'I'm not talking about everybody! I'm not talking about the Osbournes or Jessica Simpson or Tommy fucking Lee. Maybe they liked it, maybe they wanted it but I'm talking about *me!*'

'And didn't you like it? All the parties and the limos? You certainly looked as if you liked it.'

'Everybody likes parties, Mom, but you can't party all the time.'

'Why not?'

'I wanted to do something. I wanted to see if I *could* do something. So I decided to find out what you really thought. And now I know. I sang my very best for you guys. I did "Wind Beneath My Wings" like I was born to sing it and you thought it sucked! Why did you let me make an album, Mom, if you thought my voice sucked?'

'I didn't think your voice sucked, darling,' Beryl tried to explain, 'I thought Shaiana's voice sucked.'

'Shaiana's voice *is* my voice!'

'No, it isn't! I'm sorry but the two are different. I know you were being Shaiana but that doesn't make you the same thing. It's just different, it's about the whole package . . .'

'Exactly! When I'm Priscilla Blenheim, world-famous reality TV star, I'm worth an album deal. But

455

when I'm just *me* . . . just a voice, a woman alone, singing a song, I suck like a fucking rent boy.'

Beryl could find no words to reply.

'You could have stopped me, Mom. You could have said, don't make an album, darling, you have no musical talent. But no. There might have been a buck in it so you let me do it. You *encouraged me* to do it. Not content with stealing my adolescence . . .'

'Now hang on a minute, Priscilla.'

'*With stealing my adolescence*, Mom!' Priscilla insisted. 'I was fourteen. That's a time when most kids get a lock on their door so they can be self-obsessed brats in private. You invited the whole fucking world in! Just when me and Lisa Marie were beginning to grow up and trying to find out who we were, suddenly everyone else in the world had already made up their minds. We will *never* get away from what you did to us, Mom. We are fixed for ever. You were responsible for my welfare and you put me to work just as sure as if you'd stuck me down a mine or up a chimney. And now it turns out you didn't even think I had any fucking talent anyway!'

'No! That was Shaiana.'

'I am Shaiana, Mom!'

'You're Priscilla.'

'I'm Shaiana *and* Priscilla, Mom, and now the two of us have made you pay.'

'Yes, all right then! You've made me fucking pay! You've given me the fright of my life, thank you very much, and by the way don't come running to me next time you need help picking out a lawyer or a rehab unit . . .'

'You have no idea yet how we've made you pay.'

'Stop staying "we", Priscilla, you're beginning to sound as crazy as that bitch you made up.'

'I am as crazy as her, Mom. And like I say, you

456

have no idea how me and Shaiana have made you pay.'

'What are you talking about?'

'I'm talking about surgery, Mom. The thing you love most on this earth. Trying to look younger, trying to look better. It's a fucking obsession with you, a disease. I swear you have spent more time with your cosmetic surgeon these last few years than you have spent with your supposedly beloved family.'

'That's not—'

'It *is* true, Mom, and here's the thing. You know that surgeon I booked for you?'

'Yes. What about him?'

'Well, I'm afraid he turned out to be not quite as good at his job as I thought.'

'What are you talking about?'

'Yeah. Oh and by the way, it's not the morning after the show either, Mom. It's actually two weeks later. We've had you unconscious for two weeks.'

'Priscilla, what are you . . .'

'We needed the time, you see. We had to keep working on you, I'm afraid, because my guy just *kept* making one mistake after another and the more he tried to put right what he'd got wrong, the more he fucked up. Sometimes it seemed like he was almost doing it deliberately. But why would anyone do that, Mom? Why would anyone try to fuck you up?'

'Priscilla, this is the sickest joke I ever . . .'

'Do you remember Damian, Mom?'

'What?'

'Damian, buck teeth and glasses. He was a Minger quickie.'

'No, of course I don't remember him. How the hell do you expect . . .'

The door opened and a young man entered. He was wearing a white coat which had a lot of blood on it. The man had buck teeth and wore glasses.

'I'm a veterinary student, Mrs Blenheim, if you'd forgotten,' said Damian. 'So I suppose it was a bit of a stretch to imagine I'd be much cop as a cosmetic surgeon but Shaiana did insist and she's such a persuasive girl. I've done quite a bit to you, I'm afraid. I expect it all feels numb at the moment but that's the nerve suppressant. Later on you're going to be in the most excruciating pain.'

Beryl swallowed hard as Priscilla produced a mirror and held it in front of her face.

Then she screamed. A huge scream, a scream which tore the air with shock and horror. The reflection she saw in the mirror was of a face mutilated, red, bloody, criss-crossed with scars and stitches, livid with bruises and scabs.

'Like I say,' Damian went on, 'when the anaesthetic wears off I imagine it's going to be agony.'

The scream was over but now Beryl was gasping, gagging and choking with the appalled realization of what had been done to her.

'Ugly, Mom. Ugly!' Priscilla shouted. 'Think about it. Ugly! Because that's what you are now. Now that my pal Damian has finished cutting you up. Ugly!'

Beryl seemed about to be sick.

'Ugly and fat!' Priscilla screeched.

This last word was a sufficiently powerful one to focus Beryl's spinning mind for a moment.

'Fat?' she gulped, still half choking.

'Yes, fat!' Priscilla screamed. 'The worst thing on earth, eh? The thing you've fought against for years! You've spent half your life sucking it out, cutting it off and stapling it down! Well, guess what? It's back! Damian has put it all back!'

'No!'

'Yes!' Priscilla shouted in triumph. 'Lipo in reverse! How's that, *Mom*! He invented the process himself.'

With that Priscilla tore away the sheet that covered

Beryl and revealed a vast, sagging, obese and wounded body, red, purple and yellow all over with cuts, bruises and pus.

'It's a temporary effect, I imagine,' said Damian modestly. 'I doubt the new fat will actually bond with the existing tissue, I just injected it wherever I could. As I say, when the anaesthetic wears off the agony will begin but I doubt it will last long because I can't imagine that a human system can survive what I've been doing to it. We've really only kept you alive so that you could see what we've done to you.'

'Yes,' said Priscilla, 'so how's that, Mom? You're going to die, hideously ugly and very, very fat. The two things you have always feared most. That's the price you're paying for stealing my life, Mom. I'm stealing yours in return. No more TV now!'

Beryl stared down at the ruination of her body. She looked once more into the mirror at the grotesque mask of horror that had once been her face.

She couldn't do it. Words failed her. Her lip quivered, her nostrils flared and a watery film spread across her eyes. The lids closed in an agonized grimace and squeezed out a glistening tear.

'It's . . . it's . . .' she said but could speak no more.

'It's a bodysuit actually,' Priscilla replied.

Beryl looked at her, uncomprehending.

'It's a fat bodysuit, Mom. I got it from the BBC, from one of their sketch shows. Damian and I painted the wounds and bruises on it.'

'What?' Beryl still did not seem to understand.

'And this is make-up,' Priscilla continued, taking up a packet of Wet Wipes and rubbing roughly at Beryl's face. The Wet Wipe was soon covered in red and purple and yellow, and much of the apparent bruising and stitching that had disfigured Beryl had disappeared.

'We didn't do anything to you, Mom. We just scared

you. You haven't been unconscious for two weeks either. It's the morning after the *Chart Throb* final and you're fine.'

'You fucking bitch!' Beryl screamed.

'Damian was good, wasn't he?' Priscilla smiled.

'Thanks, Priscilla,' said Damian.

Beryl laid her head back on her pillow for a moment. 'Untie me,' she said.

Priscilla and Damian duly undid the straps that had held Beryl down.

'This really is a fat suit?' she said. 'You're sure?'

'Yes, the zip's at the back.'

'And you haven't done a single thing to me?'

'Of course not.'

Beryl considered the matter once more.

'You're a fucking bitch,' she said.

'Takes one to know one, Mom.'

'I can't believe you did this!'

'I can't believe anything you do.'

'Fuck.'

'Yeah.'

Once again Beryl lay silent for a moment.

'Oh well, I suppose that's rock 'n' roll, isn't it?'

'Yeah, I guess.'

'And all's well that ends well, eh? I forgive you, Priscilla.'

'Thanks. Of course it isn't over yet, Mom.'

'What do you mean?'

'You haven't been punished yet. You haven't been made to pay.'

'For God's sake. What fucking now?'

'You remember how you wanted to postpone the first episode of the new season? So you could get the eye surgery done? And some more work on your vagina?'

'Yes. I suppose none of that's happened, has it?'

'No and I didn't postpone the show either.'

'What do you mean?'

'I postponed the postponement! Look!'

Priscilla moved a lamp so that the light was no longer shining so harshly into Beryl's eyes. Instead a small television camera was suddenly revealed in the corner of the room, mounted on a tripod.

'Hi, Mom,' said Lisa Marie Blenheim, who was operating the camera.

'What the hell are you doing here?' Beryl demanded.

'Helping Priscilla out,' Lisa Marie replied. 'We're a family, remember.'

'And we just made the first episode of the new series,' Priscilla cried. 'You, me and Lisa Marie. A stepmom and her daughters together.'

'You haven't!'

'I have. For the first time in the history of TV we're going to put the "real" into reality and you are going to be seen as you truly are.'

Lisa Marie keyed in a time code and turned a video monitor towards Beryl.

'Shaiana, please, listen to me . . .' Beryl could see herself saying. '*Chart Throb* is an *entertainment* show . . . It's not about talent . . . it's just a laugh . . . Calvin doesn't care about your dreams . . . Do you know what he calls you? Mingers, Clingers and Blingers, that's what. We all do . . . You put your faith in the wrong people, Shaiana. Don't trust us, and don't believe in us.'

Lisa Marie turned off the monitor.

'I don't think Calvin's going to be very pleased when that little bit of reality is broadcast in full, do you?' said Priscilla. 'And I don't think the nation is going to think much of their favourite mom being utterly humiliated by her stepdaughter in revenge for ruining her life.'

'And mine,' said Lisa Marie.

'But that's what they're going to see in the first and final episode of this year's season, Mom.'

'Priscilla,' Beryl said. 'You can't broadcast this. I have no make-up on. I absolutely forbid it!'

And Still to Come

As a result of his exposure on the final episode of *The Blenheims*, Damian was offered a reality project for Cable TV about cosmetic dental surgery entitled *The Buck Stops Here*.

Michelle from Peroxide is a stripper. She feels her work empowers her as a woman and is hoping to make a reality documentary on the subject.

Latiffa appeared in series twelve of *I'm a Celebrity Get Me Out of Here!* and published an autobiography entitled *Being Me*.

Georgie managed finally to achieve the average weight for a young woman but only by moving to Beverly Hills. She continues to have severe eating disorders and is the envy of all her new friends.

Millicent and Graham could not rekindle their love in the bruising aftermath of *Chart Throb* and went their separate ways. They have been offered an undisclosed sum by a Birmingham radio station to get married live on air.

Tabitha appeared alongside Latiffa in *I'm a Celebrity Get Me Out of Here!* where they snogged in a hammock. Latiffa later explained to *Heat* magazine that she was no lezza but that her career needed the boost of a lesbian kiss.

Tabitha's girlfriend got her own reality show in which she lived on a desert island with a series of male hunks who were tasked with trying to turn her. The show was entitled *Breaching the Dyke*.

Vicky and her mum blamed each other for their

disastrous *Chart Throb* experience and are regularly to be seen shouting at each other on Jerry Springer-style confrontation shows.

Suki got her longed-for second pair of new tits and hence feels newly empowered as a woman. The removal of the old implants was filmed for a reality TV show entitled *Suki: Tits Out for the Lads*. She has written her autobiography, *Still Growing*.

Bloke made a reality TV show about their whirlwind post-*Chart Throb* existence entitled *Bloke Live the Dream*. They are available for party bookings and can be contacted via their website.

Michael from The Four-Z appeared in series eighteen of *Celebrity Big Brother*, in which he, the Foreign Secretary and the Bishop of Bath and Wells were tasked to put on miniskirts and do an impression of Bananarama.

Stanley, the single dad, released a cover of 'The Greatest Love Of All' which got to number six. The process of making the single was recorded for a reality TV show entitled *The Greatest Dad of All*.

Blossom has made a reality TV series for the Addiction and Recovery Channel called *How to Live with an Infectious Laugh* and has written an autobiography entitled *Loud Woman*.

The Quasar now gives motivational seminars dressed only in a thong. His autobiography is entitled *Wake Up and Dream*.

Shetland Mist got a massive boost from Iona's second placing on *Chart Throb*. They are now huge on the Scottish folk rock circuit and are to be the subject of a reality TV show entitled *Big in the Outer Hebrides*.

Dakota received a hundred-million-pound divorce settlement from Calvin and the following day married a trillionaire gun dealer with whom she was 'hopelessly in lerve'. She has since worked her way thro an oil sheikh and an insider trader and is curre be found at major charity fundraisers trying to bump into Bill Gates.

Beryl's television career survived Priscilla's efforts to destroy it and she was showered with TV offers ranging from reading the news to playing Elizabeth Bennet in a star-studded new adaptation of *Pride and Prejudice*. Each new development in Beryl's life is covered by its own separate documentary series and there is no moment of the day or night when Beryl Blenheim is not on television.

Rodney recently fulfilled a lifelong ambition by becoming the 'face' of a budget supermarket.

Priscilla became Shaiana and is big on the gay diva disco circuit.

The Prince of Wales never did inherit the throne, the position of head of state having been flogged off by the government to some Russian bloke in order to raise money for spin doctors.

Emma is single and keeps herself nice.

Calvin married Chelsie. *Chart Throb* remained a hit and CALonic TV continued to grow. At the current rate of expansion it is reckoned that by the year 2050 everybody in the world will be either a pop star or the subject of their own reality TV show.

THE END